BALDUR'S CHILDREN

Baldur's Children

DAVID LINGARD

Denise Boorman

David Lingard

Baldur's Children

A note from the author

I just wanted to say here, thank you, whoever you are for however you have arrived at this book and my story. It makes a big difference to authors like me, who like to feel as though their hard work and dedication is appreciated when our work is read.

Your investment of your own time and money is as always, well appreciated. It takes a long time and a lot of effort to write, edit and release a book, so please, I ask that you **rate** and **review** everything that you read – and not just this book, so that lesser-known authors can grow their audience and gain the credibility that they deserve.

Also, I have a website that is usually kept up to date with current works, reviews and a few extra little bits. You'll find it at: www.davidlingard.com

This is a work of fiction and any similarities to real people or copyrighted works is purely coincidental. This work, as well as the cover are is the ©Copyright of David Lingard 2023

-

A message from David Lingard

It may become apparent if you have read some of the books that I have written over the last few years, that a resounding theme underlies the stories that I have told, has been that of family bonds. This has not happened by accident, rather it is a thanks to those people who have supported me on my journey to write my books. These are the people who stand by me for better or for worse.

For Jaimie & Yas

Act 1 – Baldur's Children

Jarl peered across the void separating the wild and untamed Westlands from the unknown and unforgiving East. He had grown up knowing only one small section of the land he knew humans inhabited, as that was the clan's way. The way it was and the way that it would forever be. His father had named him Jarl because he had wanted his son to become ruler of whatever clan he chose to join as he aged. However, it was never meant to be, and the boy who had been named chief at birth was, nonetheless, a mighty warrior but no clan leader.

It was dusk, the light was fading, and it was both still and quiet.

People crossed the God's Chasm, of course, though it was not easy. The sheer drop on the Western side was over one hundred metres of jagged rock, straight down, and if someone wasn't careful where it met the ground, they could easily impale themselves on the spines below.

Assuming that a person willing to cross the Chasm had made it that far, one would then have to walk a clear mile across the flat, barren ground before reaching the other side and face another sheer cliff face. This time though, one would have to climb *up* the wall to reach the greenery that sat atop the cliff's edge and hid everything that lay beyond.

People had tried to leave the Western side in the distant past and some had made it, but not even once had a single person ventured from the East to try to make it to the West. It was the way it was and the way that Jarl had always known it to be.

"Quiet out there today, brother," Eric said as he watched the nothingness alongside Jarl. They had grown up together and were as brothers in arms. They had fought in many battles, never losing to their combined foes. Jarl knew how Eric would move and Eric, in turn, could anticipate Jarl's strikes and parries. This was why the result was never a foregone conclusion when they trained together.

Jarl always preferred to wield a pair of wooden hand axes with sharpened iron heads. He had wrapped leather straps along the shafts, crossing over and over all the way up until they fastened over the metal head. Then, as though these fearsome weapons weren't already terrifying enough, Jarl had carved symbols, patterns and runes onto each of the weapons, on their blades and down the handles. These were the runes that would give the weapons their magical properties, or so it was believed.

Eric took a more traditional approach to his arms. His single axe was larger than Jarl's two combined, and it seemed as if some master craftsman had created the iron head. There were no misplaced edges, no dull sections on the razor-sharp edge, and if anyone were to examine the weapon closely, they would not find the tell-tale hammer marks of a piece of metal forced into shape against its will.

Both men wore furs covering cloth and leather armour atop leather trousers to protect themselves from their foes and the environment.

The climate in the Westlands was mild, though it would vary throughout the year from very cold to very warm. The clan knew, though, that if they ventured too far to the north, where the snow-covered mountains lay, the wind, snow and ice were too harsh for any mortal man to bear.

To the south sat simply miles and miles of desert, and it had been more than one generation since a visitor had arrived from there.

"It is always quiet here at the Chasm, brother," Jarl replied without looking at his best friend. "Nobody dares attempt to cross any longer, not now that they are aware of the dangers."

"It is not that they fear the danger, brother; our people fear the unknown. Plenty of men and women have crossed the God's Chasm, and never once has it proven to be fatal once the other side has been reached. They simply do not return." Eric replied.

"And why do you think that is, brother? Do you think our Western ways mean that once we see that the grass grows taller on the far side of the world, we do not return to beckon others to our side? These people do not turn back to us because they are killed the very moment they reach the eastern forests." Jarl almost spat his last words out; he knew that Eric was simply attempting to bait him, and he was ashamed of himself that he had been played so easily.

"You lack humour today, brother," Eric said calmly with a smile, not looking to begin more conversations about how the Chasm was a mystery that needed unravelling. "You and Sigrid are still having trouble starting a family of your own?"

Jarl stared away across the great Chasm as though it would provide an answer to Eric's question.

"The Gods have not seen fit to bless Sigrid with a child... but we pray to the Allfather that one day our time will come and that a child will be gifted to us."

Eric slapped Jarl on his shoulder and smiled. "Do not worry, brother, the Gods have their ways, and I am sure they will see fit to deliver a child to you and your wife. So keep faith in your mind and an axe in your hands, and you will see."

"Go back to the clan, Eric. Tell them that, once again, there is nothing to report from the Chasm," Jarl ordered, doing his best to change the subject. He knew that he had no superiority over his friend, but it was not an unreasonable request and truth be told, he had had enough of their conversation. He and Sigrid had been trying to conceive a child for so long that a little bit more of the hope that had already almost disappeared left him whenever he thought about it.

Eric and Jarl's clan, the Rakki, were one of the border clans that were sworn to protect the crossing between east and west. The Rakki were a particularly large clan compared to the others, with hundreds of men, women and children who all lived in a wide-open camp spanning an area of about a square mile.

The other clans were spread out along the God's Chasm and back to the west, though there was very little interaction between them save for a little trade when the climate dictated it. The clans kept mostly to themselves and seldom crossed the invisible borders between hunting grounds. On the rare occasion, a warband would meet out in the field, and the two clans would pass fleeting words between one another before returning to their people.

Eric took hold of Jarl's forearm, a gesture which Jarl returned warmly.

"Brother," Eric said, nodding to his friend. "I fear that the mists arrive tonight, do not find yourself without shelter on your watch."

"I have never been one who is afraid of the tears of the Gods, but perhaps this time they may bring me answers if I only ask my questions loud enough," Jarl replied. It had been a while since the last mists, though each time they arrived, it was known that accompanying them was the sound of distant rumbling crying. This sound, it was told, was that of the Gods mourning the passing of one of their own, though there was speculation of which God they wept for.

The Rakki believed that the tears were Frigg's, Odin's wife, and they were shed for the two sons they had lost, Baldur and Hodur.

Jarl waited for Eric to leave and stood to watch the Chasm once again. His duty was sacred and one that he would never take lightly. He could see that. Indeed, the mists were beginning to roll behind the darkness of the night that was due to arrive within the next hour or so, and he instinctively gripped the leather handles of both his axes by his side as he waited for them to arrive.

In the distance, a rumble shuddered the clouds from the very skies, and then a flash lit up the world around Jarl. He knew that following this would come the rains of the Gods and the sobs that the mists brought. Jarl had never seen the tears of the Gods accompanied by the crying mists before, but he was not afraid. It would take more than the weather to move Jarl of the Rakki clan.

Within minutes, both the rains and the mists arrived to assault him. The rain fell hard on him and made his furs heavy to bear, but he remained standing stalwart, peering out into the Chasm. He could barely see, but he was bold to his task.

Then he heard a sound. It was the only thing he could hear over the offending rain and rumbling thunder above, and it was unmistakable. From within the Chasm, he could hear the sound of crying.

"The mists bring the sadness of the Gods again," he muttered to himself and looked up into the sky. A flash of lightning made him wince.

Then he heard it again, the crying, though this time it sounded as though it was closer and not coming from some divine being. It sounded more like it was a baby crying.

Jarl moved a few steps forward, closer to the edge of the Chasm and peered over the edge, forcing his eyesight to cut through the mist and rain.

Then as though out of nowhere, he saw a dirty, bloodied hand stretch out and grip the Chasm wall. He thought about reaching out to help whoever it was, but before he could do so, a second hand was raised toward him and a tiny, crying baby girl rested on it.

Jarl withdrew from the hand and the baby. It was the last thing he had been expecting to see, and it scared him. Then he heard a faint voice from below the arms.

"Please... I beg of you... take my child..." It was the sound of a desperate mother, and he knew that the only choice he had at this very moment was to take the baby and deposit her to safety.

The burden of choice, though, was removed from him. The mother pushed the baby up towards Jarl with all her might, and Jarl had just enough time to see her tear-stained face before she disintegrated into dust and was blown away by the wind. Then he looked down at his hands, and realised that he had caught this fragile baby girl, and that he had no choice now but to ensure her safety.

"Who's out there?" he called into the Chasm. "Are there any more of you?"

No reply came.

Jarl moved along the Chasm's edge with baby in arm, searching for any sign of another coming to retrieve this child, but no matter how hard he looked or for how long, nobody came.

Then the rains stopped, the mist passed, and the world again turned silent, save for the tiny baby girl crying in his arms.

Jarl looked down at her. She was wrapped in a short fur though it was enough to engulf her. He hadn't had the chance to look at her mother clearly enough to see if she had looked as the baby did, but that didn't matter. Jarl knew that his sacred duty was to prevent the crossing of the God's Chasm from one way or the other.

It was strange, though; his duty was to guard against members from the clans of the west crossing the Chasm, not against ingress from the east. For there had never been such an event, and Jarl didn't know what the right thing to do was.

As Jarl looked down at the baby, who was still wet and crying, he felt his heart inside his chest skip a beat, and at that moment, he felt the absolute need to keep this little girl safe. He didn't know what it was that had caused the feeling, whether this was a normal thing when saving a child from a near-death experience, but he knew that this little girl was his own to protect above everything else.

And then, all of a sudden, she stopped crying.

"What am I to do with you?" Jarl asked the girl. "By the Gods..."

Jarl looked back across the Chasm to the far side again, now that the mist and rains had disappeared, searching for any signs of life on the far side, but as usual, not a single pinprick of light betrayed any human life from beyond the Chasm. Atop the far side sat a dense woodland, but beyond that, the east was a mystery to the clans of the west.

Jarl spent a long time holding the baby girl in his arms, swaying her gently back and forth until she fell asleep. He knew that eventually, he would have to return home to his wife

Sigrid, but he did not know what her reaction would be when he appeared with a baby when they had been so far unable to conceive a child of their own.

Jarl could not leave this helpless life behind though. His mind swayed to-and-fro between his duty and his morality although he already knew which would win this internal battle; Jarl would take this girl home and do his best to keep her safe, though he knew that this could also mean keeping her hidden.

If Jarl reported that this child had come from the east, even if his clan members believed the story of her mother's passing – which even Jarl hadn't begun to unravel yet – then they could send the child back to where she came from, or worse, take her life and end the threat that she posed to their ways. After all, if the child had been an adult, she would not have even made it past Jarl.

Eric would return to the Chasm soon though, and Jarl could not risk that his brother would see him sheltering this child. If he asked too many questions or harboured any suspicions, then he could demand that Jarl hand over the baby – something that Jarl did not think that he could do.

The only choice that Jarl had was to take the baby back to his home and try to talk with Sigrid before he made any further decisions. He only hoped that his wife would understand and not attempt to remove the child from him. He knew Sigrid well, though, and he would not have married her if he had thought she would ever stand against him.

Jarl covered the baby as well as he could with the furs that wrapped her and began his journey back to the settlement and his home. It would not take long to reach the clan, at least twenty minutes or so, but he wanted to do his best to try to avoid anyone else witnessing his return and having to field questions that he would rather not have to answer.

It was dark as Jarl reached the outskirts of the clan, torches spread throughout illuminating the settlement in their dim orange glow. The settlement was essentially a series of farmlands separated by small wooden fences encircling a wooden longhouse. Most of the clan members slept within the longhouse, although the few who had married had been allowed to build their own smaller wooden huts on the outside of the farmland to give the couples their own slice of privacy away from the rest of the clan.

Jarl and Sigrid had been married for five years, and it was expected that the pair would soon parent a child though their relations had yet proved fruitless.

Jarl peered into the settlement, watching for any sign of movement coming from anyone else who happened to be awake and moving about. Then he took a deep breath and moved quickly toward his hut, where Sigrid would be asleep inside.

Thankfully, he made it inside and closed the door before anyone saw that he had returned from his post early. He knew that Eric would realise that fact and would come looking for him eventually, but he paid that no mind because right now he had more important things on his mind.

"I have been awaiting your return," Sigrid's voice came from behind Jarl as he shut the door, making him start. "I was visited in my sleep with a dream of conflict."

Jarl did not turn to face her, though he replied: "And what did this dream speak of with you?"

"It was of a great war, fighting and death," Sigrid replied. "I do not know where this place was, but I felt it was a warning of impending chaos within our clan."

Jarl let his shoulders drop, then turned to face Sigrid. As he did so, the wet fur cradling the baby fell away to reveal her peaceful, sleeping face, and Sigrid gasped sharply.

"What is this, Jarl?" Sigrid asked in a pressured whisper. "Which bed did you remove this child from? You must take it back immediately!"

Jarl opened his mouth to speak, but he realised that the words just wouldn't come. He knew that he loved Sigrid and trusted her with everything that he was, but now... now he had a new duty: to protect this child, and he did not want to find himself in a situation where he would have to choose between the two.

"Give her to me, Jarl," Sigrid ordered.

Jarl recoiled slightly, his body language portraying protection for the baby though he did not say a word to his wife.

Sigrid took a step closer to Jarl, her hands outstretched, and he felt his body letting the child go to her. She was his wife, and he knew there would be nothing he could do to betray her.

Sigrid took the child from Jarl and cradled her in her arms. Jarl could feel the warmth pass between them, and then he realised that his wife wasn't looking to take the baby from him to cause her harm; rather, he could also sense the need to protect the baby emanating from his wife.

"Does she have a name?" Sigrid asked softly, her gaze not rising from the baby.

Jarl did not respond for a long moment. "She does not," he said simply. It was the only answer he could give, given the circumstances surrounding how he had found himself with the child.

Sigrid nodded. "We shall name her for my mother," she said. "Little Sylfia. I will remain inside the hut until two months have passed and then we will tell the clan that I have given birth to the child."

Jarl did not know what to say. He had been expecting to fight for the baby's protection, but Sigrid had simply accepted the situation they had found themselves in. She had even gone so far as to concoct a lie to tell the rest of the clan on their behalf.

Jarl moved towards Sigrid and wrapped his arms around her and Sylfia. They were a family together, and no person could get in the way of their combined futures.

"I must visit Elder Wise before the night is done," Jarl whispered to Sigrid. He knew that he was standing close to both his wife and Sylfia and he did not want to give either a start with his deep tone.

Sigrid nodded slightly in response and moved back away from Jarl, sitting on the furs on the ground with little Sylfia still in her arms.

Jarl quietly left his new and unexpected family to their rest, closing the door behind him.

"Where have you been, brother? I return to our duty to find you missing, and here you are, taking time to visit your wife?" Eric's voice caused Jarl to start, though he was thankful he had managed to close his door before his friend had appeared.

"Forgiveness, brother. Sigrid has not been feeling well lately so I came to check on her. I shall return to duty shortly," Jarl said.

"Ah, there is no need to return, brother. The night is still, and the Chasm is quiet as it always is. I will take a shortened shift, and we will call the night done. Then tomorrow, you will owe me a drink!" Eric replied with a beaming smile.

Jarl responded with a smile of his own and made his move to leave Eric to get back to his duty.

Elder Wise lived in her own hut near the centre of the settlement. She was old and could not move quickly, but when any clan member needed guidance in times of uncertainty or need, she was the one they called upon; she had a connection to the Gods that no clan member could understand.

The Elder would provide foresight into what would become of a raiding party or if the coming harvests were to be bountiful. To the clan, she was invaluable, although more than a few gave her hut a wide birth through fear for what she may tell them.

As Jarl neared the Elder's hut, he automatically clutched the axe hanging down his right leg until his fingers turned white. It was where he always found comfort in situations where he lacked confidence – when things were difficult, his way out was to fight, so his hands searched for their weapons.

"It has been a long time since Jarl Ulfson has graced the Elder with his presence, but no raid into the west is on the horizon, is it?" The Elder's voice was loud and clear, though Jarl had not yet made any move to enter the Elder's hut. Somehow, she knew he was there, and she had spoken loudly enough for him to hear.

"I come to ask for your guidance, Elder Wise," Jarl announced as loudly as he dared so that the Elder would hear though it would not alert the rest of the clan.

"But he doesn't come in when it is clear that he is supposed to," the Elder replied.

Jarl absorbed the statement for a second, opened the wooden door and stepped inside.

He had been in the Elder's hut on several occasions, but he never enjoyed it. Elder Wise had a penchant for bones, and she hung them around the hut as though they were some morbid reminders of life and death. The fire that burned brightly in the centre of the hut cast shadows on the walls, and they danced as though the creatures that had given her hut its bones were full of life.

"No, no raid in the coming days, and the harvest is still weeks away. He is here for another reason, I can tell... but what is that sound that the mist carries?" Elder Wise continued speaking as though to herself.

"Elder Wise, please, I come to ask for your guidance for the future," Jarl started but Elder Wise held up a single hand to stop him.

The Elder was a wizened older lady, her nose crooked with age and her hair white, wild and un-braided. She stood with a bend in her back on the far side of the fire and looked directly at Jarl.

"There are always two plain routes for a hero to take in this world, Jarl Ulfson. One easy and one difficult. Tell me, Jarl, what route do you prefer to travel?"

Jarl thought about the question and decided that logic was the only way to answer. "If one sea is wild and the other smooth, then I would take the calmer waters," he replied.

"But do you not need wind in your sails to reach your destination?" Elder Wise asked quickly.

"Then, without wind, my warband would lower the oars and row to where we needed to get to," Jarl said.

"So you would place your fortune in the hands of men and fly in the face of the Gods? You would choose the strength of your warband over the will of Njord? Tell me, Jarl Ulfson, what makes you think that your will is stronger than that of the sea?"

Jarl did not know how to answer this question. He had never really thought about it; he and his warband would row to where they needed to go, and if a wind took them, they would let it do so.

"Forgive me, Elder," Jarl said, "I do not understand the question."

"My question is," Elder Wise held Jarl's gaze for a long moment, "do you think that the will of man can compete with that of the Gods?" But before Jarl could answer, the Elder followed up with another question.

"Do you know why we guard the God's Chasm?" She asked.

"Yes, Elder," Jarl answered with a bow. "We guard to protect those wishing to cross from meeting an untimely end. Not a single person who has sought to cross the Chasm has ever returned...."

"Not a single person, hmm?" Elder Wise interrupted Jarl.

Jarl shut his mouth with a click of his teeth. Was there any way that this Elder knew about the arrival of Sylfia and what he and Sigrid had planned for the child?

The Elder did not speak for a moment but held Jarl's gaze with a knowing expression. Then she seemed to conclude that he was not going to reveal any further information on the subject.

Elder Wise began to pull bones from thin wires around the hut and gather them up in her hands. Whispering something inaudible to the collection, she threw them into a metal bowl and pulled them above the fire.

Jarl watched as the Elder shook the bowl, and the tiny white bones leapt into position, finally resting and crossing over each other in the centre of the bowl. The symbol they formed was unmistakable, and Jarl took a step back.

"Ragnarök," he breathed.

"See now, does he? Actions taken in the face of the Gods have consequences," Elder Wise spoke again as though Jarl was not there.

"Forgiveness," Jarl said quietly, though the Elder interrupted him again.

This foretelling does not speak of Ragnarök as it is brought to this realm," she said. "The path that you have chosen has two possible outcomes, and it is within you to guide your own path. The first is that your actions will bring about Ragnarök, the first signs of which have already come to pass."

Jarl did not know this. He had assumed that when Ragnarök came, it would be quick and sudden, not something that arrived with early warning.

"The second path is that your actions directly prevent the passing of Ragnarök. It is yet unclear which path will bear fruit, but these are the two options you face," the Elder said.

Jarl had never been one to shirk his responsibilities; in fact, he was one member of the clan who took his duty as seriously as he could, though it didn't stop him from asking the question. "And if I refuse to play with fate? If I sit on the ground and do nothing?" He twisted his brown braided moustache as he spoke – the only sign he would ever give that he was either uncomfortable or deep in thought.

"He thinks he can sit by and watch does he?" Elder Wise replied. "You would prefer to sit and do nothing as the longhouse burns to the ground with your family inside, all the while a river of water runs by your feet?"

"I... I would aid those in need; I would save my family," Jarl replied quickly, as though this was all happening as they spoke.

"And if it was the will of the Gods that your family should die?" Elder Wise asked.

"Then I would fight against the very Gods themselves," Jarl replied. Then he closed his mouth quickly. He hadn't known what was happening to this point, but he was sure now that the entire conversation had led to him making that very statement.

Elder Wise smiled at Jarl. "You should remember those words, Jarl Ulfson, that is not an oath to be taken lightly."

Then the Elder sat down on the ground and closed her eyes. It was what she usually did when her foretellings had been completed, and Jarl knew that he would not receive any further wisdom from her.

·

-

2

"Do you know why we guard the God's Chasm, Sylfia?" Jarl asked his daughter. She had grown tall and strong over the last ten years. Jarl and Sigrid had kept her safe and well-trained during her first years, and the Rakki clan had welcomed her as one of their own, for it was the story they had been told.

Sylfia was cared for greatly within the settlement, with many clan members doing what they could to help her with her training or daily tasks. She would never shirk her duties, though, and where she needed no help, she asked for none.

"We guard the Chasm so that nobody tries to cross over to the other side because when they do, they do not come back," Sylfia recounted for her father.

Jarl placed a hand on her head and tousled her thick blonde hair. It had a single braid on either side that kept it out of her eyes. As he did so, the same thought that he had on a number of occasions occurred to him – that neither he nor Sigrid had fair hair, and he was still shocked that nobody had yet mentioned that fact.

"Do you think that one day we will build a bridge to the other side so that we may learn the secrets of the east?" Sylfia asked.

Jarl stroked his beard and peered out across the God's Chasm. "I do not think the Gods would like our clans to travel to the east, daughter. This is why they made the Chasm, and why we never cross."

"But is it not our way to explore the unknown and bring back with us the things that these distant lands hold sacred?" Sylfia pushed. She had always been inquisitive and had taken the teachings of the clan to heart.

"You are correct, daughter. We are a people of exploration, but we must also respect our sacred duties for these are in place for the safety of all mortal beings."

Sylfia looked thoughtful as she stared at the far side of the God's Chasm. It was not the first time she would ask such questions of her father and they both knew that it would not be the last.

Jarl and Sigrid had both told Sylfia where she had come from when she had been old enough to understand, and they had made it clear to her that she could never repeat those words to another within the clan for fear of what may happen to the three of them. Sylfia, to her credit, had never spoken a word about her own origins.

"Come, Sylfia," Jarl said as he turned away from the Chasm. "You are to learn our ways of tanning today with your mother."

The pair walked back to the settlement in search of Sigrid, who had already agreed to teach their daughter how the clan created their furs and leathers for clothing and bedding. It was the way of the Rakki clan to pass on the knowledge they had gained over generations so that the future of their people would be assured.

"Sylfia!" Sigrid called to her daughter as the three saw each other. "I hope you learned something new from your father this morning?"

"Yes, father taught me that if the Gods will something, you should not fight against it," Sylfia said.

"That... is not entirely true," Jarl replied, though neither Sylfia nor Sigrid seemed to hear him.

"Come then, treat these furs with me so that you may learn to keep yourself warm in the colder months," Sigrid ordered. Sigrid was an expert in creating furs and warm clothing and Jarl knew of nobody better to teach their daughter this skill.

Sigrid had a large animal skin on the ground in front of her, and as she spoke she cleaned the underside of the pelt to make it smooth and free of any debris or sinews.

"Mother... what is that smell?" Sylfia asked as her mother worked her way across the pelt with a small, sharp blade. She couldn't help but pinch her nose as she spoke.

"Sylfia, remove your hand from your face; this is a smell that you must get used to if you wish to survive," Sigrid said. Sylfia had not failed to notice that Jarl had walked away from them. This pelt has been prepared for us over the last few months. We soak it in urine and dry it to what you see here."

Sylfia listened and fought the urge to pinch her nostrils again. It was not an easy task though.

"Now we work the droppings of the animals into the skin to make it supple," Sigrid continued.

She stood up and walked towards a skin she had already prepared, stretched out across a wooden frame.

"We use tannin that we take from the oak trees and submerge the skin here, then it is made more flexible and will last without rotting."

As always Sylfia listened to the instruction and did her best to remember what she was being told.

Sigrid and Sylfia spent the rest of the day working with leathers, furs and skins until Sylfia could work on the items without guidance. It was the way that she had always been taught and the way that Sigrid had found most effective.

The sound of heavy footsteps approaching eventually wrenched their attention from their work.

"Tormod, what is happening?" Sigrid asked the large Viking as he approached, running toward them with his huge Warhammer held between his hands.

"They come from the east, come quickly!" he called and both Sigrid and Sylfia leapt to their feet and began to run toward the God's Chasm without any further explanation.

Tormod disappeared into the settlement proper shouting his warning as he ran, his voice growing quieter the further toward the Chasm both Sigrid and Sylfia ran.

"Mother, what is happening?" Sylfia breathed as she struggled to keep up with Sigrid.

"I do not know Sylfia, but we will find out and put a stop to this madness. It is forbidden for anyone to cross the God's Chasm." She winced as she spoke, realising what she had said, but Sylfia did not reply with a word of objection.

When the pair reached the Chasm, they came to a halt beside both Eric and Jarl who stood looking out into the depths below.

"Jarl, what is happening here? Tormod came to warn..." Sigrid started to ask, but stopped when Jarl raised a hand to silence her. Both Sigrid and Sylfia stepped forward to look to where Jarl's gaze had fallen and they too realised they could see a woman carrying a child in her arms across the divide between east and west.

"Turn back!" Eric's voice abruptly boomed down into the Chasm. "It is our sacred duty to protect against ingress from the west! You are not welcome here!" He turned to smile at Jarl, Sigrid and Sylfia, but he was greeted with three stern and worried faces.

"What causes you concern, brother?" Eric asked, picking up on Jarl's expression.

Jarl stroked his beard but did not respond.

"Who is it? What are they doing?" Sylfia asked excitedly, the only member of her family willing to speak at this given moment.

"I do not know, little Sylfia, but do not worry, we will turn them back one way or another," Eric stated with a warm smile.

"Can we not help them?" Sylfia asked. "They come from an unknown place and could have answers to questions to which we have yet to learn the answers."

"It is not our place to question our sacred duty, little Sylfia," Eric explained. "The rules we live by must be followed to ensure the safety of every clan member."

"But why..." Sylfia started.

"Enough, Sylfia," Jarl interrupted. "This is the way that we must follow. Do you understand?"

"Yes but..."

"Then no more questions," Jarl said, giving her a stern look. Sylfia backed away from her father's gaze and closed her mouth. Jarl could tell that she was upset and wanted to say more, but he could not risk the truth of her own crossing coming out – even to Eric, his brother. He trusted Eric of course, though like Jarl, Eric's loyalty to duty and the clan could potentially outweigh his oath to his brother.

The Rakki clan members watched as the pair below made their way across the Chasm - if they had heard Eric's warning, they did not betray that fact. Eventually, the pair made it to the Chasm wall and began climbing up towards the clan members who stood awaiting their arrival.

Sylfia watched silently as Eric and Jarl drew their axes and adopted a defensive posture, ready for the pair's arrival.

Above everything else though, Sylfia was amazed at how this woman was climbing the sheer wall with a baby in her arms. She wondered if her own mother had been able to climb the wall so expertly, though she shook the thought from her mind in case anyone could overhear her thoughts.

Sylfia stood by her mother and wondered what Sigrid thought of what was happening before them. She wanted to ask, but knew better than to make a sound after her father had told her enough was enough.

Then Sylfia saw a hand reaching up from the Chasm, begging for aid and to her surprise, Jarl reached down and grasped it around the wrist.

"Jarl Ulfson let go of that arm immediately!" The Rakki clan chief, Halvard's voice boomed from behind the group. It had all happened so fast that Eric had seemingly forgotten what he was doing, and had not moved to stop Jarl, although the arrival of the clan chief and most of the rest of the settlement led by Tormod certainly changed things.

Jarl, though, did not let go of the arm. Once again, he found himself unable to let a mother and baby fall to their death.

Sylfia watched as the clan chief's face began to redden in Jarl's defiance of his orders, although the choice was removed from Jarl because despite his strong grasp, the arm that he was holding disintegrated into dust and both the mother and the baby floated away into the wind, dissipating into a dark cloud as they went.

"What is this, Jarl?" Halvard growled. The chief rarely appeared at the Chasm in person, leaving the rest to their duty, although in truth this was because he was afraid of the place above anything else.

A long time ago before Halvard had become chief, Elder Wise had prophesied that the Chasm would be the cause of his death. Unfortunately, there was no wider elaboration and the chief had never spoken of this foretelling, but as a result, he had spent his entire life keeping as much distance between it and him as possible.

Jarl could not think of anything to say to defend himself. If the woman and child had remained in his grasp, then surely he would have had to have made a choice, but as it was, there was no law broken and certainly no course of action to be taken.

"What are you thinking, Jarl?" Halvard asked again. "You endanger the clan and for what? Some interlopers from the East? Do not be so foolish!"

"He was not being foolish!" Sylfia called out. "He was doing what he thought was right and if any of you would have done anything differently, then next time you can be the one who tries to save the woman and child from certain death!"

"Sylfia be quiet!" Sigrid berated her daughter and placed a hand on her shoulder. "This is not the time for such words."

"It is never the time for such words!" Sylfia objected.

"Sylfia, quiet!" Jarl boomed and Sylfia obediently shut her mouth.

"Jarl, you anger me with your disobedience, "Halvard said, his anger visibly abating. "You have sworn an oath to our ways, and you move against your own words."

"This time I will choose to look the other way, but your actions have been noted and witnessed by the entire settlement," he gestured to the clan members around him, most stern-faced and some nodding slowly in agreement. "If you choose to disobey your duty again, it will be the last thing that you do within the Rakki clan."

Jarl let his head fall in obedience. The truth was that he was happy that he did not have to make the decision because he was still unsure of what he would do.

The chief and the other clan members slowly filtered away, leaving Jarl, Sigrid, Eric and Sylfia alone at the edge of the Chasm.

"What were you thinking, Jarl?" Eric asked in a whisper. "You could have been killed for your actions."

"I do not know brother, I looked down at the child and did not have the heart to let go. Perhaps my heart grows weak as the years pass." He smiled at Sigrid and Sylfia, though the smile did not reach his eyes.

"Next time I only hope that you do as you know you are supposed, brother, I will not be able to protect you from the rest of the clan," Eric said.

"I need no protection brother, but perhaps a long drink and a good night's sleep," Jarl replied.

"To hell with sleep, Jarl. Tonight is your watch and do not even think about trying to help anyone else cross the Chasm," Eric said with a smile.

Sylfia opened her mouth but a quick stern look from her mother forced her to shut it again quickly. Eric had made a joke, but there was no way he could have known how close to the truth he actually was.

3

Another ten years passed since what the Rakki clan remembered as the 'day of the crossing', though the majority would not know that it was the second such crossing of the God's Chasm, Sylfia being the first.

Sylfia had since become an integral part of the Rakki clan, and both of her parents had continued their duties given to them as part of daily life. Sylfia had moved into the longhouse with the majority of the clan as customs dictated, leaving her parents to enjoy their time alone within their hut. If she ever took a husband, she would also be afforded a hut of her own to begin her own family, but there were no indications of such.

There had been a prolonged period of peace between the clans of the west, for harvests had been bountiful, seasons mild and, by all accounts, nothing much had changed over the last decade. This was all to change however with the news that Elder Wise was approaching her final breath; time, an adversary who could be held at bay for a while but never beaten, having finally caught up with her.

The passing of the Elder would mark a significant shift in the structure of the Rakki clan for there was nobody to take the mantle of foresight from the Elder. Although there were other Elders within the clan, these were the ones who had fought battles or had guided the clan economically over the years and had grown to such an age that their positions were less active and more honorary. Without Elder Wise, the clan would essentially be blinded to the future.

Elder Wise had foretold of her own passing on more than one occasion, though many did not believe her words. Most had assumed that she was simply losing her mind in her old age, or was otherwise mixing up the signals that she had been given by her gift as her mind grew dull through old age.

The Elder was brought out to the centre of the settlement so the clan could surround her and witness her passing, as customs dictated. There would be three fires lit to symbolise the birth, life and death of the Elder and each clan member would have their chance to speak with her before she left the mortal realm to walk the hallways into the beyond. The Elder would not grace the halls of Valhalla because she had not fallen in battle, rather she would be sent to Helheim, where those who died of old age and sickness resided for all of time.

Jarl, Sylfia and Sigrid stood together as a family and watched as members of the clan spoke with Elder Wise. The words they all exchanged were pleasant though ordinary; most offered words of comfort or thanks and on a few occasions the Elder would nod slightly and breathe out single-word replies.

Eventually, it was the turn of Jarl's family to speak with the Elder and Sylfia stepped forward first, being the youngest member of the family and therefore with the most years ahead of her.

Sylfia had never spoken with the Elder in her entire life. It was not by accident, however; she had kept her distance in case anything was said that would betray her true origins.

The young girl approached her Elder, her blonde hair still braided on both sides though she was nothing like the girl that had been delivered to this clan so many years ago.

When she reached the Elder's side, the older, dying woman did something that not a single member of the clan had been expecting: she turned to face Sylfia within her bed and grabbed hold of her shoulder. The Elder then pulled with all her might to lean her frail body close to Sylfia to whisper directly into her ear. As she did so, Sylfia saw that the Elder's eyes glowed with a bright golden hue before fading back to their original dark brown. Then the Elder spoke.

"I have seen what you are capable of, child of the east. I know that my soul will travel to Helheim and the Underworld, where I will await my return to the mortal realm. I have seen too that you have two paths before you. You can free me from that place or you can damn the mortal realm with the arrival of Ragnarök. You must choose the difficult path. You must always swim upstream to fight the will of the Gods. Save me, child. Save us all. Swear your oath to me now that you will do all you can to help me."

Then Elder Wise released her grip on Sylfia, rolled back and breathed her last, strained breath. The clan fell silent and all that Sylfia could hear was the crackle of the three burning fires surrounding her. She stepped back, a single tear rolling down her cheek as her mother and father wrapped their arms around her.

"I swear it," Sylfia breathed.

The funeral for Elder Wise would be carried out over the next few days, when the clan as a whole would again have the chance to say goodbye to their lost foreseer, but Sylfia had something else on her mind. The words that the Elder had spoken to her kept circling her mind as she tried to figure out their meaning. There was definitely something within those words, though Sylfia needed help deciphering them.

"Father, I wish to ask you about something that Elder Wise said to me before she died," Sylfia said to Jarl once she had followed her parents back to their hut. Jarl knew this had been coming, because Sylfia seldom returned with them unless she wanted to learn something.

"What did the Elder say to you?" Jarl asked suspiciously.

"She told me to take the difficult path so that I could help avoid Ragnarök, I think," she added quickly. "I do not think that I am so important that I alone can avoid the coming of Ragnarök, but her words sounded sincere..."

Jarl stroked his beard uncomfortably. "Elder Wise has spoken to me of Ragnarök in the past, and also of taking the difficult path in the face of the will of the Gods. The day you came to me she told me that your life would lead to one of two paths, one easy and one difficult, though to me she also said that the difficult path would lead to the more fortunate result." Jarl saw no need to lie to Sylfia now, she was old enough to hear the truth and come to her own conclusions.

"But what docs it mean, father?" Sylfia asked with wide eyes. Jarl simply shrugged his shoulders. He had no idea how to interpret the Elder's words either, and any way he tried he knew would mean hardship for either his family, his clan, or Sylfia alone. All of these outcomes were not favourable, so did not bear thinking about.

"Father?" Sylfia asked when Jarl did not respond.

"Your father and I do not possess the answers to these questions, Sylfia," Sigrid answered on Jarl's behalf. "We have spoken of these words before and we will do so again, but the result has always been the same: we do not know their meaning nor intent and until one becomes clear, we can do nothing to heed them."

It sounded a little too casual for Sylfia's mind to bear though. How could she receive such a warning and simply ignore it until something happened? It sounded very much as though unless she did something active, it could mean the end of the world.

"So I am just supposed to ignore these dire words? I am to forget what I have been told because there is nothing I can do about it? How does that fit with the way of the clan?" Sylfia asked, her voice raising and pulse quickening. "I need to do something to prevent the passing of Ragnarök do I not?"

"Sylfia, these should not be the worries of one as young as you. You should not worry yourself with these grand efforts that could simply prove to be the ramblings of a dying foreseer," Sigrid placated her daughter.

"Would this not be the easy path? To sit back and do nothing while the mortal realm crumbles under Ragnarök? Would the difficult task not be to do *something?* Anything at all?"

Jarl stepped forward with his arms outstretched to take Sylfia in a warm embrace.

"Child, we need not worry about such events right now and besides, we are but few in a realm of many. What is it that you think we can do?" Jarl liked to call Sylfia 'child' not to belittle her, but rather as a sign of his adoration for her.

Sylfia hated it when her father called her child though, and she could do nothing more to prevent her anger and frustration from boiling over. Before Jarl could embrace her properly, she spun on her heels and stormed from the hut, slamming the door behind her.

Sylfia walked purposefully back to the centre of the settlement, though she knew that it was not her parents' fault that she felt this way. She simply felt that she was supposed to be doing something and that *something* was just out of reach.

That night when Sylfia was back in the longhouse with the rest of the clan and her anger had abated, lying on the furs spread out across the wide-open floor, Elder Wise's words floated around her mind and snapped at her as though their meaning was so obvious though she was blind to it.

All she seemed able to piece together was that she was supposed to take the more difficult of two paths, though she knew not what these choices were, if they had already passed or even if they would come to pass in the near future. And to say that one young Rakki girl could prevent Ragnarök? It was just all too much to even begin to think about.

And then something did come to mind. There was one rule that the Rakki and all the clans to the west followed. One task that was so difficult that not a single clan member had managed to complete it and live to tell the tale. One thing that would mean flying directly in the face of the will of the Gods: to cross their Chasm and explore the eastern continent.

The idea was preposterous though. Sylfia had been raised to follow this one central rule of the Rakki clan and her father was even sworn to prevent the crossing of the Chasm from either west to east or east to west, though that would simply make it more difficult, would it not?

Sylfia tried her hardest to force away the thought. She knew that it was the wrong thing to do and to even think about attempting such a thing could be enough to get her entire family thrown out of the clan, left to fend for themselves in the wilderness in the best-case scenario. But then again, if the fate of the world hung in the balance, would the risk not be worth the reward?

It was not the night to have such thoughts though and Sylfia knew that. Eventually, she would be able to fall into slumber and forget about her ideas of breaking the one rule that her people held in the highest regard. Her slumber though, would not be dreamless.

Sylfia walked through her dreamscape as though she knew she had to keep going, though the place where she found herself was unknown. She was within a field of green grass atop the edge of a cliff that overlooked a wide, flat sea. She could hear the loud sobs of somebody crying nearby but she could not see where they were coming from. Then the skies above her, which had been bright and blue, opened up to allow huge droplets of water to cascade down to the ground.

Sylfia stopped walking and looked up at the sky, which was still bright and blue. Then, as though from nowhere, an axe the size of an entire continent flew down from the sky and impacted the ground a short distance from where she stood. The head of the weapon buried itself deep into the ground and she almost fell over when the shockwave that shifted the very earth hit her seconds later.

Once Sylfia had removed her defensive forearm from before her face, she peered across the expanse at the weapon, trying to figure out where it had come from and why it was so massive, although there did not seem to be anything else extraordinary about it.

With no choice but to continue onwards, Sylfia walked towards the mighty axe, though it seemed to take an age for her to reach it. When she did, the sheer scale of the weapon struck her with complete awe.

Reaching a hand out to touch the axe that spanned upwards like a huge metal wall, Sylfia could feel warmth emanating from it and it made her hesitate for a second. In that moment, a red rooster flew down from the sky to stand on the ground beside her. It crowed loudly at Sylfia and she woke with a start. But in the instant before she awoke, she saw the face of a giant high above her, his hair and beard a jet black and his eyes as white as the moon.

Sylfia could only guess what all of this meant, but her mind was wide awake once more. There was only one explanation for all of this: the Gods had sent her this dream as a warning not to sit idly by when she was supposed to be working. Too many times already she had been told not to take the easy path and again she thought of the Chasm that separated east and west. Her desire to break the one sacred law had been burned into her mind, and no matter how she tried to avoid the thought, it remained as clear as day.

4

Sylfia wrestled with her inner thoughts throughout the next day. She worked as she was supposed to and kept her focus on her tasks, though whenever she had thought that she had finally managed to remove the idea of crossing the Chasm from the forefront of her thoughts, it came back within a moment.

It was not until the late evening that she decided that the only way to appease her conscience and heed the warnings of her dreams and the foreseer, was to cross the Chasm. Just once, to see what lies beyond. It would not be an easy task physically and knowing that she would betray everything her clan held dear was mentally draining and filled her mind with dread and foreboding.

She waited until the darkness rolled in and the long shadows within the settlement arrived to starve out the daylight. Her pulse was racing at the mere thought of what she would do this night, but she pushed down on her anxieties as she had always been taught.

She fastened her two short swords to her back so they could be quickly drawn in times of danger. they would not hang down her sides as they traditionally did but would remain out of the way once she started climbing.

Sylfia was an excellent climber. She had practised for years climbing up and down trees in the sparse woodland while learning to hunt with an axe or spear. However, no weapon ever felt more at home in her hands than the pair of short swords she always kept close by.

Once she was sure that nobody else in the settlement was paying any attention to her, Sylfia slipped out of the longhouse and disappeared into the darkness. She crept along the outside wall, keeping her back to the wooden wall and her footfalls as slow and as silent as they had ever been. Once she reached the corner, she walked straight forward and away from the clan, towards her most difficult and dangerous of tasks.

Sylfia did not plan on crossing the Chasm and disappearing into the east, so she had no need to carry rations of food or water. She would be gone and back again before daylight would break, so she would not waste time with unnecessary preparations.

There was a short stretch of woodland between the Rakki clan's settlement and the edge of the Chasm. During the early evening, torches were spread out along the Chasm's western edge which would remain burning for several hours. Some of the clan members would relight these torches during their patrols as they passed, though Sylfia knew that Eric and her father did not like to do this.

It took a short while for Sylfia to emerge from the woodland and take her position next to the Chasm, which now felt like it was her single reason for being.

She peered out into the darkness, trying to will her mind to see where her father and Uncle Eric, stood watch over the God's Chasm. She knew that the expanse was hundreds of miles long, though the clan members on guard duty generally had their favoured position to stand guard.

Jarl and Eric would light only their post with torches; they would never start a larger fire for warmth as they deemed it too dangerous, and if the need arose to conceal their presence it was easier to extinguish torches than it was to quash a roaring blaze, as Jarl had always explained to Sylfia.

As Sylfia moved closer towards the Chasm, she spotted the telltale pinprick of light off in the distance where her father and Eric were watching for signs of movement down in the darkness. She felt lucky that they were so far away, but somewhere deep down inside she had wanted her father to catch her, to tell her how ridiculous she was being, and take her home safely.

This was clearly the most difficult of paths though, for with each step that Sylfia took she felt the need to turn back around and return to the clan she was leaving behind. Her mind was so fragmented that she had to reason with herself to keep herself focused on her task.

"You can do this, Sylfia. You *must* do this."

Then she heard a sound moving towards her from the east and across the Chasm. It was the distant sound of somebody crying being carried on the wind and she recognised it for what it was. These were the God's tears that would come paired with the mists and she took it as a sign to move onward; she had already been told to follow the tears and took this as a clear sign that she was moving in the right direction.

Sylfia took one last look at where Eric and Jarl stood and then lowered herself slowly and silently over the edge of the Chasm.

If she had thought that climbing up a tree would have been good practice for descending the Chasm, Sylfia would have been dead wrong; the jagged cliff face offered irregular and sharp handholds that barely offered any protrusions and cut her hands as she fought for her grips.

But Sylfia was descending the chasm regardless and with each step she knew that she was getting closer and closer to the bottom.

She reached for a wide, flat rock and let it hold all of her weight. It crumbled to nothing in her hand.

Sylfia's heart lurched as she felt the world around her spin, to fall into the abyss and to her death. She scrambled with her hands and feet, searching for something, anything, to arrest her fall and then her hand grabbed onto the cliff face. Something was cutting into her palm, and she knew that she had lost at least two fingernails as she had scrambled but she clung on for her life.

She let her heart rate calm and her breathing return to normal although she had failed to notice that the rock that had fallen as she panicked had bounced off the Chasm wall and landed with a loud crack that had echoed off into the distance. Looking up, she could now see the shadows cast by Eric and her father's torches moving quickly along the cliff edge *towards* where she remained still. She now had just three choices: she could stay still where she was in the hope that her father would not notice her hugging the wall, she could climb back up and try to explain herself, or she could keep descending into the Chasm and forget everything that her mind was telling her about right and wrong.

Sylfia, though, was strong-bodied and strong-willed. She would not turn back. She would continue along the path she had chosen, the most difficult of paths and the one she believed would bring salvation to all the mortal realm. She closed her eyes, gritted her teeth and took another cautious step downwards.

She made an effort to check all the hand and footholds before she used them now, not wanting to alert Eric and her father to her position, although she knew that it was just a matter of time before they would discover her in the Chasm: the pair would now be alert and would search for the source of the falling rock. Even if they didn't see her scaling the wall, they would surely see her as she attempted to cross the base of the God's chasm to the other side.

Sylfia continued to descend slowly and carefully though when she looked up again she could see her clansmen looking down at where she hugged the wall. She could see them clearly but it was evident that they could not see her. She froze, unsure how to proceed until the pair stepped back and away from the Chasm's edge.

Not long after, Sylfia made it to the bottom and took a moment to catch her breath before she made any move to cross to the other side. Her hands burned with pain, her heart was racing and her mind was telling her that what she was doing was everything that she had ever been told not to do.

It didn't matter. Sylfia knew that if she wanted to take the most difficult of paths then this was certainly the way she was meant to go and the more she thought she needed to stop and turn back, the more she knew that this was the path that was foretold for her.

Then she stepped out onto the flat expanse between east and west.

"Who is down there?" Eric's voice carried down into the Chasm as soon as Sylfia had taken her single step. She did not answer and simply carried on walking straight ahead.

Then she heard her father's voice and that made her pause.

"It is our sacred duty to prevent the crossing of the God's Chasm. Whoever you are, you must turn back now!"

Sylfia then made the biggest mistake she may have ever made in her entire life: she turned and looked back up the Chasm wall to where Eric and her father both stood. They were unmistakable and apparently, so was she.

"Sylfia! What are you doing?" Jarl called out in exasperation. "Come back before it is too late!"

Sylfia knew as well as Jarl did that it was already too late for her. By simply crossing over the edge of the Chasm she had broken the one sacred rule that all of the clans of the west held in the highest regard. Before discovery she would have been able to rejoin the Rakki clan as nobody would have known what she had done, but now she had just one choice: to continue onward.

"I need to do this father; I believe that it is what I have been told to do. I know that I cannot return to the clan and that is the price I am willing to pay for my actions," Sylfia called back up, hearing her own voice carry and echo as she called.

"Sylfia, please!" Jarl cried. "It is my vow to keep you safe..."

"It is already too late father. I will always be thankful for what you have done but now my path is set in stone," she replied before he could end his statement. Then she wiped a single tear from her cheek and turned her back on the west, facing her future to the east. One way or another, that was where she needed to go; for better or worse, she simply had no choice.

"Sylfia!" Jarl called from behind her, but she did not turn to look back. She presumed that Eric was either holding her father back or comforting him, but either way she could not concern herself with that now because her journey was only one third complete.

Sylfia looked down at her hands in the darkness; even without light, she could tell that she was badly injured. Climbing up the eastern wall was going to be difficult but at least she thought it would be easier than the descent of the west.

She heard her father call out to her three more times before the Chasm fell silent, and that made her walk across the expanse even heavier. Guilt weighed down upon her and again she fought the desire to turn back and pray that all of this had been some terrible dream.

When Sylfia reached the sheer incline of the eastern wall and placed her bloodied hands against it, it became clear that this was no dream. No dream could cause as much pain as this, both emotionally and physically as her hands burned at the very touch of the wall.

Sylfia again closed her eyes tightly and gritted her teeth. If she did not make this journey now as the adrenaline coursed through her body, it would only become more and more difficult as she wasted her time. She had not brought provisions with her and the Chasm was devoid of life, so if she did not go to the other side where she could hunt or forage, she might never make it out alive. It made her think about her mother – her real mother - who had made this journey carrying her the entire way with no promise of salvation. Could this unknown west have been worth the risk of escape from whatever she was running from in the east? Some things were better not thought about, Sylfia decided as she slowly began to ascend the eastern wall.

Climbing up was easier for Sylfia, she could look to where her next handholds were to be without much effort, although her hands bled and burned with each new release and grip on the wall. Sylfia wanted to give up. She wanted to simply let go and fall back down to the sweet salvation of death below, but she knew how important this journey was; this was not just her own life and hardship that she worked for. If she let go now, she would have dishonoured her clan and her family for nothing.

Sylfia pushed the pain to the back of her mind and locked it away. It was all she could do to keep it from begging her to turn back and forget about everything else and she kept that door locked as tightly as she could. It was a coping mechanism that she had developed on her own and she was good at it.

Reaching for the top of the sheer face, Sylfia realised that finally, she had done it; she had made it to the eastern side of the God's Chasm and she was still alive. She was bloody and bruised and she could not close her hands into fists anymore, but she had made it.

That fact alone was a bit of a surprise to Sylfia, for a big part of her had wondered what really happened to the people who crossed the Chasm. Would they simply disintegrate into nothingness, struck down by the vengeful Gods once they crossed, or was something far more nefarious on the horizon? Either way, it did not matter, Sylfia had made it across and now she knelt on all fours on the ground, panting and willing the pain in her hands, arms and knees to abate.

Sylfia breathed deeply and held it in, allowing the air to circulate through her lungs properly before exhaling, a process which she repeated three times before raising herself back to her feet. Before her stood a treeline of dense woodland and she knew that if she turned to look behind her to the west, the pull to go back would grow within her once more.

It was dark in the forest before her, and Sylfia knew that darkness in an unknown place was dangerous, but she had no choice. Because she could no longer return to the west, she would need to find food, water and shelter above anything else, and the longer she waited the more difficult that task would become.

There was no alternative. Sylfia walked straight into the forest and her life as she knew it was over. Eric and her father would have seen everything that had happened and even if her father did not want to, then Eric would have told the rest of the Rakki clan what she had done.

She moved slowly, much slower than she had ever moved before because this was the first time she had been alone, in the dark and in some unknown place. It made the adrenaline that had surged through her body earlier return to keep her alert, although she knew that it would not last long. If she did not find something useful shortly then everything would become increasingly difficult until it would eventually become impossible.

It was not long though, and not especially far into the forest, when Sylfia noticed that a dense mist had begun to roll in and surround her. Even in the darkness, she had been able to see the trees surrounding her but now it was like she was walking through thick white smoke. She knew what this was though, even before the sound of crying that accompanied the mists reached her ears.

Sylfia had no choice though. The mists never brought anything dire with them, though they would make her passage more difficult. She could block out the noise of the distant crying, but minimal visibility would make hunting so much harder for her.

Then as though in answer to that thought, a patch of the mists cleared not twenty feet from her and through the darkness, illuminated as though by some divine light, stood a single doe, beautiful and proud.

It would not be the first time Sylfia had to kill an animal to survive, and she knew it would not be the last.

Although the Rakki clan respected nature and everything that the Gods provided for them, killing beasts of the land was a simple fact of life. They were always thankful for what they were given, utilising every part of each animal they had to kill and leaving nothing to waste.

This time would be no different. This single doe's meat could sustain her for weeks if she preserved and prepared it in just the right way. The skin too would provide additional warmth should the need arise if she dried and smoked it.

Sylfia grasped one of her short, shining swords from over her shoulder ready to attack the animal. As she did so a pain of pure fire erupted from her hand as it made contact with the weapon's hilt. It felt as though someone had stabbed her through the hand and in that moment she realised the truth: Sylfia's hands were too damaged from the journey across the Chasm to be effective in wielding her weapons.

The deer looked up as though it had heard some movement off in the distance that Sylfia herself had not heard, and then in a flash, as though out of nowhere, a huge grey blur took hold of the doe and the pair rolled onto the ground with a yelp that echoed away into the ether.

Sylfia remained motionless as she watched, trying to discern whatever this creature was that was now taking down her prey but the deer remained alive and struggling and all that she could see was grey fur, claws and teeth. The creature too was at least the size of a bear.

Then with a single spray of blood, the deer squeaked out its final protest, the other creature having won the battle - not that it had been any kind of fair fight - the thing hadn't even seemed to have put any effort into the ordeal. But it was over now but rather than feast on its meal, the creature turned to face Sylfia directly.

It was clear now that it was a wolf. It was much larger than any she had seen before, bigger than a full-grown bear. Its dark grey muzzle and long, sharp teeth were stained red with blood and its eyes were shining pinpricks to match.

The wolf lowered into a deep bow, its front legs bending low and then snarled, allowing the blood and spittle to spill out from its mouth and dangle down onto the ground as long tendrils of death and anger.

Sylfia had no choice now but to reach again for her weapons. The wolf was ready to charge at her and without weapons in hand she would have no way to defend herself. She knew too though that even with weapons in hand, this was not a foe that she would take down easily. Perhaps if she had a war party from the Rakki clan with her and her hands weren't entirely broken she may have had a chance. Right now though, there was no way this battle was going to end favourably for her.

As she gingerly grasped the hilts of her swords between her fingertips the thought occurred to her that perhaps this very creature was the reason that nobody ever came back from the east. Perhaps it had some lair nearby where all of the bones of the clan members of the west were laid to rest once their meat had been removed from their bodies.

But perhaps she was just unlucky.

The wolf lunged at her before she had another second to think or plan. There was nothing she could do anyway and as it crossed the distance between them , she knew that this was to be her end.

Her hands loosened around her swords as she could no longer hold onto them, and they fell to the ground with a dull thud. They would be of no more or less use where they lie on the ground than they would be in her hands and she knew it.

The animal's front paws hit Sylfia with the force of a wooden building and the impact threw her and the beast back a full ten feet before she came to a halt. She could feel her breathing laboured and pain erupted from her back and chest, and when she opened her eyes all she could see was blood, teeth and drool.

The wolf stared down at her, its teeth bared, and if Sylfia didn't know any better it seemed as if it was pleased with itself, having taken down another foe as its prey.

At that moment Sylfia thought about her life. She thought about all the events that had led her to this very moment: her mother's struggle to get her across the Chasm, her adopted father's risk of keeping her a secret from the rest of the clan. Every single lesson she had ever been taught and now it had all been thrown away as if none of it even mattered.

The wolf reared back, opened its terrible bloodied maw and prepared to strike. Sylfia only hoped that the beast would take her head clean off in one bite to save her from the pain of a slow demise.

But then, in the moment before the wolf could strike, a jet-black raven swooped down from the darkness behind it and landed on the ground just by Sylfia's shoulder. It made no movement other than to make unblinking eye contact with the huge beast.

Sylfia was frozen in panic, because the wolf's attention was now squarely upon the raven, who by all accounts should have been nothing more than an annoyance to the situation. The wolf, though, seemed to be completely absorbed by this small, unassuming bird.

And then the wolf stepped back and off Sylfia, snapped its jaws once and slinked away into the darkness.

Sylfia did not want to move. She did not know what had just happened. She did not wish to interfere or bring the wrath of the wolf back upon her, or indeed that of the raven which seemed to have somehow saved her life. Before she could even think of what to say, however, the bird was gone, fleeing into the darkness and out of sight.

The direction the bird had flown off into was to the east, away from the Chasm and further into the woodlands. Her eyes traced what she had seen of its path and then she saw a distant pinprick of light away through the trees and into the distance. It was the telltale sign of people.

Bringing herself up to her knees and then gingerly to her feet, Sylfia wobbled unsteadily before taking a single knee. As well as her broken hands, she was sure that more than a handful of her bones had been broken when the wolf had pounced on her. Her breathing was laboured, and she could taste the telltale signs of blood in her mouth. But she was so close, so close to salvation and to discovering the secrets of the east.

But there was no more that she could do; she could no longer move and her body was far too broken to let her move onward to salvation.

She collapsed to the ground and the blood from her wounds began to seep out of her body, pooling all around her. The last thing that she saw was the wolf's terrible eyes as it watched her silently from afar.

5

Jarl and Eric had been guarding the God's Chasm as they always had together. Their duty was taken seriously, and neither man would ever be challenged on the severity with which they approached their task. The problem was that the Chasm was long, and the night was dark.

The brothers-in-arms had never favoured lighting the smaller torches along the cliff edge as others did because both had learnt over the years that to a real warrior, darkness was their friend. It was important when dealing with a possible or unknown enemy that the element of surprise was always on your side.

They had patrolled their section of the Chasm for a few hours before darkness had descended and, as usual, nothing out of the ordinary had happened. It was a seldom occurrence that someone would try to cross the Chasm, and on the very rare occasion that a clan member had attempted it, there always seemed to be an air of anxiety within the settlement as though everyone knew that it was coming.

Tonight would be different.

The air was still, and all around the pair, the night was silent. They stood talking over forgotten battles when a sound echoed up from within the Chasm, not far from where they stood. Sounds would sometimes happen; animals could knock loose rocks from the cliff face and the like, but Jarl immediately stood to attention. He would never ignore a sound like that because it was the easy thing to do.

Jarl moved first and Eric followed behind him.

"It will be nothing, brother, the birds or something similar causing us to look down into the abyss," Eric called out after Jarl, though he too followed his friend to where the noise had come from.

"We must never forget our duties, brother," Jarl called over his shoulder. "It will be the will of Loki that the one occasion we ignore such a sound, that will be the time we should have moved to action!"

Eric shrugged to himself as he moved, and with the mention of the trickster God Loki, both men drew their axes, the smaller pair by Jarl and the single large battle-axe by Eric. Both men knew that whenever Loki's name was mentioned out loud, sinister happenings followed.

"I tell you, brother, there is nothing there," Eric said quietly as the pair stood and peered down into the darkness. Jarl's eyes searched as though his life depended upon discovering the source of the noise, although Eric did not seem to want to put the same amount of effort in.

Then, as though a dagger had struck deep into his heart, Jarl saw someone step out into the faded light at the base of the Chasm. He knew, though, that this was not just any person down there; he could tell without a shadow of a doubt that this person down in the Chasm was his Sylfia.

"Who is down there?" Eric's voice startled Jarl, and he could tell that his brother did not recognise his daughter. Sylfia, though, simply kept on moving away from the western wall.

Jarl knew that he had to do something to get Sylfia to turn back - all was not lost yet.

"It is our sacred duty to prevent the crossing of the God's Chasm. Whoever you are, you must turn back now!" Jarl called down to Sylfia.

Sylfia then turned her head and looked up at both Eric and Jarl, and Jarl knew that Eric could now see just who this person was.

Jarl quickly spoke before Eric had the chance. "Sylfia! What are you doing?" He called out in exasperation. "Come back before it is too late!"

Jarl knew though that it was already too late for her. Eric had seen her as clear as day, and that would only mean one thing: Sylfia would never be welcomed back into the Rakki clan, even if she came back right now. She had already gone too far.

To Jarl's surprise though, his daughter called back up towards them.

"I need to do this, father; I believe that it is what I have been told to do. I know that I cannot return to the clan, and that is the price that I am willing to pay for my actions."

"Sylfia, please!" Jarl cried. "It is my vow to keep you safe..."

"It is already too late, father. I will always be thankful for what you have done, but now my path is set in stone," Sylfia replied before he could finish his statement. Then she turned her back on her father.

"Sylfia!" Jarl called after her four times but not once did she turn back. His daughter was lost, and there was nothing left that Jarl could do.

Eric placed a large hand on Jarl's shoulder. He had not yet said a word and Jarl dreaded the moment when he would decide to speak and the words that would follow.

"Your daughter is gone now, Jarl. I am sorry that this has happened," Eric said simply.

Jarl had been expecting harsher words but these cut just as deep. He knew that his daughter was gone, but hearing that fact out loud just seemed to make it so much more real.

"If the Gods see fit, she will find what she is looking for in the east, brother. She will become happy, and you will meet her again in the afterlife," Eric said softly.

There was something about those words though, that Jarl could not quite accept. He believed that it was the Gods who had sent his daughter to him all those years ago, the Gods that allowed her to survive the crossing, the Gods that told him and Sylfia through Elder Wise that Sylfia's life would have some grand meaning. There was no way that it was now the God's will that Sylfia should be taken away, never to be heard from again.

There was only one thing that Jarl could think of: that Sylfia's calling from the eastern side of the Chasm was of a higher nature.

Turning to meet Eric's gaze, Jarl finally replied to his brother. "I must leave my duty here tonight, brother; I cannot continue my watch with what has happened. Please will you see that nobody else follows my daughter across the Chasm tonight."

Eric grasped Jarl's forearm and nodded once. He did not have to speak any words to convey his acceptance of this task.

Jarl then took off at a fast walk away from the Chasm and his brother. He did not wish to seem too keen to get away from this place, but he also knew that there was the possibility that time was slowly slipping away from him, and somewhere deep down inside his heart he could sense that Sylfia was in danger.

"Sigrid, wake up, wake up!" Jarl spoke in a strained whisper once he had entered his hut on the outskirts of the settlement.

"...what, why do you wake me so?" Sigrid replied groggily after Jarl had shaken her shoulder. When she looked at his face though, she could tell that something was very wrong.

"What has happened, husband, why do you look so troubled?"

"It is Sylfia... the Chasm.... Sylfia has crossed the Chasm and is no longer with the western clans," Jarl started to explain though he was having trouble forming coherent sentences. "Eric and I caught her in her crossing and she has refused to turn back. I do not know if she is safe but Sigrid, I fear..."

Sigrid then placed a single hand on Jarl's cheek and he stopped before he could finish his sentence.

"You know what you need to do," Sigrid said with a single tear forming in the corner of her eye. "You must go and save our daughter and bring her back home safe. Do not delay in your task, husband."

"You know the laws, Sigrid. Sylfia will not be allowed..."

"Then we will change the laws!" Sigrid replied sternly. "Our daughter will not be left to die alone out in some wilderness. Go and bring her home, Jarl, and if we must leave the clan and the settlement upon your return, then that is what we shall do." Sigrid pulled Jarl's face to her own and their foreheads met softly.

"Come back to me, husband. Save our Sylfia and bring her back home safe."

Jarl had nothing more to say, although he was unable to prevent a tear from rolling down his own cheek. Both he and Sigrid knew that if Jarl followed Sylfia across the Chasm, he would not be allowed to return, no matter what they had both said. Even if he was not seen as he crossed the Chasm, it would be all too obvious that he had followed after his daughter. Jarl could only hope that the clan would not choose to punish Sigrid for what he and Sylfia had done to betray their people.

Jarl finally broke away from Sigrid, and as he walked through the door out into the darkness, away from the only family and clan he had ever known, he stroked his braided beard.

Family to Jarl was now a thing of the past and he knew it; he would need to fend for himself out in the wild and as long as he had his weapons, armour and furs he knew that he at least would have a fighting chance at keeping Sylfia alive.

When Jarl arrived back at the God's Chasm, Eric was nowhere to be seen. Jarl had planned on sneaking past his brother-in-arms so that he wouldn't have to explain himself, but this way did seem a little easier.

Jarl walked to the edge of the Chasm and peered down into the darkness. He had looked down there on so many occasions but this time the deep, black nothingness seemed to carry so much more meaning. Doing what he planned to do would mean leaving behind his entire life, betraying his sacred duty, an action never to be undone. He wondered if Sylfia had felt this way before she had climbed down the wall.

Turning to begin his descent, Jarl came face to face with the stern, blonde-bearded face of his brother Eric standing over him.

"I could have stopped you, brother. Or I could have pushed you over. There was once a time when you would not have allowed me to sneak up behind you," Eric said in a stern tone.

"Brother I..." Jarl began to speak but Eric cleared his throat to stop him.

"I did not see you here tonight brother. I know what it is that you must do. Just one thing I ask from you, if you do survive then please, let me know what is on the other side. Do not fade into the east and forget about your brother Eric."

Jarl nodded silently.

"Brother," Jarl eventually said once his voice had returned. "I will not forget what you have done for my family and for me."

Eric held a hand up again, interrupting Jarl, and then the pair clasped their wrists as they had done on countless occasions before. Both men knew that this was, in almost all certainty, the last time that they would lay eyes upon each other.

Jarl did not need to prolong this goodbye, and he turned his gaze away from Eric, his attention squarely placed upon the chasm wall below him and he began his descent.

The climb downwards was not easy for Jarl, although he did have experience in scaling walls when he and his war parties had been out on raids, but it felt to Jarl as though that was all a lifetime ago now. The skill returned to him quickly, though and as he regained his rhythm in his descent, he spared a moment to think about how easy it had all come back to him; his hands and feet seemed as though they had not forgotten for a moment what they were looking for when they searched for the next hand or foothold.

Within just a few minutes, Jarl had reached the base of the Chasm, and as he was about to step out from the shadow he spared a moment to look back up the wall to see if his brother was watching his progress. It was no surprise though that Eric was nowhere to be seen; he could not implicate himself in what was happening here, otherwise he could be punished for his inaction at the very least.

Then Jarl made to take his first step towards the east, marking the furthest eastward he would have ever travelled from the Rakki settlement, but then he stopped. Looking down, he could see the definite imprint of Sylfia's shoe in the soft ground and he realised that he had managed to descend in the exact same place as his daughter. He wondered how she was feeling, where she was and if she was in trouble.

Then Jarl broke into a run across the Chasm. The thought of his daughter was enough to bring his full attention back to his task. It did not matter what was going to happen to him or, indeed even Eric because there was just one person that he needed to be there for in this very moment, and that was Sylfia, out there and alone in the east.

Jarl could feel the pull of his daughter as his hands reached the eastern wall, and he didn't spare a moment to plan his route upwards carefully. He could feel in his heart that there was something wrong, that she was in trouble and he climbed faster and faster until he reached the top and practically leapt into the darkness of the woods before him.

It was so dense, but Jarl ran as fast as he could through the branches, trees and undergrowth that appeared all around him. The dull glow of the moon grew dimmer as it was blotted out by the canopy above until he was almost in total blackness. As he arrived in a small clearing, the moon again shone to illuminate a figure lying on the ground with two short swords by her side.

Jarl knew immediately that this was the body of his daughter and he fell to his knees beside her, letting out a low moan. "What has happened here, Sylfia?" he asked his daughter.

6

"By the Gods, Sylfia, NO!" Jarl cried louder now as the situation caught up with him. He placed his hands on his daughter's shoulders and the moment his hands fell upon her he knew she was still alive. She was warm to the touch and breathing, although it was shallow and laboured.

"Sylfia! You are alive, and I am here to help you," Jarl announced to his daughter, attempting to turn her over so that she could see him, although as he did so, he saw the blood pooling all around her. There was so much blood. He had seen less come from men he had killed in battle, but there was nothing he could do to help her out here in the wild. He could not take her back to the settlement to the west because even if he could carry her down the wall and back up the other side of the Chasm, they would not be welcome there.

Then Jarl looked up and around at his surroundings, and off in the distance and to the east, he could see a pinprick of light, a tell-tale sign of civilisation and perhaps even salvation for his daughter.

"I am going to have to lift and carry you, daughter," Jarl said softly as he slid his hands beneath Sylfia. Picking her up, she felt so light. Too light in fact. It felt as though Jarl had picked up an animal skin without the body still attached.

It did not matter to Jarl. He cradled his daughter in his arms and began his run towards the light, salvation, and anything that could save Sylfia from her demise. He could do little to make the journey comfortable for Sylfia but failing that, at least he would make it quick.

The woods around them eventually became sparser, and after a short while there was nothing left of them; they travelled across wide open plains that felt hard underfoot, though now before them, Jarl could see that they had indeed reached some kind of settlement.

Marking the outer borders of whatever this place was stood a short stone wall that trailed off into the darkness both left and right, and directly before Jarl stood a tall stone archway, denoting the entranceway to the settlement.

There were no buildings or people directly behind the wall. However, there was an area of farmland peppered with small torches that did nothing more than illuminate the ground directly around themselves, but the message was clear to Jarl. There were civilised people here, and that meant that surely there would be somebody that could help Sylfia.

Jarl kept moving forward, through the farmland and toward the settlement proper. Eventually, he came to a series of wooden buildings, and he could think of nothing other than to call out to the people of this place and hope that someone would help.

He sat on the ground carefully and held Sylfia delicately as though he did not wish to break her, and then he started to cry out.

"Please, somebody help my daughter! She has been wounded and may be close to death. Please!"

It only took a moment and the wooden doors of the huts all around opened, and people began to surround Jarl and Sylfia. Each of them wore concern upon their faces, and as Jarl scanned them, he realised that not a single one took a defensive posture or even looked as though they felt threatened. They all wore leathers and furs although only a couple carried weapons of any kind that he could see – small hand axes much smaller than his own.

"What is making all this noise?" a deep voice boomed from behind the crowd, and they parted to allow a much larger, older man to walk straight up to Jarl and Sylfia.

"I beg of you, chief of this settlement, please... help my daughter," Jarl begged. He knew that he had nothing to bargain with and these people had no reason to help this pair of interlopers, but he simply had no choice but to beg and to hope.

"There is no need to beg here, friend," the larger man replied. He was at least fifteen years Jarl's senior though his movements did not seem to betray any ageing of the body or joints. "Place your daughter on the ground before me, and I will aid her." The man's face was warm and kind, and Jarl did not need to think twice.

If this man promised aid, he would have leapt through a burning hedge backwards if it had been asked of him. Anything to save his daughter.

"These people are going to help you," Jarl whispered to Sylfia as he lowered her head gently down onto the ground. "By the Gods, your life will be saved."

The large man then knelt on the ground before Sylfia, rubbed his hands together vigorously and then held them just above Sylfia's slowly rising and falling chest.

Jarl's eyes filled with tears as he took the chance to look at his daughter's dire state. But somehow, he could not take his eyes away from the strange new display unfolding before him. He had been about to ask the man to help, not to sit and waste time, but then a faint blue glow had emanated from the space between Sylfia's chest and the man's hands.

Then the light began to glow brighter and brighter until the entire space between the wooden huts was illuminated in the otherworldly glow. Then, as though it had never been there at all, the glow disappeared, and the only light of the place came from the small torches lit sporadically around them.

"What did..." Jarl started to speak, but as he did so, Sylfia coughed and sat bolt upright.

"Easy, easy child," the larger man soothed. Then he handed Sylfia a leather flask from his hip, and she drank the contents without hesitation. Then she turned to look at her father and passed him the flask so he could drink. There was not much left inside after Sylfia had taken her fill, but Jarl was grateful for the gesture nonetheless and drank until nothing was left.

The water was cool, and Jarl felt it soothe his throat and cool his stomach as it trickled down into his body. It was an odd sensation and not one he had ever felt when drinking simple water. It was as though it was searching his body as it moved, leaving behind some tingly, warm feeling. Once the water had completed its journey, Jarl could feel that it sat in his stomach like a warm ball of light, but rather than make him feel uncomfortable or uneasy, it felt good.

"How do you feel now, child?" the man asked Sylfia, and it brought Jarl's attention back from his own body to the situation before them. What had just happened? What had he witnessed? And how was Sylfia now brought back from the precipice of death and able to move and speak? Whatever had happened, Jarl could do nothing more than to feel that whoever this person was, he owed more than his life to them.

"Please, honoured chief," Jarl said, bowing his head to the ground before the man. "You have saved my child from death, and there is nothing I can do to repay you this kindness. All I can do is offer my life in return for hers, in servitude to you and however you see fit."

The man, though, seemed to ignore Jarl completely and after a long, awkward moment of silence, Sylfia realised that he was still waiting for her to respond."

"I... I am much better. I do not know what you did, but..." Sylfia searched for the words, but none seemed appropriate. What could anyone say to the person who had just saved their life? So instead, she opted to tell the people still around her how she came to bear these wounds. When she looked down she was shocked to see that although her clothes were still stained with blood and dirt, the wounds beneath had disappeared, and her skin bore no marks that betrayed any sign of their presence.

"I... I was attacked just out in the woodland to the west," she started to explain. "It was a wolf I think, only much, much bigger than any I have ever seen before."

The large man looked down at her with an inquisitive look on his face. "There are no beasts in the woods to the west, and it is not normal to see many come from the east either. For miles the lands are barren. Are you sure that it was not something else that caused you these wounds?"

Jarl realised that the man had subtly gestured to him, and it made his blood boil.

"Hold on just a minute now," Jarl said angrily, raising himself to his feet. "If you are saying what I think that you are saying, I think that you had better speak more plainly, so that I do not misinterpret your words."

The man held up his hands in a placating gesture. "I did not mean to offend you, friend, but let us forget about this for now. My name is Bjorn, and I am a healer here in Baldur's Circle."

The change of tact placated Jarl, although he was still irked at what had been suggested. Not only had this man called Sylfia a liar, but he also all but said that Jarl had been the one to injure her on purpose, for whatever reason Jarl could not fathom.

"My name is Jarl, and this is my daughter," Jarl replied quietly. "We come from the west, across the Chasm, and we are of the Rakki clan, though I fear now that we may never return."

"I am afraid to say, friend, that I do not believe that going back will be an issue for your previous clan to worry about. There is something you must know about Baldur's Circle and us: Baldur's Children. Now that you are here, you can never leave this place," Bjorn said matter-of-factly.

"What do you mean?" Sylfia asked before her father could get right back onto the offensive. "Are you going to keep us here as prisoners, or is it just too dangerous out here in the east? Our clans in the west have known people to cross the Chasm to the east, but not once has one ever returned or was even heard from again."

"I come from the west!" a woman called out.

"I too travelled across the Chasm!" another voice called from the crowd. Then three more followed, one after the other.

Sylfia looked up to see who had spoken, although the crowd around the three of them were all anonymous faces, each as unknown as the rest.

"Do you recognise any of these people? Apologies, friend. I do not remember your name," Bjorn said.

Jarl looked at the faces in the crowds and studied the people who had spoken.

"There is something familiar about some of these people, but I do not believe I can place any of them, " Jarl replied.

"And that is because there is more to our settlement than meets the eye. I am afraid that when I say that you cannot leave, it is a factual statement and not a threat. If anyone does attempt to leave Baldur's Circle and cross the threshold through the stone archways, they simply turn to dust where they stand and are carried off by the wind."

"Father, that is just how..." Sylfia started to speak excitedly, looking at her father but Jarl held up a hand to silence her.

"You say that the people who arrive here must stay within your settlement?" Jarl asked. "How do you hunt or forage? How is it possible that you can lead your lives within this small settlement?"

"With time, you will come to see how we survive here, but for now you must rest. We can talk again once the morning light has come, but you are safe here my friends. At first light you may speak with our settlement's Elder and he will give you the answers that you seek."

Jarl and Sylfia both wanted to reply to Bjorn, but before they could even open their mouths to get their words out, the large man, together with almost all the crowd, had walked away and disappeared into the settlement.

"You may stay in this hut for the night," a woman with long blonde braided hair said as she gestured to the nearest hut to Jarl and Sylfia. "I will collect you in the morning and everything will become clearer then."

"What is this place?" Jarl asked quickly, but the woman had already turned away from him. When Jarl looked around Sylfia and himself, he realised that they were once again alone, and the settlement had become silent and still.

"What is happening, father?" Sylfia asked in a hushed whisper. "What is this place? And do you think that they are serious that we cannot leave?"

Jarl opened his mouth to reply. He was about to say that there was no way that such a thing would happen to people for simply trying to leave a settlement, but then he thought of something that he had not thought about for many years. It was the way that Sylfia's own mother – her real mother – had simply floated away into the wind, just as this man had warned them.

"I do not know Sylfia. But this man healed you when you were close to death and to me that bears meaning. I am grateful to these people for what they have done but I do not trust them. So for now, Sylfia, we must rest and make better plans in the morning."

Sylfia nodded silently and walked to the hut that they had been given to sleep in. The door was not locked and inside were two wooden beds covered with large, warm furs. The interior of the hut was illuminated by three torches that burned bright and straight.

"Where do you think they get the furs from if they cannot leave and the lands are barren?" Sylfia asked, gesturing to the inside of the hut.

"There are answers that will need to be given, Sylfia. But now we cannot speak at length," Jarl responded solemnly; the severity of their situation weighed heavy on him and occupied a large portion of his mind. Sylfia understood her father's undertone and remained quiet.

Sylfia and Jarl moved into the hut and to the beds within. It would be surprising to Jarl that he would find he had fallen asleep almost immediately, although Sylfia found herself within her own mind, thinking through all of the events in her life that had led her to this very moment.

7

"Wake up, Sylfia. The light is upon us, and we have questions to ask this day," Jarl said as he stood over his daughter.

Sylfia had eventually managed to sleep, though it had been a short and restless sleep due to all of the information that flowed through her mind like an unwieldy river. She had thought about her real mother, the words of Elder Wise, the wolf, the raven and not least, how this huge stranger, Bjorn, had decided to help her in her hour of need. She had not had time, however, to think upon his words of staying within this settlement, this 'Baldur's Circle'.

Jarl opened the door to the hut and was greeted by the hulking form of Bjorn, who stood not more than a foot from the door with a warm smile plastered across his face.

"You have questions for Baldur's Children, and the best place to find answers is with Elder Hugi. Come, follow me, and he will see you," Bjorn said.

Jarl and Sylfia did not need to be asked a second time, but despite knowing that their destination would give them answers, they were not shy in asking questions of Bjorn as they walked.

"How do you defend yourself from invaders in this settlement? All that I can see is farmland and huts," Jarl started.

"What did you do to heal my wounds? I was close to death," Sylfia added.

"You say that the lands are barren here. What do you hunt for food?" Jarl asked.

"And the furs? Where do they come from?" Sylfia responded.

Bjorn did not give a single response though and simply replied that with time the Elder would answer all of their questions.

Jarl and Sylfia both knew that back in the west, and within the Rakki clan, if there were situations that required the sage advice of a foreseer, Elder Wise would be approached for commentary, so this was similar. What was interesting, though, was that he and Sylfia - who were essentially invaders into this settlement – were allowed an audience with a clan Elder, someone who would surely be missed if anything were to happen to them.

The Elder's hut was at the centre of the settlement and was the only round building that Jarl could see. Bjorn did not knock on the door and await a response as Jarl would have; rather he simply pulled it open and gestured for Sylfia and Jarl to enter. He did not follow them inside but closed the door after them.

The hut was completely empty except that, dead in the centre of the room, sat a very old man with long white hair and a long white beard hanging down onto his chest. He wore the furs of a large animal across his shoulders, and his eyes were tightly closed.

"Greetings, clan Elder," Jarl said officially, as though this was completely normal to him.

The Elder did not respond.

"Uh, greetings," Sylfia parroted, though it was clear that she was far less comfortable in this situation than her father.

A long moment of silence passed. Then Sylfia couldn't help but speak again.

"We had an Elder back in the settlement in the west too, Elder Wise was her name. People would always ask her for advice because she could see the future."

Elder Hugi opened his eyes and regarded Sylfia with mild interest. Eventually he smiled a crooked smile and the action sent a shiver down her spine.

"How fares my sister?" The Elder asked.

Sylfia abruptly shut her mouth with a crack.

"I must tell you that Elder Wise no longer walks in the realm of mortals," Jarl said before Sylfia could answer. "She was old and passed peacefully according to clan traditions."

Elder Hugi closed his eyes again though as he did so, a single tear fell from each and rolled down his cheeks.

"I regret that I have not been able to see my sister in so many long years," Elder Hugi sighed sadly. "It was my hope that we would meet again, but the Gods seem to have conspired against us as they sometimes enjoy. Tell me, child, did my sister tell you of your future?"

"She said some things to me, as she did to many of the clan. Before she died, she told me to take the most difficult path before me so that I may prevent the passing of Ragnarök. It is what has led me here to the east."

Elder Hugi looked at Sylfia again as though he was trying to peer straight into her soul.

"Do you believe this prophecy to be true? That you alone, a young girl no older than twenty-some years, can prevent the end of all things?" Hugi asked.

"... no," Sylfia said slowly and in a small voice. "But I believe that my calling was to travel east to find meaning in my life. I do not believe that staying within the Rakki settlement and being a good clan member was all I was destined for. I listened to Elder Wise and although do not believe in the severity of her words, I believe that she saw something within me, and it is the search for that something that I have embarked upon."

Jarl almost fell backwards at those words. He had never heard Sylfia express that she wanted more out of her life. He, too, had remembered what Elder Wise had told him about his adopted daughter but like her, he had chosen to believe more in the melodrama than to take the words at their plain face value.

"My sister had a way with which she could see into the futures of those around her. It was a gift that she provided many years ago, as all of Baldur's Children have been given. These gifts are the reward we are given for remaining here within Baldur's Circle."

"Forgive me Elder," Sylfia said. "But if nobody can leave the settlement, how did Elder Wise manage to leave to join the Rakki clan in the west? And if the gift was given because she was supposed to stay, why was it not taken away from her?"

Jarl had been thinking the same thing, though he was also wondering why Sylfia herself had been spared during her own pilgrimage to the west over twenty years ago.

"My sister had a way of seeing what the future would bring to those around her – including herself. She told me years ago that she would be able to cross safely. The reason why was unknown to us both, but I knew that what she had said was the truth and did not question the will of the Gods. She would travel to the west and become the foreseer for your clan, and that is what came to pass, is it not?"

"This is true," Jarl brought himself into the conversation again. "But it does not explain how this has come to pass. Elder Wise was a talented foreseer, although nearing her end, her words were not as clear as they may have once been."

"I am afraid that fatigue and age are both concerns that every mortal being has to deal with. But I believe your words, Jarl, and I know that you speak the truth," Elder Hugi replied.

"That is your gift then?" Jarl asked slowly, picking apart what the Elder had just said. "You have the ability to see the truth in the words of those you observe?"

Elder Hugi smiled warmly. "You are as perceptive as I believed you to be the moment I laid eyes upon you, Jarl of the Rakki clan."

"I am not of the Rakki any longer," Jarl replied. "Once the God's Chasm is crossed, the reward is a life of exile enforced by all of the clans of the west."

"I know, I know," Hugi replied. "Many of our number hail from the clans of the west and none have returned to tell their story to their former clans. The Rakki, The Haukr, The Draugurs, The Aris, The Dreyja, The Bjarns, all clans of the west that would see if they only accepted that they should open their eyes rather than guard that abyss." Elder Hugi said with a sigh. "Do you know how the Chasm was forged?"

Jarl shook his head slowly. "We have been told stories, passed across the clans though they change and warp with each passing year. I was told that the Chasm was created when Thor fought alone, bravely, against an ice giant and his killing blow was so powerful that the earth had absorbed his magic for centuries to come. That is why we cannot cross, and anyone who does dies once they reach the far side."

Elder Hugi laughed aloud. His laugh was rattling although a little strained. Both Jarl and Sylfia awaited the end of his humour.

"A battle did not create the God's Chasm!" Elder Hugi announced jovially. "I will tell you the truth of what this place is if you would listen to an ageing Elder, whose words may or may not be as clear to others as he reaches his end." He gave Jarl a purposeful glare as he spoke his last statement, and it made Jarl feel ashamed for what he had said about Elder Wise, although he'd had no way of knowing that the two were siblings.

"I apologise, Elder Hugi," Jarl said with a slight nod of his head. The Elder nodded back slightly, appeased by the response.

"The Chasm was formed long ago when the Gods walked the earth. It was the axe head of Hodur that created the Chasm, driven deep into the ground in frustration and anger at the passing of his brother Baldur," Elder Hugi explained.

"There is no axe so large as to create such a chasm," Sylfia objected. "The Chasm is as long as the eye can see and wider than anything manufactured that I have ever heard of. How could you mean what you say?"

"These are the weapons of the Gods, child," Elder Hugi replied and continued with a dismissive wave of his hand. "Not of mortal construction. Baldur was the most beloved of all of the Gods, the son of Odin and the Allfather's wife, Frigg. Baldur and his mother both suffered the same dream, that of Baldur's fast-approaching death. To the Gods, dreams are more prophecy than something to be ignored and forgotten. On the strength of this dream, Frigg set out into the world and convinced every single object never to harm her beautiful son, the shining Baldur. Each and every object in turn promised her this vow, and as a result, nothing would ever be able to harm Baldur. Of course, this was except for one insignificant object:

the mistletoe. The feeble plant was too unimportant and non-threatening for Frigg to ask to make the vow."

Elder Hugi paused for a moment to let the information penetrate the pair before him.

"All of the Gods would then pass their time hurling objects at Baldur, and each and every single one of them would fall away harmlessly, unable to affect the most perfect of the Gods. Loki, the mischief-maker, learned of the vows that had been made and set out to manufacture a spear of pure mistletoe. Handing it to Baldur's brother, Hodur, who was blind, Loki told Hodur that it would show all of the Gods how strong Baldur was if he would withstand the spear, and Loki himself helped to guide Hodur's hand. Hodur threw the spear of pure mistletoe and killed his own brother, tricked by Loki. He was devastated, as you may understand. Hodur came to this place and drove his axe into the ground as he wept for his Baldur for days, weeks and months."

"What happened to Hodur?" Sylfia interrupted.

"Oh, it was said that Hodur was killed for his actions, but some believe that he still walks the mortal realm in search of his brother's final resting place. That is not of any importance now. What happened next, though, is what you must attempt to understand. The tears of the Gods are not something that mortal beings should be able to consume, and it is because of Hodur's tears that we, Baldur's Children are able to do the things that seem so extraordinary."

"Like Bjorn, who had the power to heal?" Sylfia asked.

Elder Hugi nodded. "And the reason that your Elder Wise became a foreseer."

"And the reason you are a truth seeker," Jarl added as a statement and not a question.

"You are correct, friend," Elder Hugi replied. "I was blessed with the power to tell if what was in front of me was truth or lies. This is the blessing that I have received from Hodur's tears."

"Then why is this place not called Hodur's Circle, and you Hodur's Children?" Sylfia asked. Jarl would never have been so brash to ask such a question although he was interested in the Elder's answer.

"The story is not yet complete, have patience," Elder Hugi replied. "After Baldur was taken to Helheim to reside in the underworld for the rest of time, Frigg spoke to Hel to attempt to free her son, so that he may once again walk amongst the Gods. Frigg told Hel of how Baldur was loved by everything on earth and that an unrelenting torrent of tears fell for him each and every day. It was not much of an exaggeration as Baldur was loved and missed dearly. Hel was moved by Frigg's words and agreed that if Baldur was so loved and that Frigg could prove it, she would not hold him in the underworld but would allow him to return to the Gods. If the entire world wept for Baldur, he would be set free. When Frigg returned with this news, Loki once again caused issues for the Gods. The trickster God said that he would never shed a tear for Baldur, and it is for this very reason that Hel still holds Baldur in the underworld. This was the first sign of Ragnarök coming to pass. Baldur's Children know that we are gifted these magical powers so that we may better spread the word to the rest of the world, so that every living thing will shed a tear for Baldur and return him from the clutches of Hel, undoing the coming of Ragnarök and saving Gods and mortals alike."

The hut fell silent once Elder Hugi had stopped speaking; neither Jarl nor Sylfia could think of anything they could say in response to such a claim, and both wondered silently if this Elder had, like Elder Wise, started to speak in twisted riddles, as she had nearing her end.

"The time will come when Baldur's Children will break forth from the Circle and spread this message, for it has been told, and it is how it must come to pass," Elder Hugi punctuated. "You will see."

Then the wooden door to the hut crashed open, and the huge form of Bjorn the healer entered.

"You must follow me now, and you will discover what it means to be one of Baldur's Children. Elder Hugi requires rest, and he has told you everything that you need to know for now."

"Of course," Jarl replied and in truth, he was grateful to be able to exit the hut without offending the clan Elder; this Elder's words were of little importance if their truth was questionable. Jarl had watched as Elder Wise had deteriorated, and he had no desire to listen to another who walked the very same path.

Jarl and Sylfia nodded deeply to the Elder, though he had already closed his eyes again, either deep in thought or simply sleeping. The three then walked out of the hut and into the settlement once more. In the daylight, though, there was just so much more to see.

The sun shone down on Baldur's Circle and it warmed the faces of both Jarl and Sylfia. The settlement was much larger than either of them had assumed, and as they looked across the farmland they could see how many people called Baldur's Circle their home. What was apparent, though, was that although this did seem much like a 'normal' settlement, there were very few children; in the Rakki clan, play and laughter would have been commonplace, but here in Baldur's Circle there was a quiet calm that seemed alien to both Sylfia and Jarl's ears.

"There are some things that you will need to know before we proceed," Bjorn said as the three stopped in a clearing between three wooden huts. "We will not tolerate violence between our clan members. Any breaking of the rules will result in your exile – and for all of us, that would mean death. Do you understand?"

Sylfia nodded quickly, although Jarl was more forthcoming. "What do you mean, all of us? I do not remember agreeing to be a part of this clan."

"The moment you shared our waters, accepted our hospitality and help, you became one of Baldur's Children," Bjorn explained calmly. "You are a part of the clan now and forever, so you must now obey the clan rules."

Jarl looked as though he was about to object, though Sylfia gently nudged him. She knew there was nothing they could do anyway, but her father often needed a little push to bridge his stubbornness.

"We live by simple rules in Baldur's Circle. You must cause no harm to any of Baldur's Children, you must strive to spread the word of Baldur's passing to the rest of the world, and you must do what you can to aid in the daily life of all of the clan members. Do you understand?"

Sylfia nodded.

"How can we be expected to spread the word if we cannot leave this place?" Jarl asked.

Bjorn smiled. "It is a rule that we live by, but that does not mean it happens very often. So by telling you these things now, the clan and even I are fulfilling this duty."

Jarl frowned at the answer but decided not to press any further. Things were definitely strange here, but there was nothing he could do to challenge Baldur's Children back to normalcy.

The three stood in silence for a long moment and Sylfia felt as though the two men were engaged in some silent battle waged entirely in undertones, but she too found it difficult to believe that these people had some higher calling that was practically impossible to achieve. Even if they could make it out of the settlement, how could they possibly convince everything in existence to cry for something that they had never known?

"I think the best way is for us to show you the things that the Gods have allowed us to do. Then you may understand better," Bjorn said to break the deadlock, though Jarl did not respond; he simply stared daggers at the larger man as though he was about to pounce on him like a wild animal.

Bjorn then pulled a short knife from his waistband, and Sylfia took a small step back. Jarl did not move.

The large man placed the blade into his hand, closed his fingers around the sharp side of the weapon and quickly drew it back, causing deep, red blood to flow freely.

Jarl's stare did not leave Bjorn's face, but as both he and Sylfia watched, Bjorn's hands glowed a bright blue, and the deep cut that spewed blood into his open hand simply vanished.

Sylfia exhaled in surprise, but Jarl did not seem moved by the feat.

"You think that cheap tricks are going to convince us that the Gods bless you?" he growled.

"Father, this man helped me when I was close to death. You saw with your own two eyes," Sylfia said, her mouth slightly agape.

"I have seen many things in my life, and many things that were not as true as they would first seem. I do not know what these people want, but it would seem they would like us to stay, and whatever show this is, is their way of making it seem like a good idea."

Then Bjorn held the knife out to Jarl by the blade. It was clear that Jarl was supposed to take the weapon, though he hesitated.

"Take it. If you require more proof, then I shall give it to you," Bjorn said.

"Father?" Sylfia began to speak, but before she could either encourage or object, Jarl took hold of the handle and held the knife as though ready to strike with it.

"Cut yourself however you like and as deep as you like," Bjorn ordered.

Jarl looked down at the knife and tossed it from hand to hand. It was of adequate construction and obviously sharp, but he had never before intentionally wounded himself. However, if this was the way to prove that this place was full of lies and magic tricks, it would be worth the small amount of pain.

Jarl didn't lose eye contact with Bjorn, although he cut his hand the very same way that the larger man had. There was no denying the pain that it caused, and the blood that flowed from the wound was certainly authentic.

"Now give me your hand," Bjorn ordered, and Jarl held out his heavily bleeding hand. He had purposely cut deeper than Bjorn had in a way to prove himself, but he need not have bothered.

Bjorn took hold of Jarl's hand and clasped it tightly within his own. The bright blue light once again flashed into existence before fading away to nothing, and when Jarl opened his hand once more he could see that the wound had entirely healed. There was no scar, nor any signs that there had been a deep wound there just moments ago, and Jarl could do nothing more than stare at his hand in shock and amazement.

"It is an excellent trick, no?" Bjorn asked with a smile. Jarl could not respond.

"Father? How did it feel?" Sylfia asked slowly, peering at her father's outstretched hand.

"It... it was no trick, Sylfia. You were right, this place does have the magic of the Gods and we would be wise to do as they say." The look that Sylfia saw within her father's eyes was one of shock and fear, one that she had not seen on many occasions.

"This is what I have been attempting to tell you, brother. We are as one in this place and my power to heal is nothing compared to what others are able to do with their gifts from the Gods. Elder Hugi, you may already know, is able to tell when truth or lies are spoken."

"Yes, I understand that the Elder has this power. Tell me, though, can all of Baldur's Children heal others?" Jarl asked. "Do you all share this divine ability?"

Bjorn laughed a booming laugh at the question, then settled himself quickly. "Of course not! Each member of the clan is afforded a different ability to the last. How the Gods decide on what that power should be is still a mystery to even the Children, though it does seem that each ability gifted is one that the individual requires most at the very moment it is given."

"So everyone here has some magical power?" Sylfia asked.

"That is how all of this seems to work," Bjorn replied. "Once you drink of the water within the Circle, you are afforded an ability that your heart and soul most desire. I was with my brother when I found my way into Baldur's Circle. He was close to death, and I needed more than anything a way to help him, so that is what the Gods saw fit to bless me with. My brother, though, wanted revenge above anything else, and he received the ability to cause harm to those who had wronged him."

"But... we drank the water," Sylfia said slowly. "And you did not think that it would be a good idea to warn us about these things first?"

"No, he did not think that it was a good idea, he did this on purpose Sylfia, to keep us here. As I already have said, not everything that meets the eye here is the truth," Jarl growled and took a large step towards Bjorn and in front of Sylfia. His shock had completely worn off and now he was angry.

"You would not have believed me if it had not happened this way, friend," Bjorn replied calmly. "Why not try to see what you can do now, then tell me if you think it has all been worth it."

Jarl could see nothing past the anger that he felt in his heart. He felt his hands reaching for his twin hand-axes, but before they reached their destination, Bjorn spoke again.

"What is it that you desire most in the world? What is it that your heart and soul crave, brother?"

Jarl then paused for a moment before he wrenched the twin axes from by his side and held them aloft.

"I want to protect my daughter!" he announced, but before he could strike out at Bjorn, the axes burst into bright orange flames. Sylfia could feel the heat radiating off the weapons, though as Jarl lowered them curiously to his eyeline, it was clear that the heat had no effect on him.

"So deep down, you believe that to protect your daughter, you must be stronger, better with the weapons you hold dear. I have seen it before, and this is nothing new to me," Bjorn said appraisingly.

The larger man's words seemed to disarm Jarl completely, who stood open-mouthed for a long moment before his axes abruptly extinguished themselves, and he let them drop to his sides. The metal heads sizzled when they touched the leather of his trousers, and he winced as he moved them away to cool.

"And you, little sister. What is it that your heart craves the most?" Bjorn asked Sylfia, who was watching Jarl's hand axes as though they were about to grow heads.

"I... I do not know," Sylfia replied honestly. "Does everyone know what they want from life? I have never thought upon the question."

"You are correct, little sister. Of course, not everyone has either an immediate need or a desire for their life, but is there anything that you can think of that you would desire?" Bjorn asked.

Sylfia thought about her desire to flee the settlements on the western side of the God's Chasm, her conversation with Elder Wise, the wolf that had almost killed her, and she answered with the only statement that she could think to make.

"I want to prevent Ragnarök. Or at least help to prevent it," she said quietly.

Bjorn laughed loudly again and this time Jarl couldn't help but chuckle along with him.

"That is a tall order - even the power of the Gods cannot interfere with the coming of Ragnarök, Sylfia," Bjorn announced.

"Then what would you have me do, turn my swords into flame like my father?" Sylfia gestured to her sides, but she had forgotten that her weapons had been left behind in her encounter with the wolf. "Perhaps I could copy your ability and heal anyone on the brink of death? See the future? See truth through forests of lies? Why do you not tell me what I should ask for, and we can be done with whatever this is?"

"Little sister, it does not work like this," Bjorn replied softly. "One is given the gift they require the most and nothing more or less. No person may ask for an ability that they desire. However, if you concentrate your mind inward, then you will eventually see what it is that you have been given."

Sylfia closed her eyes. She had become frustrated at the man before her as well as the situation she had found herself in, but having some ability – that sounded like it was something that she could use.

She turned her mind to the inside, searching all corners of her mental and physical faculties. She searched for a feeling of power or rage like her father had displayed, she tried to see into the future, and she tried to analyse Bjorn's words for truth or deception, but she could only feel blackness. There was nothing within her to draw upon, nothing new at least.

8

"There is still nothing there, father," Sylfia said long after Bjorn had left them to search within themselves. Jarl had no trouble controlling his new gift, turning his axes into flames over and over as though it was the easiest and most natural thing in the world to do. Sylfia seemed to have either no ability or, at the very least, she had no way of controlling whatever it was that she could do.

"It is simple, Sylfia. Once you have discovered your gift, it is nothing more than a thought to use it," Jarl said. "That is, of course, if each gift works in the same way."

Sylfia sat down on the ground with a sigh. "But do you really think this is a gift from the Gods? And you do not expect me to believe that you are planning to spread the word of Baldur to the rest of the world, do you? Will you stop doing that?" she asked as Jarl's axes exploded into flame again. "You do not believe that these people are correct in their plight. We should be looking for a way to get out of here, not playing with our new toys!"

Jarl let the axes extinguish themselves, and he looked down at his daughter who was sitting on the floor, looking as depressed as he had ever seen her.

"Sylfia, daughter. I do not believe that these people are answering a calling from the Gods, but there is no denying this power that I have been given. Ever since I was small, I wanted to become more powerful, to be able to fight in any fight and know that I held the advantage. So many of my brothers and sisters have been lost over the years, and I have always known that if I was more powerful, I would have been able to help them. You will have a power within you, Sylfia, but I do not know what it may be or when you may find it."

Sylfia let her head drop a little further. She had been wallowing in her own pity in not having an apparent ability, but as she thought about the words her father had used, a thought occurred to her.

"There is something that I can do that no other has done," Sylfia exclaimed. "I have left Baldur's Circle before, when my mother carried me as a baby across the Chasm and to the west. Perhaps that is my ability – to be able to leave this place without turning to ash to be carried away by the wind!"

"This is true, Sylfia. This may not have been the first time that you drank of the magical water that affords you your abilities, and so you may not have known that you have had one all along." Jarl then took a knee in front of his daughter. "I have always known that you are special, my daughter and I will never let any harm come to you for as long as I shall live."

Sylfia met her father's eyes, and in them she could see nothing but love and sincerity. It gave her both hope and strength, and she raised herself to her feet once more.

"I must test to see if this is my power," she said levelly. "I know what you will say, but father I..."

"You must learn what it is that you can do," Jarl interrupted. "But later, once it is dark. This could be something that we do not want others to see."

Sylfia nodded silently. Her expression had changed from sadness to determination; she knew that if this was her calling, it had profound meaning. If nobody could leave Baldur's Circle but her, then what did that mean for her usefulness to the settlement? She could carry messages, and arrange trade routes, amongst a handful of other things that these de-facto prisoners would not be able to do without her.

Jarl and Sylfia then spent the rest of the daylight hours alone. The pair sparred as they had done during Sylfia's lessons, although she stood without her swords and Jarl would occasionally turn his axes into balls of flame as they cut through the air. To Jarl, the motion was quick and easy, and he knew within just a few hours how useful his gift could become.

Sylfia had been well-trained in combat without weapons. Not all Rakki children had been trained as such, but Jarl fought with hand axes that he would sometimes throw and he had learnt these lessons for himself the hard way, and that was something that would benefit Sylfia.

Jarl swung his axe at Sylfia at head height, and she stepped back and away from the strike. Usually, this would mean a short pause before the next strike because most warriors used heavy, two-handed weapons but Jarl's second axe came at her in an upward arc. It was the way they had always trained: with actual weapons so that hits were real, and the danger of battle was instilled into her. Of course, Jarl would pull his attacks and more often than not, if he knew a strike was going to make contact, he would do his best to ensure minimal damage was dealt. Because of this danger, though, Sylfia had become nimble on her feet and very used to dodging out of the way of her father's quick strikes. That was partly learned through watching Sigrid fight, as she was much quicker on her feet than the large and powerful Jarl.

Sylfia watched as Jarl twirled the axes around himself to bring them back between the two warriors, held menacingly toward Sylfia.

"It would be fairer if you would let me take one of your axes," Sylfia said through gritted teeth.

"You know the rules," Jarl replied with a smile. "We fight with what we have as it would be in a real battle. If you could not protect your weapons as you should have, that is nobody's fault but your own."

Sylfia blinked slowly. She had been told this on many occasions, but she had seldom been without her swords to face her father when he was fully armed.

Jarl stepped forward again, and the feint caused Sylfia to skip backwards. Jarl laughed at her jitteriness and stepped in again. Sylfia, expecting another feint, let Jarl close the gap between them, and he kicked a flat boot out towards her.

Sylfia spun out of the way of the attack and caught Jarl's ankle before his kick could cause her any damage, but before she could do anything to respond to the attack, she caught sight of one of Jarl's axes travelling toward her wrist where she grasped her father's ankle.

Sylfia let go and again spun out of the way, stepping back to keep the distance between them.

"Good, you must not let me strike you. Without weapons, there is nothing for your opponent to break other than your bones," Jarl narrated. "Though just because you are quicker than a falling axe, does not mean that you will win every contest."

"I may not win every contest," Sylfia said nonchalantly, though panting. "I only need to win one. Did you mean to set your arm on fire with that last attack?" she asked.

Jarl looked down at his arms though there was no fire there and Sylfia took the opportunity that her distraction had afforded and lunged at her father. She shot down onto a single knee and wrapped her arms around her father's waist before he could do anything to prevent it. Jarl was much larger and heavier than Sylfia, but he could do nothing to stop the momentum that Sylfia had generated from lifting him from the ground and depositing him onto his back. Jarl moved to raise his axes from his sides but before he could do so, Sylfia had placed her knees onto his arms, preventing him from moving at all.

Jarl, though, was a seasoned warrior, and he knew that when disarmed there were always alternatives. He planted his feet on the ground and arched his back, forcing Sylfia to roll off of him over his head. Jarl did not stop there and simply accept his escape. He rolled backwards, following Sylfia and came to a halt atop her this time, pinning her down with his axes raised above his head, brightly aflame.

Sylfia closed her eyes. She could do nothing more to protect herself, and Jarl took her gesture as one of surrender. He removed his weight from Sylfia and raised himself back up to his feet, still smiling.

"Distractions are always welcome, though you should never treat a battle as over until the last attack has been thrown," Jarl said.

Sylfia smiled back at her father. She had always enjoyed learning from Jarl, and each time she had managed to get a little closer to besting the larger man, he had always stepped up his defence just a little to keep her out of reach. She knew that eventually, on the steps of battle, he would have to stop raising himself up above her, and she would be able to take the mantle from him. This was the way of life for the Rakki people and of most of the clans in general.

The day was drawing on now, and neither Jarl nor Sylfia had eaten anything all day. It was more of an inconvenience than a real problem to go for long stretches of time without food though because it was a way of life for the hunter. Food stores were generally stocked from the farms so that backup sustenance was always available, but if the clan hunters did not make a kill during a hunt, then it would mean a less nutritious meal for the entire clan. Jarl suspected that in Baldur's Circle, it was probably the same.

"Brother and sister, you have been training for a long time this day. Please, join me for a meal to keep your strength up," Bjorn said as he approached the pair. It was as though he had read Jarl's mind, but Jarl would not question the man's perfect timing; he was hungry, and he was sure that Sylfia would be too.

The only problem was that as he walked, he remembered that Bjorn had already told them that the lands were barren – and that meant that with the clan members unable to leave the boundaries of the settlement, he was sure that there would be no hunted animal to eat.

For the first time, Jarl and Sylfia were led into what was easily the largest building in the settlement: the wooden longhouse that stood off to the side of the central buildings. It was not any taller than the other wooden buildings, but it was at least four times as long as any other, and when the three of them stepped inside, they were greeted with the hum of over one hundred men and women talking, eating and drinking.

There were wooden plates and metal drinking vessels covering all of the long tables within the building, and through the centre of each sat a veritable banquet of all of the foods that Jarl and Sylfia had ever heard of and many things that they simply did not recognise.

There were fruits of all varieties, shapes and sizes, plates and bowls of vegetables that seemed to go on and on, and above everything else, there was a plethora of perfectly browned, steaming meats.

"What is this, father?" Sylfia breathed as she took in all of the aromas within the hall. Her mouth watered, and she fought the urge to simply dive in and take her fill.

"Something is not right here, daughter," Jarl replied, his eyes narrowing. "I do not understand."

"Brother! Sister!" Bjorn announced loudly and placed a large arm around Jarl's shoulders. "You must join us in our feast! Take as much as you like and leave nothing in wanting!"

"I do not understand, Bjorn," Jarl replied quietly. "You say that the lands are barren, and I have seen your farmland. You do not grow the things that you have placed on these tables."

"Ah, I see why you stand away from the tables and the rest of Baldur's Children, brother. The bounty you see before you is a gift of the Gods, as are many of the things you see around you. There are many among us that received the ability to manifest food as their power through the tears. This is something that we do know how to influence when one drinks the tears and gains their ability for the first time: if they are hungry to the point of starvation, they will become able to conjure food. If they are thirsty and near death, they will be able to create water from where there was none. "

"So this is how you discovered how the tears work?" Sylfia asked in an excited tone. "It was easy because you saw that the people were gaining the things they needed most at that very moment!"

Bjorn shared Sylfia's smile and nodded.

"So if someone was freezing to death, they could gain the ability to create fire or clothes!" she exclaimed.

"That is exactly it!" Bjorn replied, raising his hands into the air. The Gods smile down upon those in need who ask for help.

But we must remember the cost of gaining such abilities, little sister. We make our promises to avert the coming of Ragnarök, which means we must do what we can to make the world cry for Baldur."

"If the Gods wanted us to carry out this task," Jarl interrupted, "then why would they trap us within this settlement? Surely we would be better placed if we could leave to spread the word?"

"We do not question how the Gods work, brother," Bjorn replied, still smiling. "We trust that when the time comes for us to carry out our duties, we will be ready. But for now, come as members of Baldur's Children: Join us and take your fill."

Sylfia stepped forward but Jarl placed a hand on her back to stop her. "Sylfia... we do not know what will happen if we eat this food. We drank their water and then were told that we could never leave. This may not be a good idea."

It did make sense to her, but what choice did they have? They were already stuck within this settlement as it was, and they were going to have to eat something eventually.

"Do not worry, brother. I promise you that there is nothing that this food will do for you other than fill your belly. Now join us and enjoy what the Gods have given us."

Sylfia and Jarl walked forward and took a seat at the end of a long wooden table. The other people that they could see were engrossed in their own conversations, some arm wrestling, some attempting to outdrink others, and a few sat silently. Not one of them though would even look at the two new additions to their clan. As soon as the larger Bjorn saw Sylfia and Jarl had taken their seats, he, too disappeared into the crowds.

Sylfia had never seen such a bounty of food and drink before, and she began filling her wooden bowl with anything and everything that she could reach. The metal tankard held only water although it was both cool and refreshing as she drank, but through mouthfuls of the most delicious food that she had ever tasted, she did notice that her father was only taking the food that they had eaten whilst in the Rakki clan.

"You must try this, father," Sylfia said through mouthfuls of food. "The tastes are unlike anything I have experienced before!"

Jarl did not answer his daughter. Rather he chewed slowly and did not let his gaze drop from the other people within the longhouse. It was as though he was awaiting a battle, and he would not let his concentration falter for even a minute.

Eventually, a woman with red hair tied into tight braids approached Jarl and Sylfia from the crowd. She looked taller than even Jarl although she did not quite reach the lofty heights of Bjorn's stature. She held out a hand for Jarl to take and smiled.

"My name is Hilda," she said.

Jarl did not release his gaze from the crowd of other people, nor did he take Hilda's hand.

"My name is Sylfia, and this is my father, Jarl. We come from the west," Sylfia replied with a smile of her own. "Please forgive my father, he does not always know when he is being a rude old man."

Jarl's gaze faltered for just a moment before his frown grew even deeper, and he redoubled his attention to its purpose.

"You know, Jarl," Hilda said, still smiling. "I made a lot of the food in this place, so you do not just have to eat the meat."

Jarl looked down at the meat as though seeing it for the first time, and then he opened his mouth and let the chewed mass he already had in there spill out onto his beard and then onto the table. He looked up at Hilda, still frowning. "Tastes bad," he proclaimed.

"Oh, that is not a worry. Would you prefer something that tastes as though it has been cooked a little longer?" Hilda replied. Then she cupped her hands over a wooden bowl before Jarl, and both he and Sylfia watched as a familiar white-blue glow seeped through the gaps in her fingers. When she removed her hands, there was a perfectly cooked slab of steak sat within the bowl.

"We can all do tricks here," Jarl growled and picked the steak up in his bare hands and placed it on one of his axe heads. Within a second, the meat burst into a blaze of orange-red flame that, when extinguished, left the steak blackened and charred.

Jarl hadn't noticed, though, that his action had silenced the entire longhouse, with each and every clan member staring silently at him.

"Father, do not be so rude!" Sylfia berated Jarl through the silence. "These people have been nothing but kind to us, and you repay them with suspicion and anger?"

"You think that they are kind to us?" Jarl raised his own voice back at Sylfia. "Do not be so naïve, daughter. These people tricked us into drinking some potion that they say is of the Gods, but as far as we know, it is a potion of the damned! They tell us that we cannot leave, yet they proclaim to be messengers of the Gods! Sylfia, I thought that I had raised you to think better than this!" Jarl then picked up a tankard and slammed it down on the table with a loud thud.

Sylfia then saw the huge hulking figure of Bjorn stand from one of the wooden benches and make his way towards where they sat. The smile was no longer on his face, and Sylfia began to worry about what was to happen next.

"Here comes the man himself," Jarl exclaimed as he spotted Bjorn's approach. "Come to tell us more about how we are unable to leave? Or was that just another trick to keep us here?"

Bjorn stopped dead in his tracks. It seemed that Jarl's words had caused him to rethink whatever it was that he was about to say, and his dark grimace faded away as he seemed to come to some inward conclusion.

"You think that I tell half-truths, Rakki?" Bjorn said flatly, though it was clear that he meant no pleasantries in his words. "Then follow me now, and we shall see who is untruthful."

Jarl stood up from his bench and followed Bjorn through the doors to the longhouse. It had become dusk outside already although not yet dark enough for the torches within the settlement to be lit for the night.

Sylfia followed the pair out of the longhouse and into the settlement proper, and as she moved, she realised that many of the people who had been eating their food had also stood up and started to follow. Sylfia knew that this was not going to be a good thing.

Bjorn strode purposely towards where Sylfia and Jarl had entered into Baldur's Circle, and the pair eventually came to a silent stop before the archway that denoted the boundary of the settlement. Catching up with the pair, Sylfia could now see words carved onto the interior of the archway that she had not taken the time to notice before.

For any who reach this archway that do not know of its significance, you are urged to turn back now.

There will come a time when this point is passable, though until the Gods see fit for us to all to be allowed to do so, it is only your end that you will find beyond this point.

We are forever Baldur's Children, destined to remain within his Circle until we are freed to return that mercy to Baldur himself.

One day Baldur's Children will rule the world and bring about a new age to all of mankind.

Go with the blessings of the Gods, and forever be at peace.

The words were as clear as day, and Sylfia read them through twice to ensure that she had missed nothing of their meaning.

"Do you think that simple words are enough to convince me of this curse?" Jarl said aloud as the rest of the followers arrived to watch what was happening.

"No, brother, I do not expect you to believe. I expect you to attempt to pass through the boundary and join your ancestors as they walk in their next lives," Bjorn replied solemnly.

Jarl took a single step towards the archway and faced it completely.

"Father!" Sylfia called out after him. Jarl did not respond.

Then Jarl walked directly up to the archway and reached a single hand through the imagined barrier, and held it there for all to see.

For a short moment, nothing happened. But then Jarl watched as his hand began to disintegrate into a cloud of grey dust, swirling as though it was not connected to his arm any longer.

"Father, please!" Sylfia cried out and leapt forward, taking hold of Jarl's shoulders and pulling him back and away from the archway. As his hand returned to the interior of the boundary, it quickly reformed into the natural body part that it was.

Sylfia had pulled so hard that Jarl had fallen backwards and on top of her, and she could not help but begin to sob as she realised just how close she had just come to losing her father.

Bjorn and the rest of Baldur's Children slowly left the pair to deal with their thoughts, and whilst Jarl was silent, Sylfia could not control her sobbing.

9

Jarl and Sylfia had eventually left the archway to return to the hut they had been allowed to rest in the night before. They were curious if this was to be a long-term arrangement, though every member of the settlement seemed to be staying very far away from them since they had received proof of the dire boundary.

"Did it hurt?" Sylfia eventually asked once they had each lay upon their furs. Neither one of them had said a single word to each other since the incident at the archway.

"I do not wish to speak on this, Sylfia," Jarl replied.

"But you must now believe in what these people have been telling you?" Sylfia pressed.

"I said I do not wish to speak."

"But they have given you proof again and again. Father, you must believe your own two eyes!"

"I have said what I have needed to say on the matter, daughter, and you will listen to me. Do you not understand the meaning of this?"

"And do you not understand the meaning of being wrong? Why can you not simply admit when you are wrong?" Sylfia asked.

"Because," Jarl let his voice drop in volume. "Because if I admit that what we have been told is the truth, it means that we must remain here forever. I... we will never see Sigrid again, and that... that is a difficult thing to ask of me. You do not understand the connection that I share with your mother. To be apart from her and to still feel her in my heart is akin to torture."

Sylfia had not expected that response. She had been waiting for another flat refusal to speak about the matter, but her father had opened up to her and given her a reason for his behaviour. And it was a good reason too.

The response had thrown her off her trail, and suddenly Sylfia realised that she too missed her mother. The reality of their situation weighed down upon them both, and they sat in silence for a long while before Sylfia spoke again, when a sudden realisation had struck her.

"But I can leave the settlement, I have done it before!" she exclaimed.

"That was a long time ago, Sylfia. We do not yet know how any of this works, but that feeling... a part of you floating away into nothingness... that is not something that I would wish upon a stranger, let alone my own child. It is certainly not something that I wish to experience for a second time."

"But if I can leave the settlement," Sylfia began to plead.

"I said NO, Sylfia. Why must you always try to bend or break the rules?" Jarl said. He stopped short of blaming Sylfia for being in the situation that they were in, but the silence he let hang in the air spoke volumes.

Eventually, Sylfia spoke under her breath, quiet enough that she thought that Jarl would not be able to hear her.

"I know I can leave this place, and I shall prove it."

Sylfia spent a long while in silence then, thinking through everything she thought she knew about the people who called themselves 'Baldur's Children' and the place where they had been told they would both have to spend the rest of their lives. Her father had been so adamant that he wanted to leave, but she hadn't truly thought about what that actually meant. She missed her mother, though. If she was right and could leave, it would bring her hope.

Eventually, when the night was dark and still, Sylfia slipped off of her bed furs and crept towards the wooden door. She looked at her father, who was breathing heavily in his sleep, and grimaced as she pulled lightly on the wooden door. Thankfully, it did not creak as it opened; rather it swung open easily as though it was a sign that she was doing the right thing.

The night outside was cool and dark, and it reminded Sylfia of the time that she had snuck out from the Rakki settlement to face the God's Chasm alone. This was no different: she was planning on doing something that she knew would be dangerous, but again she felt it was the right thing to do.

The paths around the settlement were again lit by burning torches, and Sylfia skirted the edges of these to remain hidden by shadow as much as possible. Within a few moments she was out of the settlement and approaching the archway.

Even in the darkness she could see the words carved into the stone and it made her heart beat faster. She halted beneath the archway and slowly pushed her hand through the imaginary boundary just as her father had. But unlike her father's, her hand did not begin to flow away from her; rather, it remained solid, with nothing at all affecting her. She waited for a long moment and then stepped confidently through the archway, taking a deep breath as she moved.

Sylfia felt no different once she had passed through the threshold to the other side of the archway, and she tried her best not to think about how many other people had done the exact same thing only to fade away into the ether. Her mother - her real mother - was one of those people, and she could only hope that her passing hadn't been painful.

With just one thing on her mind, Sylfia shook off all thoughts of the past and any doubts that she had and began her walk into the darkness in search of her previously discarded short swords. This would certainly be an excellent way to prove that she could pass through the invisible boundary and out into the east proper.

She did not remember the way back to where the wolf had attacked her the last time she was in the eastern wilds, but she knew that her journey should be in as straight a path as possible from the settlement, as Jarl had carried her to safety and would not have taken anything but the most direct path.

Thankfully, after a few strides, Sylfia recognised the footfalls that still indented the mud underfoot. She could tell from their size that they were most probably her father's, and the depth that indicated that he had been carrying another reinforced her notion. She knew now that all she needed to do was to follow these prints back into the forest, and she would have her weapons – and her proof that she could leave the settlement – back in no time.

Sylfia was surprised that after a few minutes of calmly walking through the dark woods, the trail still continued. She had not been aware of just how far her father had carried her, and that had begun to make her feel guilty. Eventually though, as she knew it would, her path ended in a small clearing illuminated by the moonlight, and on the ground in the centre of the clearing, lying where they had been dropped were her two short swords.

Sylfia straightened her shoulders and walked out into the moonlight towards her discarded weapons. Something stopped her in her tracks. She could not be sure exactly what it was, but something was moving in the periphery of her vision.

Stopping abruptly, Sylfia turned her head and saw slumped against a large tree trunk, the form of another person. She tried her best to see if the person was watching her or not, but after a moment she realised that whoever this was, they were either uninterested or simply had not seen her yet.

"Hello?" Sylfia called out softly. "I thought these lands were barren. Have you come from the west?"

The figure did not respond, and Sylfia had no choice but to move closer to the person to see them more clearly.

"Are you OK?" Sylfia tried.

Still no answer.

Sylfia had reached just shy of touching distance when she realised that the person was a woman, and terribly wounded. She was wearing a white tunic stained a deep red by some hidden dire wound. Her dark hair was matted and wet as though she had been running and her breathing was shallow and strained.

"What happened?" Sylfia asked as she placed a hand on the woman's shoulders. The woman's eyes opened quickly and betrayed her fear as she realised another person was so close to her.

"Please... I do not know if the beast is coming back. I beg of you, please..." the woman said in a panicked tone.

"It is alright, I am a friend, and there is nothing in these woods with us," Sylfia said. But as she spoke, a low growl came from somewhere in the distance. She recognised it for what it was, and it made her hairs stand on end. The woman let out a feeble whimper.

"We need to go," Sylfia announced. "Quickly, before that thing finds us."

Sylfia had no intention of standing to face the giant wolf again, but she was not sure that this woman could move as quickly as she could back to the sanctuary of Baldur's Circle.

"I... I do not think that I can move. Please, leave me; I know that this will be over quickly."

Sylfia looked behind to see where the growl had come from but there were not yet any signs of the wolf. Her swords, though, still lay on the ground, glistening in the moonlight and Sylfia knew that this was a choice that the Gods were providing her with. She could run back to the settlement alone and save herself, or she could turn and fight. She would be protecting a stranger against a foe that she knew she had no hope of defeating, but as she had been told on several occasions already, if she wanted to make a difference in this world, she was going to have to take the most difficult of paths. This again would be a path that would provide difficulty beyond measure.

Moving quickly yet silently to where her swords lay, Sylfia stood over them and peered into the darkness. She still had no idea where the creature was or from which direction it would approach, but at least she knew she would be in a better position to fight with her familiar weapons in hand.

But something was stopping her from picking up the pair of short swords lying on the ground. She could not place what was preventing her from being able to defend herself but a feeling deep down inside herself was warning her of something.

And then Sylfia realised something - the woman, bloodied and broken and slumped against the tree, was watching her intently. No, not watching, staring directly at her as though she was waiting for Sylfia to make her move. Even from this distance Sylfia could see that the woman had bright, piercing golden eyes, and their gaze made her feel cold and judged.

Sylfia stopped over and reached out a hand to the first sword, though she kept her gaze on the woman who was watching her. As her fingers reached for its hilt, a quiet whispering coming from the woman reached her ears

"Yes, go on, pick it up," she was whispering, and Sylfia knew that if she had not been paying attention, she never would have heard the sound. Sylfia stopped and stood upright without her weapon.

"Please!" The woman begged again. "It is approaching, you must!" Then almost immediately, an ear-piercing howl emanated from the woods behind Sylfia and the realisation that the beast and this woman were somehow connected dawned on her.

"What is your name?" Sylfia called out to the woman.

"Does it matter? Help me!" The woman cried back.

"Tell me your name, or I will not help you," Sylfia replied.

"My name is Elli. Please now pick up your swords and protect us both from that beast!" Elli cried and pointed to some place beyond Sylfia.

The treeline in the clearing rustled, giving Sylfia no alternative but to leap into action. She dropped to her knees in one fell swoop and collected both of her swords as though they had never left her hands. She regained her footing and adopted a warrior's stance, but whatever had made the noise had disappeared although she could still sense something approaching.

She spun on her heels just in time to see Elli reaching out for her but she could do nothing to prevent the woman from placing her hands on Sylfia's shoulders. The woman's weight was extreme and her eyes were closed again. Sylfia struggled to remain on her feet, but it was just all too difficult.

Sylfia had no choice but to drop to a single knee.

"It is so nice of you to kneel before me," Elli said softly, and then, before Sylfia's eyes, the woman aged a hundred years or more. Her skin creased and cracked, her stature bent, and her hair thinned and fell out. This was no normal injured woman; this was a woman of advanced age with no visible injuries and still she held Sylfia down on her knees.

"What is happening?" Sylfia grunted through the strain that should not have been there.

"I am afraid that no mortal being can withstand old age," Elli explained in a hoarse, wizened voice.

"I... do not... kneel to time..." Sylfia managed to reply through gritted teeth, but she knew that her time was near. If she did not move soon, the weight of this woman's hands would crush her and end her life.

Sylfia then had a thought. She had been fighting against this unbearable pressure as though it was the only thing she could do, but it wasn't; she could go with the force on her shoulders and use that moment of freedom to escape.

She did better than escape, though.

She let go of her efforts to hold herself up, fell backwards to the ground then raised a sword swiftly through Elli's arm severing it perfectly at the elbow. The older woman howled in pain as a spray of blood coated Sylfia's face, but she did not take a moment to assess the damage she had caused but turned and ran, back to Baldur's Circle, back to her father and back to safety.

It did not sound as if the shrill screaming behind Sylfia was remaining in the woods - it sounded as if she was being followed through the trees. Surely it could not be true, the woman had seemed so elderly, and with the serious would that Sylfia had inflicted there was little chance that she would survive, let alone follow in Sylfia's nimble footsteps.

Gradually the trees faded to nothing behind Sylfia, and she ran panting as Baldur's Circle appeared in her field of view.

The torches looked welcoming now, and the stone archway centred in the small wall she knew would be her salvation; she had done what she needed to prove that she could leave the settlement and collect her weapons.

Sylfia was just feet away from her salvation when she turned to look behind her. She would not have usually done so, but a voice carried on the wind, making her turn.

"You are a weak human..." it carried. "I will show you just what happens when insects require punishment!"

The elderly woman was just a few yards behind her, but now she had both of her arms again and held a long, wooden spear to the ready.

Before Sylfia could do anything about it, Elli launched the spear at her and it flew through the air between them, straight and true. Then just before the tip hit Sylfia, Elli faded into dust and was carried away by the wind.

10

The tip of the wooden spear hit Sylfia as though it was made of steel. She was so close to the salvation of Baldur's Circle, but close was not enough. The spear penetrated beneath her shoulder blade through her back and protruded from her front. Sylfia looked down and saw the sharpened end, stained in blood, and the cackling laughter from Elli faded away along with Sylfia's vision, which faded to black. The last thing she thought as her life faded away was just how stupid she had been.

~

Jarl had known that Sylfia was planning on doing something that he did not wholly agree with. It was always her way and as her father, he could always tell that something was coming. It was partly why he was so harsh on himself when he hadn't realised that his daughter had planned on crossing the God's Chasm in the first place.

But after she had spoken of her notion that she may have been able to leave Baldur's Circle unharmed, he knew that it was precisely what she planned to do, and knowing Sylfia, she was going to attempt this sooner rather than later.

When Sylfia had slipped from the furs and crept out of the wooden hut, Jarl had been awake, waiting in the darkness for that very moment.

Waiting for a long moment for Sylfia to assume she was alone out in the darkness, Jarl crept out of his furs and followed in his daughter's footsteps. He did not want Sylfia to know that he was following her, but he wished to be there when she realised that she, like him, could not cross through the boundary of the archway. He would remind her that he had told her so and that, again, she should listen to her father above all else.

Sylfia had stopped at the archway and pushed her arm through the invisible barrier, but unlike when he had performed this very act, she had not been affected. Then, before he could do anything to prevent it, Sylfia walked right through.

Jarl was shocked at her ability to cross over and was tempted to call out to her, but he knew it would do no good. Instead, he would await her return and pretend he had not noticed her leaving.

Jarl waited for a long while for Sylfia to return. He knew that she would probably go to fetch her pair of short swords and then come straight back to the settlement, but as time passed he became increasingly worried and agitated. He thought about crossing the boundary himself to go and look for her – if that creature that had attacked her last time had returned, she could have found herself in trouble, and this time without anyone there to save her.

It was silent beyond the archway, and Jarl did not know if that was a part of the magic of the place or if it was simply the fact that nothing was happening.

But just as Jarl was about to try to wave his hand through the threshold once more, he saw Sylfia emerge from the treeline to the west at a full sprint, coming right towards him.

Breathing a sigh of relief, he was about to move into full view within the archway so that Sylfia would know that he had foiled her plans, but he saw the look of utter fear on her face. And then he saw the red blood staining one of the swords in her hands.

"Sylfia!" Jarl called out at the top of his voice, but his daughter could not hear him. Standing within the archway, he was unsure if she could even see him.

Then Jarl saw a second figure emerge from the woods, and any hope he had evaporated. The woman was elderly, crooked even, but she moved as though she had the grace of the Gods. She held a hand out to her side, and suddenly a long, wooden spear appeared there. She drew it back and threw it powerfully, straight and true at Sylfia, who had made it to within a mere few feet of where Jarl stood.

The spear hit his daughter with a sickening wet thud, and Jarl watched as it stuck her through like a roasted hog.

Jarl acted without thinking. He leapt through the archway without a single thought for his own safety and caught Sylfia's limp and lifeless body before she hit the ground. The elderly woman was still cackling, but she had faded into the woods now that her work was done. Jarl fought the urge to chase her, but he knew he had more important things to worry about.

For the second time in as many days, Jarl carried his daughter into Baldur's Circle and shouted out for help.

Bjorn was again the first one to aid in Sylfia's plight. The large man seemed able to sense pain and injuries, and as soon as he arrived at Sylfia lying on the ground next to Jarl's kneeling form, he again placed his hands over her body.

"You must remove the spear," Bjorn instructed Jarl. "As soon as you do, I must heal her, or she may lose too much blood for me to prevent her journey to the afterlife."

Jarl nodded once. This was not the time for anger or arguments, and he knew it.

As he pulled the spear from his daughter, a spray of blood coated his hands and forearms, but he did not care. Bjorn's hands had illuminated as before, and he knew his daughter, would be safe again.

At least, that was what he thought.

The strain became evident on Bjorn's face as he struggled with whatever it was that he was doing to control his power. The veins on his neck and temples bulged and the light beneath his hands grew to an almost unbearable brightness. Bjorn did not stop, though. He gritted his teeth and growled as he put in every ounce of effort that his body could afford until, eventually, he fell to the ground with his eyes closed. The illuminating light faded away to nothing.

"Bjorn? Sylfia?" Jarl asked, but neither replied.

Jarl looked up at the blank faces now surrounding the three on the ground. Not a single one offered a hand to help, and Jarl fought to keep his tears on the inside. He did not know what to do and was about to ask for help when four people picked up Bjorn and another two Sylfia, and gently carried them away from sight.

Jarl saw that Sylfia was to be taken to their usual hut, but he did not see Bjorn's destination. He spared a moment to hope that the large healer would be well, then returned his attention to his daughter, who had not yet opened her eyes.

"Where are you taking them?" Jarl called out the first thing he thought of to nobody in particular.

No reply came.

Jarl remained on his knees with his face in his hands for a moment before realising that his daughter's blood was now smeared over his skin. There was nothing more he could do other than to follow, and sit by his daughter's side as she fought to return to the land of the living.

Sylfia had been placed in their hut, but nobody remained to keep watch over her. Jarl would be there, though, from now until the moment that she awakened.

Jarl spoke in a hushed tone as he knelt over his daughter. "I am sorry, my daughter. I should have accepted your words more readily rather than leave you to disobey. I am sorry that you feel the need to challenge me, but I know that it is who you are. You have so much fire in you. I am sorry that you are here on the eastern side of the Chasm, Sylfia. I wish I could do something to change the hands of time, but I promise you that I will never stop protecting you. I will always be there for you no matter what happens. Just please come back to me, Sylfia."

Sylfia did not reply. As she lay on the furs, Jarl could see that her wounds had closed and her breathing had returned — albeit weak and shallow. She looked peaceful, even if she had no consciousness.

Jarl watched over his daughter all night, and by the time daylight had arrived, he had fallen asleep. There was only so much a man could do in this situation, and Jarl needed his rest too.

Jarl was awoken by the creak of someone opening the wooden door to the hut and the sound of their footsteps as they walked inside.

He opened his eyes and met the gaze of the old man with long white hair atop his head and a long white beard hanging down onto his chest. Elder Hugi still wore the furs of some large animal across his shoulders, and Jarl could still not figure out exactly what animal it was. Behind the Elder stepped Bjorn into the hut.

"I suppose you have experienced a long night?" Elder Hugi asked with a smile. "I have not been in this situation in a very long time. Not since Bjorn here, at least," he trailed off.

Jarl looked at Bjorn. The large man looked pale, as though he was severely ill. He was sweating and could barely stand, although he managed to do so under his own power.

"What... what happened?" Jarl asked, directing his question more to Bjorn than the Elder.

"I do not know. This has never happened to me before. As I was healing Sylfia, I could feel her wounds closing, and everything was as it should normally be. Then I felt something inside her like a poison, and I tried to remove it, but it fought against me. I tried my best to push it away but I felt it engulf me and then I fell. I am still not myself."

"Our friend here requires rest," Elder Hugi interrupted. "I believe what has happened here was that your daughter has been struck by a spear that was curiously constructed of pure mistletoe, as was the weapon that felled our God Baldur. I do not think that the magic we all use here in the Circle is effective against any weaponry of such construction, and I do not know if your daughter will survive this."

Jarl looked at Sylfia, who was still lying silently on the bed.

"She has healed and rests now," Jarl said. "There has been no change." It sounded as though he had pushed all emotion from his words as he spoke; this was the time for action and not for feeling.

"And I do not know if her presentation will remain stable or not," Elder Hugi replied. "She may yet heal, or she may not. We are all servants of time in one way or another."

"And you came here to simply tell me this?" Jarl growled. It seemed to him that if they had nothing constructive to tell him, why were they even there at all?

"No," the Elder replied with a grin. "I am here to divine what happened last night. We are aware that you are unable to leave the Circle. However, it would appear that both you and your daughter were able to leave last night, and we would like to know why. It is foretold that one day we shall leave, and when that day comes, we will be able to spread the word of Baldur's situation to the world and undo the first sign of Ragnarök."

"Do you not think there are more important things to consider?" Jarl replied, careful not to let his voice raise to a shout. "Do you not think that I would rather tend to my daughter than answer questions about the Gods?"

"And do you not see what is happening before your eyes?" Bjorn practically hissed. It was the first time that Jarl had seen him without a jovial attitude. "Even in the west you must have heard that to the north the winters are unending. This coldness creeps closer to our borders with every passing moon. Do you not see that this is the coming of the Fimbulwinter?"

"We do not care for fairy tales and children's stories in the west," Jarl growled back, raising himself to his feet. His straight gaze only reached Bjorn's neck, but Jarl had felled larger opponents in the past.

"Children's stories or not, even you cannot deny what you see with your own two eyes. I do not wish to have this discussion with you again, brother. There are more important things to mind than arguments between men. Let us agree on the most basic of things: that your daughter is in trouble and requires care. I believe that I am the only one able to help her, but I do not know if it will be enough," Bjorn replied, his tone turning solemn.

Jarl could not argue. He knew that he needed these people, and Bjorn specifically, to help Sylfia, and fighting with them would not force them to help him. But it was true that he had indeed seen the winters growing longer in the north, and their coldness searched further south with each passing each season. He had secretly wondered if this could indeed be the beginning of Fimbulwinter, though he had never voiced his concerns out loud.

"Please, what do you need to help my daughter?" Jarl asked, putting all else to the back of his mind.

Elder Hugi spoke before Bjorn could this time. "We need to keep her out of the daylight, warm and under constant watch to ensure she does not become any worse. I believe we will save her, but it will not be an easy task."

"I beg you, do whatever you can... she is all I have left in this world," Jarl replied quietly, his voice cracking.

The Elder nodded. "You must trust us to do as we shall and not interfere, Jarl of the west. Do you accept these terms?"

Jarl did not even hesitate to give his answer. "I will always do whatever it takes to save my daughter."

"You are both members of Baldur's Children now, as you have been from the moment you entered our settlement. We will do what we can to save Sylfia as she is one of our own," Bjorn announced before lifting Sylfia easily and carefully from her furs and walking out of the hut. Jarl made a move to follow his daughter, but Elder Hugi stood in his way.

"You must leave her in the hands of the clan, brother. The healing process, I believe, will take weeks or months and not hours, from this wound, as your daughter must be healed with a combination of methods. Forget your daughter, for now, Jarl. The clan will take care of her."

Jarl felt his face redden at that statement. "You wish me to forget the one thing I care most for in this world? And what would you have me do instead, sit back and await your words?"

"No, Jarl. You are to become an active clan member along with every other inhabitant of Baldur's Circle. You must use your gift as best suits the clan and do what you can to spread the word of Baldur to the rest of the world."

"So that is how it is to be? You will hold my daughter hostage so that I will work within your clan?" Jarl practically spat back. He could see what the Elder was asking of him, and he did not enjoy the thought.

"Do not misunderstand me, Jarl," The Elder replied calmly. "We are not your enemies, nor do we intend to hold your daughter to ransom. This attitude of malice that you hold towards our clan is unfounded, and if you do not change this soon, you will eventually see that you have been foolish. You will see, Jarl of Baldur's Children."

11

A month had passed since the last words that Jarl and Sylfia had shared. Jarl had spent a long while in solitude, but eventually the Elder's words penetrated his mind, and belief began to override suspicion. Jarl knew that if he was to repay the clan for their mercy and kindness, he would have to do something to pull his weight around the settlement.

Jarl found it interesting that no single clan member had asked him to do anything specifically. He had been told that 'helping' was expected of him in return for his food and shelter, but he did not have much idea of what that meant.

In the Rakki clan, Jarl had been a warrior, a raider and later, a sentinel to guard the God's Chasm. Since Jarl had been in

Baldur's Circle, though, he had not seen a single enemy, threat or danger whatsoever. In essence, all he had really seen were farmers doing a small amount of work to keep the farmland fertile and really not much else.

Each day, Jarl had arranged with Elder Hugi and Bjorn to visit his daughter and spend some time with her, and as the sun set on each day he would fulfil that duty. Sylfia was peaceful each time Jarl saw her, and she seemed to breathe easily though she never opened her eyes. The Elder and the healer had both told Jarl that they did not know if or when Sylfia would awaken.

For the first few days, Jarl chose not to leave his hut until the moment that he could see his daughter, but eventually he had started to leave earlier and earlier, collecting food from the longhouse and retreating quickly to his solitude.

By the second week, Jarl had started to put his skills to good use and had begun to patrol the wall that surrounded Baldur's Circle, keeping a lookout both in and out of the settlement. After all, it was what he knew best, and was comfortable doing.

It was strange, though, that in the time that Jarl had been carrying out this task, he did not come across a single individual looking to either leave or enter the settlement. It was as if the place was in the middle of nowhere, in some barren land and the fact that Sylfia had managed to get herself almost killed not once but twice out there was a mystery to Jarl.

This night was dark on the outskirts of Baldur's Circle, and Jarl was patrolling as he always did, in a clockwise direction. The torches had been lit in the centre of the settlement, but nobody seemed to care too much about anything that may have entered the outer reaches.

The sound of footsteps on the farmland to his right made him stop. The torches made the person simply a silhouette, and though he tried to see who it was, the darkness on his side kept the individual in shadow.

"Brother, you do not have to do this," A woman's voice came from the figure as it reached speaking distance. "You should come back to the settlement and find other ways that you can be helpful to us all."

The voice was familiar, but Jarl could not place it straight away. He closed his eyes and tried to remember where he had heard it before, but the memory would not come.

"I do what I know," Jarl replied in a gruff tone. "This is what I have always done and will always do. My task is to protect."

"But you are not using your gift! This is the one thing that the Gods have seen fit to bless you with, and you shun it in favour of what you have known in a life lived without their aid?" Jarl now recognised the voice: it was Hilda, the tall, red-haired cook who had spoken to him in the longhouse.

"And using your gift to cook is more important than keeping raiders, murderers or rapists out of the settlement? Or to keep those inside who wish to cause themselves harm by attempting to leave?" Jarl asked.

"Yes. I am using the gift that I was given by the Gods, to provide food for those who need it. It is what I have been tasked to do, and I do not question it," Hilda replied as she handed Jarl a lump of meat the size of his fist. "This is what I do here, for our people and on behalf of the Gods. What do you do, Jarl?"

"I stand guard," Jarl replied without hesitating for a second. "I do this to prevent harm coming to those for whom I stand guard."

"That was your purpose before, in your old life," Hilda said. "You have been given a gift, and it is your task to use that gift to help this settlement and all of Baldur's Children."

"What would you have me do then? I can control the flame but to what end? Would you have me light torches or fires? Create bonfires for warmth? My gift is not as useful as yours is, sister; my gift saves time, but it is not something that we cannot live without."

"Oh, so you do not think that I am unable to cook without my gift, then?" Hilda asked, her voice raising slightly. Jarl could hear the smile on her face through her words, and he could not help but feel warm inside.

Taken aback by the abruptness of the question and the change in Hilda's demeanour, Jarl was left speechless. He had been expecting to keep fighting his corner as he had always done, but the woman was just so disarming.

"I am going to show you how things are supposed to work around here, Jarl of the Rakki clan," Hilda replied, still smiling. "Now sit," she ordered.

Jarl obediently lowered himself to the ground. He was not above taking orders from others, and he had no reason not to listen to Hilda, who seemed as though she had only ever tried to help him.

Hilda cupped her hands together, and Jarl watched as light filtered through her fingers again. It was so bright that he could see the outline of her veins and bones beneath her skin and the light illuminated her soft face that showed determination but no malice. Jarl waited in silence until the light faded to nothing, and when Hilda parted her hands, between them was a round, flat chunk of meat.

Jarl could not tell what kind of meat this was, but if he was pressed, he would have guessed that it came from a cow. It was red, juicy and uncooked.

"Now, this is where your gift is required," Hilda said. "Hold one of your axes beneath this meat and the other above so that I have something to cook upon."

Jarl obediently obliged, holding his two axes, as instructed. He knew what was coming next, so before Hilda could ask, Jarl channelled his gift into the bottom axe, doing his best to keep the blaze small and controlled so that Hilda would have a small yet effective cooking fire and grill.

In the new orange light that the flaming axe provided, Hilda's expression was warm and caring. He had not taken the time to see what she looked like before, past her hair and annoying interruptions.

Hilda silently placed the meat on the axe prepared for cooking, and between them they cooked the meat to a perfect brown on the outside and pink in the middle.

Hilda was the first to test it, using her teeth to tear off a chunk and chewing it whilst making appreciative noises. Then she offered the other half to Jarl, who couldn't resist the combination of hunger and the aroma of the meat cooking. His mouth had been watering for minutes already.

When the flavour exploded in his mouth at the first bite, Jarl's first thought was that this had to be another divine gift afforded to Hilda, who was watching him silently and patiently.

"You can make *anything* taste as though it was from the Gods themselves?" he queried.

Hilda could not help but laugh heartily. The sound was like music to Jarl's ears, and it made him smile. Eventually, Hilda managed to gather herself enough to speak again.

"No! I am an excellent cook without whatever it is that the Gods have done for me! My ability is an extension of myself and not the other way around, and let that be a lesson to you, Jarl: Your gift is not what defines you, do you understand?"

"Yes, I do," Jarl responded slowly, and it was the truth. He knew now what these people were trying to say to him all along: They were together working towards the same goal. He was not a captive in their foreign lands, he was one of Baldur's Children and now he knew that he needed to do what he could for the good of the clan.

And with this realisation, it dawned on Jarl that he could never go home, and that meant that he would never see Sigrid again, regardless of the fact that he could still feel her presence in this world, deep within his heart.

"Now let me show you just what I can do with these powers," Hilda continued as she cupped her hands again, and when she opened them again, she held a perfectly cooked chunk of meat in her hands.

The pair spent a long while together, with Hilda conjuring all kinds of different foods ranging from meats to fruits and vegetables. The items were never particularly large, but they were always delicious. Then subtly her mood changed.

"You must do what you can to prove yourself useful in the clan, Jarl," she said with a look in her eyes that Jarl did not like. "People... people need to be useful here, do you understand?"

"No, I do not understand," Jarl replied quickly. "What are you trying to tell me?"

"Not to worry now," Hilda replied in a renewed, chirpy tone. "Anyway, what do you know about Ragnarök?"

Jarl blinked a few times; he felt as though his head had just been spun around and he was now talking to a different person.

"As much as the next man," he said. "I know that it is the end of days and that we cannot prevent it once it has begun. That the planes will all form as one in mighty battle and left behind will be nothing but scorched earth and death."

"You are partly correct, brother, but I must enlighten you with more of the truth that we live by in Baldur's Circle," Hilda explained. "I trust that Bjorn or Elder Hugi has told you about the history of our settlement, the powers that we have been afforded and the plight of Baldur?"

Jarl nodded and added a: "But..." though Hilda ignored him.

"There are four signs of the approach of Ragnarök. The first is that Baldur, the shining God, has passed. This is the most important sign to us here as Baldur's Children because we believe that if we can bring him back from Helheim as Frigg had sought to do, then Ragnarök will be unable to occur."

Jarl nodded as Hilda spoke.

"The second sign is the arrival of Fimbulwinter. This is the dire frost, the severity of which man has never experienced before. Three winters will follow each other without a summer among them. Animals and crops will perish along with the weaker clan members across the world. Eventually, the warmth from the sun will disappear for good, and all that will be left behind will be a bitter cold." She paused to allow her words to sink in, then continued. "Thirdly, the great wolf Fenrir will devour the sun and the moon, and the world will be forever plunged into darkness."

"But these are just tales that are told to scare children into obedience. They hold no truth," Jarl tried to speak, but again Hilda interrupted him.

"The last sign is that Yggdrasil will be shaken so violently by the Midgard Serpent, Jörmungandr, that it will launch the unlaunched ship. The Naglfar Ship, constructed of the bones and fingernails of the fallen will release the armies of the dead from the underworld to join the great battle." Hilda paused, and again Jarl spoke.

"But these tales are not true, sister. We know better than to believe in such fantasies, do we not?"

"Then tell me what these powers are that you have seen with your own eyes? The foods that you have eaten and the flames that you can create from nothing? Tell me what this is if it is not borne from the hands of the Gods?"

Jarl did not have an adequate answer to give to Hilda, so remained silent, but after a time, he spoke.

"Then tell me, sister, you know so much of me, but how was it that you came to be a part of this place?"

Hilda took a long, deep breath, and decided to share her truth with Jarl.

"I had a husband where I come from. You do not know this, but like many of the clan, I have left someone behind whom I do not think I will ever see again." She paused for a long moment as though the words still hurt her. "I come from the north, where the climate is different from here. The winters are long and cold, but we always found ways to survive. It was no longer than two years ago, our lands were becoming broken and infertile, the animals that we hunted for food and warmth grew scarcer, and my clan knew that if we did not find new grounds soon, we would be no more. So I travelled south with a party of five to search for fertile ground and a new home for my people. As we travelled, we were supposed to hunt, but after many days of journey, we found the lands to be barren and my party wanted to return to the settlement. I knew that if we turned back, it would be the end for us. We would never survive the journey back north if we found no prey."

Jarl waited for Hilda to continue, not making a sound to interrupt her.

"I heard a voice carrying on the mists as I walked alone, and I knew that my salvation and hope for my people was close by and that I needed to keep on going. When I arrived at this place, it was dark, and I was alone. I did not want to tempt fate, so I crept into a hut that I could see was empty. Inside I drank of a flask there to quench my thirst, and I prayed to Andhrimnir that I may share in the beast that the God had slaughtered that day in Valhalla. I prayed with all of my being, and when I looked down into my hands, I could see that I had been blessed by the Gods."

"So the Gods simply answered your question and gave you food when you needed it most? I can see now why your people believe that the power you are given is what you covet most," Jarl replied. "Though why then has Sylfia not been given a power? My daughter must not be destined to spend her life in slumber, I am sure of it."

"The powers that we are given are not always apparent. I would not question the will of the Gods, but I would not be surprised if your daughter has some power that you do not know of," Hilda said with a smile. Although her words went some way to soothe Jarl, they made him think about something else: what did Sylfia want most in the world?

The only conclusion that Jarl could make was that Sylfia had wanted to leave the Rakki clan and travel west, and once inside Baldur's Circle she had wanted to leave again to prove that she could – so perhaps her power was that she was able to escape from places that others could not? There was no way for Jarl to test this though and the thought of Sylfia brought back a sense of helplessness and loss. He would see her again tomorrow though.

"I would like you to meet some of the other clan members tomorrow. I believe that you have spent enough time attempting to be the outsider," Hilda announced to cut the silence again.

Jarl nodded slowly, but his gaze did not raise from the small fire that he had started so that the pair had somewhere warm to sit while they spoke.

"After I visit Sylfia, I will come to the longhouse for food," he agreed. "Then you can tell me more about this place that I am destined to call home."

12

Sylfia remembered what her father had done for her in the moments that she had assumed were his last, making her feel both sad and confused. She had been told that she was destined for great things, but since she had decided to take the most challenging path as she had been directed, everything seemed to have gone wrong.

She had crossed the forbidden Chasm, left the unescapable settlement, put her family in danger and fought off unimaginable foes – so what more was she supposed to do?

Sylfia knew that she was dreaming though. She had dreamed so many times before, but this time she had a feeling that she would not awaken until the time was right. She was stuck and she had no option but to simply wait and see what was to happen to her.

The world around her was dark, although when Sylfia looked up to the sky, the stars were bright and the moon was full. The glow of the universe above illuminated her surroundings, and Sylfia could see that she stood in a flat, wide-open field that spanned as far away as she could see until it returned to darkness.

As she looked up at the stars, though, the formations were not as she remembered. She knew which bright stars to look for in the sky to find her way home, but now she could not find those familiar pinpricks of light.

"Where am I?" Sylfia muttered to herself, and her voice was carried off into the wind, echoing over and over as it drifted away from her into the ether.

Sylfia patted her thighs where she usually kept her swords close to her hands, but the weapons were missing too. In fact, now that she took more notice of herself, she realised that she was wearing nothing but the simplest leathers and cloth; her furs were gone along with anything else that she may have carried.

"Hello?" she called out, and the word echoed and faded away into the distance without reply.

And then she felt something. It was as though the entire world around her was shaking to its very core, and she had to squat slightly to steady herself. She could feel her heart begin to race, and then abruptly the motion stopped.

And then a voice reached her, as if it was being carried on the wind, although she could feel no breeze. She listened intently and eventually she could make the words out, as distant as they were.

"I am sorry, Sylfia. I should have listened to you."

Sylfia recognised her father's voice immediately but could not tell from which direction it was being carried.

"Please, daughter. Come back to me," he said.

Sylfia picked a direction at random without knowing where to go and began running as fast as she could. She ran as though her life depended on it but her surroundings never changed. The grass still stood beneath her feet, glowing in the moonlight, and the darkness seemed to move around her as though she was in some divine spotlight.

Eventually, she halted as she realised that her endeavour was futile. She had run for so long and so far that if this place was real, her surroundings should have been at least a little different.

Something was different now though. Not in her physical surroundings, but more of a feeling. It was as though she was being watched.

Sylfia stopped moving and held her breath. It was what she had always been taught to do in this very situation so that she could hear anything approaching but also remain hidden if her enemy was not entirely sure where she was. She could only last for so long, though, and it would be futile if her stalker made no moves towards her.

This time though her enemy made its presence known.

Evolving from the darkness itself, not far from her and directly in front, two bright yellow eyes appeared to cut the darkness apart. These were no human eyes, and behind them followed the shadow of the dire wolf she was now meeting for the third time.

Sylfia's feet anchored to the ground with fear as the beast stalked closer. Even at thirty feet away and in the darkness, she could see the drool dripping from its terrible maw, its sharpened teeth protruding from its mouth, and hear its deep, low growl as it moved slowly toward her.

The wolf must have known somehow that Sylfia could not move because it made no attempt to run towards her as it had done before. 'No', Sylfia thought; this creature was torturing her, and there was nothing she could do about it - nowhere to run, nowhere to hide and no weapons to use to fight it. She could only hope that it would make her death quick and painless.

The wolf kept its head low to the ground, face contorted into an evil smile as it approached. It came within mere feet of Sylfia, who still could not move, petrified to the spot. She had willed her legs to uproot themselves so she could run from this creature, but the more she asked them to oblige, the faster they stuck.

Coming to a halt inches away from Sylfia, the wolf bared all its teeth for her to see. They were longer and sharper than any animal's she had ever seen in the past, and the beast slowly moved its open mouth towards her face.

Sylfia closed her eyes as she felt the wolf's hot breath touch her skin. It was simply too much, and all she could do was let out a quiet whimper.

"Help me," she begged in a tiny whisper.

Her words had been so small when they had slipped from her mouth, but instantly she heard them carry on the wind and echo loudly into the distance. It was strange, almost as though the echo was working in reverse, becoming louder and louder as they carried.

Then came the sound of fluttering feathers, and the wolf abruptly stopped in its advance and when Sylfia finally picked up the courage to open her eyes, sitting on one of the wolf's bottom fangs, just inches from her face, was a jet-black raven.

The raven seemed nonchalant and simply sat there as though it was the most normal perch in the world, but the wolf had stopped. It growled deeply at the bird, all attention gone from Sylfia, and as soon it reared up high into the air, trying to shake the raven free from its mouth, Sylfia fell to the ground behind her.

She watched from her back, still unable to convince her body to take her away from here as the wolf shook its head from side to side to try to dislodge the raven. No matter how hard it tried or how fast it whipped its head back and forth, the raven did not budge from its seat for even an inch.

The wolf howled in frustration, and Sylfia could not figure out why the giant beast did not simply bite down on the bird which sat perfectly within the wolf's mouth. All it had to do was bite down and it could return to the task at hand – her own death.

When the wolf realised it could not shake the raven free, it turned from Sylfia and ran in the opposite direction. After a short burst, the raven flew from the wolf's mouth high into the air and out of sight. As soon as the wolf was free from its passenger, it returned its focus to Sylfia and she could see its full length as it began to circle her. It watched her following its path, and then abruptly it turned to run directly at her again.

Sylfia let out a gasp as the wolf again bore down on her, but after it had taken just a few steps toward her, the raven shot down from the sky and stood directly in its path. Again, the wolf screeched to a halt before it could reach her for the killing blow and turned back to stalk its perimeter around Sylfia once again.

Sylfia was now sure that somehow this raven was protecting her from the giant wolf, as it had done before in the eastern woods. She did not know what the raven was doing or why the wolf could not bring itself to harm the bird, but it gave her newfound confidence and with it, she rose back to her feet.

"Scared of a little bird, are you?" Sylfia called to the wolf as it thundered around her, the bird again out of sight. The wolf snarled in response and turned towards Sylfia, but again the raven appeared as quick as a flash to intercept its charge.

This time the wolf stopped dead in its tracks and sat on the ground before the raven. It looked to Sylfia as though they were communicating as some time passed with neither of them doing anything other than staring silently at each other. Then the wolf threw its head up to the sky and howled an ear-piercing, shattering howl.

The raven abruptly spread its wings and flew off high into the sky, disappearing once again. The wolf lowered its head, and the eyes that had been yellow before were now a deep, shining golden. It made eye contact with Sylfia, and she could see in those eyes an intelligence that she had not noticed before.

The wolf howled again and ran in a wide arc around Sylfia, growing no closer each time it passed her. Sylfia, though, still did not move.

Then the wolf lunged.

Sylfia's first instinct was to throw herself to the side so that the wolf would miss her, but she knew better; she had been paying attention to the interaction between the wolf and the raven, and she was now certain that as long as she made no moves at all, the wolf would not be allowed to touch her.

The wolf thundered toward her on all fours, not slowing for a second. Sylfia fought her instinct to close her eyes, and as she watched the wolf came to an abrupt halt just an inch from her face. It bared its teeth at her, and spittle landed on her face, but still she did nothing.

Then Sylfia had an idea. Slowly, gingerly, she held a hand before her and placed it inside the wolf's open mouth. She was sure that this very gesture had come from a story she had been told as a child, but she could not remember exactly where.

The wolf did not bite down on Sylfia's hand though. It kept its eyes locked on Sylfia and watched, waiting for her to make the next move.

Again, Sylfia knew better.

Once she was sure the wolf would not harm her, she withdrew her hand from the beast's mouth and smiled at it.

"You cannot harm me, can you?" she asked warmly. "Each time we meet, you attempt to have me draw my weapons against you, and that is when you can kill me. But you cannot harm me if I am calm, subdued, and submissive. The raven is here to remind you of that, is it not?"

The wolf, of course, did not respond, though it turned its head away from Sylfia, which was admission enough for her.

"Then leave me. Stop trying to fight me because I will never fight back. You will never scare me away from my task because I know that each time I find a new obstacle in my path, I am on the correct one," she ordered.

Then to her surprise, the wolf turned away from her and bounded away without so much as a snarl, and she watched until it had disappeared into the darkness.

"How long have you been watching me?" Sylfia asked aloud. She would not mistake the presence of footsteps behind her when they belonged to another human being.

"My child, I have watched you for longer than you could imagine and will continue to watch you until the day that you are taken to the underworld," a croaky, wizened female voice replied from behind Sylfia.

Sylfia turned quickly as she attempted to place the voice, and came face to face with Elli, the woman who had all but killed her this night.

Her first thought was to attack, but she had already seen what the old woman was capable of. Sylfia's blood ran cold as she realised that she would not be leaving this place alive.

"Is it everything around this place that wants me dead, or do I simply have terrible luck?" Sylfia asked.

"Not everything is trying to kill you, child," Elli replied. "In fact, of the three beings you have encountered within 'this place', as you call it, not one has meant you harm."

Sylfia thought for a moment. "But the wolf?" she asked.

Elli nodded. "Though the wolf you have just seen, which I have to say you handled expertly, was the same wolf you have already encountered. And I am afraid to say that it was that same entity who stole my guise to hit you with his spear."

"What?" Sylfia replied.

"The one who wears the guise of the wolf is in fact, the trickster God Loki. He is forbidden to bring harm to any living thing unless it is in self-defence, and perhaps that is why he baits you into attacking him. Loki also laid the trap that caused you your dire wound, and he pretended to be me, too."

"Loki, The God Loki?" Sylfia asked in bemusement. "And I am supposed to believe that a God has taken an interest in me?"

"I tell no lies, child, and Loki is not the only being of power that watches you as you travel along your path," Elli replied.

Sylfia couldn't help but let out a snort. Having face-to-face meetings with literal Gods was not something that she believed happened regularly, and much less to her, although something in the back of her mind was nagging at her, the tiny suspicion of 'what if'.

Sylfia decided to leave that particular line of conversation for the moment in favour of things that she may have actually believed in.

"Then who are you, really, old woman?" Sylfia asked.

"If you think I am so old and frail," Elli replied, "Then I will allow you to attempt to wrestle me to the ground. If you win, I will tell you everything you have ever wanted to know about any being in existence, but if you lose, then you must continue along your path to the very end, no matter how difficult that may seem."

This seemed like a no-brainer to Sylfia; either she would win and learn everything she had ever wanted, or she would lose and simply continue with her life. It did not really matter though, Elli looked as old and as frail as anyone Sylfia had ever seen in the past, and she was young and strong – there was no way that Elli would beat her in a fair fight.

"I will not go easy on you, old woman," Sylfia said quietly. "I only hope that you do not hold a grudge for this."

"Then I will make it easier for you, child," Ellie replied with a smile. "If you can push me back by one single step before your knees hit the ground, then we shall say that you have won. Do we have a deal?"

Sylfia was bewildered by the situation, but she knew that it was necessary, and if that meant pushing back an elderly woman, then that was exactly what she was going to have to do.

Sylfia held her arms outstretched towards Elli, who did not return the gesture.

"If you are not going to fight back, then this is going to be over quickly," Sylfia said.

"Things, as they tend to, will be over exactly when they are meant to be and not a single moment sooner," Elli replied.

Sylfia simply shrugged and placed both of her hands on Elli's shoulders. She had a fleeting thought that perhaps, like the wolf, Elli could not fight back until Sylfia had threatened her, but something reassured that this was not the case here.

Elli's leather tunic did not cover her shoulders, and when Sylfia's hands contacted the older woman's bare skin, it felt paper thin and cold, and the bones beneath were clearly frail. Sylfia did not want to hurt the woman but at least a gentle push would be no hardship to her.

Elli, however, did not budge.

Sylfia frowned. The gentle push should have been enough to knock the older woman back, but it seemed to have had no effect on her at all.

Doubling her efforts, Sylfia pushed harder, and though it still felt as though the old woman's skin was ready to tear at the slightest touch, it felt to Sylfia as though she was trying to move a mountain of stone.

Elli smiled, but she did not raise a hand toward Sylfia.

Sylfia realised there must be some magic here to keep this woman upright, so she planted her feet into the perfectly balanced combat stance that she had been taught, bent at the waist and pushed with every single inch of effort that she could muster. Elli still did not move, not even an inch.

Then as Sylfia began to think of new ways to coax the old woman to take a step back, Elli took a single tiny step forward. It was a fraction of a step, but as soon as her leg had moved, Sylfia took the opportunity whilst her opponent was off-balance, to push her back again.

Her plan did not work, as rather than push Elli back or over, the sheer dominant force of Elli's frail leg pushed Sylfia back, her feet sliding along the ground as they searched for purchase. Then as Elli's foot planted itself softly onto the ground, her other leg began to move.

With each tiny step, Elli moved just inches, though the more Sylfia tried to fight against her, the harder it seemed to get.

Eventually, Sylfia thought of a new tactic. She only had to get Elli to move a single step back, so she stood away from the older woman to gain a running start, then launched herself into a sprint. Sylfia impacted Elli around the waist, but where she had expected something to give, it was as though she had run into a tree. Sylfia's feet slipped away on the ground beneath her, and her knees impacted the ground with a thud.

"As many before you have tried, you have failed to interrupt my slow advance," Elli announced with a smile. "Do not feel ashamed though, child; no being will ever push back the steps I have taken."

"Who... who are you?" Sylfia panted. She was mad at herself for her loss, although her mind again told her that everything was not as it seemed.

"I am not the poor facsimile the trickster was pretending to be. My name is Elli, and I am what you know as 'old age'.

"You are old age?" Sylfia asked. "But that is just a concept, is it not? Not a being or a person?"

"I am not quite a being, child. But I will bear down on all, be them on this plane or the next. None can stand before me for long," Elli replied. "I am afraid that you have lost your match with me, and you must keep your promise."

"I will keep it," Sylfia said sincerely. "I will do whatever it takes to keep to the most difficult of paths, but please, is there anything you can do or give me to help me along my way?"

"I am afraid that, like Loki, we are bound by a set of rules and if those rules are broken, then where we have helped, Loki would be able to hurt."

Sylfia was about to beg for something more when the jet-black raven fluttered down from the dark sky and landed on Elli's shoulder.

Elli looked pensive for a moment, then turned her attention back to Sylfia.

"There is something that we can do for you, though it may neither help nor hinder. This raven is named Muninn, and he has the power to tell you of the things that may come to pass. However, these things may not be clear in their meaning and may change upon the actions of others. Would you like Muninn to show you what he knows?"

Sylfia looked at the raven curiously. As its head moved about quickly as though it was listening and watching everything around it, she noticed that one of its eyes was missing.

It didn't matter. If there was information to be had about the future, then Sylfia needed to know it.

She nodded confidently, and immediately the raven turned to face her, and she could not help but stare into the hole where its left eye should have been.

Then her own vision began to change and morph, as if the whole world around her was being twisted. She could sense the sun and moon chasing each other across the sky as time passed faster than it ever had before. She did not know what this raven was doing, but somewhere deep inside her, she understood that this was not just her future but that of the entire world too.

Then Sylfia saw a scene in the raven's eye, as clear as day. She could not be sure where this place was, but judging by the long stretch of white snow-covered mountains, she believed it must have been the frozen north. She did not know what was significant about this place, but as she watched, the cold and the snow began to creep slowly into the south where the grass was still green and the vegetation living and vibrant.

As the cold spread its tendrils ever southward, the land changed quickly to a barren vision of white death, the cold transforming everything it touched into uninhabitable and barren plains.

"Fimbulwinter will bring death to many as it spreads across the lands from north to south. The process has already begun, but only once they feel its effects will the people understand what is happening to them," A man's voice seemed to carry on the wind toward Sylfia, and it startled her. She did not reply but continued watching with morbid interest.

Something then caught Sylfia's attention. High above the whitening plains, as Fimbulwinter rolled in to overcome the land, the sun and the moon shone together brightly in the sky.

Sylfia had always been taught that no matter how hard the sun or the moon tried, neither could catch the other, but here they were together, as though they were partners in bringing light to the world.

Then Sylfia saw a creature leap from atop a snow-capped mountain into the sky. As it flew into the sky towards the sun and the moon it was clear that it was a great wolf, and when it reached its final destination it opened its mouth wide and the sun and the moon both disappeared as they were eaten by the animal. The world plunged into darkness and Sylfia held her breath, not knowing exactly what was happening.

The world had turned dark and cold.

Then the vision faded to darkness, and Sylfia tried to peer through it to see what was happening without the light of the sun and the moon. As she watched intently, something shifted ever so slightly.

Whatever this was, it was monstrous. First, she saw the scales, and then as a single mountainous eye passed her by, Sylfia realised that she was looking at some kind of snake.

She had heard stories of the Midgard Serpent in her youth, but she had believed that these were simply fables. But there was no denying that this serpent looked as though it would be large enough to encircle the entire world.

Sylfia could not tell what had awoken the giant serpent. Perhaps it had unconsciously recognised a change in the world – that the light had disappeared or the cold had consumed the lands. It could have been something else altogether, but the result was always the same: the serpent had awoken, and now it was moving.

The serpent uncoiled itself from around the world, and the world began to shake, and that movement caused another sleeping serpent to stir. Nidhogg, who had slumbered beneath the great ash tree Yggdrasil, stirred and sank his teeth into the roots of the world's tree.

The roots turned black as the Nidhogg's venom spread throughout its circulatory system and the tree itself began to shake as Yggdrasil was leeched of its life.

Sylfia knew what this meant. The falling of the great tree was the end of the world, but she still could not turn away from the vision in the raven's eye. Though the images were clear, they were not exactly as she had been taught. She knew of Ragnarök, a wolf eating the sun and the moon and the felling of the world's tree, but the rest was confusing, and the versions she had heard throughout her life had been different or augmented to suit some other purpose.

The giant ash fell to the ground, and the land shook to its very foundations. Every inch of the world felt the falling of Yggdrasil, but the vision within the raven's eye turned far, far away to the north, where the snow-covered mountains hid their secret deep below, frozen in the underworld.

In the distance, Jörmungandr's monstrous serpent head breached the oceans causing a tidal wave to spread across all of the world's oceans, but the raven's attention remained focused on the mountainside.

Deep within the mountains of the north, the shockwave caused by the falling of the great ash tree had made a single tiny crack form between the base of two great mountains. As Sylfia watched, as though it all happened in an instant, the crack grew to thousands of feet long and a great chasm formed as the mountains separated.

Within this new Chasm sat a great wooden ship that looked as though it had been stuck there for centuries and had now been released by this dire chain of events.

The ship appeared to move.

Sylfia tried to peer closer to see what was happening because it was not the ship that was moving; rather there were people aboard – and they were moving. To help her to see, the raven's vision moved closer so that Sylfia could see what was happening for herself.

The ship itself was constructed of some materials that she could not make out at this distance, although the closer the raven's gaze moved, the easier it was for her to distinguish the parts of the ship. It had been constructed of bones and finger or toenails and they covered it as though they were in unlimited supply, and Sylfia had to stop herself from retching at the sight.

Then she saw the crew in better detail. They were not human, but were clearly the dead reanimated back to life, and a good proportion of them seemed to be some kind of giants.

The ebb and flow of the oceans and the colossal wave that the Midgard Serpent had caused upon its awakening reached the ship, and at first, nothing happened. And then, as if it were a cork flying from a shaken bottle, the ship launched. It rocketed from its deep resting place beneath the mountain and broke free into the dark ocean, for the sun and moon were still not there to light the way.

As the ship sailed the thrashing oceans, Sylfia watched as the serpent, the giant wolf and the ship all came together as the army of the damned. These creatures spelled the end of the world and the passing of Ragnarök.

"Do you see now, child?" Elli asked with a smile still on her lips. "Do you see what will come to pass? The end of everything, everything except me, for you see..."

"Because nothing can beat old age and the passage of time forever?" Sylfia interrupted. The old lady tended to be a little dramatic and right now, Sylfia needed clarity, not flourish.

"I do not understand what all of these creatures are, and what they are doing," she said softly.

"There are many things that you would never come to understand within a million lifetimes," Elli began and then caught Sylfia's plea for simplicity. "The ship that you saw launching is the Naglfar ship, and it carries Draugr and the damned to join Loki and his children as the world is ended. This is the final sign of Ragnarök. Before this, you saw the awakening of the Midgard Serpent, which causes the wave that releases the ship, the Nidhogg gnawing at the roots of the great ash tree, Ygraddsil, until it fell to shake the earth to awaken Jörmungandr. Have I missed anything?" Elli asked.

Sylfia shook her head slowly.

"And this must all come to pass?" she asked quietly, though before Elli could answer, the raven crowed loudly.

"These are the things that are destined to pass. Ragnarök will come eventually, just as everything in imagination will happen, given enough time," Elli answered. The raven crowed again, louder this time.

Elli huffed in annoyance. "But these are simply visions of a possible future and not what is destined to happen. The coming of Ragnarök may be prevented, but it will not be an easy task."

Where had Sylfia heard that before? It seemed that every time she had asked a question about the future, hers or otherwise, she had been told that she must always choose the most challenging path before her. She did not, however, know how she was supposed to fight against a literal God, his mutant children and a ship full of terrifying warriors.

"But... how...?" Sylfia asked in frustration, not quite knowing where to start.

"Our deal was not for me to give you all of the information you seek," Elli replied, "and I have already told you so much, child. I will see you again, though. I am sure of it."

And with those last words, Elli simply vanished. The raven remained though and as Elli left, it hopped onto Sylfia's shoulder and placed its beak next to her ear.

Before Sylfia could react, it whispered into her ear.

"Take the most difficult of paths and never give up. You have a destiny that no man can fulfil. Trust in yourself and ask every question that you can."

And then it spread its wings and flew off, high into the darkness, before disappearing altogether.

Sylfia watched the darkness as it closed in towards her, and when it was just a few feet away, it abruptly stopped, ebbing and flowing as though it were the waters of the oceans.

"Help me!" came the call from the darkness, and Sylfia recognised it immediately as her father's.

"Father? Where are you?!" Sylfia called back into the darkness, searching around her for some sign of where the sound had come from.

"I have found the ship. I think I can destroy it!" Jarl's voice returned.

"No, father! It is too dangerous!" Sylfia cried as she started running into the darkness in her best guess direction.

Suddenly, a bright light cut through the mists, and then her father was there. Flames had engulfed his entire body, and he was stumbling toward her, off balance and clearly in distress.

His skin was bubbling and boiling and he was moaning as though he had nothing left to give. His head seemed to simply fall from his shoulders, his knees hit the ground, and he crumpled onto the ground, the flames still dancing over his lifeless body.

Her first instinct was to try to help her father, but Sylfia knew it was already too late. Beyond everything, despite the pain and mental anguish that seeing her father perish in such a way had caused, she knew that this was not a real place. And she knew what this was.

"Your tricks do not fool me. I know what you are, Loki, son of Odin," Sylfia announced confidently.

The flames covering Jarl's body took a moment to extinguish themselves, but as soon as they did, his burnt and bloody face upon his decapitated head contorted into a smile, and then he laughed.

"It is only fair that if the others get to toy with you, then so do I," Jarl announced, though the voice was not his own; it was formal, almost regal even. "Tell me, why do you think that you are so important in this world that you can address a God in such a way?" he asked.

Sylfia thought for a moment. "I do not think that I am so important, but you clearly do," then she paused, and Loki, in the guise of her father, peered at her curiously to listen to what she had to say.

"Now there is an answer that I was not expecting," Loki replied. "What makes you say that?"

"Because you have repeatedly tried to get me to halt on my path. You tried to get me to fight you as the wolf in the woods, you tried to kill me dressed as Elli, and you have tried to kill me here in my dream, although the raven stopped you. I can only guess that this show was intended to make me worry about the safety of my father as well. That if I continue as I intend, then my father will perish?"

"Come, child. Do you not think that a God such as I would have the power to kill a tiny mortal if I so chose to? This is all simply a game to me so that I may simply pass the time until Ragnarök comes, and my family is returned to me. There is nothing that you can do to prevent Ragnarök. Even if you were to travel to the very depths of Helheim and burn the Naglfar ship to the ground, it would change nothing."

"If that is what it will take, then we shall see what difference one tiny mortal can make," Sylfia announced. "And Elli told me that you are unable to harm me unless it is in your own defence, so I announce to you now that I have no intention of harming you, so you will have no need to defend yourself against me," Sylfia said with her arms spread wide and her empty hands open.

"Ah," Loki replied with a smile, "That is correct. But you know there are always other ways I could have reached you. Not to worry about that anyway, as it seems that my father and Elli have taken it upon themselves to interfere with the lives of mortals, which is against those rules you seem to hold so dear. You must know what that means?"

Sylfia felt a shiver run down her spine. Had Elli and the raven's explanation and visions of the future broken the single rule that had prevented Loki from killing her outright? She remained silent and inwardly braced herself to receive the full might of this God; after all, if she was to die right here and now, then that was the way that it was supposed to be.

"It means that if they can tell you what happens in the future, then so can I," Loki said with a smile.

Sylfia exhaled quietly at that statement. Even if this was in a dream, she would rather not have been killed. Besides, she did not know if her death would carry over to the real world or not.

"I can tell you that the Naglfar ship is indeed to the north although it is not within the mortal realm. It remains stuck beneath a mountain as you have seen already, though I know that your plan to prevent Ragnarök involves you destroying that ship – it is the most difficult of tasks after all, is it not?" Loki's voice inflected and trailed off at the end of his sentence as though it was a question that needed no answer. In truth, though, Sylfia had not even begun to think about how she was going to prevent Ragnarök, but it did sound as though it was something she would need to do, and Loki seemed to mention this Naglfar ship as though it was key in his story.

"You will never find the ship without the help of those who mean the most to you," Loki gestured to himself, still in the guise of Jarl. "But once you find my ship and my family, it will be the death of your father. Is that a price that you are willing to pay?"

Sylfia remained silent.

"Your father will die for your actions, and Ragnarök will still come to pass. I tell you this as balance for what my father and Elli have told you this night," Loki said, all humour gone from his voice. Sylfia could detect nothing but the truth in his words.

"I do not believe you," Sylfia said angrily. "You would tell me anything to keep me from preventing Ragnarök!"

"Then let me give you something more than words as I tell you your future. I will allow my poison to dissipate, and your slumber will be over. You will awaken in an unknown place, and your father will already be in danger. You will need to choose to save him or continue along your path. I could keep you sleeping for as long as time, but I know you will never succeed. This is how sure I am of your failure," Loki sneered, and then Jarl burst into flame, screaming again before his body fell to the ground limply, and quiet filled the world around Sylfia again.

13

"Jarl, come and sit with me," Hilda invited as Jarl entered the longhouse. The hall was illuminated by a plethora of torches around its perimeter, and Jarl could see every person within. It was the first time that he had actually looked at these people, though, and what he saw was not a collection of angry faces or ones that gave him no attention at all; now Jarl could see the smiles that these people wore, and many of them faced in his direction.

Where once these faces were blurs to him, just more potential enemies and threats, Jarl had now started to regard each and every one of them as though they were his people. The peculiar thing was that they no longer felt like warriors or deadly foes; these people seemed more like farmers, labourers, cooks and the like. Amongst them, he could not see many scars or obvious battle wounds, and it made him wonder exactly how these people had survived all this time.

"Are you just going to stand there, or are you going to join our table?" Hilda asked once it was clear that Jarl had stopped in his tracks.

"Apologies, sister," Jarl replied, looking at Hilda and the four clan members who sat nearest her at the long wooden table. And apologies to the four of you," he added sincerely. I know I have not been the most appreciative of guests here in Baldur's Circle, but now Hilda has seen me return to the right path. Please, forgive me."

The four men's faces had been soft before Jarl had spoken, but his words made them all positively beam. They all wore long, braided beards, and Jarl had the smallest of the stomachs of the six people now sitting together. It seemed to Jarl that life and the comforts of the clan had made them soft. He did not dislike the men for it, but he vowed to never allow that to happen to his own body.

"Anders, Garald, Janson and Ragnar," Hilda announced their names, and they each in turn nodded to Jarl as their name was called. Jarl would like to eat with us today. Do you all agree?"

The men all nodded again, and all still wore smiles on their faces.

"But the real question is, will he be able to keep toe to toe with the four men who have the power to eat until there is simply no food left!?" Janson announced loudly.

Jarl looked sideways to Hilda and whispered in a low tone: "They have been given the power to eat their fill?" he asked.

"No!" Hilda replied in a jovial tone. They will share with you their divine gifts if they so choose, but the ability to eat is not a gift from the Gods!"

The six sat down, filled their bowls and ate what they had before refilling their bowls and finishing that. Janson and Garald then went back for a third helping whilst Jarl wondered how he had ever fit into his leathers and furs.

"Tell me, brothers," Jarl asked. He found it difficult to speak after eating so much food, but he soldiered on nonetheless. Why is it that none of you carries weapons? In western clans, finding a clan member absent his weapon is a very rare thing."

Jarl watched as the expressions on the five people's faces, with whom he had been laughing and joking not long before, turned serious. Jarl also could not help but notice Garald's gaze flicker to Hilda's for just a second before Anders spoke.

"What... would we need weapons for, brother? The lands are barren, and when we do receive guests, they quickly learn that they cannot leave. We have not had to defend this settlement in many years."

His response sounded a little forced to Jarl's ears, and he was about to follow his question up when Anders spoke again.

"Besides, we are farmers and cooks for the most part here. We keep to ourselves, and we have all we need."

"I understand," Jarl said, trying his best to push all suspicion from his tone. It is just odd to me, though I am sure that I will get used to all this one day." He slapped his hands on the table loudly. So tell me, what abilities have the Gods blessed you with?"

Anders was the first to smile at Jarl and offer him an answer. When I arrived here in the Circle, I was starving and close to death. It is a common story here, I am sure you will find. The Gods afforded me the ability to eat anything and everything, and it would sustain me always." He patted his stomach happily, and Hilda snorted.

"I have the talent to make plants grow quicker than you have ever seen. I can harvest a crop of wheat from seed to table in a day," Garald offered. I have been a farmer for my whole life and it brings me great joy to watch things grow. This is the blessing that the Gods afforded me and I am forever grateful for that."

"Just make sure some of what you grow actually makes it to the table," Hilda said with a laugh. This one would take your fingers off if you offered him a handful of meat!"

"Apologies, brothers. Your abilities seem useful, truly they do, only… it seems they are only useful in feeding yourselves and others within the clan. Even you, sister, your gift is to provide food. Surely there is more that the Gods have provided?"

"Yes!" Janson announced in a booming tone. When I arrived from the northern plains, I was also close to death. But for me, it was the cold that was killing me. My fingers had all turned as black as night, and I had lost all feeling in both of my feet. My beard was covered in ice, and my breath was shallow and pained. It all went away when I drank of the God's tears in the Circle."

"The tears cured you?" Jarl asked.

"Yes, I was cured by the Gods, but that was not all. I was given the ability to never feel the effects of the heat or the cold. I could strip down to my bare skin and walk out into the darkness in the dead of Fimbulwinter and I would not feel even a bit uncomfortable!"

"But nobody wants to see that!" Hilda chirped in. The group all roared with laughter though Janson looked a little upset at the ridicule. Eventually, they all simmered down and Jarl looked to the last man at the table.

"And you, Ragnar?" Jarl asked when the man did not offer an answer on his own. Are you able to walk about the settlements without any clothes, or are you another cook?"

Hilda's gaze spun around to Jarl, and she looked worried about what Jarl had just asked. In fact, all of the other five seemed to wear a stern expression now, and the laughter had all but disappeared.

"You do not know what you ask," Hilda started, but Ragnar stopped her with a raised hand.

"It is OK, sister. I have told my story before, and I will tell it again. I do not fear the past and it will not be what pains me."

Now Jarl was even more confused than before. He was about to ask what Ragnar had meant, but before he could open his mouth, the large man spoke again.

"When I arrived here, I was with my son. His name was Herleif. He was so strong."

Jarl noticed that as Ragnar spoke, all of the others had dipped their heads.

"So strong. But he believed that he could do anything without thought or aid. He had been hunting out to the east, and he had climbed to the top of a tall tree to look for signs of our next prey. It was so tall that I told him it was not necessary. He was only fourteen years." Ragnar took a long pause and then inhaled sharply.

"Herleif saw the light to the west, from this very settlement. He called down, but as he looked to me he slipped from the branch and fell. I called out and tried to help but he was too far away from me, and when I caught him, he was bloodied and broken. Our hunt had taken us days from home, but I remembered that he had seen this settlement, so I thought to come and beg for aid as it would be quicker, and he was fading away from me so quickly. We were brought water as soon as we arrived, and I drank first."

"What happened to Herleif?" Jarl asked in a hushed tone, remembering how he and Sylfia had arrived and the pain he had felt in his heart at seeing his daughter close to death.

"I... my power was not to heal my son," Ragnar said with his gaze fixed down on the table. If I could go back and change but one thing, then it would be to beg for the power that Bjorn was afforded by the Gods, but I did not know of the power of the tears. My desire, above anything else in the world, was...

was to be able to take my son's pain away from him. That is the power that I was given. Not to heal, simply to remove the pain that another feels so they can move on with peace."

Jarl did not know what to say to Ragnar once he had stopped talking, and a silence fell over the small group. His emotions felt so conflicted; on the one hand, the Gods had seen fit to play some cruel joke on Ragnar, but on the other hand, the people of Baldur's Circle could have warned Ragnar about what he was going to receive beforehand in case it would have made a difference.

"Was there no healer to aid your son?" Jarl asked quietly. Was Bjorn not ready in waiting as he was for Sylfia and me when I arrived carrying my child in my arms, close to death?"

Ragnar shook his head slowly. We have been here for a long time, and the clan is not what it once was. Where there are many now, there were once few, and some were simply luckier than others in their arrivals," Ragnar replied. Then he brought his gaze up to meet Jarl's with a defiant look in his eye.

"Tell me, Jarl. Is there anything that you find suspicious within the settlement? Anything that you feel in your heart that should not be?"

Jarl stared back at Ragnar plainly. There was something in the man's eyes that he did not like, something that suggested that if he were to ask the right questions, he would find answers that were now obscured from plain sight.

"Do not listen to Ragnar," Hilda interrupted quickly. He does not know what he is saying; perhaps he has had a little too much of the ale this night, hmm?"

"Ah, forgive me, brother," Ragnar said. He let his gaze drop back to the table as if he had been knocked back into his facade. I have spoken out of turn. Pay me no mind."

It was too late to ignore now though, but Jarl placed his unease to the forefront of his mind. He had known he was correct to be suspicious of these people, and now Ragnar had let on that something else was going on with the settlement.

Jarl decided to press his questioning, although he knew that he needed to continue in a way that would not cause the group to hide their secrets from him.

"Do not worry, brother," Jarl said softly to Ragnar. I know the difficulties in caring for a child. I cannot imagine the pain in your loss." He took a long drink of the ale in his tankard and turned his attention to Hilda.

"Tell me, sister, is it a rare occurrence for people to arrive here in Baldur's Circle?"

"It is a rare thing, but we have new clan members join almost every season when they are wandering, lost in the wild," Hilda replied, though her voice was low and her head dipped, as though she did not wish to be overheard. Why do you ask?"

Jarl smiled warmly. "Only through curiosity. It seems the clan is destined to grow and grow if new members arrive regularly and cannot leave, especially with Bjorn on hand to heal the sick or wounded." He paused as though for dramatic effect. "Though from all of the powers or abilities that I have seen that the Gods have given to the members of the clan, I have not seen any with divine strength, nor anything to provide greater prowess in battle. Why is that?"

Hilda looked at Jarl for a long while without saying a word, and Jarl could not tell if it was because she did not have a good answer to his question or if she was trying to cover something else up. Eventually, though, she spoke, but again in a hushed tone.

"The powers afforded by the tears are those the individual requires most at that moment. That their heart desires. Tell me, do you think one who has the time to drink his fill has battle on their mind first and foremost?" Hilda asked.

It was actually a good explanation and one that Jarl had not thought about. As he had wandered the perimeter of the settlement, he had thought about how these abilities would have benefited a warring clan. How its warriors could possess greater strength, invulnerability, even the fire magic that he now had, and how that could make such a force practically unbeatable.

"Do not misunderstand me," Hilda added before Jarl finished his thought trail. Many of Baldur's Children have known war and have come from clans and settlements that have never known peace. But as you will see as time passes, we seek no battle, and we need not defend ourselves."

There was still something that was not adding up for Jarl. He had never known a place that did not need to defend itself; the idea was alien to him and again he had the feeling that something about the place was being hidden.

He opened his mouth to speak again, but before he could ask any more questions, Hilda announced that they should all drink and forget about the troubles of the outside world. He could tell from the warning look in her eye that this was something that he should not pursue, so he decided that if he was going to continue to learn more about Baldur's Children, he was going to have to do it alone.

14

"Please, daughter. It is time for you to return to me," Jarl grumbled as he knelt by Sylfia's bed. "I do not think that this place holds our future but I cannot leave without you."

Sylfia had been left to rest in an empty cabin, where Jarl was allowed to visit her during the evening hours before it turned dark. He had been told by Bjorn that Sylfia required rest so that her body could attempt to repair the damage that the mistletoe spear had caused, and although he did not take well the idea of being told that he could not see his daughter whenever he liked, he would do nothing that could have jeopardised her safety.

Sylfia's cheek twitched as Jarl spoke. It was not the first time that it had happened – the first time he had thought that she was about to wake upon hearing his voice. Now though he understood that this was simply a natural reaction to her sleeping body being disturbed, and when it happened, he felt guilty that he was potentially interrupting her rest.

"I hope that you can hear my voice down there, Sylfia. I hope that you know that I will always do everything in my power to protect you."

As she had every time Jarl had spoken to her, Sylfia remained quiet and asleep. To Jarl, she looked peaceful, but all that he could wish for was for his daughter to be returned to him.

Jarl did the only thing that he could think of to do in this situation, and what he had already done on a number of occasions as he looked down at his daughter. Jarl prayed to the Gods.

Each time Jarl had prayed for his daughter, he had prayed to a different God in the hope that one would take pity on him and Sylfia and allow her to wake up. The last time he had prayed to Odin as the Allfather, but this time he prayed to Frigg, as she would be merciful and understanding of a parent's need to reunite with their child. No response came though, and eventually he had to respect the wishes of the Gods: if and when they would see fit, Sylfia would be returned but not a moment sooner.

Jarl raised himself from his knees beside his peaceful daughter, gave her one last look and left the building. He had seen her like this every day, and he knew that his presence did not make any difference to her.

This would be another night in which Jarl would patrol the settlement for an hour or so before he would feel comfortable enough to return to his own hut to sleep. He knew that he did not have to carry out this duty, and had been told that on a number of occasions, but something about falling into his old role just seemed to calm him. It was as though he had a purpose, a duty to fulfil and that gave him peace.

Jarl walked the perimeter of Baldur's Circle twice before something started to wear on him. He could not place what it was but it felt as though he had forgotten something. Then it dawned on him: each night previously, when he had left Sylfia, he had kissed her forehead softly so that she would know that he loved her. This night he had forgotten.

Rushing back to the hut where Sylfia slept, Jarl shook his head, wondering how exactly it was that he had forgotten such an important thing. He swung the door open and walked inside purposefully.

But the bed was empty.

Jarl stared at the furs that covered the small wooden bed for a moment, trying to grasp that Sylfia was not there, and two emotions fought for headspace. Sylfia was gone, and that was a bad thing, but it could also mean that Sylfia was awake.

Jarl looked around for signs that Sylfia may have simply awoken and walked off in her confusion, but he could see nothing to suggest it. He threw open the door and ran back into the night, peering about to see if she was anywhere within sight, but the settlement was empty.

His heart rate quickened, and running to the longhouse where he knew the rest of the clan would be, Jarl began to worry about what state his daughter would be in. Would she be confused? Angry? Hurt? After all, the last thing that she had done was to disobey him again simply to prove a point.

When Jarl reached the longhouse, the low hum of clan members met him, as it always did in the building, and a quick scan revealed that his daughter was not present.

"Has anyone seen Sylfia?" Jarl boomed. "Where is my daughter?"

The room fell silent and all of the faces within turned to look at Jarl. Nobody made a sound.

"My daughter has left her bed, please, has anyone seen her?" he repeated.

Again nobody replied.

Then just at that very moment, Bjorn entered the longhouse behind Jarl and placed a large hand on his shoulder.

"Brother, what is it that I can help you with?" Bjorn asked sincerely.

"My daughter, Sylfia..." Jarl managed to repeat. He could not think straight, and these were the only words that he could force out of his mouth.

Bjorn looked as though he had been expecting this moment and before he spoke, he let out a solemn sigh.

"I am sorry, brother, but this has been how it had to be. I did not wish to tell you this, but your daughter fares worse than we have told you," he exhaled loudly, and to Jarl it felt as though a dagger had been plunged into his heart. "Sylfia requires more care and attention than we first assumed, and she is now under constant care. She is brought to the hut for you to visit and is then taken back to be cared for properly."

But Jarl could see something behind those words. The pain of the thought of his daughter slipping away from him was engulfed by the distinct feeling that he was being lied to. He had no special ability to detect falsehoods like Elder Hugi, but he could sense that something simply wasn't adding up. He remained silent for a long while as he attempted to arrange his thoughts correctly.

"But... she will still get better?" Jarl managed to ask. He had quickly concluded that the best thing he could do would be to play along with whatever it was that they were doing. After all, he had no way of knowing their plans and what it could mean for Sylfia if they discovered that he mistrusted them.

"We think that in time, she will grow back to herself, but for now, we do not know how long that is going to take. I can promise you, though, brother, that we are doing everything we can for Sylfia."

Jarl should have dropped the matter right there, and he knew it, but he heard the words slip from his mouth before he could stop them: "and why would you want to aid an outsider?"

"We have no outsiders here," Hilda's voice came from beside Bjorn as she joined the conversation. "You and Sylfia are as much members of this clan as you have ever been in any other, and the quicker you accept that fact, the quicker we can move on to more important things."

Those words struck Jarl now. He thought about what these 'more important things' were in a place that had few visitors and from where nobody could leave, but frustratingly he just did not have enough information to connect all of the dots.

Jarl did not want to speak with any of these people any longer, so he let his head hang down in false embarrassment, turned and walked straight out of the longhouse. He was now convinced that these people were not telling him whole truths, but the only thing in the world that mattered was finding Sylfia. They would then find a way out of this place - Sylfia could certainly do it after all, and he had also done it once.

The air seemed colder again, and the dark kept Jarl peering around every corner, wishing he would see his daughter walking up to him. He knew that would not happen though, and he resigned himself to trying to find her by peering into every building within Baldur's Circle.

There were at least forty wooden buildings scattered about the place, and Jarl already knew that at least a handful were empty. Elder Hugi had his own hut, and the longhouse was occupied by many of the clansmen. That left thirty-something huts to check, and once that task was completed, he would ensure that he and Sylfia would do whatever they could to leave this place far behind.

Jarl moved from hut to hut, slowly keeping within the shadows as best he could and peering through cracks in the exterior woodwork or through windows or doors wherever he could. He saw families, men and women in these huts, faces that he had already seen within the camp, but as the number of possible locations for Sylfia dwindled to nothing, Jarl had the sneaking suspicion that he was not destined to find his daughter this night.

It did not make sense to him. The clan could have moved Sylfia to a secret location, or they could have told him the truth, that she was being looked after. Either way, he had now searched the entire settlement and had not seen a single trace of her, and knowing that nobody could leave this place where could she have gone?

"Jarl! What are you doing?" Hilda's voice reached Jarl as he moved away from the last place he had searched for Sylfia.

"I am looking for my daughter," he practically growled back to her. "If she requires constant care, then I wish to know where she sleeps."

"You cannot keep doing this, Jarl. You have no idea the..." Hilda stopped herself before she continued speaking, as though she was about to say something terrible but had managed to catch herself.

"What?" Jarl asked with his hands held out to his sides. "What if I were to ask the wrong question? I am a prisoner here already, am I not? I cannot leave, I do not know these people, and my daughter, my daughter is being hidden from me, and I do not know why!"

"Come now, Jarl, you must leave this mistrust in the past," Hilda said with a tone that indicated she was tired of having the same conversation over and over. "Your daughter is not being hidden from you; she is being healed as you have always been told."

"Then take me to her!" Jarl almost shouted. "Either tell me where she is or take me to her now!"

Hilda paused for a moment as she contemplated her answer, but this time she did not give any sign that she would be telling Jarl some hidden truth.

"It is just not for the best, Jarl. Your daughter is not well, and she needs her rest; you must understand," Hilda said.

Jarl practically growled in response but did not argue with the woman. Instead, he turned his back on her and stormed away. Hilda did not call out, nor did she follow; she knew better than to poke an angry bear.

Jarl walked away quickly whilst muttering to himself. He would not simply accept that he was not allowed to see his daughter, but these people were still standing in his way.

He walked to the archway out of the settlement and along the inside of the stone wall. He did not try to cross the boundary to the other side, not that he really wanted to, but his mind whirled as he tried to figure out just how many lies he had been told.

Walking furiously, his anger grew until he could contain it no longer, and eventually he turned back to the settlement and walked straight to the room where he had last seen Sylfia. There must be some sign in there of where she was going or how they were moving her to and from the hut without being seen.

The hut and the bed that his daughter had slept on remained empty, but this time Jarl stomped over to the bed and pulled the furs off the wooden bed frame. The furs hit the wall behind him and slumped to the ground in a heap, but Jarl ignored them because now he could see something he had not before. A small, round iron ring was attached to the floor underneath the bed.

Jarl stood up and pulled the bed frame off whatever this was, and this revealed two heavy metal hinges attached to the floor. It was now clear that this was no ordinary floor; this was a doorway to something beneath.

Jarl took a moment before his curiosity, mixed with his anger, demanded that he follow this new path that presented itself to him. He knew deep down that behind this door he would find his daughter one way or another and it all made sense to him right now.

Beneath the door stood a wooden ladder that travelled down a narrow tunnel until it eventually reached the dirt below. Jarl could not see where the light was coming from that illuminated the path, though it flickered lazily, suggesting that there were either torches or candles that lit the way beyond the ladder.

Tentatively, and as quietly as he could manage, Jarl lowered himself down the ladder rung by rung until his feet touched the soft dirt below.

Upon reaching the bottom, he could see that a single tunnel led away from the entrance and the ladder. On both sides of the wooden walls sat torches that burned brightly within the silence, and every ten or so metres there was a supporting timber frame that Jarl assumed must have helped to keep the tunnel open.

Jarl knew that no good ever came from secret tunnels, and even less one that he was sure that these people were using to keep his daughter from him. With all of his being, he wanted to sprint to the end where he knew Sylfia would be, but he had to be wary of the dangers that could lurk within.

Moving slowly along the tunnel, Jarl found that it was much taller than he had expected and when he walked fully upright, there was still room above his head. He moved quietly and slowly, and after a few minutes, he wondered if there would ever be an end to the place.

Eventually, Jarl heard noises carrying from the tunnel before him, so he slowed even further and crouched down to make himself seem smaller. What he had not been expecting though, was the noise of not just a few people talking in hushed voices; it sounded like many, many people were in the tunnel ahead.

Jarl moved further forward, and suddenly the tunnel around him opened up. He now stood on a stone ledge that overlooked a sheer drop down, hundreds of feet onto wide open sands. The flat sand beneath him covered thousands of square feet and was covered by a literal army of thousands of men and women.

Taking a moment to look around the outside of the wide open area that had somehow been carved from the very earth, Jarl realised that the perimeter of the sands were not sheer faces; the entire construction was a spiral that was lined with hundreds of tiny rooms fronted with iron bars, some of which stood open while others were locked shut with their inhabitants leaning against them, watching what was happening below.

Jarl could now see that some of the noise that assaulted him was coming from what must have been prisoners rattling the bars or shouting, demanding or begging for their freedom, although most of the noise came from the army of men below.

These men were not standing idle, Jarl could see as he watched. They were training.

Each person that Jarl could see from his perch wore heavy leather armour and carried deadly-looking weapons - axes, swords, daggers, spears and bows. Warriors screamed war cries as they dove at their opponents with their raised weapons. Their attacks would be parried and redirected, with counter strikes following swiftly behind. Although Jarl could tell that nobody was attempting to kill each other, their training was well-organised and very serious.

Then Jarl focussed on a pair in the centre of the sands, a man and a woman who were fighting, having been given a wide berth by the other participants of the event.

The woman held a long thin sword in one hand but nothing in the other, her open hand clearly sending the message that it was not a threat. On the other hand, the man gripped a single, giant axe in both hands, and Jarl could only assume that with his superior size and weapon, he would simply overpower the woman.

The man swung his axe behind him and bore down on the woman, preparing a deadly overhead strike and Jarl held his breath as he watched.

The axe came down at the woman who seemed to make no move to avoid the strike, but at the last moment she dropped her shoulder, and the axe sailed harmlessly past her and embedded itself into the ground. In a flash, the woman's elbow crunched into the side of the man's face and he stumbled away from her, while from her open palm shot a bright orb of fire.

The orb whipped through the air in an instant and if the man had not reacted, it would surely have set him ablaze. He waved both of his hands before him, and the fireball impacted a bright blue shield of water that splashed out of existence along with the flame.

Jarl could not see the expressions of the warriors or the other people around them. They should have been just as surprised as he was at the display, but their actions betrayed no surprise, it was as if this was simply a normal event for them.

As Jarl watched the rest of the sparring partners around the training sands, he realised that almost all were using similar abilities to either attack or defend themselves. This was an army of enhanced beings and the thought of these people actually fighting out in the real world with these powers made him think just how much of an advantage they would have.

At least these people could never leave Baldur's Circle, was the first thought that entered Jarl's mind, but then he remembered why he was there in the first place - to find his daughter.

The army below looked as though they would be occupied for at least a while longer, so he decided to try to walk the perimeter of the route down to the sands and look as if he belonged there. He did have a similar ability to the rest of these people, after all, and the huge number of them meant that was no way that they would recognise that he was not one of their number.

Jarl moved along the outer wall to his right on a slight decline, walking as naturally as he could. Initially he had thought to plant his back against the wall and hope that nobody would see him, but he knew that acting suspiciously would not serve him well if he was seen.

At the very first cell that he came to, Jarl slowly peered in and around the corner, hoping that if anyone was inside they would either not see him or not raise the alarm.

To his surprise and relief, Jarl found himself staring at his daughter, alone in this first cell. "Sylfia, my daughter, what have they done to you?" Jarl practically moaned as he saw Sylfia lying on a flat stone table.

Though the iron bars were not locked shut, she had her own tiny cell. It appeared that she was still sleeping, although leather straps held her arms and legs to the table and another had been wrapped tightly over her forehead. It looked as though whoever had placed her there had been attempting to keep her still.

"Quickly, I must get you out of this place," he whispered. He knew that she was not in any state to respond to him but talking to her just seemed to make him feel better. He also had no idea where he should go once he freed her from her restraints, but any place would surely be better than here.

Jarl began to tug at the leather bindings that held Sylfia in place. They were tight against her skin as her clothes had been mostly removed although she still had her cloth undergarments on. The bindings around her wrists came away easily, and Jarl was just about to start to work on the pair that held her ankles when he felt a huge hand plant itself on his shoulder.

"What are you doing here, brother?" Bjorn's unmistakable voice came to Jarl. With heart thumping, he poured everything he had into his one ability. He felt the power within him yearning to release itself, and the moment he felt that he could put nothing more into it, he took hold of the handle of one of his axes hanging down by his side, spun around and pushed it as hard as he could into the giant man's face.

Jarl would have liked to have swung the weapon for a proper strike, but he knew that he did not have the time, and this was his only option as Bjorn was so close to him.

Bjorn let out a surprised and angry howl as his skin burnt and blistered where the axe contacted it, and Jarl could not help but smile at his small victory. He then raised his burning axe high over his head as Bjorn brought his hands up to his damaged face, readying his final killing blow.

Then, before he could swing his axe, a second man, whom Jarl had not noticed entering the cell stepped between the two men and placed his hand tightly around Jarl's bicep. The man was slender and wore a straight expression on his shaven face, and Jarl tried to meet his gaze. It was fruitless though – the axe above Jarl's head abruptly extinguished itself, and weakness flooded through him. He tried to push the man back but no matter how hard he tried, his body felt like it had nothing left to give.

The man then abruptly punched Jarl square on the nose, and he crumpled to the ground.

It felt as though the weight of the world was bearing down on Jarl as he tried with all his might to right himself, but he simply could not. Whatever this person had done to him had rendered him unable to focus properly, although he managed to watch as Bjorn brought his hands up to his face and healed his burns. The large man then planted a huge boot onto Jarl's nose, and he felt the crunch and explosion of blood that followed.

"You do not think you are the only one here with a gift, do you?" Bjorn asked through gritted teeth. "Birger here has a very interesting gift: he is able to take the gift away from others and sap them of their strength. Do you feel like you are weak right now, Jarl?" Bjorn asked.

Jarl remained silent though he still struggled, trying his absolute hardest to at least raise himself to his knees. It was futile though, and Jarl only hoped that the effects of this ability would not last.

"Now, if you would not mind, Birger has come to relay information to me. I am sure that you will find this all very interesting," Bjorn said nonchalantly, and it was obvious that he no longer saw Jarl as any sort of threat.

"The solution to our troubles has worked," Birger said in a flat tone, with a voice that was certainly higher pitched than most. He wore just a cloth robe that covered him from head to toe.

"You are sure?" Bjorn asked excitedly. "Is it temporary or does it last?"

"It has been a day, and there is no sign of change. I have left three outside to ensure that it is still working, but I do not think that it will change. We are free, brother," Birger replied now with glee in his words.

Jarl tried to stand again, but his back would not let him move. He grunted loudly.

"Ah, and here is the man that made all of this possible," Bjorn announced, his attention turning to Jarl. "You have no idea how big a part you have played in the grander scheme, but let me enlighten you."

Jarl had no intention of listening to the man; all he wanted to do was to stand, take his daughter and escape as quickly as possible. If he could also throw an axe or two at the huge healer and possibly even his friend, that too would be fine.

Bjorn continued speaking regardless of Jarl's silence. "I saw your daughter leave Baldur's Circle, and I saw that you too were able to leave when her life was in danger. It was long ago when this very prophecy was foretold, that one would arrive within the settlement that could set us all free. Sylfia has been the one we have been waiting for these long years, and she holds the key to our salvation."

"What... have you done to her?" Jarl managed to croak out under the weight of the world.

"I have done nothing," Bjorn replied. "I have healed her to the best of my ability, though she remains asleep as she did when you returned her to the settlement."

"If you have healed her, why does she not wake?" Jarl growled.

"She does not wake because it is not the will of the Gods for her to do so," Bjorn replied matter of factly. "When and if she is supposed to awaken, then she will."

"And the lies you told me? And her restraints? Were those too the will of the Gods?" Jarl asked.

Bjorn looked at Sylfia as though he had forgotten that she was in the room.

"Ah yes, brother, there are some things that you need to be told, are there not?" Bjorn replied. "We knew your daughter was different not long after the two of you arrived in Baldur's Circle. Never before has one drunk of the God's tears and not immediately gained an ability, so we knew that this could only mean one thing: that Sylfia already had an ability. We knew that one would come with such a background to us, as it had been foretold long ago by one that we believe you know personally: your Elder Wise."

"Elder... Wise?" Jarl asked in confusion.

"Yes, before the Elder left us here in Baldur's Circle, she told us that the day would come when a child of the Circle would return and bring with her the ability to free us from our entrapment. It was believed for a long time that the Elder spoke of herself, but you brought with you the knowledge that Elder Wise had passed, so there had to have been another. Sylfia was born in Baldur's Circle, was she not?"

Jarl kept his mouth tightly shut. He knew that there was nothing that he could say to make this situation any better.

"We do not require your confirmation," Bjorn said flatly when he received no reply. "Sylfia brings with her the ability to leave Baldur's Circle; that is her ability, and that is what will allow us all to be free and avenge our God and patron: Baldur."

"You seek freedom for vengeance?" Jarl asked, picking up on the last thing that Bjorn had announced. "I thought it was the goal of Baldur's Children to ask the world to weep for the fallen God so that he may be released from Helheim? Or is this another lie you have told to keep us on your side?"

"Do not be foolish, brother," Bjorn said angrily. "We are but mortals, and as such we know that it is beyond our power to convince the world to weep for a God they have long forgotten. Instead, we look to destroy everything and everyone that does not bend to the God's cause. For if we cannot make them weep, we will make them nothing at all."

There was too much new information that Jarl needed to absorb and he closed his eyes. He tried to run through what had been said in his mind, but the thing that stood out to him now was the fact that Bjorn had told him what Sylfia's gift was.

"You believe Sylfia's gift from the Gods is the ability to leave this place?" he asked.

"We do not believe that this is so; we know that it is her gift. Understand this, brother, with the help of this gift, we have also been allowed to leave the Circle and thus passes the first in a line of prophecies that will now become reality."

"You can leave?" Jarl asked. "How?" Jarl's thoughts turned to Sigrid and the Rakki clan in the settlement to the west, to his best friend Eric and the people that he had shared his life with. He desperately wanted to go home and hoped that they would forgive him somehow. He did not care how; he would beg until his very last breath to be there with them.

Bjorn smiled at Jarl as though he was about to tell him something he was very proud of. "It was not my idea I must admit. Birger understood that as your daughter could leave the Circle, she must have had a divine power. So he thought to use her tears to see what would happen if we drank of them as we do of the God's, and that led us to this discovery. If we drink of Sylfia's tears, we are free."

Jarl looked over at his daughter, who was still partly tied to the stone table, and now he saw why her head had been strapped down; these people had been forcing tears from her eyes to drink to test their experiments.

"You are a monster," Jarl growled and redoubled his efforts to stand. "You have been milking the tears from my daughter's eyes just to see what would happen, and you drank them? Is everyone here insane?" He still could not bring himself to his feet, although he could now move his legs somewhat little.

"No, brother. We have been waiting for this moment for so long and it is our destiny, our fate. We will bring back our patron God from the underworld and the grasp of Hel and stop the path of Ragnarök before the world ends. This is why you have been brought here to us."

"This is truly madness!" Jarl countered. "You are a fool if you think that I will let you treat my daughter this way. You think I will sit and allow you to drain her eyes until they run dry, just so that you may leave this place - and what? Go to war with every clan in the entire world?"

"You may think me a fool, brother, but you may think differently of me once we have ground your western settlements into the dirt. We know that your former people will not weep for Baldur, so these will be the first sacrifices to our God. Your people will be crushed by the might of our army, and as much as you may protest, there is nothing you can do to stop us."

Jarl's anger surged through his entire body again, and as he pushed and pounded against the internal force that was preventing him from moving freely, Bjorn spoke again with a grin on his face.

"I do hope you have not left anyone you care about back in that settlement of yours."

With those words bringing the image of Sigrid to the front of Jarl's mind, he felt the barrier shatter and crumble, and as he raised himself to his full height, he picked his axe up from the ground and it ignited with his burning rage.

Jarl swung his axe at Bjorn with all the hatred and might he could muster, and as the larger man brought his arm up to defend himself, the axe cut clean through it at the bicep, and Bjorn's severed arm fell to the ground with a wet thud.

Bjorn cried out in pain as he fell back, but Jarl had forgotten that another man stood in the room with them. Birger lunged at him, and before he could raise his axe again in defence, Birger had again taken hold of Jarl's arm and the weight of the world pushed him back down to the ground. This time though, he lay face down and flat against the ground with the feeling of a thousand feet pinning him down. He was almost entirely paralysed, and something deep inside told him that this was to be his end.

Jarl could just about move his head to watch as Bjorn again healed his wound, although this time the damage was so severe that no matter how many times the healer tried to heal his missing appendage, it would simply not reattach. The wound healed and closed, but Jarl knew from the look on Bjorn's face that he would now be destined to live the rest of his days without one of his arms.

Free of pain, Bjorn rose to his feet and stepped over to Jarl where he lay. He did not say a single word but bent his right leg behind him and then kicked Jarl in the jaw as hard as he had ever been hit. Through the explosion of pain, Jarl's vision faded to black, but for one split second before he lost consciousness, he heard Sylfia's voice cutting through the darkness.

"Where am I? Father? Bjorn?"

15

Sylfia had been left where she had been restrained before Jarl had been caught by the now one-armed healer and Birger. She had woken slowly, unable to move or speak, but she could hear what was happening between the three men out in the real world.

Birger was still a bit of a mystery to her as he had not said many words, although Bjorn had shown his true colours: he planned to lead Baldur's Children on a crusade to the west, destroying everything and everyone as they went.

Her restraints were tight again against her ankles, wrists and forehead, and all she could do was stare up at the rock ceiling and wait for somebody to tell her what was happening.

"Sylfia, you have been badly wounded and we are attempting to bring you back to health," Bjorn's voice came to her low and calm. She realised that he was not aware that she had been able to hear the last conversation between him and her father, and she was not going to change that; she needed to play along with whatever this was so that she could rescue her father – if he was still alive – then head back to the west to warn the clans before the catastrophic army was unleashed upon the world.

"What... what happened?" she eventually managed to force out in a croaky voice.

"Well, it is your father, Sylfia," Bjorn replied in a sullen tone. "He did not make it. I am sorry."

His words stabbed Sylfia through her heart and the pain she felt was unlike anything she had ever experienced. She knew that her father and this man had been in a fight, but killed? That simply could not be true, could it?

"What?" Sylfia croaked again as tears began to well in the corners of her eyes, and as they started to stream down her face, she felt a cloth pressed against her skin to blot them.

"I am sorry, child," Bjorn repeated. "When you returned to the settlement you were wounded, and your father crossed the border to bring you back inside. As all of us here do, you know what happens when people cross the border, Sylfia."

She knew that the large man was lying, but that did not stop the tears from coming. In her dream world, she had just watched her father die, and to hear the words said aloud – regardless of whether it was a lie or not – was simply too much for her.

"My... father?" Sylfia managed to croak out. "He... could not..."

"I am sorry, child," Bjorn said again. "But there is something that you can do for us. His death will not be in vain." As he spoke again, Sylfia felt her tears being dabbed again by the damp cloth against her cheek.

When she did not respond, Bjorn spoke again. "You may be surprised to hear you do indeed have an ability, Sylfia. You may well be the most important person to visit us here in Baldur's Circle because your tears will enable us to leave the settlement."

Sylfia was shocked to the core by this statement, and her eyes flew open. Her vision took a long time to focus, but eventually everything stopped being simply outlines and blurs of light and dark, and she managed to assess her surroundings properly.

She tried to look down at her body, but a strap held her head firmly in place. Above her, she could only see mud and stone and her wrists and ankles were fastened to whatever it was that she was lying on. Whatever it was, it was both hard and uncomfortable.

"What... what have you done to me?" Sylfia moaned as she realised how securely she was restrained. To make it worse, she was at the mercy of this man, this liar who was keeping her from her father.

"Let me be clear, Sylfia," Bjorn said as he stood over her, now in her line of sight. "Every person that becomes a part of Baldur's Children must pay their way within the clan. Most will use their gift to make our lives easier or better, and you are no different. Your gift will set us all free, Sylfia, and that is what more than a few of the people within the settlement want." Then Bjorn's voice changed to something both more serious and sinister. "But do not think this is a choice you can make, child. Your gift will be used to give us our freedom whether you like it or not. Believe me when I say we will use your tears and leave this place, one way or another."

Sylfia closed her eyes momentarily to let those words sink in, and when she opened them again, Bjorn was still standing over her. To her mind, that was a mistake as the large healer was well within range for her to spit in his eye.

Bjorn wiped his face with a large hand, then turned away from her. He took one step away, and Sylfia could no longer see him.

"Take the tears, as many as you can. Waste little or you will be on the table next," she heard Bjorn order as he left.

"You will cry, child. One way or another, you will cry," a rather high-pitched voice reached Sylfia and she thought bitterly that this was not how she thought things would happen once she had awoken.

~

Jarl did not know when he had been carried from the cell following his fight with Bjorn, and he did not know how long he had been unconscious for. What he did know, though, was that after he had lost the fight, Bjorn had chosen not to heal Jarl's injuries, and that meant that he was in a fair amount of pain.

With double vision and his head pounding, Jarl appraised his new surroundings. He was inside a cell similar to Sylfia's, though his own had no stone table in the centre. There was nothing in it - the room was bare and thick iron bars stood between him and freedom.

The noise from the cave system was gone now too. Where once there were the sounds of battle, grunts and the clash of weapons upon armour, now there was simply silence.

Although that was not entirely true, as Jarl could hear some distant sobs and moans which he presumed were coming from the other prisoners. He was unsure how many were left as he had not taken the time to search the underground caves before he had been captured, but the quiet suggested there were not many.

"Hello?" Jarl muttered out loud. He did not want to make too much noise in case it brought punishment, but he wanted to know if anyone else was around.

"Hello?" he repeated, slightly louder this time.

The distant sobbing grew muffled and then stopped. It was clear that whoever was out there, they did not want to respond to him.

"Can anyone tell me where I am?" Jarl voiced, but no reply came.

A long time passed, and Jarl realised that nobody would reply to his questions. He had all but given up on speaking with any other prisoners when he heard distant footsteps echoing about the cave system.

Jarl listened as the footsteps walked, paused for a while, and then moved on again. It sounded as if whoever was out there was stopping at each cell. He tried to internalise what this could mean and whether it was good news or bad, and decided to remain silent until the person revealed themselves to him.

The steps stopped at a nearby cell and Jarl knew that their owner would be with him in seconds. He readied himself for a fight, but stopped short when someone he knew walked into view.

Hilda stood on the far side of the bars peering in at Jarl with an expression that betrayed her surprise.

"Jarl? What are you doing here?" Hilda asked in a whisper, leaning into the bars.

"I should ask you the very same thing," Jarl replied in his own whisper.

"I have come here to feed the prisoners and the army," Hilda said. "But you should not be here."

"I would not be here if you had told me the truth from the beginning," Jarl felt his anger beginning to rise as he spoke. Obviously, Hilda had known about this place but had neglected to tell him.

"This is where the army of Baldur's Children train. It is not important because they will never be able to leave this place. It is a symbolic place, but there must be somewhere to put those who come to our settlement that mean us harm, can you not see this? What did you think we would do with those people?"

In truth, Jarl had not thought about it. He had been told that they rarely had visitors in Baldur's Circle, and when they did, they joined the community without hassle. With hindsight, this view was juvenile. Of course every visitor would not have been friendly, so what could they do with the ones who were not? Throw them outside of the settlement to their immediate death? Kill them, perhaps? Maybe this prison system was more of a mercy than he had first thought.

"They have taken Sylfia, Hilda. They have taken my daughter and they are experimenting on her. It is not right," Jarl explained.

"This cannot be true, Jarl. You must be mistaken," Hilda replied. "Baldur's Children are a peaceful people for the most part – we do not bring harm to those that do not threaten us or our journey."

Hilda's words made her sound as though she was one of them, and mention of journeys and paths just seemed to give them an excuse to do as they wished.

"Speak plainly, Hilda, and listen," Jarl growled. "They have taken my daughter because she can leave this place. She can step outside the boundaries and not fade away into the wind as we all would. This is why they experiment on her; Bjorn believes he can take this ability from her and lead this army out into the world."

Hilda's face paled. "They have always spoken as though the day would come, but I always thought that it was a way to keep us from insanity," Hilda's voice went even quieter. "They have amassed an army here greater than any I have seen in both number and power... If they are to become free then I do not know what they will do."

"You have stood by and let this happen? You have watched an army grow and have said nothing about it?" Jarl asked incredulously.

"But they could not leave!" Hilda exclaimed." The size and power of something that could never be released did not matter!"

"They have found a way, Hilda."

Hilda remained silent for a long moment, and she seemed to be trying to make sense of something.

"This is why the army has been allowed to move out of the caverns and up into the settlement then. I came down here to ensure that the prisoners were still being fed. If they are to die, that is one thing, but leaving them to starve is inhuman."

"The army has re-joined the settlement already?" Jarl asked quickly. "How do they have enough of their potion to allow them all to pass out into the world?"

"I... I may have had something to do with that," Hilda said slowly in a very small voice. "Bjorn asked me to create a gruel that could feed the entire army at once and I watched as he added a small vial of something. I assumed it was more of the God's tears to see if it would afford the warriors power or something, but from what you are saying..."

"Those were Sylfia's tears. My daughter's tears," Jarl replied. "Those dogs have taken the ability from my daughter and are planning to use it to wage war across the entire world. The tears work, Hilda. This army is going to leave and head to the west where my clan and my family are, and there is nothing we can do to help them."

"They... they would not, would they?" Hilda began to argue.

"They believe that they must make every being in creation weep for Baldur, Hilda, and they know that it is an impossible task. They believe that if they destroy everything they find, what is left will weep! Do you not see this, Hilda? Are you so blind?"

Hilda placed her head in her hands. In her heart she knew that Jarl was right, but she had always turned a blind eye to such things; it was simply never going to happen, so it had never been a worry.

"You must set me free, Hilda. You must set me free, so my daughter and I can go back to the west and warn my family before it is too late. The clans of the west will never stand against such an army, and I will lose everything once more," Jarl pleaded.

"You... you do not understand, Jarl," Hilda replied. "Even if I could set you free from this place and you could get your daughter back, you will not be able to warn your people in time. If the army has been freed, they will leave the Circle immediately. They will not await any further sign, sunlight or nightfall. They will move now."

"Then we will pass them to the north. We will move more quickly as two than an army. Please Hilda, you must help me."

"I... I wish I could help you, Jarl, but I am afraid that I do not even have the keys to open the door to your cell. You are trapped inside, and I do not know for how long that may be," Hilda replied. But a soft voice interrupted her. "We *can* open the door," Sylfia said with a smile.

Hilda and Jarl both turned to see Sylfia arriving with a large iron key in hand, followed by a young, shorter man who looked nervous, as though he did not want to get caught doing something wrong. Both wore similar leather trousers and shirts, but beyond that, it was difficult to see if they had anything else useful with them.

"Sylfia! My daughter! But how?" Jarl exclaimed as his voice filled with relief. "It has been many days since I have seen you walk." Tears began to fill his eyes as he spoke but he did not care; he was overwhelmed with joy upon seeing his daughter alive and well again.

"I had help," Sylfia explained. "Torgen was sent to collect more of my tears once the army was taken to the surface to ready themselves for their exodus. He was to torture me as a rite of passage, but thankfully he saw the error in his ways and decided to set me free instead."

"H... hello, prisoner," Torgen said in a small and frightened voice. "Please do not judge me too harshly as I was only doing as instructed. Once your daughter had enlightened me, I knew I had to do everything I could to aid her in her next journey."

"And that is?" Jarl asked, trying to ignore the man's original purpose.

"We must prevent Ragnarök," Sylfia announced confidently.

"Sylfia, please. Not all of this again. We are but mortals in this world sent to live our lives, not to meddle in the greater workings of the Gods," Jarl started.

"Wait. You look to prevent Ragnarök as well?" Hilda asked. "This is the aim of all of Baldur's Children. Our goals seem so aligned yet still so far apart!"

Jarl sighed, being only too aware that with any encouragement, Sylfia would not drop this. He did not care for the greater happenings of the world; he now had simply one task to carry out: to warn the west of Baldur's Children and hope to save the lives of his wife, his best friend and the rest of the settlement that he had once called home. They would never be able to withstand the might of this army.

"Sylfia, please," Jarl started to say.

"Father," Sylfia said sternly before Jarl could say another word. "I have been told throughout my entire life that I am to carry out this task. I was chosen by the Gods to cross their Chasm, and within the dreams I have had, I have spoken with beings that are beyond our comprehension. If I am not supposed to do this, I would have died a hundred times already.

I ask you, father, listen to me now, trust me, and you will see what I am supposed to do with my life."

The four fell silent; there was simply nothing that any of them could say to try to either agree or disagree with Sylfia's proclamation.

Eventually Jarl sighed. "I will not bring up this matter again, Sylfia. Sometimes I know that in attempting to keep you safe from harm, I forget that you are your own person with your own path. Forgive me, daughter."

Sylfia could hardly believe what she had just heard. This was the first and only time that her father had admitted that he had been so wrong about something, and she could say nothing.

"We must warn the west, though. Whatever your path is, daughter, we must do right by our family first. Then I will follow you on your journey."

"And so will I," Hilda spoke confidently. "If our goals are so aligned, it would be foolish for me not to try to aid you."

The three pairs of eyes turned to Torgen, who stood quiet and still behind Sylfia and Hilda.

He did not need to pledge his allegiance to Sylfia as they already knew his position. He simply unlocked Jarl's cell door and allowed father and daughter to wrap their arms around each other in a reuniting embrace.

The group then made their way back up through the winding cave system until they reached the place where Jarl had entered through the trap door. It was clear that the entire army had not used this exit from the caverns, as leaving one by one would have taken an unholy amount of time, so Jarl presumed that there must be a much larger entrance somewhere else, but neither Hilda nor Torgen could say where it was. Or they would not say; Jarl was still unsure of just how trustworthy these people were.

The group breached the trapdoor into the empty wooden hut, and daylight filtered through the gaps and cracks in the walls. That suited Jarl perfectly, as it would make tracking their enemy's footsteps far easier.

They were not planning on tracking the army per se, though Jarl recognised the need to keep an eye on their progress as they moved to the west to ensure that there were no nasty surprises on the horizon.

Activity in the settlement was carrying on as usual once the group left the hut. They walked out tentatively, not knowing precisely what would be on the other side to greet them; would the entire army or Baldur's Children be standing there awaiting their exit? Fortunately, nothing out of the ordinary was happening outside. None of the more important people – or the ones that Jarl had come to think of as such – were present - the workers were tending to their farms, people were tanning leathers, starting fires, creating furs, and doing everything that Jarl recognised as 'normal life'. It was strange when he reflected on how he had been told on more than one occasion that these lands were barren, and he spared a moment to think about where these people had found their furs and animals. Eventually he left it with the will of the Gods and started to move away from the settlement with his group, heading to the west, and home.

"Why is it so quiet here?" Sylfia asked in a low whisper as they moved.

Jarl had not been paying attention to sound over sight, but now that his daughter had brought his attention to it, the place was as quiet as a grave.

"It is not the quiet you need to be wary of," Torgen interrupted, "rather what the mists bring."

Sylfia looked out into the distance and focused on a rolling mist headed from west to east. It flowed and danced as though it was searching for something to encapsulate, and as the group moved slowly toward the small stone boundary of Baldur's Circle, the mist grew closer and thicker.

"What is in the mist?" Sylfia asked, almost whispering now.

"The mist is a symbol of intervention from the Gods. Each time the mists have rolled across these lands, it has brought with it trouble or change and I do not remember a time when these changes have been a good thing," Torgen replied.

His words made Jarl think about his old clan's thoughts about the mists when he was a part of the settlements of the west. They too had believed that they contained a magical power, and he recalled hearing a child crying within them before Sylfia had been given to him by the Gods.

"We do not need to listen to such superstition now," Jarl growled, keeping his voice low and controlled. "We must find in which direction this army has left and try to pass them before they arrive at the Chasm."

"They will not be able to stop them, even with proper warning," Hilda warned. "These are not normal warriors that threaten your former lands; these are Baldur's Children, and they have the will and power of the Gods on their side."

"Beating the army is not my main concern at this moment. We must warn the clans so that they can retreat to safety before they are left to go to Valhalla in defeat. In the west, we do not make decisions for others, and such matters are left to those of importance. We will warn them, and then we will aid them in what they decide to do."

A moment later, the group arrived at the stone archway and again Jarl took a moment to read the inscription upon it.

Jarl snorted as he read. The words spoke of peace and freedom, yet he knew that all these people wanted was war and death.

"Wait," Sylfia said abruptly to the group. Then she reached underneath her leather shirt and retrieved two small glass vials with small leathers pushed inside them to act as stoppers. "You must all drink this before you attempt to leave the settlement; it will stop you from, well, you know."

They did not need to be told what was in the vials as they all knew the power that Sylfia's tears would afford them, for without this very liquid, the army that had broken forth from Baldur's Circle would still have been very much contained.

16

The group had quickly found traces of the army's movement through the dense woodlands despite the thickening mist, helped by the daylight attempting to break through the canopies above. It was not difficult; a force of that size that was moving slowly westward would leave a path of destruction in its wake.

Jarl and his small group followed the army's path and it became progressively more evident; the warriors had taken to destroying the woodland as they passed and, in some cases, even burning patches down to the ground. Jarl did not know if this was due to excitement or boredom, or whether it was necessary to allow their passage. Either way, Jarl and his group did nothing to disturb the trees and vegetation around them as they moved; none of them had ever been fond of senseless violence or destruction.

It was not long before they caught up with Baldur's Children, although it was quite unexpected. The army seemed to have set up a kind of camp in a small clearing at the end of their path of destruction. It was just a few hundred metres from the edge of the Gods' Chasm, but Jarl could not figure out what they were waiting for. The army had superior numbers and warriors endowed with the divine powers of the Gods, and if they chose to move against the western clans, the west would not be able to stand up against this threat.

"They wait for nightfall," Torgen announced quietly. "It is to make the raid easier for them and to minimise their potential losses."

Jarl did not need to be told why nightfall was a good thing for a raiding party; he had been on more than a few raids himself. This was no raid, though – this army was there for one thing and one thing alone: complete and utter destruction.

"They do not know how strong the western clans are, brother," Hilda spoke as though she had read Jarl's mind. "They will wait and attack only when they are sure of their victory."

"There are no clans that could stand against such an army," Jarl growled back. "They fight as though they are cowards. They remain hidden until they are to be set free, and they will attack under cover of darkness, using surprise to aid them. This is not the way for warriors to enter Valhalla."

"They do not wish to enter Valhalla, father," Sylfia replied. "They plan to remove their enemies with the least possible risk or damage to their ranks. I know that you are a traditional man, father, but you must see that the ways of old are not always the best. If we are to change the future, we must learn from our past mistakes, not repeat them."

Jarl had not thought about the situation in that way. In truth, he had always thought about war, battles and fighting as glorious epics to recount later with friends and allies. Still, Baldur's Children had a task to complete and rather than see them as cowardly for their actions, Jarl knew that he needed to focus on the fact that these people were going to do whatever it took to complete their task.

"Then at least we still have time to pass them," Jarl announced, letting his daughter's words permeate his mind. "We pass them to the north, giving them a wide berth in case they have scouts at the perimeter, and we will cross the God's Chasm alone. There will be guards in the west, and we will warn them of what will come behind us."

"And then what?" Hilda asked quietly. It was an unexpected question but one that nobody had thought of an answer to thus far.

"Then the clans must unite and decide if they are to stand and fight or run and hide," Jarl replied quietly. He knew that it was much more likely that the clans would all believe that they could defend themselves well while remaining separate, but he knew that option would lead to their downfall.

As the group walked away from the camped army and around it to the north, Sylfia tried her best to keep in step with Jarl, who seemed to be quickening with every step he took. His footsteps were soft and silent on the grass beneath him, and Sylfia, Hilda and Torgen all did their best to keep up with him although that was not an easy task as the larger man had trained for situations such as this.

It was only a matter of minutes before Baldur's Children were out of sight, and the small group of five was confident that if they turned back towards the west, they would avoid running into any scouts. They knew, though, that ahead of them now was another task that was going to challenge them.

As expected, Jarl breached the tree line and walked out to the Chasm's edge slowly and cautiously. He looked along the ridge both left and right though nobody was there to witness his arrival. Across the Chasm, he tried to see the other side, but the mist had thickened and the visibility was simply too poor to make out anything over a few metres away. Even looking down towards the base of the Chasm, he could see nothing but a foreboding and dark abyss.

"Do you think they are there awaiting us, father?" Sylfia's voice reached Jarl as she approached from behind him.

"I do not know, Sylfia. There will likely be a lookout, but in this mist I do not think our approach will be seen until the very last minute."

Both Jarl and Sylfia knew how difficult the crossing of the Chasm was going to be, as both had recently struggled through that very task. Sylfia shuddered as she remembered the difficulty that she had had, and fervently hoped that a second crossing would be easier. She planned on letting her father descend the sheer wall first and would simply copy his hand and footholds so that she would not find herself in the same situation as the last time.

"It is a long way down to the bottom?" Torgen asked as he joined the pair looking out into the Chasm.

"It is. Deep and wide the God's Chasm, but the cover of this mist will help us greatly. Do not expect to be greeted with smiles and handshakes once we have reached the far side, though. Crossing the God's Chasm is but the easiest in a line of difficult tasks before us all," Jarl said.

"Then we need to keep our strength with us," Hilda said brightly, handing each of the group a freshly cooked steak big enough for them to hold in their hands. "Climbing is not easy on an empty stomach!"

Jarl could not have agreed more with Hilda's sentiment, and once he had finished his snack, he moved to the edge of the

Chasm and turned to face the rest of the group. But it felt different this time as he placed his first foot over the edge and searched for a protrusion to begin his descent. The last time he had done this, he had been following Sylfia to try to save her, but this time he was leading a group willingly across the God's Chasm – the one place that he had always sworn never to cross.

Silence was their only companion as they descended the sheer Chasm wall, and it felt right to Jarl. It was not simply that none of the group was speaking to each other as they concentrated on their task; rather it seemed that the world around them had turned silent as though it had been swallowed by the mist.

It took a short while, but eventually, Jarl's leather boot hit the solid ground of the Chasm floor. "I am at the bottom," he called up to the rest. He knew that it was probably unnecessary and the mist was swallowing up the sounds around them, but at least he had no fear that his call would be carried anywhere else.

Sylfia arrived on the ground a moment later, followed by Torgen and then Hilda. Hilda let out a small cry of victory once she had let go of the Chasm wall, and Sylfia knew exactly how she felt; the descent was not easy nor pleasant, but Sylfia knew that the climb up the far side of the Chasm would not be easy either.

The group stepped out into the flat chasm floor as one, side by side in silence again, for they knew that their task was not yet complete. Suddenly, a noise above them cut through the silence making them all to look up as one.

Cutting through the mist, a jet-black raven swirled silently overhead, allowing sunlight to pour into the Chasm all around them, and for a moment Sylfia could see the blue sky high above them. The raven circled overhead a few times before disappearing into the mist again, and Sylfia watched to see if it would return. She wondered if it had been the same raven that belonged to Odin, but from this distance there was no way to tell.

"The Gods watch over us," Torgen announced from the back of the group as they all followed Jarl across the Chasm floor. The sudden announcement made Sylfia jump, and she turned back to look at him.

"What do you mean?" she asked, coming to a halt.

Torgen pointed up towards where the raven had flown. "This is a sign of the Gods is it not?" he asked as though it was common knowledge. "Ravens always come to those as a sign that they have brought the attention of the Gods."

Sylfia looked back up to where the raven had flown with an inquisitive look on her face. Whatever Torgen had learnt about ravens was not too far from what she had learnt herself, and it made her wonder just how many things she could learn from cultures removed from the Rakki clan and the teachings of the west.

"Do not fill her head with more talk of the Gods and their plans," Jarl ordered from the front without looking back. The gap between the front and the back of the party was growing, and Sylfia and Torgen increased their stride to catch back up.

Sylfia was about to object, but her father had anticipated that she was about to speak and held a single hand up. She decided that it was better to drop the matter, for now at least.

The party stopped; they were now face to face with the sheer Chasm wall that ascended straight upwards above their heads. They all knew that it was the only route they could take, and this was the climb they had come for. Once they had scaled this wall, they would be in the west and at the end of their path.

Jarl again led the party. He took the first hand and footholds and pulled himself up the wall, hand by hand, foot by foot, and before long, he, Sylfia, Hilda and Torgen had made significant progress upwards.

As they climbed, a few words were called back and forth between them – generally warnings regarding loose protrusions or difficult places to climb - but as they ascended, their calls grew more and more muted; if any guards were patrolling on the western edge of the Chasm, they needed to be able to say their piece quickly, as anyone caught climbing up the Chasm and crossing over from the east, could very possibly be killed there and then. Their best hope was to reach the top - and safety - and then make their way into the Rakki settlement so that they could tell the chief or anyone else who would listen about the danger approaching.

Jarl, having been at the front of the group for the duration of their journey from east to west, breached the top of the Chasm first. As he pulled himself up and looked around, he noticed that the mists that had covered their path had not abated on the western side of the Chasm and he gave a sigh of relief. As far as he could see both left and right along the Chasm – which was not very far at all – he could not even see the slightest betrayal of another living soul, a lit torch or fire. He realised that this being the daytime, they may not have seen the need to light any fires for the watch, but with the mist as thick as it was, personally he would have lit something just so that he knew where he was going.

Behind Jarl, Sylfia, Hilda and Torgen pulled themselves up from the Chasm. For Sylfia, it felt much easier this time, mainly because she carried no weapons with her, her swords having been long lost in Baldur's Circle. It had been hard to leave them behind, but it would have been far worse to have wasted the time to go and look for them. She was not alone in this though, as not another member of the party carried any weapons that she could see.

Jarl had also reflected on the same fact but had not mentioned it to the group. Without a weapon on his person, he always felt so naked, but he too had had to weigh up the pro and cons of attempting to search for weapons and armour when the priority had been for him and his daughter to leave the settlement. Plus, any time wasted in warning the Rakki clan about their impending war could have meant many lives lost.

"Who goes there?" A loud shout carried through the mist to snap Jarl back to his reality, but it was a familiar voice that quickly brought a smile to his face.

"Eric!" He called back into the mist. He was sure that the man approached from the right and he was excited to once again see his brother and friend.

"I told you that I would come back and..." Jarl started speaking, but as he walked towards the sound of Eric's call, no less than five figures emerged into view through the mist.

Eric was the first to show his face and where Jarl wore a faltering smile, Eric was straight-faced and his stare was fixed above Jarl's head. Behind Eric, the other four Rakki clan members were all people he knew and cared for: Erland, Leif, Egil and Steinar.

Jarl was flanked by his daughter and the two former Baldur's Children as he began to speak.

"Eric, we bring news from the east. It is vitally important that..."

Eric held up a hand to stop Jarl. "You have broken the most sacred of our laws, and by order of our clan chief, I have been asked to place you under arrest."

"You cannot!" Sylfia exclaimed loudly, and the other four men stepped forward threateningly. Not only were all four of the men huge underneath their dark furs and long braided hair, but they each carried very sharp-looking battle axes. Even if each of Jarl's party carried weapons, it probably would not have been a fair fight.

"Brother, you know who I am and the beliefs that I hold," Jarl tried to speak sense into Eric, but his friend would not even look him in the eye.

"Look at me, brother!" Jarl shouted, but still Eric did not amend his gaze.

"We are to take you back to the clan where you will be tried and held until it is decided what the clan will do with you and your friends," Eric announced as though talking to nobody in particular. "Please give us your weapons and hold out your hands in front of you now."

Not a single member of Jarl's party moved a muscle, though when the armed warriors took hold of their hands, they did not attempt to resist their binding. Each of them received a length of rope tied tightly around their wrists which was joined by a short length of rope to the next so that they could not try to run.

"Please brother, you can see that we are no threat; we have come to warn you," Jarl spoke pleadingly to Eric who walked alongside him.

Eric did not respond and kept his gaze firmly on the path before the group.

"Brother," Jarl spoke again after a short pause, and this time he managed to garner a response.

Eric turned his head to face Jarl and Jarl could see the hatred in his friend's eyes. "You do not get to call me brother any longer. The moment you left our settlement to head east, you gave up that right. You are a prisoner and if you do not stop talking, then I will make you."

Jarl could hardly bear his friend's coldness, but he was convinced that if he could just speak with him alone, everything would be made clear.

Jarl lowered his voice to a whisper. "Eric, brother. You can speak plainly with me," but before Jarl could finish his sentence, Eric drove his elbow into Jarl's cheek, and pain erupted from the strike. Jarl's immediate instinct was to retaliate in anger, but after a short pause and a deep breath, he knew that it was not the correct cause of action and would not help. He would continue along as a prisoner – quietly – until he reached his former home and could talk with others.

The journey felt a little longer than Jarl had been used to, and he was not sure if it was because of the silence, the mist, or the fact that he was now a prisoner when he had expected to be able to relay what was happening. He found it strange, too, that his party had all remained silent during their capture. Either they thought better of it or were simply following his lead.

Eventually, the familiar sight of the Rakki settlement came into view through the relentless mist. Jarl felt the tug of coming home, and wondered if Sylfia felt the same.

Although Sylfia did feel a sense of homeliness for the settlement, her mind was elsewhere. In her heart she knew that this could not possibly be the end of her journey but was simply another steppingstone along the way; there were more important things for her in store.

Torgen and Hilda were both silent and kept their vision trained on the ground. They knew what it was like to be an outsider in a new place and they recognised that the way they had been greeted meant that things were more than likely to go from bad to worse.

"You have returned from the east, Jarl Ulfson," the Rakki clan chief Halvard announced in a booming tone, his voice arriving before the mist swirled about his huge frame. "You have broken the one rule that we hold in the highest regard, and you have turned your back on the oath that you once swore. Tell me now," his voice deepened into a growl as the chief grew angrier as he spoke, "why should we not kill you where you all stand?"

Jarl looked the chief dead in the eye. He had never seen him so angry before. His face had turned a deep red, and a vein bulged on the side of his neck as he forced his words out.

"Because we have come here to deliver a warning," Jarl said loud and clear for all present to hear. "We have crossed the God's Chasm and seen what lies to the east. There is a settlement there that was damned by the Gods, and all who resided there were trapped inside. There was an army within of a size and power that the west has never seen, and now they are free. They are coming for us all, and we do not have the power to stop them. This is why we have returned, against your laws. Against our laws, which I swore to uphold." Jarl remained precise and level with his words, "To deliver this warning."

"The laws are there to appease the Gods!" Halvard practically shouted. "It is your crossing west to east and east to west that will damn us all! The Rakki clan and the others of the west have fought in many battles over the decades, and not once have we ever been overpowered. You speak as though mortal man can reduce us to fire and ash but it is the Gods who decide our fate, and this is how you will kill us all."

Jarl had never heard the Rakki chief speak this way – so unable to hear and, at the same time, so fearful of the Gods. The clan had always appreciated the old teachings and respected the Gods of old, but they had never blamed them for hardships or even thought that they would have a hand in the future downfall of man.

Jarl lowered his voice to speak directly to the chief. "What is this, Halvard? Why are you so concerned with the will of the Gods when a real threat is knocking on your door?"

Halvard did not seem to accept Jarl's words. In fact, he seemed not to have heard them at all, and simply turned his back on Jarl and his group without any kind of reply.

"Halvard, you must listen!" Jarl objected to the chief's back.'

"These four have crossed the God's Chasm and have returned with news of impending doom. They have broken our most sacred of laws, and they question our position. We have no choice but to punish them as severely as our customs dictate."

"Wait!" Sylfia protested before Halvard could complete his decree. "Can you not see that we have come back to try to help you, all of you?"

Halvard slowly turned back to look at Sylfia, and she could tell that at least some of her words had made it through his hardened exterior.

"We came to warn you!" she repeated. "You must listen to us or you will be caught unprepared for what is coming!"

Halvard's gaze shifted away from her to the ground as though he was trying to make sense of the words through his own emotions. Jarl had worried that his daughter's interruption when the chief was in this state could bring nothing good, but he could see something now: the chief was listening to Sylfia and was hearing what she was saying. Even though the words were the same as his own, Halvard was listening to Sylfia.

Halvard eventually waved a hand dismissively and shrugged. "I do not see why we should send these four to their deaths. They will be restrained until we decide what we are to do with them. If this army arrives, we will talk about what happens next, but until then, they are prisoners of the Rakki clan.

17

Jarl, Sylfia, Hilda and Torgen were placed in a wooden cage the Rakki clan had assembled for these situations, within the settlement but outside the buildings. The enclosures had seen little use throughout Jarl and Sylfia's lifetime – usually, they would be called upon when minor discretions required a resolution. Still, the punishment had not yet been decided. Jarl could not help but feel as though the Gods were laughing at him, having been imprisoned twice in as many days, but he could not help thinking that without Sylfia's intervention, the Rakki clan chief may have thrown them back into the Chasm to their deaths.

The daylight that had been attempting but failing to break through the thick mist was waning, and although it was still light, the night would soon roll in and Jarl knew that it would bring with it the arrival of Baldur's Children. He was desperate to do more to warn these people, but the chief clearly was not going to listen to him. He clung onto the thought that once Sylfia had spoken, the chief had listened, and he wondered if that would work with any of the other members of the Rakki clan. After all, he did not need to warn everyone, just enough so that they could have a discussion and come to a real, informed decision.

The small wooden cage was barely enough for all of the group to fit in, though it did not seem to matter to the Rakki clan. The group had arrived together, so they would be jailed together.

"I take it that this was not the reception you were hoping for?" Hilda asked as the group sat on the ground. It was not cold and as they sat, the grass warmed a little beneath them. Jarl thought at least this cell was far better, albeit smaller, than what he had been provided with in Baldur's Circle.

"I do not understand why the chief is so set on this path," Jarl replied quietly. "To guard the God's Chasm is one of our most sacred traditions, but I expected the chief to at least listen to what we have to say. He knows that we would not come back here to risk our lives if it was unimportant. It is as though he is afraid of what our crossing means to him."

"So you knew that there was a chance that crossing back over the Chasm could have led to our deaths here?" Hilda asked in shock.

"It was always possible, though I did not expect it of us," Jarl replied slowly.

"I grew up in this settlement," Sylfia interjected. "These people are our friends and our family. I thought that maybe the laws were in place to stop outsiders from crossing over to the west, not punish us for seeing what is out there in the wider world."

Jarl nodded.

"But what do we do if they do not listen to your warning?" Torgen asked. "If they keep us in here until nightfall and the army arrives, we will be unable to defend ourselves, and we'll be slaughtered without a thought!"

Jarl exhaled loudly before he spoke. "There is nothing more we can do other than wait and hope that the clan will see sense in all this."

The four sat sombrely together, lost in their own thoughts. Eventually, a large figure materialised through the mist that the sunlight was still fighting a losing battle against. It was Eric, Jarl's former friend and clan member.

"Eric, I knew that you would return!" Jarl announced happily as he stood to his full height. Jarl extended a hand through the wooden bars of the cell, but Eric did not grasp it in greeting.

"Why did you return?" he whispered angrily, "have you not done enough damage to this clan already?"

Jarl was at a loss at how to respond; as far as he knew, he had not caused any damage to anyone apart from himself and the three who shared his small wooden cell.

"What do you mean, brother?" Jarl asked.

Eric took a moment to compose himself before he looked Jarl dead in the eye as though he was searching for something within.

"Please, uncle. We do not know what has happened since we travelled east. Tell us why you are so upset," Sylfia said as she joined her father.

Eric took one look at Sylfia, and his entire being softened visibly. Jarl and Sylfia had both noticed but neither commented as he began to speak again.

"It was... things were not the same once you left," Eric explained. "When Halvard heard you had crossed the Chasm, he became angry and agitated. He doubled the guard on the edge and said that any who crossed from either side would be punished. His anger was mostly directed at your family though. It was as if you had all personally insulted him, Sigrid..."

"Mother!" Sylfia grasped the bars at the mention of her mother. She had not yet seen Sigrid and longed to see her smiling face once again. Jarl, too wanted nothing more than to see his wife, but the dire tone with which Eric spoke worried him.

Eric continued speaking without looking at Sylfia, who regained her silence, having also read the look on Eric's face.

"Your wife, Sigrid..." Eric said slowly, as though he was having trouble processing the information for himself.

"Please, Eric, you must tell me what has happened to Sigrid!" Jarl could already feel the tears starting to well in the corners of his eyes. If Sigrid had been executed for his crossing of the God's Chasm, he did not know if he could live with himself. Deep down in his heart though he knew his wife still lived. He could feel her presence, and that was all the confirmation that he had ever needed.

"Sigrid was exiled, Jarl," Eric said quietly. "She was sent from the settlement to fight for herself out in the wilds as punishment for what your family had done to the clan. This was your fault, Jarl," Eric concluded.

But Sylfia had heard those words and come to a different conclusion – this was *her* fault. She had chosen to cross the Chasm and had chosen to break the most sacred law of her people. Her father had simply crossed after her to either try to protect her or to bring her home. This was all her fault, not her father's.

"Your punishment for breaking the law here was for your family members to be exiled?" Hilda asked in shock

"There must be punishment where punishment is due," Jarl explained over his shoulder. "We were not here to receive punishment, so it passed on to the family."

"And you knew this?" Hilda replied. "You knew this, and you still crossed the Chasm?"

Jarl did not respond. He knew that whatever he could say would only make Sylfia feel as though she had been the cause of all of this. And she was the cause, but Sylfia already knew this and saying anything to make her feel worse would not be helpful.

"Do you know where she went?" Jarl asked Eric.

Eric shook his head. "Halvard ensured she would not join another clan to the west or the south. He sent word of the trouble that your family has caused, and they will not aid her if she arrives at any of the other clans. When she left, she was heading north and into the cold. I do not believe that she will be able to survive for long." Eric's head hung as he finished his sentence. The news had clearly affected him.

"Then we must find her," Jarl announced. Deep down he knew that surviving a journey northward was difficult even for groups of warriors and Sigrid would have little chance on her own, but he knew that she lived, so it was a matter of time and not a foregone conclusion.

A knocking sound interrupted them, and Jarl and Sylfia turned to see what was happening. Torgen was banging his fist on the wooden bars.

"If you have not noticed, we will not be going anywhere. We are trapped in this place, and before the daylight arrives in the morning, we will be dead." He continued knocking rhythmically as though it was some morbid heartbeat.

"Eric, brother, you must free us from this place, The army approaches and we cannot defend ourselves or the settlement if we are trapped here," Jarl said.

Eric shook his head, and it did not even seem to Jarl as though Eric even had to think about releasing them. "I will not disobey the word of the clan chief," he said sternly. "My family will not pay for my treachery as yours has."

"Eric... uncle..." Sylfia said softly. "We are not asking for you to help us in such a grand way that you be punished, but why not simply unlock the cage and later, when you are eating with the rest of the clan, we will make our own escape? You would not be blamed, and we would be free to rescue my mother".

Eric stared at Sylfia for a long moment, but eventually, he shook his head, turned and walked away, back through the mist, and the four captives were left alone once more.

"Can you not use your power to burn the ropes that bind the wood?" Hilda asked Jarl, who was still staring after his brother in the mist.

"I have tried," Jarl said slowly. "I do not know exactly how my powers work, but unless I hold a true weapon in my hands I am unable to do anything more than I was before."

Hilda looked down at her own hands, cupped them and then opened them to reveal a slab of perfectly cooked meat.

"My ability is still with me, at least," she said as she began handing out meat. She knew how important it was going to be for the group to keep their strength up.

"And what is your power, boy?" Jarl asked Torgen. "You must have one although you keep this secret for yourself."

"It is... it is not something that has been helpful to us on this journey so far," Torgen explained cryptically. "When I arrived within Baldur's Circle, I was much younger than I am now, just a small boy. I was scared and alone. I came from the east after my family had been killed by a raiding party. I had travelled alone for so long..." Recounting the story was obviously hard for Torgen, and where Jarl felt frustration, Sylfia placed a hand on Torgen's shoulder.

"I did not know what these people wanted or what they were like. I remained hidden for the longest time and even managed to steal some food and water."

"You drank of the tears," Hilda concluded for him, "and that granted you your power. The power that you are granted is always that which your heart desires the most."

"Well, yes," Torgen replied... and then abruptly vanished.

This was not something that Jarl had been expecting at all. The boy had been there one moment and had simply disappeared in the next without sound, fanfare or warning.

"I cannot hold this for very long though, and if another touches me I become visible again..." Torgen trailed off as he reappeared. "It is useful for remaining out of sight or for stealing food where it is not offered though!"

Jarl looked at Torgen more closely, he looked as though he was above twenty years but Jarl could see a childlike innocence within him, as though he had indeed kept his contact with others to a minimum. Then he had a thought.

"How did you gain your place in the caverns underneath Baldur's Circle if you have kept yourself to yourself for so long?" Jarl asked.

Torgen's cheeks reddened slightly. "It was kind of an accident, actually," he said. "I followed some of the clan into the caves once, and when I was inside, they found me. I acted as though I was supposed to be there, and they kind of just let me be. I do not present much of a threat, and after I had run a few errands for them they trusted me. I did not like that place much though, especially when prisoners were brought in from the outside world."

Jarl chose to ignore that last part. He already knew that prisoners were held in the caverns but did not know how many or what they did with them after Baldur's Children had decided that they had no use for them.

"So you are able to turn invisible?" Sylfia asked, knowing just how useful that could be for so many things.

"I can, but not for long," Torgen repeated. "Anyway, it does not matter now; it is of no help to us, is it."

Jarl had to agree. The group had already been trapped, and being invisible was not going to change that. He did wonder, though, why the boy had not used his power to avoid capture in the first place, but it was no use pondering the things that had already come to pass.

"Does anyone have any other ideas?" Hilda asked, but the group remained silent. There was nothing that they could do other than wait and hope.

Before long, dusk had begun to settle through the mist that still covered the Rakki clan settlement, and the group trapped within the wooden cell sat on the ground next to each other to share at least some of their warmth. Jarl wished he could have started a fire, but without his powers, he knew that was impossible.

Hilda was able to keep the group well-fed with her own gift, but beyond that, although they each held divine powers, they could do nothing to break free from their incarceration.

A noise above them made them look up as one. It was again the gurgling croak of a raven high above them, and along with the call came the sound of its ruffling feathers as it descended towards them. It faded into view through the dancing mist, and as it flew, it cleared the air to reveal the sky above. It could not have been long before darkness would truly take hold of the settlement, bringing with it the end of all they had known.

The raven landed on the wooden cage and perched there as though it was the most normal thing in the world, and as it appraised its new surroundings, Jarl could see that the creature was missing its left eye.

Sylfia squealed in excitement, "The Gods have come to look down upon us! This raven is a messenger of what is to come!"

Jarl was about to ask what his daughter was talking about, but before he could open his mouth, the raven spread its wings. The mist around them thickened, and he could barely see past his own nose. Then he heard the sound of footsteps approaching, amplified as though it was the only sound in the world.

18

Jarl held his breath, and he knew that Sylfia, Hilda and Torgen had too. He wondered if Torgen would turn invisible to hide from whatever was approaching, though they probably would not have been able to see him through the thick mists anyway.

The footsteps grew closer and closer, crunching through the grass below, and they all knew they needed to remain silent. Jarl knew instinctively that this must be the beginning of the attack on the settlement, and the raven had arrived to hide them from this first incursion.

Dark shadows began to pass by the wooden cage, and Jarl watched their gait as they did their best to sneak through the mist, as though they were stalking their prey. He wanted to call out, to warn the Rakki clan of this enemy's approach, but he knew that there was nothing he could do right now that would not result in his death.

Far fewer shadows passed than Jarl had expected, and once their figures had all but disappeared, the raven opened its wings and took to the skies. Behind it followed a trail of the thick mist, and the visibility around Jarl and his companions rose with the raven to a few metres once more. It was clear that whoever these people were, the raven had just shielded the party from discovery, and Jarl was thankful.

Then suddenly, a hand gripped the wooden bar next to Jarl, and Eric stood on the outside of the cage, cutting through the rope that bound the entrance to the cell shut.

Eric's eyes met Jarl's as they shared a silent understanding: he was here to free them, but they were to not make a sound and in a moment, the wooden door swung open. The group spilt out into freedom. Jarl took hold of Eric's wrist but Eric did not seem enthused by the action. He did not swat Jarl's hand away though, and for the first time since he had returned, Jarl felt as though he had his brother back again.

"It has begun," Eric said quietly, then turned and gestured for the group to follow him towards the settlement and to where the figures had gone. Jarl worried that he had no weapons with which to defend himself properly, but freedom had been the biggest hurdle he had had to overcome, and now he and his group were free.

Led by Eric, the group found themselves in the centre of the settlement in less than a minute, and they flattened themselves as one against the exterior wall of the wooden longhouse. Jarl could hear voices from within, although he did not recognise them and it did not sound as if there was any kind of fight happening within.

Eric opened the door slowly and walked inside, followed by Jarl, Sylfia, Hilda and Torgen. Five robed figures knelt before the Chief, and Chief Halvard stood at the far end of the longhouse. The chief had his axes strapped to his sides, and Jarl could see Halvard had another attached to his back, though the five robed figures were on their knees before them, eating from small wooden bowls.

"What is happening here?" Eric announced before Jarl could do anything to stop him. Had Eric had forgotten that Jarl and his party were still supposed to be locked in their cell?

Halvard's face darkened when his eyes fell upon Jarl. "WHAT IS THIS, ERIC?" he practically screamed at the Rakki clansman. "IS THIS YOUR DOING?"

Eric glanced behind him to look at Jarl. Seeing these five men kneeling on the ground in tattered robes, hungry and weak seemed to snap him back to his reality and the reason why his brother had been imprisoned in the first place rushed to his mind.

"I... I do not know... I was not expecting...." Eric stuttered though he could think of no good excuse for freeing Jarl. If these five had been a part of some invading army, perhaps he could justify his actions, but as it was, this was not what he had expected.

"And you," Halvard turned his attention towards Jarl and practically spat his words at him as though they were arrows. "Is this the invading army come to kill us all? Do they look as though they are threatening, mighty warriors to you?"

Jarl opened his mouth but no words would come. What could he possibly say? That he was mistaken? That these were some other people? But how could that be? This was far too much of a coincidence, was it not? And the raven had concealed them from these people. Why would it have done so if this was not the threat that approached?

Then one of the weak and weary travellers turned his head to face Eric and Jarl, just for a second, and that is where Jarl saw it. He recognised the man's face, but his body was different. The man that knelt before Halvard, begging for food and salvation, was Bjorn, the leader of Baldur's Children.

Jarl reached for the axe he usually kept attached to his side but his fingers met fresh air; he had forgotten that he carried nothing but the clothes on his back.

"These people are not what they seem!" Jarl protested loudly. "They are disguised as beggars and are here to kill us all!"

Halvard looked down at the five people before him and then back up to Jarl, and laughed.

"You think that I am a fool? I can see what is happening here. You search for your place back amongst our people." He turned to Eric. " Take these prisoners back to their cell, and if they become free again, you are to kill them where they stand. As for how they gained their freedom in the first place, we will talk about that later."

Eric paused for a moment and nodded, keeping his gaze dipped. He was not sure what had happened, how he had been convinced to help these prisoners, but now he had a new task and he was going to follow it to the letter.

Just as Eric turned to face Jarl and his group, Jarl leapt straight at the five beggars. There was some distance between them, Jarl being at one end of the longhouse and the five, plus Halvard at the other, but Jarl knew that he had no choice; he needed to show the chief and Eric exactly who these people were.

In a flash, one of the beggars raised himself to his feet and buried a short dagger into Halvard's stomach before he could do anything to prevent it. The large clan chief held his stomach as blood began to redden his hands, and groaned as he fell to his knees, and then flat onto the ground.

Jarl had been so close, and by the time he had reached the figures, who now all seemed far more menacing than they once had, he could do nothing to save Halvard.

Unarmed, Jarl ploughed into the closest of the five figures, who were now all on their feet. Jarl recognised two of the faces in the group: Bjorn, the large healer, and the woman he had seen practising in the caverns with the army, and he knew that whatever was about to happen next, it was not going to be easy.

Jarl barrelled into Bjorn. It was not by choice, he was simply the closest of the group, and as the pair fell to the ground the disguise that the large healer had been wearing faded away as if some magical cloak. Bjorn now looked both large and menacing, although Jarl noticed that he was still without one of his arms – no matter how skilled a healer he was, there was apparently nothing he could do to regrow it.

Bjorn and Jarl clattered to the ground, with Jarl landing on top. Neither of them had any weapons as Jarl had not had one to begin with, and he presumed that in the commotion, Bjorn needed more time to retrieve whatever it was that he may have been carrying.

Jarl pinned Bjorn down onto the ground, raised his balled fists above his head, and drove them down onto his opponent's face once, twice. On the third time, he was tackled by another member of the group.

Jarl fell to the ground this time and looked up to see the point of a dagger careering towards his face. Fearing his life was over, at the very last second, a large double-sided battle axe cut through the air and sliced through the arm of Jarl's would-be assassin. Jarl looked up and watched as Eric, who held the axe that had just saved his life, pulled it in a powerful back swing and decapitated the disarmed man without fanfare.

"Take this," Eric commanded as he passed Jarl a single, small hand axe. It did not look as though it was a menacing primary weapon such as the battle axe, but it was far better than nothing.

With Bjorn still on the ground, three warriors remained for Jarl and his party to deal with. Now though, Jarl, Eric, Sylfia, Hilda and Torgen stood between the three outsiders and the exit from the longhouse. Only Eric and Jarl were armed, and as they watched their opponents carefully, two of the three men drew their weapons, one a small axe and another a short sword, and the woman that Jarl had previously seen fighting drew her own short, thin sword and opened her other hand again as though it held no threat.

Eric and Jarl stepped forward as they had done so many times in the past, each knowing how they had always fought and both confident that neither would get in the other's way. Their three opponents took a single step apart to gain their own space. Jarl smiled as he realised what this meant: this group was not used to fighting together, and that meant that Jarl and Eric had the advantage.

The woman with the sword stepped towards Eric and Jarl was left to face off against his counterpart with the axe. The man with the sword moved towards Sylfia, Hilda and Torgen – he was mistaken if he thought that his weapon would give him an advantage and Jarl was not worried; he knew that Sylfia was skilful even empty-handed.

Jarl, Eric and their opponents were engaged in their battles as the man approaching the three unarmed members of the group smiled, slowly holding his short sword out towards them. Torgen abruptly vanished, leaving two to fight one.

Sylfia knew what she had to do: she was faced with an opponent who held a weapon whereas she held none, and she had no idea how skilled the man was, so before Hilda could more in front of her and before her opponent could gain a solid footing, Sylfia lunged forward at the man.

He raised his blade and thrust it out straight and true towards Sylfia, but she dropped her leading knee to the ground and shifted her centre of gravity underneath the sword and the man's killing strike. Within a moment, Sylfia had made contact with the man's waist. She had passed the reach of his weapon so had immediately removed it from the fight; with her arms wrapped around the man's waist, there was little he could do with the sword.

The man tried to hit Sylfia's back with the hilt of the sword, but as it was both short and light, it did not have much effect on the warrior. The momentum was already with Sylfia's strike though, and she lifted the man's feet clear off the ground before depositing him onto his back with a loud thud against the wooden floor. Clearly winded, he dropped his sword as his attention turned to his pain and away from the fight and Sylfia took the opportunity to place a knee on the man's bicep and grasp his hand tightly in her own. She bent his hand forwards, towards his own forearm, leaning her weight into it, and after a moment his wrist snapped and he howled in pain. This was the first lesson that Sylfia had been taught: disarm your opponent and prevent them from taking up new weapons against you.

Hilda could fight, although she had not had to for many years and as much as she wanted to help, there was little that she could actually do. She watched as Sylfia swiftly bested her opponent, she watched as Eric and Jarl faced off in their own bouts, and she wondered exactly what she could do to help. Then she saw Bjorn stirring on the ground, and she knew that she had a true purpose.

Eric and his opponent had traded blows, and they were evenly matched. Where Eric held his mighty battle axe, his opponent held a small hand axe, and although it looked unfair to the untrained eye, where Eric's attacks were far more powerful than anything that the small axe could muster, they were obvious, lumbering, slow even. The tiny hand axe was, of course, far less devastating but it could be swung, swung and swung again before Eric could wind up even a single attack. The pair were locked in a stalemate, and as far as Jarl could see as he took fleeting note of the bout, that suited him down to the ground. He knew that his own opponent, though, had more tricks up her sleeve.

It seemed as if the woman facing Jarl did not want to fight. In her face, Jarl could see nothing but hatred and a burning desire for his blood, but there was nothing aggressive in her actions. She stepped forward and backwards in tow with Jarl. She mirrored his stance and even raised and lowered the sword as he did his axe and eventually, he realised he would have to make the first move in this fight.

Jarl raised his small hand axe high over his head to ready his strike. He knew that it would telegraph his intent, but he wanted to know what the woman would do against such an attack. Too late he remembered that he had seen this woman deal with this very attack once before.

As the axe came down toward her, the woman dropped her shoulder and the weapon sailed harmlessly past her. Had it been larger, like Eric's, it would have embedded itself into the ground, leaving Jarl open for her counter. The woman did manage to counter, though it was not as devastating as it could have been. She again drove her elbow into the side of Jarl's face, though as his weapon was free to move he was able to roll with the strike, so what could have been a devastating blow was merely glancing.

Jarl saw the woman open her free hand, and a ball of fire grew into existence within her palm. He dropped to the ground just as the fireball sailed over his head and crashed into the wall behind him. It was pure luck that the longhouse was not set ablaze.

Taking a moment to compose himself and figure out exactly how he was supposed to best this woman in combat, Jarl jumped to his feet and faced her again. He found it strange that she had not attacked him while he had been vulnerable, although at least it had given him the time to think and plan his next move. The woman extended her sword arm towards him again, but this time Jarl knew that telegraphing an obvious attack was going to get him nowhere. Instead, he took a sideways stance, with one hand outstretched and his axe poised to strike by his chest.

Knowing that his empty hand would be no match against the extended and very sharp-looking sword that the woman held, Jarl did not place much hope in defending her attacks in this stance. Still, he needed to be adaptable in this fight, especially with the added danger of the woman's fireballs. But Jarl, too had a divine gift up his sleeve, and before he made his next move, his small hand axe burst into flame. He could feel the heat radiating from the end of his arm but it did not hurt him.

Jarl jerked forwards and brought the axe upwards in a quick uppercut, but the woman raised her chin and extended her body so that the strike fell short of her face. She followed through with a kick and Jarl had to jump backwards to save from being caught under his own chin. He barely had a moment to see a fist-sized ball of fire heading directly at his chest, and he did the only thing he could think of: he brought his axe before him to block the attack.

As the fireball hurled towards his axe, Jarl had no idea what would happen - whether he would be burnt, or his axe destroyed or if he would be thrown back by some divine blast. He did not have the time to change his mind, though, and as the fireball impacted his flaming axe, he was surprised to note that nothing happened. The fireball was simply absorbed by his axe with no more effect than a drop of rainwater in the ocean.

For the first time, the woman did not look confident in her approach to the fight and her face betrayed the fact that she had no idea how to deal with Jarl's own divine ability.

Jarl lunged forward at her and as he did so, he passed his flaming axe from his right hand to his left. He smiled internally as he saw her gaze follow the deadly weapon and ignore what he was actually doing. Jarl slammed his leading shoulder into her face and she flew back to the ground behind her. However, this one would not be as simple to remove from the fight as Bjorn had been and she was back on her feet in an instant. Again she held her sword to the ready and this time she did not wait for Jarl to make his attack.

The woman whipped her sword from left to right as she stepped forward. She made quick jabs and trusts that forced Jarl to block and parry as she tried to find an opening in his defences. As the fight continued on, though, something happened that Jarl had not been expecting: the flames that engulfed his axe had begun to dull and reduce, and he knew that soon he would be without his divine gift in this fight. Just as Torgen had said his ability did not last long, it appeared that Jarl's own power had a similar limitation.

Jarl knew that as his advantage waned, he would need to regain control of the fight and the only thing that he knew that he could rely upon now was his brute strength. He would have to try to overpower the woman and hope that her own ability was diminishing as his was. He suddenly swung his axe with wild abandon, trying to catch her off guard with the sheer force and surprise of the attack.

The woman was too quick for Jarl though, and as she evaded his attack she spun a full three hundred and sixty degrees and led a counter with the back of her fist. It caught Jarl in the jaw, and his vision blurred as his body fought to keep a hold of his consciousness.

Jarl stumbled back, but before he could refocus on the fight before him, the woman followed up her attack with another kick that sent him back to the ground. His landing was not as soft as the woman's had been, and although he tried to will his body to right itself, it would not obey his commands.

The woman stood over Jarl with her sword held to the ready and a sneer on her face. He was to be the next casualty of the crusade of Baldur's Children, and there was nothing that he could do to prevent it. Jarl looked up at her from the ground with determination still blazing in his eyes but could do nothing more. She drew her sword back ready to strike, when suddenly the tip of a sword thrust from her chest and her eyes grew wide at the realisation that someone had just ended her life.

Behind the woman's frozen form appeared Torgen, holding a short sword with a mix of sorrow and relief on his face. Torgen had taken no pleasure in this act, but it had saved Jarl's life, and he would be forever grateful for that.

The woman fell to the side and Jarl eventually managed to raise himself back to his feet. Torgen abruptly disappeared again, and Jarl took a moment to survey the longhouse. Blood and death stained the floor all around. Eric had bested his opponent, the woman Jarl had faced lay dead in a pool of her own blood, Sylfia had either killed or rendered her opponent unconscious, and Halvard was lying still on the ground surrounded by blood. Jarl knew that Bjorn had left the fight before it had even begun.

But that was not strictly true.

He had overlooked Hilda on the first glance around the room, but now she stood with her arms down by her side with Bjorn's single arm wrapped around her, holding a knife to her throat. Jarl's blood ran cold.

"Do not think that Baldur's Children are so easy to best," Bjorn growled with menace in his eyes. "We fight with the divine will of the Gods on our side, and there is nothing you can do to stand against us."

Before Jarl could respond, a rumbling growl came from Halvard, who had not yet passed and Bjorn turned to look at him. Within a second, Jarl saw what was happening. Halvard had picked up one of the small hand axes that had been discarded on the ground, and holding his bleeding stomach with his left hand, he hurled it directly at Bjorn.

Jarl knew that he would never have been so reckless while Hilda stood hostage, but if the chief was anything, he was a fierce warrior and Jarl had seen him throw axes with deadly precision before.

This time, though, Bjorn had been able to watch the whole attack unfold as Halvard had taken an age to wind up his throw.

Thankfully, Hilda, too had seen the attack unfolding and she dropped her weight onto Bjorn's single arm and twisted herself from his grasp at the very last second before the axe would have buried itself into her face, killing her for sure. To Jarl's dismay, though, Bjorn also managed to shift himself out of the way at the last minute.

Bjorn evaded the axe but where it should have flown straight past his face and harmlessly embedded itself in the wooden wall behind them, there was a sickening thud and it remained suspended in the air.

A trickle of blood leaked from the base of the axe and slowly, from the top of his head and progressing downwards, Torgen faded into existence with a shocked look upon his unmoving face. He fell to the ground without a single breath; his death had been instant.

"No!" Jarl moaned, but before he could step forward and wreak revenge on Bjorn, Sylfia lunged with the two swords she now held in her hands. She was so angry that her knuckles had turned white, and within an instant she had slashed a deep cut into Bjorn's face with one of the swords and cut his throat with the second. The large healer was the last of Baldur's Children present to fall to the ground, dead.

Sadly, Torgen was well past the point of being able to be healed, even if Bjorn had been allowed to live on the proviso that he would heal him.

Amongst the carnage stood Jarl, Sylfia, Eric, Hilda and the bleeding-out form of Halvard, who had slumped back to the ground.

"J... Jarl..." Halvard managed to breathe, and Jarl rushed to the dying man.

Jarl took a knee by the clan chief, although he would not hold that title for much longer as the man neared his dying breath.

"Yes, chief?" Jarl said softly, managing to pour all his respect within his tone.

"I must... tell you something," Halvard rattled. "Jarl, my time has come. I am dying, and soon I will leave this world for the next. But before I go, I must tell you something important."

Jarl leaned in closer, his eyes filled with concern and respect for his chief. "What is it, chief? What do you need to tell me? Do you speak of Sigrid?"

Halvard looked confused for a fleeting moment, then shook his head slowly. He then took a deep, rattling breath and began to speak again.

"When I was a younger man, Elder Wise told me that my death would come from the east, across the God's Chasm. And so, I made the decision to ban all travel across the Chasm to protect myself and our lands from that threat. When you returned, I did not want to believe..."

Jarl's heart sank at this revelation. "Chief, why did you not tell any of the clan this before? Why did you keep this secret for so long? We could have changed things or protected the Chasm more completely..."

The chief looked at Jarl with regret in his eyes. "I am sorry, Jarl. I did not wish to burden you with this knowledge. But now, with my time coming to an end..."

The chief smiled weakly and reached out to grasp Jarl's hand. "I know you have always held the Rakki clan at the front of your heart. I am sorry for how we have treated you this past day. You are now, and forever will be, a member of this clan. May the Gods watch over you and guide you on your path."

And with those final words, Halvard took his last breath and passed into the afterlife, leaving Jarl to turn and face his friends who had been watching over him.

19

The group knew they did not have the time to mourn the passing of either Torgen or Halvard. With the failure of whatever this plan had been, the rest of the army was sure to follow quickly, and that would mean death for everyone left within the Rakki settlement.

Jarl, Hilda, Eric and Sylfia left the longhouse alone, the carnage and death behind them, although where they had entered unarmed, they each now carried weapons. Eric still carried his large battle axe, Jarl had attached two axes to his sides while Hilda carried just one, and Sylfia had liberated two short swords, which suited her well as it was how she had trained. It was all they could do, in the hope that if the enemy was more numerous than they had expected, at least they would be able to defend themselves.

"What do we do now?" Eric asked quietly as the group walked out into the darkness. The mist had abated since their victory over the advanced raiding party, and Jarl wondered if that was some divine intervention or simply a coincidence.

"I do not know, brother, but I fear the approaching army will be too large and too strong for the Rakki clan to stand against alone. They are here to destroy every living thing, and they have powers that you can only imagine," Jarl replied.

"I saw what you did, brother," Eric replied slowly. "I do not know how you did this or if it was some trick, but..."

"This was no trick," Hilda interrupted. Baldur's Children are able to call on the divine might of the Gods, and this is what you have seen. Jarl has also gained this ability, and there is a way for you also to do so."

Eric looked both sceptical and wary at Hilda's words. He had never really trusted outsiders, and his built-in caution for anything coming from the east screamed at him to distrust this woman, but before he could reply, Sylfia spoke.

"It is true, Uncle. The powers that are given by the Gods are great, and they will serve you well as a warrior. I do not know what powers they will bless you with, but from what we have seen, they could be useful for the path before us."

"And what path is that, little Sylfia?" Eric responded, giving his full attention to Jarl's daughter. "What would you have us do next?"

"We must travel north and find my mother. There is nothing there for her beyond death and misery. We must find her, and we must warn all those we find along our path of the army that comes in our wake."

Eric handled his beard the way Jarl did when he was thinking, and the action made Sylfia smile. It was the small things like this that reminded her of home and of happier times.

Before Eric could respond, though, Jarl cried out in exclamation.

"What is this, brother?"

Eric turned to see where Jarl was looking, and as he did so, he too was taken aback. Approaching them from the west, not too far away in the distance, was a long, winding line of bright pinpricks of light.

"It is a fire serpent!" Hilda whispered, her voice filled with panic and fear.

The group watched as the line of light moved towards them, winding slowly as though it really was a serpent whipping its tail. Eventually the long, thin line amassed into a single large group and Jarl realised just what this was. It was not a serpent sent to either help or hinder; this was an army, the size of which he did not know was possible to amass in the western realms.

"That is no fire serpent," Eric stated before Jarl could provide his input, having come to the same conclusion as Jarl. "That is the combined forces of the western clans. Halvard must have sent word."

Jarl placed a hand on Eric's shoulder. "There is always hope where there is the will to fight for what is your own," he said.

"So, there is a chance that we may stand against this army?" Sylfia asked with a newfound excitement in her voice.

"I do not..." Hilda began but Jarl interrupted her.

"Where there is hope, there is always a chance for victory, and now, rather than wait in their beds to die alone, the western clans will fight for what is rightfully theirs. If there were any chance that these Baldur's Children were to be defeated, there would be none greater."

Hilda still did not look convinced but she did not argue. The group needed this small ray of hope and she would not be the one to extinguish it.

It did not take long for a small group that represented the leadership of the western clan's alliance to arrive in the Rakki clan settlement, and Eric, Jarl, Sylfia and Hilda were there to greet them. The group explained the situation in detail, showed them the bodies of the fallen invaders and the former clan chief, and described where this new army lay in wait. There was no point in telling them what these people were capable of though; the armies of the west would require all of the confidence they had brought with them if they were to stand against this foe.

"We will greet this army in battle as close to the God's Chasm as we can so that they cannot retreat like the dogs that they are once we defeat them," one of the clan leaders intoned. He was a fair bit shorter than Jarl and Eric, but he made up for it in his muscular stature, with a large round wooden shield attached to his back and a particularly menacing broadsword that he carried in a single hand.

In fact, when Jarl looked at the small group that had come to the settlement, they all carried large, imposing and deadly-looking weapons. It had been a long time since Jarl had seen a battle waged between armies and never one on this scale. It was just now that he realised how much of a factor the perception of your opponent may play in the fight to come.

"When their armies lay defeated, and their survivors turn on their heels to run, I want their only choice to be met with a blade or to fall to their deaths into the Chasm that they should never have crossed in the first place," another of the leaders added.

Jarl reflected that these leaders all respected and planned to uphold the laws that the Rakki clan chief Halvard had put into place a long time ago, and it made him wonder if they had been given a similar prophecy to what Halvard had been told: that the east would bring their deaths.

"Before we head into battle," Jarl said quickly. "Why do we not allow visitors to wander from east to west? Do we not wish to help these people where they need help? Or to open trade routes where before there were none?"

The group of western chiefs looked at Jarl as though he had uttered a question that they simply could not comprehend and there was a long pause before one of them finally spoke.

"The prophecies of old have led us along our path to prosperity and safety and have granted us all years beyond our fathers. We will not question what has given us so much," Then, as one, the group turned and began their march past the Rakki settlement and towards the army of Baldur's Children at the God's Chasm.

It sounded to Jarl as though the men were scared, as if they had been given the same warning as Halvard, and if they had, then seeing his lifeless body at the beginning of this invasion from the east was surely not going to fill any of them with confidence.

As the group watched the combined armies of the western clans march slowly past their settlement, they were amazed at just how sizable a force had been mustered. There were thousands of warriors ready for battle, and if pressed, Jarl would have admitted that he could never imagine such a force losing a battle in an open field. He knew though that this battle was going to be anything but ordinary.

"Let us join our brothers and sisters then," Eric announced as he began to move to join the ranks of warriors in passing. "And we shall see what it is to be victorious in battle once more, brother!"

Sylfia was the first to step forward and follow Eric, but Jarl placed a hand on her shoulder and slowed her to his own pace. He spoke softly so that nobody else could hear his words.

"Daughter, I will not lose you again. If this battle begins to fall out of our favour, you must head north and begin your search for Sigrid. I will follow if I am not with you, but you must not come to find me. Do not stop to look back at the battle, continue your path until you find your mother; she is waiting for you."

Sylfia nodded slightly at her father's words. She had not intended to leave the battle if things were not going their way, but she also knew that her mother would need her help, if she did not already.

Sylfia caught up to Eric and handed him a water flask as they walked. As he drank, it spilt out onto his bright beard, and he wiped the excess away with his forearm.

"Do not be scared, Sylfia," Eric said with a smile. "Victory in battle is not a fleeting thing, and afterwards we will either drink and recount our tales of victory or dine in the halls of Valhalla."

But Sylfia knew that this battle was not to be the end of her path. She knew that her destiny lay in the north, but if she could help in the fight to come, then she would.

Eventually, the western alliance reached the God's Chasm and the clearing where Baldur's Children had amassed their forces. The armies of the west formed into ranks as they shouted, chanted and battered their weapons against the ground and their armour. Baldur's Children, though, remained silent.

The night was dark and cold, and the battlefield was shrouded in a new, thick fog that seemed to seep into the very bones of the warriors who stood on either side facing each other. Baldur's Children were still making their way up the sheer Chasm wall behind them, their full number not yet ready to fight. Their force was massive, but not quite as large as the total allied forces of the west although there was not much between them, and with a steady stream of reinforcements coming from the rear, the numbers would soon swing to the favour of the invading army.

The heavy air awaited the smell of blood and death, and the ground underfoot was slick with the dew that the swirling mists and abrasive cold had caused.

Baldur's Children kept their stoic faces hard and determined as they prepared to carry out their divine task. They stood before the Chasm to shield their allies' entrance to the field of battle. Even as an incomplete army, they were a fearsome sight, clad in their imposing armour and wielding powerful magical abilities that granted them strength and speed beyond that of mere mortals at the least, and far more apparent divine abilities at the most.

Jarl did not know what these people were actually capable of, but from what he had already seen, this was going to be anything but a fair fight. At least if the western clans had not answered the call of alliance and union, even that small shed of hope for victory, or perhaps even survival, would not have been present in his mind.

The western alliance was the first army to make their move. They knew that if they struck early and pushed their foe back before their total numbers had arrived then they would have a chance for a quick and decisive victory. As they moved to rush their invaders to take advantage, the ground shook beneath their feet and the sound of impending doom filled the air.

The sound of steel clashing against steel quickly filled the battlefield as Baldur's Children met the clans of the west beside the Chasm. The western clans finally allied against a common foe, with fierce battle cries and towering shields and weapons charged towards the enemy line, determined to claim victory and defend their homelands.

As the two armies met, Jarl could see no tell-tale signs of divine intervention or even whatever powers these warriors had been given. Rather the war had started as though between two mortal armies, with the clashing of sword and axe against shield.

Chaos quickly overwhelmed the battlefield. Warriors stabbed at each other in smaller breakaway battles, axes were thrown into crowds of enemy forces and large battleaxes were swung in devastating arcs. All the time, the mist swirled menacingly, always threatening to close in and remove all sight from the warring parties.

Amid the chaos, a fierce warrior wielding a flaming axe cut a swathe through the mist, driving down enemy warrior upon warrior. This was not one of Baldur's Children using their power though, Jarl could see as his friend made his heroic charge. Eric's long braided blonde hair streamed behind him as he swung his weapon with deadly precision, striking down anyone who dared to stand in his way. The gift that the God's tears had bestowed upon Eric was well placed, Jarl knew, and if he had been given the ability to spread the gift to others, then perhaps they would have been afforded a better chance of survival in all of this. As it was, he knew that although it still remained hidden, this enemy was far more powerful than any of the west had realised.

Baldur's Children, though, with the instilled belief that they had divine will on their side, fought with equal ferocity, their swords, axes and spears flashing in the moonlight. The battle continued, and neither side seemed to gain nor lose ground.

Jarl realised that Eric's marauding path through the enemy forces would not last for much longer and he ran towards his brother-in-arms to give him aid. As he ran, he held both of his hand axes high over his head and called on his divine power to set them ablaze and they burst into life immediately.

Jarl shrugged off the feeble enemy attacks as he made a path that mirrored Eric's own, his axes whipping out periodically to send his foes flying away, either mortally wounded or too injured to pursue.

"This is unimaginable, brother," Eric practically laughed as he swung his flaming axe in a wide circumference around himself, but Jarl could see that while Eric seemed to be enjoying all of this, the enemy was slowly surrounding him as his allies could not match his newfound prowess.

"Brother, we must retreat before we are entirely surrounded," Jarl growled under his breath so that the enemy would not hear.

"Surrounded? Surrounded? Do you not see what is happening here before you, brother?" Eric called back with glee. "The powers that I have been afforded have not been given to be washed away at the beginning of the very first battle. The Gods are with us, and we must press our advantage!"

One of Baldur's Children wielding a long spear attempted to swipe at Eric from a safe distance, but Jarl saw the attack coming and cracked one of his axes into the weapon, shattering it before it could deal any damage to Eric.

"Now brother, we must regroup with the others!"

"You go, brother, I will remain here and teach these dogs to leave be what is not theirs," Eric called back, still with a smile in his voice, and Jarl knew that there would be no convincing him. He also knew that if he left now, Eric would surely perish. He had no choice but to remain with his friend.

Sylfia remained with the bulk of the western allies at the rear of the battle. She had borrowed a large bow and a quiver of arrows that she wore across one shoulder, her twin swords attached to her waist for use later.

It was difficult to see through the mist where the enemy was, but that fact worked both ways and it was one that Sylfia planned on taking advantage of.

She walked slowly forward into the mist with her longbow drawn. As well as reducing her vision, the phenomenon seemed to dampen the sounds of battle, though she knew that war still raged on. The warriors were slowly moving forward as a group towards the main battle now, a part of their tactic: they would continue to crush their enemy forces with weight in numbers until they could be pushed back no further and would be forced back down into the Chasm, one way or another.

Then from the mist, a shout reached Sylfia's ears and a warrior charged at her, emerging just feet from where she walked. Sylfia had but a fraction of a second to act, releasing her arrow which travelled momentarily free from the longbow and through her would-be attacker's neck with a spray of blood. The man fell before Sylfia's feet and she quickly nocked another arrow, pulling the string taught and continued walking slowly forwards.

Jarl and Eric had begun fighting almost back-to-back with their flaming weapons, and although not a single foe had managed to so much as land a scratch on either of them, Jarl was beginning to worry why Baldur's Children had not used any of their own divine powers.

Then suddenly, as Jarl pushed back the warrior before him with overwhelming strength, the mists around them began to wane. Jarl knew that something momentous was about to happen; the very air around him felt as though it had become charged and the sounds of battle began to quieten as though the world had paused for a moment, and Jarl did not understand what was happening.

Then a rushing sound slowly filled the air. It was quiet at first before developing into an almost deafening roar, and Jarl noticed that the enemy warriors all around had each dropped down onto one knee. This left the allied clans of the west looking around themselves not knowing how to proceed, some even claiming victory as it seemed their enemy had surrendered.

Suddenly, from behind the kneeling army, a tidal wave rose from the God's Chasm and atop it stood hundreds of warriors, many of their weapons ablaze by the will of the Gods, and Jarl's heart sank as he realised that the battle had now only just begun. The true army of Baldur's Children had been dropped into the fight, and things were going to get far more difficult than they had been so far.

The tidal wave towered high over the battle before crashing down onto the ground before the Chasm and depositing the new warriors into the fight. A moment passed and then the Baldur's Children who had remained on one knee, looked back up from the ground and raised themselves to their feet.

The lull in activity was over, and now the real battle had begun.

"Brother, we must retreat from this place!" Jarl called to Eric as the pair watched their enemy about to gain reinforcements. The mist had not returned to the field of battle, and the pair could see at least a dozen warriors running straight at them, their weapons blazing brightly through the darkness.

This time Eric did not show the same bravado as he had before. Regardless of how simple it was to cut down a ring of enemies who had no divine power on their side, he knew that standing against this new enemy would be suicide. There was no honour in suicide.

Eric and Jarl both turned their backs towards their new approaching foe and cut down the warriors that had encircled them to the rear. Eric swung his mighty battle axe at three of their opponents and it sliced through all of them easily, severing their upper halves from their lower. Jarl swung an overhead strike with the axe in his right hand at one and unleashed a ferocious backhand swipe at a second and within a moment the pair had felled five enemy warriors.

And then they ran. They knew that this was not the way of their people, but they had to regroup with the main fighting force, or they would not last to fight for another moment.

Then Jarl heard a call come that almost made him stumble.

"Archers! Present shields!"

The order came from somewhere in front of Jarl, but he knew what it meant: either the new enemies that had joined the battle had come equipped with bow and arrows, or the enemy was pursuing a new tactic launched at the change of tide in this battle. It did not matter; the result was the same: Jarl and Eric were both advanced targets, and neither carried a shield to present as the order suggested.

The first arrow sliced through the air beside Jarl and embedded itself into the ground with a thud. It had missed by mere feet, and he picked up his gait and willed his legs to press onwards and away from this new danger. His pulse quickened and his breath shortened as he moved, but he did not care; he needed to break the range of the archers.

A second, third and fourth arrow screeched past him as he ran. He darted left and right erratically as he moved to present a more difficult target; he knew the simple fact was that the further he ran, the better his chances became.

A hail of arrows then began to fall all around him and he did his best to block out their deafening call of death. The arrows struck closer and closer to him as he moved; it was simply a matter of time before one struck him and he could only hope that the wound would not be terrible enough to stop his escape.

As he ran, Sylfia came into view standing in front a line of shield-bearers. Beckoning him to join them in their safe area, although he could not hear her. He knew that he would be safe if he could just make it to that line of wooden shields studded with arrows that they had successfully deflected, and the armies of the west could regroup and counter.

And then he was there. He had made it without a single wound upon his person. Turning to look back across the battlefield, his mouth dropped as he saw that Eric had not been so fortunate. His brother had not yet been hit by any arrows, although with Jarl not presenting a dividing target any longer, all of the enemy's focus was now on Eric, who juked left and right, avoiding the rain of arrows. "Brother, quickly!" Jarl called out and his eyes locked with Eric's. Jarl could see the fear and panic within those eyes, but he knew that Eric could do this if he just kept moving.

Then the world turned silent as Jarl watched Eric's mouth hang open into a silent shout as a single arrow pierced his calf. The pain it caused must have been immense, and the look on Eric's face did nothing to hide that fact. The worst part in all of this, though, was that Eric had stopped moving as he had cried out.

Jarl moved to leave the shield wall to fetch his brother but was held back by a group of hands and he was forced to watch, helpless, as three arrows impacted Eric's back, each with a deafening thud, their bloodied tips protruding from his chest as he fell silently to the ground.

Act 2 - Fimbulwinter & The North

The battlefield that had played its part as Baldur's Children's first task was smoking in the distance amidst the beginnings of the morning light. By the time that morning had come and the sun had risen, the armies of the west had been soundly beaten by their new foe, who had seized upon their advantage in both size and power. In truth, Jarl had always known that there was nothing that they could do to stand up to such an enemy but at the very least, he thought they had dealt them a blow that they would not easily recover from. Their tactics were strange to him, and the only thing that he could think of that made any sense was that this army was not as all-powerful as it had once seemed. It was large, for sure, but if every member did not have divine powers, perhaps that left a small ray of hope for the rest of the western lands beyond the allied clans.

Jarl, Sylfia and Hilda had escaped from the battle before Baldur's Children had begun to systematically destroy the ranks of the western alliance. They were sure that their calling was to the north and their path was not to end in battle at the God's Chasm, so they had left once Eric had fallen. They had managed to watch much of the battle as they began their retreat to the north, but it was a morose endeavour, and eventually they simply turned their backs and walked mostly in silence.

"Do you think that there are any other survivors, father?" Sylfia asked as they stopped to watch the smoke rising from the battlefield. They knew that the next time they saw smoke, it would be from the Rakki clan settlement, the furthest east of all of the western clans, but Jarl wanted to see if he could discern movement in the distance. It was a morbid thought though, and he knew it; if there was any movement to be seen, it would surely be the murder of the remaining members of the Rakki clan who had been too weak or too young to fight in the preceding battle.

"We can only hope that is the case, Sylfia," Jarl mumbled as he turned his gaze from his former home. He had harboured many thoughts recently of his triumphant return to his people, his reunion with his wife, his friends and his clansmen, but it was not to be, and once again Jarl found himself in unknown lands.

No man, woman or child had travelled north over the past decade. It was a simple matter of survival: as time had passed, the lands had become less and less bountiful, and of the few clans that had called the north their home, only the hardiest had survived. Eventually, those clans had broken contact with the rest of civilisation to the south as they sought to protect their own existence.

The north was cold, and the further north one travelled, the harsher the weather turned. Jarl knew that after a few days' travel the ground beneath them would turn white as the snow began to cover it, and when that happened it was a sure sign that anyone attempting to survive on their own would have a much harder time trying to do so. The thought made him reflect on why the group was travelling north: to find his wife and Sylfia's mother, Sigrid, and find somewhere to shelter and plan their next move.

In the past there had been tens of thousands of people inhabiting the northern plains before the winters had become as dire and barren as they had been of late. Each year the snow and ice would travel further south, coming thicker and colder to the Rakki clan and the others. It was of little concern to Jarl and his people, though he knew that each time the temperature dropped further, it would mean a harsher existence for any of those people to the north.

"So where do we go now?" Hilda asked. She had remained the quietest of the three as they had travelled, and both Jarl and Sylfia had assumed that she had felt guilty for the loss of their people.

"We travel north," Sylfia answered before Jarl could speak. "We must find my mother and help her. She is probably all alone out here, but if I know her, she will be fine."

"And then?" Hilda asked. "We all just return to the embers of your former clan and move on as though nothing has happened? Baldur's Children will not rest until their work is done, and you must know that their work will never be done."

"No... I do not wish to return to the south..." Sylfia said slowly. "My path is to the north and leads to a snow-covered mountain," she cut her sentence short before revealing any more information, as she knew that her father would try to convince her not to get involved in such matters.

Jarl had picked up on what Sylfia had been saying though and contemplated the snow-covered mountain. He knew that if it was Sylfia's desire to travel there, then within must surely be a danger but to Jarl it did not matter what would happen once the group had rescued Sigrid. This was his one and only task, and he would not stop to think about anything else until it had been completed. He would deal with Sylfia afterwards.

"I will do whatever I can to aid you," Hilda said softly, the pair almost entirely ignoring Jarl and with those words Hilda passed each of them a thick slab of cooked meat. At least they would not go hungry as they travelled.

Jarl found that he was able to use his divine power to melt snow in leather flasks so that they would have water to drink and warmth to huddle around as the nights rolled in. It seemed that this small group of three had been perfectly assembled to make a journey of this difficulty a little simpler.

As the group trudged quietly onward, the drop in temperature quickly became apparent, and Jarl hoped that it would not continue. Singular flakes of soft white snow had begun to fall throughout the day, and the longer the group travelled, the more the snow began to hide the green grass underfoot. By the time the sun had started to set, and the group stopped to make camp for the night, there was not a shred of greenery to be seen anywhere. And where once there had been trees lining their path, there now seemed to be nothing before them but a sea of flat, white snow.

There had still been no sign of Sigrid.

The darkness brought a renewed vigour to the cold and the three travellers huddled together around Jarl's burning axes to keep warm while the howling winds bit at their faces, hands and feet. It was all that they could do to group as closely as they could to each other.

"Tomorrow, we must find proper shelter," Jarl announced through gritted teeth. He was terrified of falling asleep and letting his flames extinguish themselves, or else the group may not see a tomorrow at all. The group's spirits were low, and without any hope of properly tracking Sigrid, sadness was taking hold.

Eventually, the group fell asleep, and with the will of the Gods Jarl managed to keep his flaming axes alight. It was not the blazing inferno that he could call upon during battle, but it was enough to keep the cold from taking them on to the beyond before their time.

The morning came and with it, the realisation that they had no choice but to continue with their perilous journey. Long hours passed once again without anything happening to draw their attention.

As Jarl, Sylfia, and Hilda trudged slowly across the barren landscape, they eventually passed a series of crumbling stone walls and wooden buildings, long abandoned and left to decay and covered in thick white snow.

It was clear that this had once been a large northern settlement, a place where their kin had lived and thrived.

They stopped to look around, taking in the ruins of the old settlement, searching all the time, trying to guard the smallest flicker of hope in their hearts.

Eventually, Jarl stepped forward and placed his hand on a crumbling stone wall. "This surely was once a great place," he said, his voice filled with pain, "but Sigrid is not here, surviving in this harsh land. It is a shame that this place has been abandoned and left to rot."

Hilda and Sylfia nodded in silent agreement, their faces etched with sorrow, respect and fear. They stood silently for a moment, paying their respects to the memory of those who had come before them.

Then, as the winds howled and the snow swirled around them, the group turned away from the ruined settlement and continued their journey north, the memory of this once-great place burned in their hearts and minds, but still without answers on Sigrid's whereabouts, their beloved wife and mother.

They had thought about making camp there to use the meagre shelter that it offered, but there were still hours left in the day, and each time the group stopped, they knew their chances of survival, and therefore Sigrid's, would drop. If they did not keep moving as far as they could for as long as they could, it could mean the end of everything.

It was not ten minutes from the settlement when the group heard something that they had not heard for what felt like days: the call of nature. It was distant and the winds obscured it, but after they heard the first wolf howling, it was almost all they could hear. There must have been dozens of the creatures out there, and Jarl did not know if they were being hunted by the animals which were likely starving to death, or if they did not realise that this small group was so close.

"Do you think they know we are here?" Sylfia whispered to Jarl after listening to the howl carried on the wind, and it was as though she had read his mind.

"I do not know, daughter. I have wondered the very same thing, but there is little that we can do about it now. We must press on and find your mother," and as he spoke those last words, a thought struck him. Perhaps the wolves had found Sigrid, and that was why they were howling.

"We must go towards the wolves," he announced suddenly. "Whatever they have found may need our help." He did not want to voice his fear for Sigrid, but Sylfia quickly grasped his meaning.

"Towards the wolves. Are you insane, Jarl?" Hilda asked incredulously. "We may as soon lie down here in the snow and await our deaths! Starving beasts will not welcome you into their clan as easily as others."

"Then you shall feed them if they are starving," Jarl snapped back at the woman. He was grateful for her presence and the fact that she provided food so that they did not need to hunt – which would have been very difficult with the lack of wildlife around them – but she had been one of Baldur's Children, and recently she seemed to have forgotten that fact.

"We do not leave our people to the mercy of the wild," Jarl growled.

"Is that not exactly what your clan chief did with your wife?" Hilda snapped back quickly, and in a flash, Jarl took hold of her shoulder and unsheathed one of his axes.

"You should not speak of the things you know nothing about!" he shouted louder than he had intended.

"Then you should remember that your people imprisoned you and exiled your wife to die, Jarl. You are so quick to condemn the actions of others, but are you too stubborn to see past the end of your nose?"

What Hilda was saying was, of course, true, but Jarl had loved his clan for his entire life, and he knew what the rules were. He had even upheld them himself on more than a handful of occasions.

"My father only broke the rules because of me," Sylfia said quietly. "My mother was exiled because of me. Baldur's Children were freed because of me. All of those people back there died because of me. If you want someone to shout at, then shout at me. My father was only trying to help me," by the time she had finished speaking, her voice was tiny and shaking.

The three stared at each other silently for a long moment before Jarl noticed something over Hilda's shoulder: a figure slowly walking towards them through the whipping snow.

"Sigrid!?" Jarl called out in desperation, although he should have known that this person was much too tall to have been his wife. The figure, though, did not respond and continued to walk towards the group.

Sylfia and Hilda turned to see what was happening behind them, and Hilda instinctively took a step back to stand next to Jarl while Sylfia stepped forward, peering through the snow.

"I know you," Sylfia muttered as she took another step towards the person. The figure was at least eight feet tall, and Jarl could not see how Sylfia would recognise this person when he had never before come across anyone so large.

It gradually became clear that this giant was a man, and with that revelation, Jarl drew his axes into his hands and used his divine will to set them ablaze. Hilda also drew a single straight sword and held it to the ready. Sylfia, though, took another step forward.

On the drawing of weapons, the figure stopped. It seemed he was sniffing the air as he stood motionless, mere feet from the group.

"Do you recognise me?" Sylfia asked.

"I do not recognise any who see me, for I never see them," the giant man rumbled in response. Then he took another step forward, and the entire group could now see him. His hair and beard were long and jet black, his face was aged though not overly wrinkled, and his eyes were pure, milky white, absent pupils. "For you see, I am blind."

Jarl and Hilda still held their weapons to the ready. They both knew that if this man truly was blind, the only way that he had been able to survive in these conditions was with help – and that meant that he must be far more cunning than he was giving the impression of.

"I do know you... I have seen you before," Sylfia pressed. "You were sitting by the God's Chasm... it was you, I am sure of it."

"The... God's Chasm?" the man replied. "I am unfamiliar with this place... but there is a scent on you, something most peculiar."

"You... your name..." Sylfia stammered. "You are Hodur, are you not?"

Hilda's head snapped around at the mention of that name though Jarl did not yet grasp the importance.

Hodur smiled. "It has been a long time since somebody has recognised me, child."

"I did. As I have said, I saw you in a dream, by the God's Chasm," Sylfia repeated.

"Tell me... what is this God's Chasm of which you speak?" Hodur asked.

"It is a..." Sylfia started to speak but was interrupted by Hilda.

"It is the place where the God Hodur sat and wept after killing his brother Baldur. It is the birthplace of the settlement of Baldur's Children, and I do not believe that you are this God."

Jarl quickly interrupted before Hodur could speak again. "And you think that we are simply to believe that you are this God? We are not as simple as you may believe us to be because you have found us wandering these plains without preparation, but we are no fools to believe that the first person to proclaim that they are a God is so."

Hodur stood silent for just a moment, and Sylfia thought that the God's size alone should have been proof that he was no ordinary man.

"A demonstration then, perhaps?" Hodur suggested with a smirk in his tone.

"I will not believe without seeing with my own two eyes," Jarl replied. Perhaps he should not have been so cavalier.

Hodur waved a hand in front of Jarl, and as he did so, Sylfia watched as her father's eyes turned from their usual dark circles to milk-white blindness.

"Now do you see?" Hodur asked, still smiling.

"I... I see nothing!" Jarl replied, his tone betraying his panic. "Please, I beg of you, return my sight to me! Without my vision, I will never be able to find my wife, Sigrid!"

Hodur did not need to wave his hand again for Jarl's eyes to return to their previous brown as they did so immediately.

Hodur then turned to Hilda, who had started to explain about Baldur's Children.

"That... was a lot of information to take in one go," Hodur said. "And I assure you that I am Hodur, as you know of me."

"But when I saw you, you were a giant?" Sylfia asked.

"These things change with time," Hodur explained. "Where once the Gods ruled as giants amongst mortals, now we prefer to stand as equals... well, perhaps equals plus a little extra?" he added. "Now, tell me what you saw of me in this dream of yours, child."

Sylfia tried her best to recount her dream when she had seen Hodur, trying to keep it as clear as she could and as she spoke, she realised this was the first time her father had heard this story.

"I stood within a field of green grass atop a cliffs edge that overlooked a wide and flat sea. I could hear a thundering cry nearby, and then the skies above opened up to allow vast droplets of water to fall to the ground. And then, as though from nowhere, an axe the size of which I could not truly comprehend flew down from the sky and tore the ground in two. Then I think I must have woken as a red rooster crowed, and that is all I remember."

Hodur smiled while Sylfia spoke as though this all meant something to him, and when Sylfia had finished her story, he replied.

"That is indeed the way I remember those dark days as well, child. I am afraid that once that rat Loki tricked me into killing my beloved brother Baldur, I could not deal with the feelings that my actions had brought. As I said, we Gods enjoyed portraying ourselves as giants at that time..." he trailed off as though reminiscing. "Your 'God's Chasm' was the result of nothing more than a distraught giant God driving his oversized axe into the ground whilst he sat and mourned the passing of his brother."

"And the tears, that was you crying for Baldur?" Hilda asked.

"That is correct. Like most beings in all of creation, I wept for Baldur. I do not know of any who shed more tears for his passing than I."

Hilda's mouth hung agape at Hodur's answer, and though he could not see her, he knew that she had been awestruck.

Hilda fell to a single knee. "Your tears... your tears are what have given the people of Baldur's Circle... all of us... you have given us the divine power of the Gods!" she almost cried.

"No..." Hodur replied slowly. "This was not meant to be so..."

"It is so, and with these powers, these people have amassed an army to wage war on the west. They seek to fulfil Hel's promise to release Baldur from her grasp if the world weeps for Baldur; they believe that if they destroy all who do not weep, then Baldur will return," Jarl practically growled. "This is with you, God Hodur, and the deaths of all my people."

Hodur brought a hand up to his long black beard and caressed it gently as he thought about what these mortals had told him. Could it be true that through his act of mourning, the world had been changed so dramatically?

"The Gods... would not allow this to pass," Hodur eventually replied. "We do not interfere in the dealings of man so directly."

"And why not?" Sylfia called. "You all seem to get involved in so many ways, but whenever you are asked directly to help, you say you will not!"

Hodur's attention turned to Sylfia, who had stepped towards him and his milky white eyes seemed to look straight through her.

"We do not take action for good because that would leave the path open for others to take action for evil. Do you not understand, child? No God will harm a mortal being unless they are threatened, and that single fact has saved the lives of your kind on so many occasions. If those rules were to change... it would be the end of all of humanity."

That made sense to Sylfia, and she stepped back into line with her father and Hilda.

"Can you at least tell us if you have seen my mother in these lands? Her name is Sigrid and we believe she may be here alone. It is not a safe place for anyone to be here alone."

"Child... you may have noticed that I could not have possibly seen anything or anyone... for I am blind..." Hodur repeated with a smile. Sylfia could not decide if this was a joke or not. "I, too, travel these planes when I am looking for something that cannot be found, though now I feel that the time for a successful hunt draws closer now that Fimbulwinter has arrived."

"Fimbulwinter... has already arrived?" Sylfia asked.

"Indeed, this is what we are experiencing now - the winter to destroy all life as it flows through the lands. It is unbreakable by the winter sun and will only worsen as the days, months, and years pass. This is what has been foretold, and what is now coming to pass."

"But you are a God! You can change all of this, can you not?" Sylfia pressed confidently.

"This is not something that is within the power of the Gods. Fimbulwinter was foretold to us long ago and signified another stepping stone on the path to Ragnarök. It is at Ragnarök where the Gods will make their final stand at the end of days, and we must not interfere beforehand."

Sylfia's heart clenched with worry but she did not ask another question.

"You may ask me but one more question before I leave you... I fear that if I am seen to give you more help than is normal, the wolves may change their stance of simply acting as distant observers."

Before anyone else could speak, Jarl stepped forward. "You said that you search for something that cannot be found. What is it you search for in these lands, God of winter?"

Hodur smiled again and turned towards Jarl.

"That is an excellent question, mortal being... I am searching for the caverns in which the path to the underworld resides. I look to bargain with Hel and offer myself in exchange for my brother Baldur. He did not deserve to leave this world so soon... I can smell death in these lands, and I know that it is here... but never have I found my path... I fear that it may simply be... too difficult."

To Sylfia it felt as though those last two words had been spoken purely for her benefit, but she did not voice her theory aloud. She could assume that the code was there so that Loki or his wolves – whoever was following Baldur – would not understand that this most perilous of paths was for her alone. She had been told so many times by so many different people that she must always take the most difficult path if she was the one hope for the entire world to prevent the passing of Ragnarök.

The wolves howled in the distance again, and Jarl scanned the bright white snow around them as though expecting their attack.

"With these words, I must part from you, mortal beings. You must search for shelter before the cold grasps you in a hold that you will not break free from. Remember this; the tallest peaks house the deepest roots." Then Hodur turned and walked away from the group and he disappeared as though he had never been there at all.

Jarl turned to Hilda and Sylfia, about to ask what they thought that the God had meant by his parting words, and saw that Hilda was still kneeling down on the ground with her nose practically touching the snow.

"Hilda... Hodur has left..." Jarl said slowly and in a bewildered tone.

"That... that was... we were in the presence of..." Hilda struggled to speak though she eventually raised herself to her feet.

"That was the God of winter and darkness, Hodur," Sylfia said matter of factly. "And he did nothing to help us find my mother." Sylfia lowered her voice in case anyone was listening in who should not have been. "But he did tell us where we need to head to next. We must find the tallest mountain, and within it will be the next step along our path."

Hilda nodded slightly but Jarl simply rolled his eyes. His only path right now would end with finding his wife, no matter how long that took.

"It does not matter where our path leads to after we find your mother, Sylfia," Jarl placated as he wrapped a large arm around his daughter. "We will continue to travel to the north and search for any signs of your mother. If we do find any settlements or people here, then it will all be for the better. I would very much enjoy some warm shelter and a cooked meal... a home-cooked meal," he added quickly as Hilda opened her mouth about to remind Jarl of the food that she so selflessly provided.

The wolves howled again in the distance, though the sound seemed to have come from further away, something that Jarl very much appreciated; he knew just how big wolves could grow in this area.

"So what do we do now?" Hilda asked.

"We head north in search of shelter. It is where Sigrid would have gone, and it is where we must follow," Jarl replied.

Sylfia nodded silently. She knew that what her father was saying was true, and the far north would be where her true path would eventually lead anyway.

The group once again trudged on in silence, and as they walked, the bitter weather seemed to attempt to dissuade them from their route north. The wind picked up and whipped snow and ice into their faces, making it more difficult to both move and see with every single footstep that they took, but they soldiered on, as they knew the path they walked was the only one that they had to endure.

As the night drew closer, the fierce weather did not abate. There were mere hours to go before they knew that darkness would set in, but without shelter from the wind, making camp would be almost impossible. They needed at least some kind of windbreak but had seen nothing but flat, white snow for so long that it felt like wishful thinking to look for such a place.

Then a sound was suddenly carried on the wind, and it was one that Sylfia recognised. She had heard it once before as she slept, and she knew what it meant. Before she saw the cause of the noise, into view came a short stone wall with a gap in the centre where the three could enter this unknown settlement. Sitting atop the wall as though ready to beckon them in, was a single red rooster, crowing loudly.

"Into the settlement, quickly," Jarl ordered and ploughed through the open gateway in the stone wall. Sylfia and Hilda needed no encouragement to follow him and into this new and unknown place.

Just feet behind the wall, stood a new structure and it was unlike anything that any of the party had seen before. This building was constructed from thick stone walls, standing ten feet tall with a roof made of lashed branches. It looked solid, as though it could have been there for hundreds of years, but when Sylfia looked, she could see no snow stacked upon its high roof, while everything else in the world around them was white. The door was large, thick and wooden, and the moment that Jarl pushed it open, they were greeted with a blast of hot air that cut through the cold that they had been suffering for so long.

In the centre of the room a small fire cracked and fizzed as though it had been untended for at least an hour and was dying, though it was at least a sign to all of them that somebody else was alive around here.

"This must be where mother has made her camp!" Sylfia announced gleefully. "She would go to the largest, strongest-looking building and stay there until she is rescued, no?"

Jarl looked pensive. In normal circumstances, that is exactly what he would do, and he knew that his wife would do the same, but being exiled? There would be no hope of rescue for Sigrid, unless from total strangers, or perhaps from Jarl who she had hoped would search for her. It was more likely that there was a small hunting party that had camped here and had left for the hunt, although why they would hunt at night, Jarl could not answer.

"We must not raise our hopes that this place houses Sigrid, Sylfia. I do not know what good it would do to make camp in such a place for a single person searching for salvation. If Sigrid has found this place as we have, perhaps she may have rested here for a short while, but she would have needed to find a settlement where people could help her."

"But there could be people here!" Sylfia argued. "We cannot see the rest of the settlement through the storm, but this could be a full and vibrant place when the winds do not blow, and the snow does not fall! I have never seen a building constructed such as this one; it has been built to withstand the cold, the wind and the snow. Do you not feel warm, father?"

Jarl, who was about to remove his damp furs from around his shoulders, paused for just a moment.

"I know you wish this to be easy, daughter, but we must not hope foolishly. We will take our night's rest in this place because it is built as you say, but in the morning, we must continue to search for Sigrid. Do not doubt me though, daughter, she will be alive out there in these lands, for I know not of any place that your mother will not turn to her will."

"So, who is hungry then?" Hilda interrupted with a smile, and when Jarl and Sylfia looked at their companion, they saw that she had stripped most of her clothes away and was busy arranging them around the fire so they could dry out. There was also a convenient pile of wood inside for her to bring the fire back to its former glory.

Sylfia and Jarl followed suit and placed their clothes around the fire; when they did eventually leave this place, at least they would be both warm and dry.

"Tell me about your clan, Jarl," Hilda said as the three sat by the fire and ate the meat that Hilda had prepared for them. It was the first time that they had been comfortable enough to just sit and exist, and all three of them knew that they needed this opportunity to unwind.

"The Rakki clan is a... was... a clan of great warriors and pride. We were the largest of the western clans, and our chief Halvard, was much respected far and wide from our home. We had our laws and our ways of doing things, and that is what had kept us safe for so long..." Hilda knew what was coming next but remained silent. "Only when I broke those laws and crossed the God's Chasm did the mighty Rakki clan fall... this was my fault, and I will shoulder that burden until the day I fall in battle."

"You have fought in many battles?" Hilda asked, ignoring Jarl's spiral into self-hatred.

"Yes. There was no peace between the western clans in the days of old. We fought in a great many battles. My brother Eric and I fought and raided for years before peace finally came to our lands. We were always ready to defend our clan when the threat would come once more, we had just never expected that threat to come from the east."

Sylfia put an arm around Jarl's shoulders, and Hilda mimicked the gesture on his other side. The group needed to say nothing further; Sylfia felt the guilt of knowing that it was her actions that had caused her father to break his most sacred of laws, that brought the eastern clans westwards, and that she alone was the reason that her uncle Eric was dead and her mother was missing. Hilda felt the guilt she had harboured ever since learning of the plans of Baldur's Children and agonised over how she had not seen their evil before, perhaps she could have done something to stop them, or at least less to help them.

The group sat festering in guilt and none of them could muster up a single word as they watched the flames dancing before them.

A short time had passed when a dull thud came from the door behind the group, and as all three turned to see what had made the noise, it slammed open and a figure lurched in, dropping an armful of wood onto the ground. Sylfia leapt to her feet and drew her blades and Hilda followed suit, bringing a single sword to the ready but Jarl ran to the doorway and wrapped his arms around the figure.

"I knew that you were safe, Sigrid. I knew that we would find you," he breathed.

21

Sigrid and Jarl embraced for a long time. They had been apart for what seemed to both of them an eternity, though in reality they knew it could have been much, much longer. Jarl had never admitted out loud that he had harboured worries that Sigrid may not have made it to the north alive in the first instance, but now, each and every worry that he had ever had in his entire life simply melted away.

"Mother I..." Sylfia started to speak as Sigrid and Jarl parted for a moment. Upon seeing her mother, Sylfia had felt the waves of guilt for what she had done wash over her, and she could not help but remember that all of this was her fault.

Sigrid took a step towards her daughter with a stern look upon her face, but after the tiniest of moments, she leapt at Sylfia and pulled her tightly against herself in a warm and loving hug.

"My daughter! I can see the pain in your eyes. None of this is any of your fault," Sigrid whispered into Sylfia's ear. "You have done nothing wrong, my daughter, and we are all safe as a family.

Eventually, Sigrid and Sylfia parted, and Sigrid's attention turned to Hilda, who was standing awkwardly by the wayside.

"And who is this?" Sigrid asked with a straight expression on her face.

"Mother, this is..." Sylfia began to speak, though Hilda interrupted her.

"My name is Hilda, and I have come from the Baldur's Children clan," she said with a smile.

"We have a lot to talk about," Jarl announced when he saw the look of confusion on his wife's face. Another woman was travelling with her husband and daughter, and the announcement of a clan that she had never heard of would not be easy to follow.

"When we travelled to the east, we came across mostly barren lands, but there was a settlement there like no other I have ever seen before," Jarl recounted their adventures to the east, although he struggled to remember all of the details as so much had happened. However, he managed to remember most of the events, but when Sylfia eventually spoke, he was surprised at what she had to add to the story.

"I found that I was able to leave Baldur's Circle without fading away into the wind, and so I left the settlement shortly after we had arrived. I travelled back into the woods to find my swords. When father had found me close to death the first time, it was because I had fought with a wolf. I do not know if this animal was Loki himself or he had simply been a part of the intent, though his involvement was clear."

Jarl remained silent as Sylfia spoke as he had not yet heard what she had been doing when they had been separated.

"I had dropped my swords when I fought the wolf and I thought that it would be a good idea to go and get them back. I did not know if Baldur's Children were going to be a threat to us, so I thought it would be better to have them with me."

"That was most probably a good thought, though to travel back to an area you know to be dangerous to retrieve weapons that you may or may not have needed is a little foolish, daughter," Sigrid said calmly and Sylfia realised that this comment was more to teach for the future than to discipline for the past.

"The second time I went into that forest, I could hear the beast approaching again, but this time I met someone else in need," Sylfia trailed off as she noticed that her father's astonished expression. "It was a woman, and she begged me to pick up my weapons and fight the beast. She told me that her name was Elli and that she was the Goddess of old age, but as soon as I picked up my swords, she attacked me. I found out later that the Gods cannot attack mortals unless they are threatened, and the woman was not truly Elli. It was the trickster God Loki, again in disguise."

"You make a habit of speaking with the Gods in person?" Hilda asked incredulously. "This is surely not a normal thing for the people of the west?" She looked to Sigrid and Jarl for agreement, and both shook their heads.

"Before our meeting with Hodur today, I have never thought that the Gods were anything more than stories to keep the weak in line."

Sigrid looked at Jarl questioningly, though all he said was "later"; right now, he just wanted to hear what Sylfia had to say.

"Loki almost killed me once more," Sylfia said, "and he would have done if it was not for father crossing the boundary out of the settlement to catch me and take me into safety. He should have died..."

"I did not die though, Sigrid, do not worry," Jarl said with a smile.

"This one has a bit of a talent for getting people out of the settlement," Hilda said with a gesture towards Sylfia.

Sylfia nodded. "It is true. My tears made it possible for the army of Baldur's Children to leave their captivity, but before that, whilst I was unconscious for a long time, a vision came to me."

Again, Jarl was shocked that he was only just learning of this now. He wasn't sure why Sylfia had waited for so long to say anything but thought that perhaps it was because she had worried that everyone around her was going to die, and that it would be her fault. He hoped reverently that the reunion between the three family members had alleviated some of that guilt.

"And this vision, what did it show to you?" Sigrid pressed.

"It... it showed father dying," Sylfia said with an exhale, remembering the worst part of her vision first. "It was terrible. He screamed for mercy." She raised her gaze to meet Jarl's, who was not yet sure how to respond, so remained silent.

"But one of Odin's ravens came to me," Sylfia said quickly. And Elli - the real Elli and not Loki's disguise. She told me what I had been told by Elder Wise when I was younger, that I could prevent the passing of Ragnarök if I simply chose the most difficult of paths. She told me to find the Naglfar Ship and destroy it so that the armies of the damned would never come.

"That is... that is a very big task for you to undertake," Sigrid said. "Did this vision show you anything else?"

"Loki came to me then. He said that if the other Gods could show me glimpses of my future, then he could as well. He showed me that the Naglfar ship lies to the north, stuck beneath a mountain and that I would never find it without the help of those who mean the most to me," she looked up to both of her parents.

"He said that the cost to find the Naglfar ship... the cost would be the deaths of people I love. When I told him that I did not believe him, he freed me from his curse and allowed me to return to the land of the living."

The room fell silent for a while as Sylfia completed her recount of her and Jarl's time away from the west. Jarl then told Sigrid about the army of Baldur's Children, their size and powers, everything up to the moment that Sigrid had walked through the door to this room, including the end of the clans of the west.

"And who is she?" Sigrid asked, gesturing to Hilda. "Is this a princess that you have promised to deliver to some distant lands for the promise of wealth and fame?"

Hilda laughed at Sigrid's words.

"No, friend. I am a cook!" she announced, and with that, she cupped her hands together in a gesture that both Jarl and Sylfia had seen on so many occasions, and offered Sigrid the perfectly cooked steak that she held once the light that accompanied her magic had dissipated. Jarl gave Sigrid a single nod in response to her astonished gaze to confirm it was safe to take, and Sigrid grasped it and promptly ate it as though she had been starving for weeks.

"How...?" Sigrid managed to squeeze out between mouthfuls.

"As I have told you, these are the powers that the Gods have given to us," Jarl handled one of his hand axes and willed the weapon aflame. Sigrid jumped in surprise and Jarl quickly extinguished his weapon.

"And you, daughter? Have you been given the power to speak to animals? Or perhaps even to the Gods at your leisure?" Sigrid asked with wide eyes.

"Not exactly..." Sylfia replied with a warring expression on her face. "My power is not so much something that you can see, but it gives others the power to aid me on my path. That is why Baldur's Children were able to leave their settlement once they had consumed my tears..." She did not mention that she believed it *more* than gave people the ability to help her; she had already been told that her power more than convinced people to come to her aid, and then gave them certain resistances to follow up on that desire. She was certain that it was this power that had made Jarl follow her across the Chasm in the first place, had positioned Torgen into freeing her from the Baldur's Circle prison, and was perhaps even the reason that Hilda had come along on this journey.

"Can I receive these powers?" Sigrid asked after a long pause.

Jarl shook his head in reply. "No... the powers are given by the tears of the God within Baldur's Circle. If we ever see that place again, perhaps you will be granted their divine will, although that place may not be there when we return, now that Hodur has learnt of what is happening there with his own tears."

Sigrid nodded slowly in acceptance. She seemed disappointed by the answer although it was difficult to miss something that one never had experienced. Jarl knew that if his or Hilda's powers had been taken from them, their onward journey would have been far more complicated than it stood now.

"What about you, wife. How do you find yourself here in the north? And what happened when you left the Rakki clan?" Jarl asked, and the question made Sigrid wince as though there was an actual physical pain component attached to it.

"I... after it was found that you and Sylfia had left to cross the Chasm, the clan met to deliberate upon your punishment. Halvard is... I suppose was... hell-bent on making an example of you both so that none would follow you across. He tripled the guard at the Chasm to make sure that if you returned you would never be free of imprisonment. But the clan was unhappy that they could not punish you directly, so they turned to the next best thing – something that you both loved and cared for."

Sylfia felt as though someone was crushing her heart with their bare hands as her mother spoke. The feeling of guilt was simply too much and when she looked at her father, she knew that he too was battling with the very same emotion.

"I was placed in a cell and fed nothing for two days while the clan members concluded. In the end, there was just one who objected to my punishment."

"Eric?" Jarl blurted out hopefully.

Sigrid nodded. "He did not want to see harm come to me, but there was nothing he could do."

Sylfia's head hung at the mention of her late uncle. She just hoped that he was now safe and well in the halls of Valhalla.

"The clan decided that exile from all of the western clans was the punishment that would be enforced on the families of any who cross the Gods' Chasm, breaking our most sacred of laws. All of the western clans were notified and I was set free."

Jarl's expression did not change.

"I was given food and water for a week and told that no western settlement would ever become my home. I was also not allowed to cross over the God's Chasm. I think they wanted me to eat all of the food immediately as I was so hungry, but as I left the settlement, I took not one single bite. I did not know where I was going to go but did not want to give them the satisfaction."

Jarl smiled at those words. His wife had always been both strong and stubborn, and he liked that about her.

"And you went north? Why?" Sylfia asked.

Sigrid turned her attention to Sylfia. "Because my choices were to go either south or north, and I knew there were once great clans to the north, who had no recent ties with the western lands. I could have travelled south and eventually found the open waters, but I do not enjoy boats."

"You do not enjoy boats? Who in this world does not enjoy boats?" Sylfia asked with a smile. She knew that her mother was joking, but she had not yet given a good reason for her journey to the north.

"I must confess that there was something more," Sigrid said with renewed seriousness to her tone. "Until I heard your words of the Gods and their interventions and power, I would not have believed that it was anything more than the hallucinations of a starving woman... but I believe that I heard a voice that told me to head north, where I would find family again. I did not know that the words would be so literal."

Sylfia's eyes bulged. "Who was it? Who told you to head north?"

"I do not know, daughter. But whoever they were, I will be eternally grateful to them," Sigrid replied. Despite believing her though, Sylfia could not help but think there was more to this story than met the eye.

"Then I travelled north. What else was there for me to do?" Sigrid continued. "I thought to look for settlements that the western clans would have no influence over; clans that would give me shelter, food and warmth, and in return I could work for them."

"And did you find any clans or settlements?" Sylfia asked.

Sigrid shook her head. "As I moved into the north, the cold became quickly unbearable. It was clear from the ruins of settlements that I came across that these people had all left long ago. I do not know to where they fled, but in all of my time since leaving the Rakki clan settlement, I have not seen another living soul, that is unless you count the wolves who have been circling me, of course."

"Wolves?" Jarl said quickly.

"Yes," Sigrid replied, looking at Jarl now. "For the last few days. I do not know if it is because they can sense that my food has all but run out or if it is mere coincidence, but these wolves seem to be tracking me. They are always just out of sight though they howl at the night's sky and are never too far away."

A loud howl in the distance punctuated Sigrid's last statement, and she looked at the roof as though the creatures were above them.

"These wolves, father, must have been sent by Loki to keep us from finding the mountains!" Sylfia exclaimed. "He would do anything to keep us from that place, but he cannot interfere with our journey directly. They must be here to try to scare us away!"

"And a good job of that they will do too, daughter. We have no business, the four of us fighting against a pack of wolves and we do not need to hunt or forage for food, so we can leave them be and make our camp in this place. It is warm here and safe from the vile winter beyond."

"But this is no ordinary winter, father; this is the Fimbulwinter! Hodur told you himself! This is not some storm that we can sit here in comfort and ride out, waiting for the greenery of summer to arrive!"

"We have nowhere else to go!" Jarl's voice raised to match Sylfia's. He had just got his wife back, and the last thing on his mind was to put at risk everything he held dear to follow some fairy tale into a snow-covered mountain."

"Your father is right, Sylfia," Sigrid sided with Jarl. "We must make a more permanent base before we do anything drastic and this place is as good as any. We have nowhere to go, and if that means that our new settlement shall begin with us four, then that is what we must do."

"You have spoken to an actual God, and I have been sent by the Gods to enact their will. To prevent the passing of

Ragnarök! How can you not see that we must do what is right for the world, father? What is right for every single human being in existence?!"

"Sylfia... you must listen to your parents..." Hilda spoke softly to bring the tension in the room back down to a manageable level. "They will always have your best interests at heart, and they will always do what they need to do to keep you safe. You must understand that?"

Sylfia sighed heavily. "I do understand. But right now, my path is dangerous, and in order to carry out the will of the Gods, I will have to place myself in danger..." she looked at each of the three others in the room in turn pointedly. "I am not asking you to throw your lives away on some whim. I am asking you to come with me, to aid me in my struggle to save the world from total destruction. Will you help me?"

Hilda, Sigrid and Jarl kept their mouths tightly shut. They each knew that the next words they would speak would be of total agreement with Sylfia and they did not even question why. She had asked for help, and they would each answer that call, no matter what.

Before any of them could reply, a single black raven flew down from the open ceiling above them and perched above the door. Jarl could see that it was missing an eye, and its face spoke of an unknown intelligence.

"What is this?" Jarl said as he took two steps towards the bold bird.

"Is this not proof of what I have been saying to you?" Sylfia asked. "This is one of Odin's ravens, and you can now see that he has been watching over me. Look into his eyes and see what I have seen."

"This is not..." Jarl started to speak as he took a step towards the perched bird. He was about to say that this was not proof of anything, but he stopped when the raven turned its head and Jarl could see into the hole where the bird's eye should have been.

Within the eye of the bird, the darkness grew and grew until it encompassed Jarl's entire field of vision. Blackness turned to white, and Jarl realised that he was looking at the outside of this building from above, with snow covering the entire world except for the roof. The view darted, and it took a moment for Jarl to realise that he was looking down on the world as though through the eyes of this bird. He did not know if what he saw was the past, present or future, but he knew instinctively that something important was going to happen.

Then he saw the wolves. Three giant grey beasts prowled a hundred feet to the north of the building, which stood alone, any other constructions having not ever existed or having been lost to the ravages of time.

The wolves growled and stalked low to the ground, though being larger than any wolf that Jarl had ever seen, he was unsure if this was merely to intimidate their prey. They had not seen the raven flying high above them though, as they moved closer and closer to the building.

A thought turned Jarl's blood ice cold: what if this was happening right now and these beasts were about to break into the building and kill them all, with Jarl left helpless as he watched it happen through the eyes of the raven?

But his heartbeat lowered as he remembered that the bird was inside the building with them so there was no way that this could be happening now.

The wolves reached the door to the building and stopped, huddled together. They waited for a short moment and then, in turn, they leapt at the door. The first hit made it bang and rattle loudly, while the second caused snow to shake free from the walls of the building. The third wolf, though, broke the wooden door free from its hinges, and it fell into the warm building.

The viewpoint of the raven swooped down and followed the wolves inside. Jarl could feel the warmth blast into it as the heat from the fire reached its feathers, and he saw the people inside ready themselves to fight the aggressive beasts.

Jarl saw himself first. He was holding both axes high and ablaze, standing before his wife and daughter. Next to him stood Hilda wielding her straight, short sword. The wolves had slowed in their approach but were taking small, deliberate steps forward towards the group. If they continued, the group would be backed into a corner.

Jarl watched as he lunged at the central wolf with both axes in a deadly overhead strike. He could see from the raven's viewpoint that the strike was desperate, poorly executed and would not cause the beast any real trouble if it managed to evade the obvious attack.

And the wolf did move from the path of the attack. It swung its giant head up into the air so that Jarl's axes would be able to reach nothing but its mouth, if at all anything, and as the strike came down the beast bit down hard, severing both of Jarl's arms at the elbows.

Jarl's scream was silenced within a moment as a second wolf clamped its jaws down over his head, leaving his decapitated corpse to fall to the ground with a thud.

Hilda leapt forward as Sigrid and Sylfia stood petrified with shock, their mouths hanging agape, but her own attack could do little more than Jarl's. Hilda flicked her blade back and forth at the three wolves, unsure of which to attack, but they were clearly too intelligent to fall for her bravado. Eventually, the three separated and Hilda's defences were too wide to be effective, the outer two wolves awaiting their chance to strike.

Eventually, Hilda's attention was split far enough for the outer pair to lunge together and as one bit into her chest and shoulder, the other wrapped its huge maw around both of her legs. It only took a moment and a small amount of effort from the giant wolves, but Hilda fell to the ground, broken into three bloodied pieces without so much as a scream.

Jarl had been so focused on watching the wolves that he had failed to notice that both Sylfia and Sigrid had crept around the inner wall of the building and out through the doorway the wolves had left open. Suddenly the viewpoint of the raven flew from the building, through the doorway, and high up into the sky so Jarl again had an overhead view of the white world below.

From above, he could see his wife and daughter running through the snow as fast as their legs would carry them, and he internally willed them to run faster and faster away from this place. And then he saw the wolves, all three with deep red blood covering their mouths and grey fur, bearing down on the two women. Within an instant, they were upon them. Both Sigrid and Sylfia drew their weapons, twin swords for Sylfia and a single axe to Sigrid's hand, although they did not turn to fight but kept running until the last moment.

The wolves pounced. It was over in an instant, the great beasts flattening Jarl's wife and daughter to the ground and removing their heads with their sharp teeth and powerful jaws in a moment.

22

Jarl's eyes snapped open, and his attention returned to the room. He did not know for how long he had been staring into the eyes of the raven, but he knew that what he had just witnessed, he never wanted to think about again. He stared into the eyes of Sigrid and Sylfia and reorganised his thoughts.

"Father, are you OK?" Sylfia asked slowly, her face etched with concern. "Did the raven show you a vision?"

Jarl could not yet bring himself to speak though he nodded slightly. His face was as white as snow, and it was obvious that whatever he had seen had shaken him to his very core.

Finally able to speak, Jarl grunted: "We must not stay here. It is not safe with the wolves circling." He spared a glance at the raven, worried that it might have deigned to show him more of their future, but it simply sat there, silently looking into the distance.

"I knew that you would come to understand, father!" Sylfia exclaimed with a smile. "We must head north and find the tallest mountain, and there we will find the caverns that will lead us to the Naglfar ship."

Both Sigrid and Hilda wore uneasy expressions, and it was clear that they were unsure of this path, although neither of them objected.

"I do not see another path. The future has been made clear to me if we stay in this place, it will end with all of our deaths," Jarl explained quietly. The raven cawed in agreement.

"How..." Sigrid began to say, but from the look on Jarl's face she knew that his mind would not be changed, and he would not be pressed on this matter.

"OK, then how do we proceed now, husband? Do we continue north on an aimless path until we find some huge mountain with a doorway carved into its base?" Sigrid asked.

"I do not know the answer to these questions," Jarl replied truthfully. "All that I know is that if we remain here, we will all die. The wolves circling your path will come for us, and we will not be able to beat them."

"Do you know how long we have before they come?" Sigrid asked.

Jarl shook his head. In truth, he had no idea, but he did not want to wait and find out.

"Then we shall leave this place. We will continue north and trust in the Gods, and Sylfia," Hilda announced with a smile of her own. "The Gods have given Sylfia a path to walk, and I will trust that they will see fit to keep her moving in the right direction."

The raven cawed again as if in agreement. It then flew down from its perch above the doorway and stood before the door as though to show that it was ready to go. It was still dark outside though, and Jarl had always preferred to move during the daylight hours when it was easier to see where they were going, see incoming threats, and keep an eye on each other. The dark was dangerous, and each of them knew it, but the raven had other ideas.

"Can we wait until the daylight?" Jarl asked the raven, hoping that it could understand what he was asking, but the bird simply hopped towards the door and pecked at it impatiently. They all knew what its answer was.

"Then, if we must go now, we must all be in agreement," Jarl said to the others and awaited their response.

"I will follow Sylfia on her path," Hilda announced first.

"I will not lose my husband and daughter again," Sigrid said firmly. "We will go wherever it is that we are meant to."

"Then we have no other choice but to leave," Jarl said, toying with his braided beard. He took a long look at the warm fire and all of the firewood stacked nearby. This would have been the perfect place to camp for an extended period of time, but he knew that if the threat was truly as bad as he had seen, they needed to leave as soon as possible.

Without so much as a fond farewell to the shelter the building had provided, Jarl opened the wooden door to the cold, dark air outside and the group stepped out as one into the night.

The wind was not as bitter as it had been during the previous day and the snowfall had abated somewhat, so visibility was not as poor as it had been. Jarl lit both of his axes and led the group from the front with the weapons held high overhead. They made for effective torches and Sylfia was relieved that she could see a respectable distance all around as the group moved, as it would make defending themselves against any dangers at least a little easier.

The first wolves' howls in the distance reached the group within a few minutes of their departure, and Jarl could not tell if these howls were because the animals had discovered they had left or if it was simply part of their nature. Whatever the reason, it made his blood run cold and he instinctively quickened his pace.

Once outside the door, the raven flew in a northern direction and was quickly out of sight. Sylfia had seen its direction, so she presumed that it would make its presence known when it was once again needed.

"Do you think that the wolves are coming for us?" Hilda asked in an almost whisper.

"It would take more than wolves to take my family away from me for a second time," Sigrid replied, and Hilda could hear both her smile and determination in her voice.

"These beasts are unlike anything I have ever seen before. They are wolves but they are at least three times the size they should be," Jarl said, glancing over his shoulder.

"These beasts are of Loki," Sylfia said confidently. "It was a giant wolf that attacked me once before, although then it was Loki in disguise. If there are more, I would guess that he had some hand in their creation at least."

This news did not reach Jarl well; if an actual God was going to try to stop them on their journey, then he as a mortal being, would not be able to do much to stand against it.

The wolves did not come any closer but simply howled in the distance as though to let the group know that they were still being watched. Sylfia wondered if it was the raven's presence that was keeping the group safe, but she knew that whatever their help was, it was probably going to fade especially as they came closer to the snow-covered mountain, when Loki's attempts to stop them would likely grow more frantic.

Eventually, the sun began to rise on the horizon and for a brief while, the white snow surrounding the group turned to a welcoming orange. The glowing ball of light that brought a slight warmth where there had been none before rose in the east to their right and made their shadows flow long to their left. The eerie silence of the first morning light gave Sylfia new confidence that they would somehow make it.

"Do you think that I can get a power like yours?" Sigrid called to Jarl as he strode onward. "I think it would come in useful, not just in battle. If you had been out here in the north on your own without any fire, you would know just how lucky you are."

"Do not forget mine!" Hilda nudged Sigrid. "I would be willing to wager that you would not have had as many troubles if you had not had to search for food!"

Sigrid could not agree more. If she had had both warmth and food without so much as lifting a finger, she would have had a much easier time since being exiled, and she welcomed the fact that her daughter had not had to struggle as she herself had.

"There!" Sylfia called out excitedly pointing upwards. Jarl, Sigrid and Hilda followed Sylfia's outstretched arm and saw what she was pointing at. The raven had returned, circling high above them as though it did not have a care in the world.

It flew high into the air before divebombing almost all the way to the ground, pulling up into a glide at the last minute and flying straight and true just slightly off the path that the group walked. It was clear that the raven was correcting their course and Jarl dutifully obliged.

"With the will of the Gods on our side, how could we possibly fail?" he asked with laughter in his tone. Sylfia's smile, though, was quickly wiped from her face when the howl of a wolf came from her right, followed rapidly by two more, ending in a terrifying symphony. Whatever was happening, it felt as if something had changed.

Jarl too felt the change and picked up his pace to almost a slow jog, and the rest of the group dutifully matched his speed. They did not know how far they needed to go, but dawdling in the open whilst the beasts made their next move would not serve them well.

Sylfia watched as the raven flew off high into the air again and swooped off to the right toward the wolves. She hoped that it would remain safe and give them a little time to reach somewhere a little more protected.

In the distance were the beginnings of high peaks, though they were still far far away and between them and these mountains Sylfia could see nothing but flat, open snow. There would be nowhere to shelter as far as any of them could see, and that meant that if the beasts did decide to attack, they would have no choice but to stand and fight in the open. It was this thought that kept Jarl's legs pumping into the soft snow over and over, the thought of his family's safety set firmly in his mind's eye.

The wolves howled again, louder this time, and Sylfia thought that at any moment, the beasts would appear to her right, darting towards her.

Although the landscape was mostly flat and pure white with snow, Sylfia could not see all around her for miles and miles; wherever there were gentle hills or dips, her line of sight was cut short, and this was what the wolves must have been using to mask their approach, keeping out of sight until they were ready to strike.

All the time they walked, Jarl kept his axes ablaze and to the ready, ready to defend himself and his family at any given moment.

"They are near, and they are coming," Jarl warned over his shoulder as the group moved onward. He did not want to add to their fear, but he needed everyone to be ready, and as though following instruction, each member of the party drew their weapons.

"When they come, aim all of your attacks at their eyes. If they cannot see you, they cannot attack you," Jarl ordered. Although this sounded the right thing to do, Sylfia knew that if these three wolves were anything like the single one she had fought before, her family would have little chance of survival.

It all happened so fast. To the group's right, the raven cawed and flew at immense speed towards them at head height, behind it bounding three giant grey wolves, snapping at the air. They were nowhere near the raven, although they tried to catch it as though it was their main focus. Then the wolves' eyes met Jarl's, Sylfia's, Sigrid's and Hilda's, and without missing a beat they changed their angle of approach ever so slightly to head directly for the party of mortals. The group turned and faced the beasts with their weapons to the ready.

Sylfia swallowed hard, dreading the approach of the fearsome animals. Jarl's thoughts turned back to the vision he had seen when the wolves had killed his entire party, and he struggled to remember any detail that would possibly help them in the upcoming fight. In the end, though, he could think of nothing so simply held his axes to the ready and awaited the exchange of first blows.

As they approached, the three wolves, changed their formation into one line behind a single wolf. It was a strange way to approach a battle, Jarl thought, but it at least meant that his party would only have one beast to deal with at a time to begin with. He fretted that he did not know what this tactic was though, and that was surely a disadvantage if the wolves did something unexpected.

"Behind me!" Jarl cried to his wife, daughter, and Hilda once he had made his mind up – if these beasts wanted to fight one on one, then he would stand up to that challenge.

The wolves stopped no more than a few metres from Jarl as he stood with his axes blazing white hot by his sides. His vision had already shown him that holding them high above his head would mean his arms would be torn off, so he kept them within his guard until he was ready to move.

The front wolf, a huge grey beast, stepped forward, closing the distance between it and Jarl in a moment whilst the other pair lowered their heads and snarled. It was clear that this was to be a battle between champions. The tension in the still air was palpable, and Jarl could see that the wolf's fur was bloodied and matted from a previous victorious battle. His muscles tensed as he gripped his axes as tightly as he could.

Abruptly, Jarl let out a fierce war cry and took the advantage for himself. Swinging his first axe at the giant beast, the flaming weapon flashed through the air, catching the wolf by surprise, its fur crackling as the flames licked at it. It let out a howl more of anger than pain and reared up on its hind legs. The beast showed its full height now, and standing tall it was at least three times the height of Jarl, who stepped back and readied his guard.

The wolf lunged at Jarl, but the skilled warrior was too quick and had seen the attack projected as though it had been in slow motion. He side-stepped the lunge, the wolf's sharp, bared teeth that were ready to sink into mortal flesh found nothing but cold air. Jarl swung an axe in a fierce backswing and caught the wolf's ear as it moved to avoid his counter. Jarl could tell by its movements that the beast was intelligent.

The pair once again faced off on equal footing, Jarl's shoulders rising and falling as the fatigue of battle began to set in. The wolf lunged again and as Jarl made to skip out of the way, it changed its trajectory again, darting to where Jarl had moved to. It clattered into Jarl and knocked him to the ground easily.

Jarl brought his flaming axes up before his face without a moment to spare. The wolf, fuelled by its primal instincts and sensing the end of this battle, opened its terrible maw and snapped at Jarl's face and only the intense heat of the flaming axes kept it from biting his head off in one fell swoop.

Jarl knew now that he was no match for this adversary. He was a skilled warrior with a divine power to call upon, but he was still a mortal man. He held the wolf's mouth at bay as best he could, and as he lay on the ground, he looked up above himself at Sylfia and Sigrid and did all that he could to imprint their faces into his mind's eye so that he could take the memory of their faces with him to Valhalla, if that was where he was destined to go.

The wolf seemed to sense Jarl's acceptance of his end and it stepped back and allowed him to drop his axes to the ground, where they extinguished themselves and sizzled for a moment, melting small circles of snow.

"Father, NO!" Sylfia screamed and the three wolves snarled at her as a warning not to interfere with this fight.

"It is OK, daughter. I give my life to save my family. You must go on from this place. Continue along your path."

All hope was lost. But then a sudden commotion from the east distracted the wolf. A jet-black raven, its wings flapping wildly, swooped down from the sky and landed on the forwardmost wolf's head before it could do anything to prevent it. It began to peck wildly at the wolf's eyes and face, frenziedly trying to keep the wolf from delivering the final blow.

Jarl dug into his last reserves and seized the opportunity that the raven had handed to him. He scooped up one of his hand axes and with a fierce cry, swung it at the wolf's neck, the weapon bursting into flame as it cut through the air. Although the wolf's neck was thick and wide, the blade bit deep and Jarl struck again and again, the animal's blood spurting out with each strike until he had cut through, and with a final gurgle, the wolf slumped to the ground with a thud, its head rolling away from its body. Jarl had won, but without the raven's help, he knew he would not have had the chance.

The pair of wolves that remained on their feet howled in rage as the raven flew towards them. Jarl did not know what the bird could accomplish without the element of surprise and in a two-on-one situation, but he would not squander the opportunity. He scooped his second axe from the ground and shouted "RUN!" to the rest of the group.

None of the women needed to be told twice. They turned on their heels with one last look at the raven and the pair of wolves and lifted their feet from the ground.

They had no idea how far they would need to run before reaching any kind of safety, but they all knew that nowhere could be worse than the open plains, facing off against this pair of angry wolves. Now they had proven that the animals could be killed, although no one expected that they would be given a chance for a one-on-one fight again after the unfair intervention of the helpful raven.

Above the pounding and crunching of their feet in the snow, their heavy panting breaths and the thoughts of any kind of salvation running through their heads, the group could hear the wolves howling far behind them. Although though they could not know how the raven kept the wolves busy and away from their retreat, they would be eternally grateful to the bird.

A long, steady incline added to their exhaustion. As though running in thick snow was not difficult enough, the slight incline made their legs burn with every step. The sound of heavy footsteps behind them spurred them on, and when Sylfia took a second to look back behind her, she saw the pair of very angry wolves bearing down on them, one with blood around its mouth and the lifeless form of the raven hanging out from one side. Their saviour had indeed paid the ultimate price for their one chance at escape.

Sylfia knew already though that barring some new miracle, there would be no escape for them this time. If over the crest of this incline, there was simply more snow to cross before they arrived at the tall snow-covered mountain, the wolves would easily reach and tear them apart as they had the raven.

The group raced, their speed increasing as the wolves grew nearer, their paws pounding the snow easily beneath them. The only thing the group could do at this moment was to keep running, to keep moving at all costs.

As they neared the summit of the incline, Sylfia hatched the beginnings of a plan and drew both of her swords, instructing the rest to follow suit with their own weapons.

"When we get to the other side, lie flat on the ground, and as the wolves pass us, take them out from beneath!" she gasped.

Sylfia could feel the hot breath of one of the wolves behind her and could hear its terrible sharp teeth clattering together as it tried to reach her as she ran. And suddenly, they were there at the top of the hill, and Sylfia and the others immediately slid onto their backs.

The plan would not be so easy to enact, though, as all four of them found themselves unable to stop sliding, the far side of the hill being a sheet of pure ice that led down into a deep chasm with a single wooden rope bridge spanning it.

They could not stop, and the bridge was not in the right place for them to arrive at if they were able to reach it.

The wolves, though, also found that they could not stop, and with a yelp, they scrambled to find purchase on the ice slope that would lead everyone to their doom.

Thankfully, Sylfia, Hilda, Sigrid and Jarl had taken their weapons to hand before cresting the hill, and they fought to imbed their forged and sharpened blades into the ice to combat their momentum. Fortunately, as they began to slow, the pair of great wolves were too distracted by their own plight to notice that they had passed their prey.

The group eventually came to a halt halfway down the icy slope and they watched as the wolves could not prevent themselves from falling into the dark abyss that the rope bridge spanned. The last thing they heard from the beasts was an echoey yelp followed by complete silence.

23

Sylfia could not believe they had managed to evade the wolves, but Jarl was sure this task could not have been that easy. The raven had given him a dire warning and it had helped them in their fight against the great beasts, but it just seemed far too easy.

With the last fading howl of the falling wolves, the air that had remained calm while the group had fought quickly turned once more. The first winds whipped into Jarl's face as he looked to the narrow bridge spanning the chasm below, and he wondered if the construction had not been used in years. Moreover, he wondered who had built it; had it been left from a long-forgotten settlement or was it placed there precisely for

Sylfia to carry out her task? He had questions without answers again, and to Jarl, that meant danger.

"The wind is picking up again," Sylfia announced as the group collectively raised themselves, although she was stating the obvious; the wind was almost strong enough to slide each of them along the ice if they let their attention wane, but along with the wind, it had begun to snow again. The flakes fell silently at first, but as the wind collected them and whipped them through the air, battering each of them, they knew that whatever God controlled this weather did not want this crossing to be simple.

Beyond the wood and rope bridge, before visibility narrowed and shortened, Sylfia could see that a narrow path led on towards the tallest mountain in the distance, and she instinctively knew that this singular path would lead to her intended destination and the Naglfar ship. She still did not know what was going to happen once they reached the ship and everything that it contained, but that was a problem for the future.

"We must continue forwards!" Sylfia cried above the now howling winds. "The bridge will lead us into the mountain path and to the tallest snow-covered mountain!"

Jarl had seen the path too, but was pleased that Sylfia was taking the initiative to command the group. He was a natural-born leader himself, but raising a daughter to walk in his footsteps was one of his proudest achievements.

"And then what?" Hilda called back. "The bridge does not look as though it can take our weight, let alone all of us at once!"

"It will hold," Sylfia replied confidently. "This is the way that we are supposed to go."

It made sense to Sylfia; the bridge had been provided by whatever means so their journey could continue. She would not question it nor hypothesise about its origins; it had been provided, and therefore it would be used.

Jarl sheathed one of his axes and held the other aloft. It ignited, turning into a bright yellow beacon in the blizzard that had begun to rage around them. He was grateful for the little warmth that it provided, although he knew that they could not last in this climate for long; his toes had begun to turn numb where he stood.

"Follow me!" he cried at the top of his voice. "We will find shelter, and we will rest, but we must leave this storm behind!"

No one objected to that, and as one, they followed the burning axe of their leader to the near side of the bridge.

The bridge itself was constructed of wound ropes and flat planks of wood. It appeared to have been made long ago for some long-lost settlement here in the north and had not been used for some time. Long icicles hung from the ropes and the planks all the way across its twenty or thirty-metre length, and when it reached the other side, it was tied into long wooden stakes driven deep into the ground. It hung low in the middle and if it had been pulled tighter it would have provided a more stable footing for those crossing it, but Sylfia thought silently that any bridge was better than no bridge at all – after all, when she had crossed the God's Chasm – twice – she had been forced to scale the walls.

"I will cross first," Hilda shouted to the group and strode past Jarl before he could set foot on the bridge. "If the Gods truly bless Sylfia, the bridge will not fail until she has crossed safely." The wind whipped her red braided hair as she shouted her words and in a moment of clarity, Sigrid could see why Hilda had been brought along with her husband and daughter. This woman was not a simple magical cook who kept them well-fed – she was a friend too. Sigrid could see through Hilda's deception - Hilda was putting herself at risk so that the rest of them did not have to.

"Once I have crossed, the rest of you shall follow. Do not set foot on this bridge until I have made it across, is that understood?"

The group nodded as one and Hilda stepped forward, alone and into the blizzard without a torch to light her path.

Hilda clutched the rope railings of the bridge tightly as she began to inch her way across. The wooden slats had not been densely packed and there were gaps beneath her feet, so she had to look down as she walked to ensure she didn't step straight through the slats. She could see the snow falling around her and disappearing into the dark abyss below.

Sylfia, Sigrid and Jarl watched as Hilda disappeared from their view after just a few metres, the rising storm hiding her from them as though playing some divine joke on them all. The storm swallowed her up, and she would not be seen again until they were all reunited on the far side of the bridge.

The icy winds of the blizzard howled around Hilda, continuing to whip her long red hair into a frenzy. She could neither see the other side of the bridge nor the side that she had departed from through the thick curtain of snow, but she knew that she had no choice but to press onward.

Then she heard a voice carrying on the winds and stopped, listening intently.

"This is not the path of mortals... you must turn back or face eternal damnation," the voice rasped. Hilda closed her eyes and shook her head. These were not the words that a God would speak, and she knew it.

"Hilda?! The storm is getting worse!" Jarl's voice cut through the storm and wiped away all thoughts of voices on the wind. "We must hurry!"

The bridge had begun to swing wildly, and as every second passed that Hilda inched her way across, the task was becoming more difficult as the intensity of the storm reached new levels.

Then the bridge lurched, raising her up into the air and dropping away from beneath her as though it was trying to throw her off entirely and as she fell back onto it, her foot slipped on the icy planks and she lost her footing entirely. Hilda slipped off the bridge.

She flailed her arms about searching for anything that would afford her purchase and at the last second, before falling to her doom as the wolves had before her, her fingertips felt the frozen twisted rope that ran alongside the bridge, a part of its base and she wrapped her fingers around the rope as best she could and clung on for dear life. She dangled below the bridge, hanging from the rope for a moment before the realisation struck that between her fatigue, the storm and the icy, slippery rope, she could not raise herself back onto the bridge. This was to be her end and there was nothing that she could do about it. The rest would wonder what had happened to her, though nobody would ever know the truth.

Then as all hope had filtered away, a cold, rough hand grasped her wrist and pulled her back up onto the bridge with a strength and ease that surprised her. And when she opened her eyes to meet her saviour, she found Jarl, a stern and straight expression on his face.

"We must move now," he commanded without any word or acknowledgement of how he had just saved her life.

Hilda looked beyond Jarl and saw that the others had joined her on the bridge. She knew it was foolish to test the bridge with their combined weight but realised that with the bridge now holding the four of them, where once it had danced in the wind, it hardly moved at all.

They pressed onward with haste across the bridge, not wishing to tempt fate.

Sigrid, bringing up the rear, tried to keep the group at a steady pace, but the icy wood and ropes beneath her feet made it difficult to keep her balance. "I don't know if I can do this!" she cried out, her voice shaking with fear. Her words cut through Jarl, having never heard fear in his wife's tone before.

"Do not worry mother!" Sylfia cried through the blizzard. "The Gods would not allow us to reach this far if we were to be beaten by a simple bridge!"

With those words renewing their vigour, they struggled onwards, but as they moved cautiously across the rope bridge, the winds began to grow even stronger, rocking it violently as though that was the single intent of the raging storm. Hilda felt her stomach drop as the bridge swayed beneath her again, although it was nowhere near as violent as the thrashing that had almost thrown her to her death. She closed her eyes and gritted her teeth, focusing on putting one foot in front of the other.

Finally after what felt like an eternity, the group reached the other side. Exhausted and frozen, they collapsed onto the snowy ground, each of them gasping for breath.

"We did it," Sigrid whispered, tears of relief streaming down her face.

Hilda nodded, her own breath coming in ragged gasps. "We made it across. We're safe."

Jarl released both hand axes from their sheathes and held them out, igniting them to a bright orange flame. It was the best he could do to afford them a little warmth, and as they huddled around him and his divine power, he could see their shaking, grateful faces for this small act.

As though by some divine joke, the storm now began to die down, and Jarl's visibility started to return. He scanned the area beyond the bridge whilst the group huddled for warmth, and eventually, his eyes came across a small section of the mountains beyond that was slightly different to the rest.

"There is a cave!" he announced happily. He did not add that there was also a narrow valley that ran along the centre of the mountains which looked ominous to his eyes, as he knew that the others needed time to rest before they could tackle another test of their mortality.

The women looked to where Jarl had pointed with his flaming axe and eventually, they each saw what he was looking at.

Sylfia was about to ask why they could not simply take the valley path and continue towards their intended destination, but as she opened her mouth, the world beneath their feet shook with a mighty boom. In the distance, the snow atop the mountains began to fall as avalanches triggered all around them. Jarl watched as the snow on the mountain above the cave he had spotted began to shift.

"We must go, NOW!" He shouted and pressed his feet into the snow beneath him.

The others did not need to be told twice. As one, they pounded their feet into the ground, heading towards the cave they had accepted as their destination. It went against Sylfia's nature to run towards the danger, the falling snow, but she knew that if they did not reach the cave's sanctuary then the avalanche would push them back down into the open chasm and to their deaths. They had one chance only, and this was it.

The group ran as fast as their frozen legs and aching muscles would carry them. They had been through far too much already, and this latest task was not something that any of them would have chosen.

The snow on the mountains continued to slide as the world shook beneath their feet. It was enough to make Sylfia stumble, but she managed to keep her footing and ploughed on.

As they grew nearer to the break in the mountain, the darkness beyond betrayed the secret cave. It spoke to them all of salvation, and as it grew closer, Sylfia watched from the corner of her vision as the first dustings of the avalanche began to fall across the cave entrance.

It was going to be so close and Sylfia did not know if they were going to make it, and then suddenly, she dived through the opening and into the hard rock cave beyond. She had made it, and when she looked around, she heaved a sob of relief that the others had too – her father, mother and her friend Hilda.

Jarl relit his hand axes to illuminate the cave around them. It was a small open area, though to the rear it led off into a narrow path away from the outside of the mountain. It was quiet without the wind and the snow to deafen them. There was no way of knowing where the path led, but they were left with no alternative as the avalanche had quickly covered the cave entrance entirely in at least ten feet of snow.

The sound of the storm outside had all but disappeared with the closing of the entrance, and if Jarl had not had his divine gift, they would have been in complete darkness. There did not seem to be any danger around them, but as Jarl had always said, darkness itself in unfamiliar territory was dangerous.

Hilda fell back to sit on the ground, shivering and breathing heavily. As the adrenaline of her ordeal began to wane, all that was left was fear and cold.

Jarl held his axes into the centre of the group, and each of them sank to the ground to rest their aching legs.

"I... I thought I would not make it," Hilda chattered, shaking. "The bridge... the storm..."

"It was indeed as though the Gods did not wish us to be here," Jarl agreed. "I am sorry that you had to go first and alone."

"It... it was my idea," Hilda said, though her words still did not sound confident. "I come from the north... not here, but I thought that I would be more used to dangerous and cold terrain..."

"You come from the north?" Sigrid asked with interest. "Is this your home?"

Hilda shook her head. "I come from the north, yes. The winters were always harsh and we did see some storms. I left a few years ago when the cold was becoming unbearable. That is when I found Baldur's Circle. This place was not my home, I come from far from here and my people would never attempt to cross the mountains. We had little trade with others, which is why the failing lands caused such an issue for my people."

"Why did you not cross the mountains or make trade routes with other northern settlements?" Sylfia asked.

"We did try in the beginnings of our settlements. We made trade with others, alliances and pacts, but as winter fell each year the routes would become blocked or change as some paths became impassable and others opened. We found ourselves reliant upon others, and that was just not sustainable for us. We knew that we needed to be able to survive on our own and over time, the alliances, traders, and any interaction with other settlements faded. It was not until I saw what the Fimbulwinter had done to the settlements as we passed that I realised that no settlements were left in the north any longer. My people, they are all gone."

The others fell silent momentarily as they let Hilda's words settle in.

"We have all lost everything, have we not?" Jarl asked in a low tone. "Except that is, for each other. We are a family, and that is something that can never be taken from any of us."

Hilda looked up at the faces that smiled back at her, each illuminated by the flickering orange glow of Jarl's axes. However this had happened, she had indeed found a family.

"I do not know what I would have done if I was not with you," Hilda said. "Though I think that the people of the north were gone long ago, and though some were my family, I knew that they were lost to me from the moment I entered Baldur's Circle. I am thankful to you, Jarl, for showing me that there is more to life than just surviving."

"We have all lost more than we would ever have thought possible over these last few weeks, but as long as we stay together and look out for each other, there is nothing more that we could ask the Gods for." With that, Jarl looked around the cave to assess the level of danger they were currently in. "I will remain awake and act as sentry as we rest. Then we will press on into wherever this place leads to," Jarl said commandingly.

None of the women objected to his instructions, and as one they moved closer to the large man and his flaming axes so that they could benefit fully from the heat they provided. After they had rested and allowed their weary bodies time to repair themselves, Hilda would provide food for them all to eat.

As Jarl took the first watch, he stared at the only path that led from the cave's entrance with an intensity and seriousness that only a trained sentry could muster. At the same time, he ensured he kept his axes alight so that the warmth they provided never dropped, and his family remained comfortable as they slept. He listened intently for any changes to the sounds around them or, indeed, outside the cave, but nothing happened that drew his attention. Eventually, he swapped places with Sigrid and allowed himself to rest, trying his hardest to keep his axes alight through his slumber, although inevitably the task proved too difficult, and the group was plunged into the silent darkness and cold of their sanctuary.

"Father, it is time for us all to awaken," Sylfia's voice roused Jarl, and when he opened his eyes slowly, he realised he could not see through the darkness that shrouded them and instinctively picked up both of his axes and lit them.

When he looked at his family staring down at him, he could see the cold that offended their faces and bodies. They were shivering, the moisture in their eyes and noses having frozen on their faces, and Jarl realised that his beard had also turned to ice. He guiltily realised that the others had allowed him to rest for as long as possible while they suffered without the warmth of his divine gift.

"You should have awoken me sooner; you are all freezing half to your death!" Jarl announced with shock and concern plastered across his face.

No one replied to his outburst, although they did seem to be sitting a little closer to him as he rose, the warmth from his axes almost immediately staving off the cold. Hilda beamed at him through chattering teeth and handed him a perfectly browned steak.

Jarl's demeanour softened as he took the meat. He loved nothing more than to eat a good breakfast after a long rejuvenating rest.

"Thank you, all of you," Jarl said softly to his group. "If we are all well rested, and once we have regained the feeling in our fingers and toes, we should head into the tunnel and see what lies beyond."

"It must be the way," Sylfia said. "The Gods would not have funnelled us into this cave entrance and blocked the way back if we were not supposed to go this way, would they?"

"Or perhaps it was another of the Gods, looking to keep us from our final destination that led us here and trapped us inside to die?" Hilda added, although Sylfia could see from the smile on her face that she was being at least partly sarcastic.

"Either way, the result is the same," Jarl answered Hilda, missing her tone and intent. "We must continue onward, for no other path is available."

"And who knows, we might find a new home inside these caves?" Sigrid offered, which made Sylfia snort. Sylfia felt as though she hadn't smiled properly in a long time, and as her father had done earlier, she looked around at her new family and realised that there would be nobody else in the world that she would have spent this time with.

"You do not realise how right you are," a woman's voice came from within the tunnel that led deeper into the cave.

"You have entered my domain, and not many are given the opportunity to leave."

The voice was accompanied by a figure walking towards the group. She was clearly female and of average height, but when she walked closer and into the light of the flaming axes, it was clear that she was not entirely flesh-coloured, having a blue tint to her as though she had been frozen and thawed out again.

24

"You have wandered into my domain. Now you must tell me why you have done so and I will decide if you may leave or not," the woman said.

The group stared at the woman who had appeared from seemingly nowhere, with no light of her own and showing no signs of the cold touching her skin. She looked young, as though she was in her late twenties, with straight, jet-black hair, but she spoke with a wisdom and tone that suggested she had many more years behind her than her appearance would suggest.

Jarl's first instinct was to adopt a defensive stance, facing her with both axes held to the ready and both blazing with a new level of intensity.

"What business do you have here with us?" Jarl growled in an almost inaudibly low tone.

"It is as I have said. You are the ones who have walked willingly into my domain, and it is I who will decide whether to let you leave... or not... as the case may be," the woman replied authoritatively.

"I am sick of being told that I cannot leave once I have arrived!" Jarl said more to the others than the woman who stood in their path. "If this one would like to try to stand in our way, she will meet the sharpened side of my axes."

"By all means, you are welcome to attempt to best me," the woman replied. "Though my pet will no doubt have some objections to that."

Jarl's blood froze as he heard the low guttural growl of something terrible coming from the darkness behind the woman, and two glowing yellow eyes as big as his fists appeared there. He could not help but take a wary step back. He knew what was approaching and he did not need to wait for the wolf to slink into the light of his axes to get his confirmation.

"I believe that you may have already met my pet, Garmr?" the woman asked, still with genuine question rather than sarcasm in her voice.

"That thing..." Hilda said quietly. "That... is Garmr?"

The wolf growled as though in reply and stepped into the light for the group to see. There in front of them stood the giant bloodstained wolf that Jarl had killed in front of them all not long ago, although now it looked very much alive.

Garmr growled a low rumble and lowered his head to the ground as though he was about to pounce, but an open palm from the woman kept him in his place.

"This is indeed my pet, Garmr. He has been by my side for a very long time and few have managed to pass him when he has been out hunting," the woman explained.

"Then... if that is Garmr... it makes you..." Hilda stopped as though she could not bear to say the last word. It was clear that she knew the significance of this wolf, though it was lost on Jarl, Sigrid and Sylfia.

The woman stared at Hilda for a moment as if waiting to see if she would utter her name, but after a short while, she took pity and spoke again.

"My name is Hel, and as you have already been told, this is my domain," Hel said.

"But this cannot be so!" Hilda objected. "This place is not Helheim; it simply cannot be!"

Hel smiled brightly at the mention of her domain and the recognition of her being.

"Do you know what Nilfheim is, mortal?" Hel asked Hilda, although she answered her own question before Hilda had a chance to respond. "There is another name for Nilfheim – that is the World of Mist. Nilfheim exists beneath the realms of mortals and has a tendency to bleed through as mist does as the realms become closer together. With the near coming of Ragnarök, the mists of Nilfheim have been bleeding into this plane for some time, and as such I have manifested my physical form here and now."

"But... the dead... and Helheim! And Garmr... I watched him die with my own eyes!" Hilda struggled to form a coherent sentence in the presence of the ruler of Hel; it was just too much to bear.

"You mortal beings are always concerned with things dying, aren't you? But you fail to see that what is already dead cannot be killed," Hel said.

"So you are telling us now that you are the guardian of Helheim, the God known as Hel, and this is your wolf, Garmr?" Jarl asked. "And you are also saying that Ragnarök is coming, which means that the veil between the planes of existence is falling so that Nilfheim is now present here in the mortal realm?"

Sigrid and Sylfia both studied Jarl appraisingly. If anyone was going to understand everything that Hel had just told them, each of them would have bet that it would not have been him.

"That is exactly what I am telling you, Jarl. Though tell me, why have you come all this way to the north, to my domain, and why did you think it wise to kill my beautiful Garmr?"

The wolf bared its teeth and growled again and the sound sent shivers down Jarl's spine.

"We come to speak with you!" Sylfia interrupted before Jarl could say another word. "We have come to speak of Baldur and his release back to the mortal realms."

Hel smiled sweetly at Sylfia. "You have been blessed have you not, child? I can sense something inside you, a path that will lead you to great things, but also to great loss."

Hel had offered no answers to Sylfia's statement and she knew that was intentional. She did not know why Hel would evade her question but knew that she needed to proceed.

"My path is difficult, as I have been told, but we are here to speak of Baldur. You hold him in your domain, do you not?" Sylfia asked again.

Hel nodded. "I do."

"And it is within your power to release him?"

"It is," she said.

"Then tell us, what would you have us do to have you release Baldur back to the world, to his parents and all of the mortals that miss him so?" Sylfia asked.

"A long time ago, I was asked a similar question," Hel replied. "I was asked what the price may be to set Baldur free, back to the plane that mourned his passing. My answer was then as it is now: if everything in the world sheds a tear for Baldur, then

I will willingly give back the shining God. Though since that day, not every being has shed a tear for him, and thus, no deal can be made for his return."

"Almost everything in the world did weep for Baldur though, surely you have seen that?" Hilda asked.

"Of course, I have seen what the passing of Baldur has done to the world and the pain that it has caused, but if *almost* everything has wept, then I am afraid that I must only *almost* release him from my care."

"So this deal still stands?" Jarl asked. "If everything weeps for Baldur, then he will be returned?" His thoughts had turned to Baldur's Children and what their aims had been. If Hel did indeed have the power to release Baldur and so prevent the coming of Ragnarök, then perhaps they had not been so far wrong in their plans after all.

Hel's attention turned back to Jarl. "Yes, my deal will stand until it is fulfilled or the end of time arrives. Though one being has sworn an oath to never weep for Baldur."

"Loki," Sylfia muttered under her breath.

"Yes, my father can be quite stubborn," Hel said. "I doubt that he will ever weep for the shining God, no matter the circumstances."

"Then he will die," Jarl announced. Sylfia shuddered as that particular proclamation could land the group in great trouble with Hel, but Helheim's keeper simply nodded.

"Yes, my father will eventually die. Death is inevitable to all beings, and the Gods are no exception. I suspect that if you wish harm to come to Loki, you would not be the first in line, and it would be far more likely that you would be sent to my care before him in any case."

"Then may we petition you for your aid?" Sigrid called from the rear of the group. She had always had a way with words and a way of seeing situations in a different light than her husband, who always seemed to think with his axes.

Hel thought about that for a long moment, and her head lopped from side to side animatedly as she pondered.

"This is not something I have ever been asked before," she replied slowly, and it seemed as though this was the first time she had been off-balanced. It was starting to appear as though she did not have an answer, and Sylfia wondered if the Gods had indeed given her the power to get people to help her when she needed it most, this was indeed the time when it would come in most useful.

"Please, we do not ask this of you lightly," Sylfia spoke softly and calmly. "We are begging of you to offer us any aid that you can to help us along our path. We will pay any price that you demand if it means that our journey can continue."

It felt to Sylfia that a belt that had been fastened tightly around her waist had expanded with her words and as she spoke, she could sense it growing. She felt the belt pass through Hel and Garmr, then attempt to pull against their will, bringing it back to Sylfia as it contracted once more. She had never tried so hard to use her divine will before, and she had certainly never experienced this feeling before. It made her wonder if she had ever even truly used her gift correctly. She suddenly felt the contracting belt move straight through Hel and the great wolf without reeling in whatever it was supposed to.

"I can sense your gift and your will, child, but you surely did not think that a minor divine gift like yours would work against a being such as I?" Hel asked.

"I... I did not know that this was going to happen," Sylfia admitted, half wondering and worrying if the God was about to take offence. "I apologise... I..."

Hel held up a single open palm to stop Sylfia from speaking. "Do not worry, child," she said calmly. "I can see that as the planes of the worlds grow nearer and the bonds between them stronger, these gifts have become a little more common and a little... well let us say out of control." She looked directly at Jarl and his flaming axes as she spoke those last words. "Though I will say this, it is law amongst the Gods that we do not interfere with the dealings of mortals. We must not give you aid nor hinder you on each of your paths. We must not seek to harm you or to give you the means with which to wage war with your fellow mortals."

"But you have done so, have you not?" Sigrid spoke again. "With the divine power that the Gods have given to man, there is an army of mortals with divine powers seeking to destroy everything in the world, and with these powers, nobody can stand against them!"

Hel looked at Sigrid with a bemused expression. "You believe that no mortal can stand against an army of mortals simply because they can conjure fire and water? You believe that the flaming axes of this mortal with you now will make him invulnerable to sword, spear, axe or arrow?"

Sigrid stuttered through her response, though she could see that Hel was correct; even though Jarl had power within him, he was still mortal and that power made him no more indestructible than the next man.

"These powers that this army commands - do they make them anything more than mortal beings?" Hel asked nobody in particular. "If they are struck down by mortal hands, will they rise again? Of course, the answer is no. Although these few can be seen as fortunate, they are nothing more and nothing less to a being such as myself than any other mortal, for no mortal can harm a God."

Sylfia had remained quiet whilst Hel had spoken; something that the God had said was playing on her mind.

"So if the Gods do not interfere with our paths, then I have two questions. First: why did Garmr attack us when it was clear that we were not a threat in any way to your domain, you, or the wolf itself, and secondly: if you are saying that the

Gods will not interfere with the world of mortal men, does that mean that if we continue along our path, past you and into Helheim, then you will not stop us?" Sylfia counted off both questions on her fingers as she asked them and held them up after she had finished speaking, as though challenging Hel to knock them back down again.

"Well, I must say that your questions are well formed, and they would be relevant, child, though you have missed some of the finer detail of the basis on which they are asked. First, Garmr did not attack you unfounded. He saw what Odin's raven was doing to help you on your journey – which in itself is a breach of the code that we immortal beings live by – and secondly, the rules that apply to the land of the mortals do not strictly apply to the realm of Helheim."

Hel's words turned Sylfia's blood icy cold; if what she had just said was true, then if this God decided that this conversation bored her and simply wanted to leave, she could kill them all without the fear of punishment or repercussion. That notion in itself was strange though, as Hel did not seem to have to play by any of the 'normal' rules of the mortal realm.

"Then instead answer this," Hilda interrupted the obvious sparring of the two minds. "Are you going to kill us to stop us from attempting to complete our path, or will you simply leave us be and let the bones fall where they may?"

"I have not decided," Hel lopped her head to the side as though contemplating the idea. "Your task is to free Baldur, is it not?"

Sylfia nodded.

"Then you know what you must do to make that happen, the rules have not changed.

"And if we promise not to interfere with Baldur or his release, we simply must continue along this path, will you allow that?" Sylfia asked.

"It is a strange thing to ask," Hel said, switching her head to the other side as though not entirely understanding the question. "Hel is a place that all may enter but none may leave – except of course Baldur, that is, if anyone can convince my father to shed a tear for the shining God – which again he has sworn never to do."

"So, we can just freely enter your domain?" Jarl asked, not seeing what the game was here.

"As it has been for all of time and as it will continue to be so until Ragnarök passes... and as you may feel..." As though on queue, the ground shook beneath their feet and Hel smiled. "The world's serpent has already begun to stir and each passing day brings us closer to the end of the world. It does not matter to me what mortal beings are doing, all that matters is that once Ragnarök has come to pass, those who do not make it to Valhalla will be welcomed into my domain. That being said, to me it does not matter if you wander into Hel now, or when Ragnarök has eventually come to pass. Either way, you will be unable to leave."

The words cut into Sylfia as if they had a bladed edge. Surely this was not supposed to be how this was to happen? She had been told that her path was going to be most difficult, but she had not been told that it would mean condemning herself and everyone she cared about to eternal damnation.

"The path onwards will bring you into my domain," Hel interrupted before Sylfia could answer. "Though it may not be an easy path without dangers. Whatever you decide to do next, neither I nor my pet here will stand in your way," and with those words, Hel turned and walked away, back into the darkness and into the tunnel that was still the only way out of this place. Garmr let out one last low growl, bared his teeth at the group threateningly and then turned and skulked away. The group was left alone again, though this time it was with their mouths hanging open in shock.

25

"So what do we do now?" Sigrid asked quietly once the group had taken a moment to digest the fact that they had just been speaking to Hel, and that the God had all but invited them into her domain. It was a traumatic experience for all of them, although had they thought about it of course, they could have gone to Helheim before – they would have simply had to have died outside of battle, missing out on their opportunity to go to Valhalla and instead live out their eternal lives in the normalcy that the underworld would offer.

But these had always been stories passed down through generations of men, women and children. Although the belief was there within them all, Jarl, Sylfia, Sigrid, and Hilda had never truly believed that the Gods were real and that they would be awaiting them in the afterlife exactly as they had been told.

"I... I do not see that we have any alternative than to continue," Sylfia said slowly. I can only see one path, and that is the one that lies before us..." she trailed off as though unsure of her own words.

"And then we reside in Helheim for the rest of time, daughter. Do you not see that..." Jarl started but was interrupted by Sylfia.

"Yes, I can see; I can always see, father! But I do not see an alternative path, do you?" Her father had asked Sylfia if she 'could see' on far too many occasions, and this was the last time she could take it. "I am sorry to say this to you here and now, but I am no child! I have been an adult for many years, and it is time that you understood that I do not need to be coddled in this way! The fate of the entire world rests upon our shoulders, and if we manage to prevent the coming of Ragnarök, then will our lives not have been worthwhile? Would you not give your life if it were to save just one hundred others? Would you not give your life for the lives of the Rakki clan? Father, we have the chance now to make a difference in the world, and you are worried that we may not return?"

Jarl thought for a moment on Sylfia's outburst. His instinct was to raise his voice and press his will down upon his daughter, as he had done before when she was younger, when he knew that what he was saying was right. The problem was that this time he did not know what was right. Sylfia was correct to point out that she was older now, and no matter how much he wanted to protect her at every turn, he would eventually need to allow her to make her own decisions and mistakes.

"I am sorry, Sylfia," Jarl said quietly. "Ever since you came to Sigrid and me, we have done everything we could to protect you and keep you safe. We know that sometimes this means that we can be overprotective of you and your decisions. We will try to do better for you, daughter, and listen to you with proper intent."

Sylfia could barely close her mouth at her father's admission. She did not know if he was being sincere or not, but his words did sound so, and Sigrid then arrived by her side, snaked her arm around Sylfia's shoulders, and pulled her into a tight embrace.

"We always want what is best for you, Sylfia, to help you wherever we can and ensure you have grown up correctly and safely. I can see now that we have done everything that we should have to turn you into the woman that you have become today. Jarl and I are more proud of you than you could ever imagine, and we will help you on this journey however it may take us."

Jarl stepped forward and placed a hand on Sylfia's shoulder. "Daughter, I am sorry, and your mother is right: we will follow you to the ends of the earth, and in this case, that may well be so. As a family, we have always respected the Gods, so before we continue along our path, I would like to do one more thing."

Jarl turned and stepped towards the cave entrance covered by the avalanche and placed his axes on the ground. The frigid air in the cave instantly assaulted Sylfia's skin as the axes extinguished themselves and the cave was plunged into darkness. Then a moment later, the axes reignited, and Jarl was on his knees, a smear of red blood on the frozen snow covering the entrance.

Then Jarl spoke: "Odin, mighty Allfather, I come to you today with a heavy heart and a troubled mind. My family and I are about to embark on a journey into the realm of Helheim, a place of darkness and cold. I fear for all of our safety, and I pray that you will watch over us and keep us from harm. Grant us the strength and courage to face whatever challenges may come our way and guide us safely through the treacherous lands of the dead. Protect us from the dangers that lurk in the shadows, and keep us safe from the icy claws of death. But above all, great Odin, I pray that you will see us safely home again. I long to return to the warmth and light of our home and to live my life in your glory. Please, grant me this wish, and allow us to return to the land of the living. I thank you, Allfather, for all that you have given us, and I offer you my allegiance and my loyalty. May your wisdom and your strength guide us through this difficult journey. Hail Odin."

"And I pledge to you my life now and forever," Hilda spoke from the back of the cavern. "You have given me a new family to be a part of, and I do not know how I can repay such a blessing. Where once I was lost, my family and friends gone, you have given me a new reason for being. Allfather, please see it within your blessings to keep my new family safe and return us all from the depths of Helheim."

Sylfia, so overwhelmed with emotion, could not muster a single word to say in gratitude to the group. Each of them had all but sworn their fealty to her, and she was afraid that if she said anything at all, perhaps it would break whatever spell they were all under. A memory returned to her though, that of her being told about her gift. People would do whatever they could to ensure that Sylfia was protected, and the Gods would give them the power to aid her. Sigrid though had no such power, and Sylfia wondered if, in the fullness of time, her mother would gain some divine will as a method to protect her from harm. Sylfia hoped that would happen, at least.

The group turned their collective backs away from the snow wall that separated them from the outside world and the depths of Helheim. They knew that if they spent enough time and energy they would be able to free themselves from the cavern and return to the frozen wastelands beyond, but then what would they do? The north held nothing for them, the army of Baldur's Children was most likely scouring the lands to the south and west to rid the world of any beings that Hel would need the tears to fall from in order to free Baldur from Helheim, and soon Ragnarök would come. If Ragnarök did indeed come to pass and the group was not still within Helheim attempting to prevent it, it would not matter if they were anywhere else within the realms of man, as none would be untouched by the end of days.

The tunnel before them was dark and wide and cut a winding path through the ice, so they could not see what approached around the dark corners. The ground beneath their feet was also slippery as though it had been made so purposefully, making the group move very slowly and cautiously.

"How long do you think this tunnel is?" Hilda asked as they inched along.

"I do not know," Jarl replied. "Though there is one thing that I have noticed, this path has been growing steadily shorter and narrower. I do not know how the beast Garmr would have been able to fit through now."

"Perhaps they did not come this way," Sigrid offered, though her tone lacked conviction.

"I have not seen any alternative path, have you?" Jarl asked.

"No, not as yet," she replied. "But this place may hold more secrets than we can see with our mortal eyes."

Just as she spoke those last words, the group turned a corner carved out of the ice and found themselves face to face with an ice wall covering the entire tunnel, except for a small section at the bottom, just big enough for each of them to crawl through one at a time.

"This is not big enough for that beast to crawl through," Sigrid said with wonder in her expression as she ducked down, feeling the edges of the frozen gap as she crouched beneath it.

Nobody else spoke until they had crawled through, but as they raised themselves on the other side, they were struck speechless at what awaited them; Jarl held both of his axes up to the wall before them so that they could all see the next step in their journey.

What Jarl's axes had illuminated within the new ice-covered cavern that they found themselves within were four perfectly flat ice walls around them, a flat ice ceiling above, and a shimmering frozen ground beneath them. It was as if the place had been carved into a perfect cube by some divine being. What was most interesting, though, was the stone archway that had been constructed within the far wall which had been almost entirely swallowed by the vast, thick roots of a tree that could not be seen but must have been nearby.

Hilda was the first to speak upon entering this new cave. "Surely this cannot be the Gnipa cave..." Her words were not a question, but rather a statement that she did not wish to believe.

"We have met Gods, seen visions of the future and have spoken to Hel herself," Jarl said levelly. "We come to this cave to seek Helheim and the God Baldur to free him from this curse... and you have trouble believing that we are within the Gnipa cave, the location of the gates of Hel?"

"If this truly is the Gnipa cave... then where is the beast Garmr? This is his home is it not?" Hilda asked. Her voice had fallen almost to a whisper, as she did not wish to alert the great wolf to her presence.

Jarl swung his axes around himself as though to throw their light and warmth to every corner of the Gnipa cave, eventually illuminating a dark corner that had eluded the light. Two chains, as big as those that held the anchors of longboats, lay piled on the ground as though they had released whatever it was that they had been holding.

"I was taught that Garmr would be freed at the coming of Ragnarök," Hilda whispered. "I did not think much upon it until seeing the entrance to Hel... and these chains... does this mean that we are too late? Has Ragnarök come to the world, and we simply do not know it yet?"

"No," Sylfia relied assuredly and without lowering her voice. "Ragnarök has not yet come because our path has not yet reached its conclusion. These tales have never been wholly true, and if I know anything about Loki and his family, they cannot be trusted."

"Were you also taught that the wolf howled each time a new soul entered into Helheim?" Sigrid asked. "Only because earlier, as we travelled through the north... the wolves were howling... do you think that..." she trailed off.

"What has happened in the past has already happened, and we can do nothing to change that," Sylfia reassured her mother. "But we can change what is yet to come, and what is yet to come still is the passing of Ragnarök. We must continue as we are supposed to and do what we can to save all that we can. If indeed the howling of the wolf did signify the passing of mortals into Helheim, then they are lost already, and all we can do is make sure that their sacrifice was not in vain. We are mortals, as were they, but we will give them their vengeance."

As she finished, the world beneath their feet shook violently again and the cavern creaked loudly.

"We must move now before our decision is taken," Jarl announced. "Let us move and speak later!" He grasped Sigrid's hand and ran straight at the stone archway he knew would lead them on and into Helheim.

Jarl stopped and stood at the archway as Sylfia, Sigrid, and Hilda crossed through. He wanted to ensure that his family would make it safely across before he went through himself, and as each of them stepped over the threshold into Helheim, they instantly disappeared into the darkness.

"You do not have to go through, Jarl of the Rakki clan," Hel's voice came from the cave that the group had vacated, and he turned to see Hel standing in the centre of the Gnipa cave with Garmr by her side, head lowered and snarling.

"You must know that if you cross through into my true domain, you will never leave. You will stay in that place forever, and so will your family," Hel said lightly. "They have already gone, but who will remember them if you go through? Who will mourn their passing? Do not be a fool, Jarl."

In his heart, Jarl knew that what Hel had said was the truth. He knew that if he crossed over into Helheim he would be giving his life away. He would never return, and his family would never be remembered. They would disappear as all mortals did. But Hel was allowing him to live, to remember and to tell their story.

But Jarl had already known this when he had decided to travel to Helheim with his family. It was not new information to him, and therefore it made no difference.

"Do you not see how what you ask of me is impossible?" Jarl asked. "You ask me to abandon my family to death whilst I live? And what kind of life would that be, here in the north with no food or shelter? I am not as much of a fool as you seem to think."

Hel smiled sweetly at those words. "Garmr will take you to any place on this earth for you to live out your mortal life. I can give you riches beyond your wildest dreams." As she spoke, her hands filled with gold and jewels, "and all you need to do is to not proceed through that gate."

Jarl sheathed one of his hand axes, extinguishing its blaze and brought his hand up to his dark braided beard as he pondered. His beard felt rougher than it once had, the cold, the wind and the ice taking its toll on the fine hairs. His mind wandered back to all of the pain and suffering that had accompanied his journey northwards. It was unthinkable that it could have led to his death and nothing more - he had worked too hard for this to be it.

"I do agree that if I go through this door, if I travel through to Helheim and am reunited with my family, nobody will be left to mourn for us. We have travelled through unbearable hardships and loss, and eventually, I may simply be another number."

Garmr began to growl, sensing some dire crescendo to Jarl's words.

"The problem Hel, is that you simply do not understand the mortal bonds of family. I may not know the truest version of the stories that mortals are told of the Gods, but if I am correct in saying that Loki is truly your father, then you are the one who does not see clearly. If you think that riches and an easy life are any payment worthy of losing my family, my daughter and wife, then you do not truly know what it means to be a daughter or to have a father." Jarl lowered his hand from his beard, though he did not reclaim his second axe but placed his hand across his heart as he spoke his next words. "And even if I was still a member of the Rakki clan, as you have said, the clan was destroyed, killed by members of Baldur's Children – the army trying to kill everything in the name of your deal for Baldur's release. So if I do not return from your domain and you are but the only one who can tell my story, tell people that my name was Jarl, father to Sylfia, husband to Sigrid and friend to Hilda of the north."

Before Hel could answer, Jarl launched the one axe he still held straight at Hel. He watched as it travelled through the air, the flames remaining lit and trailing behind it as though it was some divine pinwheel, and then it struck true. The axe of sharpened iron buried itself directly between Hel's eyes, and red blood spouted from her blue-tinted skin as though it was the first time the thick liquid had ever felt the cold of the air. Just before the flames extinguished themselves, Jarl saw the God fall, and Garmr let out a howl as it leapt towards him. Jarl simply crossed his arms across his chest and fell backwards through the corpse gate and into Helheim. The last thing he saw was the terrible sharp teeth and the gaping maw of the great wolf snapping at him as he fell, too late and too far away to reach him.

26

Jarl's fall backwards felt like an eternity. He had been expecting to hit solid cold ground on the far side of the archway but found himself within a sea of nothingness. He kept his arms crossed against himself while looking about to see if there was anything in the blackness that would tell of anyone or anything around him, but there was simply nothingness for as far as he could see. He was not sure though, if it was his mind's eye that was trying to see, or his physical eyes.

"Father?" Sylfia's voice cut through the darkness and Jarl grabbed onto it as though it was his one and only lifeline. "What happened? Why are you on the ground in such a manner?"

Slowly Jarl began to be aware of his body with the help of Sylfia's words. He could now feel that he had fallen to the ground as he had passed through the corpse gate, and had remained with his arms crossed against his chest. He opened his eyes and saw Sylfia peering down at him with mild concern on her face.

"I... I do not know what happened when I came through the gate... just darkness and nothingness... was it the same for you?" Jarl asked, trying to shake the feeling of loss that was building up within him.

Sylfia nodded slightly. "It was not too different, though after we walked through the gate we stepped through the darkness into this place, and did not arrive as though we had fallen here directly from the grave."

"I uh..." Jarl searched for the right way to tell the others what he had done, but he did not need to finish his statement as Hel's voice reached his ears.

"Your father thought that it would be wise to attempt to kill me," Hel said, though she had not yet arrived. Jarl awaited the snarl of the great beast Garmr, ready to bite his head clean off, but no noise came and he let out a long exhale.

Helheim, or at least where the group had arrived, was a cold place. Not as cold as the north had been before they had crossed into the afterlife, but certainly cold. Their vision was shrouded in mist too, much like the God's mist that had covered the plains of the west on occasions, and almost identical to that which had covered the battlefield when Baldur's Children had defeated the allied armies of the west. Jarl did not want to know what lay beyond this mist though, because everything that he thought he knew about Hel and Helheim told him that this place would not provide an easy life for him and his family.

Hel's shadowy form came into view through the mist and Jarl watched as she closed in on the group, trying to see if she had the dire wound on her forehead where he had thought he had killed her. Again he was thankful that the shadow of the wolf Garmr did not emerge with her.

"Father? What were you thinking?" Sylfia asked incredulously. "You attempted to kill Hel? And for what? You could have got yourself..." she did not finish her sentence because as Sylfia was speaking, she realised the ridiculousness of that statement – the group was already in Helheim, so what more could be done to them.

"I am sorry, daughter. I simply thought that if there was any small chance that I could kill Hel in the mortal realm, I was going to try. I thought that if Hel died, then perhaps Baldur would be set free from this place and we would not all have to risk everything to find him."

"And what if you had killed her? Her death would release all of the lost souls from Helheim. Did you not think of that?" Sylfia asked.

"I... did not," Jarl admitted. "I did not have the time to think everything through and I simply acted."

"Then next time you need to tell us your plan before you leap to action! The stakes here are higher than we could have ever imagined and one false step could..."

Hel cleared her throat as though to remind everyone that she was both there, and the most important person in attendance.

"I offered your father a choice, actually," Hel said sweetly as though they had not just been discussing her death. "I offered him a life of ease, simplicity and riches beyond his wildest dreams if only he would leave the rest of you to go to Helheim without him. The fact that he attempted to end my life is more of a testament to your familial ties than to his desire to act rashly... though Jarl, you must remember what you have already been told: what is already dead, cannot be killed."

"You... you could have left us for riches?" Sigrid asked. "And you chose to follow us through the corpse gate? You are such a fool Jarl, I do not know what I ever saw within you."

Jarl turned to look at his wife, shocked by her statement, but now he could see that she was smiling. She had not meant her words and, if anything, seeing her smile made him forget everything in the world around them.

"I did not understand either," Hel said to Sigrid entirely missing her sarcasm. "I would like to learn more about how your empathy for each other works, if I may?"

"We will tell you all that you need to know about family, love, empathy and anything else you desire, if for each new lesson you answer a question of our own choosing, truthfully," Hilda said quickly before any of the other three could speak. It was a clever tactic and Jarl was pleased that Hilda had spoken before he had the chance to open his mouth again.

"OK," Hel said sweetly. "Jarl, do you regret your decision to follow your family into my domain, even if I were to tell you that there is no possible means for escape, and now you are all damned for eternity rather than one of you being left to live your life with happiness, freedom and riches?"

"I do not regret it for even one second," Jarl replied without offering any further information.

"Hmm... that is... interesting," Hel purred. "Now you may ask me something."

Again Hilda was the first to speak before anyone else could ask anything of Hel. It was obvious to the rest of the group that Hilda did not want a possible valuable question to be wasted.

"Can you tell us in detail how Helheim works? I mean specifically how the place is laid out and how it can accommodate all of the fallen souls of the mortal realm?"

Hel smiled sweetly again. "This is actually information that I may have told you anyway because it does not matter what you do or do not know about my domain as you will never leave it."

"Then answer the question without commentary," Sigrid said without a smile of her own.

"As you wish," Hel replied. "Helheim is a world between worlds where the happenings of each of the realms bares no consequence on the others. It is a place where the dead come, those who do not reach the illustrious heights of Valhalla. That is to say, those who do not die in battle come here to me." Hel waited as though for some sign of comprehension, but no one said anything, hoping for further information.

"My domain is constructed from nine rings, each smaller than the last and each specifically designed to hold a different type of being within. On the first and outermost ring, mist and shadow will be found. On the second, the mortals who died of sickness or old age reside. Third is for those mortals who led foul lives, the thieves, murderers and rapists of the mortal realm. Forth is reserved for the leaders of those most foul men, those who have elevated themselves above the rest through combat, bribery or nefarious means. The fifth ring is where one may find the Jötnar, the giants of Jötunheim. Sixth is for the mightiest warriors of the Jötnar, who have gained their place on the sixth ring through ranked combat. Seventh belongs to my beast, Garmr. He uses the ring to hunt any who wish to attempt the crossing to the eighth ring, where one will find the Draugr, the undying dead, and lastly, the central the ninth ring is reserved only for the Gods."

The amount of information that had just been given by Hel was nothing short of amazing to Hilda. Her mouth hung open whilst she digested everything, and could not think what to ask next. If she had stopped to think, she could have thought of ten questions to ask next, but her mind was occupied trying to sort through the information that she had just been given and she simply drew a blank.

"Tell me," Hel said. "Why is family so important to mortals?"

"This is an easy question to answer," Jarl replied. "To us, family is everything. Whatever we do in life, we do for our families. From birth we are protected by those who love us, and as we grow old we protect those who will carry our blood to the next generations. A family bond cannot be easily broken, bought or disregarded such as you have attempted. "

"And this is a natural reaction?" Hel asked. "You each are born with this inbuilt to your being?"

Jarl nodded. "It is as so, though family is not as simple as those who you give birth to or who have given birth to you. Family is the title given to all those who a person grows to care for, regardless of their being. My wife, Sigrid is not of my blood, but I love her with all of my heart and will do anything to protect her. Hilda was not even of my clan and now she has become a part of my family. It is a natural happening and can happen to anyone at any time."

Hel stroked her chin in a very human gesture as she thought. "Is the bond between a father and daughter always as strong as it is with you and your daughter?"

Jarl shook his head. "It is a very rare thing for a man to not have love, and the desire to protect his daughter at all costs... but it does happen. I have not seen it in all of my years... but even so it does happen."

"And Sylfia, you feel this bond for Jarl even though he is not your real father?" Hel asked.

Sylfia did not even stutter. "Of course. Jarl is my father no matter what has happened or what will happen. We are family and Sigrid is my mother. Hilda is as family as my father has told you... but tell me... why do you ask these questions?"

"I ask because I have never felt this bond with my father," Hel looked directly at Sylfia. "When your father chose to die to be with you rather than to live with wealth and happiness it made me wonder if mine would do the same. It is, however, a question I cannot answer."

Sylfia immediately bit her lip to stop herself responding that Loki would not do anything so selfless, but she knew that it could do no good. Instead she held her silence and let Hel ask her next question.

"How did Hilda go from being a friend, to a member of this family," Hel asked the group.

"To us, Hilda has become a member of our family because she has proven that she will put the needs of the family as a whole before her own. She will do anything to protect any one of us, as any one of us will do for her. This is the bond of a family and together we make each other stronger," Sigrid explained and her words brought tears to Hilda's eyes. Every word was true and she could not have said it better herself.

By now Hilda had managed to arrange more questions in her mind and asked the next that she felt would be important.

"Is it possible for us to cross between these rings?"

Hel nodded. "It is possible, though it is difficult." She did not offer any further information on the subject.

"A question to all of you: would you place the safety of your family above the rest of the world? For example, if you were given the choice to all die now to prevent the passing of Ragnarök, would you take it?"

"Is that not what we have already done?" Sigrid asked. "We treasure our family but we do not believe that we are better than any others in the mortal realm. Each of us would gladly give our lives to save our fellow man," and with Sigrid's words the entire group nodded in agreement.

"Fascinating," Hel said.

"How do we cross between the rings?" Hilda asked.

"Each ring will provide a different challenge if you do look to traverse this realm to the centre as I suspect... though in the most basic sense, each ring is connected by a stone bridge to the next," Hel replied. "Now... I have an offer to make for you and afterwards you can ask me one more question before I leave you to my domain. The offer is thus: I will return all of you back to the mortal realm with more riches than you could ever imagine. You would be able to live forever as a family in comfort and happiness and I make you the promise that if Ragnarök does come to pass during your lifetime, you will be excluded from any harm caused by any who listen to me."

"No," Hilda said quickly.

"No," Sylfia agreed.

"No," Sigrid said.

"No," Jarl said.

"Then if it is your will to remain here in my domain, I will not stand in your way," Hel said and turned her back on the group.

"Wait!" Hilda shouted. "You have one more question to answer."

Hel turned back towards the group, not objecting to Hilda's call. Hilda though, did not yet know what to ask. There were so many questions that she could ask where the answer could help them on their journey, but she needed to ask something that could not be answered ambiguously. Eventually she settled on the only thing that she could think of that could not be answered with some riddle.

"Where is the Naglfar ship, exactly?" she asked.

"The Naglfar ship is located between the eighth and ninth rings of Helheim," Hel replied without hesitation. Then once again she turned away from the group, took two steps forward, and disappeared into the mist that she had emerged from.

The group stayed still for a moment after Hel had disappeared. They each wondered what they were supposed to do in this new place and whether they were supposed to simply walk blindly on, though after a short while they each thought that nothing was going to happen unless they did something for themselves.

Jarl and Sylfia were the first to take two steps forward towards the swirling mists and as they did so, Hilda and Sigrid watched them.

Then suddenly, before their very eyes, a giant hand, formed from the dark swirling mist, reached out and picked up the pair and when the mist had abated there was nothing left.

Sigrid ran forward to where Jarl and Sylfia had disappeared from, but Hilda remained standing without moving an inch; she already knew that there would be nothing that she could do to change what had happened, or to chase down the other two.

"Did you see where they went?" Sigrid gasped in a panic and Hilda shook her head.

"They have been taken by the domain and there is nothing we can do now except try to follow them and hope that we are reunited," Hilda replied. "We must take the next step and perhaps we will be taken to the same place and in the same way."

Then Hilda stepped forward to join Sigrid and within an instant the mist swirled around them, shutting out all of the light.

Both had the dreadful feeling that they were being transported to somewhere new and against their will.

27

Jarl felt himself moving through the new nothingness, but this time he sensed that Sylfia was travelling alongside him. It felt better, as though more of the world was right now that Sylfia was with him and he was not alone, although he desperately hoped that Sigrid and Hilda were not far behind them.

The world swirled and morphed as the mist carried them to wherever it deemed necessary, and a long while passed before Jarl felt as though the world had stopped moving and he had reached solid ground once again.

"Are you with me, Sylfia?" Jarl asked once he was sure that he was stable and that the ground beneath his feet was staying exactly where it should.

"I am here, father, though I do not exactly know where here is," Sylfia replied. "Can you see mother or Hilda," she asked hopefully.

"I can see nothing," Jarl replied, but as he spoke, the mist faded back and away to reveal the world around them.

Jarl and Sylfia were now alone. Looking behind themselves, they could see nothing but the dark swirling mist, hiding where they must have come from, and before them stood a dark, desolate forest of dead trees and knee-high fog.

"Do you think that they are out there somewhere?" Sylfia asked hopefully.

"I do not know," Jarl started to say, but he was interrupted by a voice that carried within the mist.

"Are you out there, brother?" the voice said. "Please. Come to my side."

To their delight, both Jarl and Sylfia immediately recognised the voice. It was Eric, Jarl's brother-in-arms from the Rakki clan and Sylfia's de-facto uncle.

"Eric! Is that you, brother?" Jarl called back excitedly into the mist. "Call out to me and I will find you!"

He readied himself to run towards his brother and Sylfia quickly followed suit.

"Brother, are you out there?" Eric called again, and this time Jarl broke into a sprint, heading directly towards the sound of his brother's voice and the desolate wasteland before them. Sylfia had no choice but to join her father in this pursuit and followed quickly behind Jarl as he sprang into action.

"Father... I do not..." Sylfia panted though she was interrupted by Eric's voice again.

"I am in need of your aid, brother. Come quickly before it is too late!" It sounded as though Eric's calls were becoming more and more urgent, but Sylfia could not help but think there was something wrong with this situation.

"Eric... died... in... battle!" Sylfia managed to call out loud enough for her father to hear, and as the words penetrated his haste, he stopped dead in his tracks. Sylfia arrived next to him and stood alongside her father.

Sylfia watched as Jarl reached down to retrieve his axes, though his hands would find nothing but air. At some point the mist must have removed his weapons without him knowing. Sylfia also found that she was unarmed after a quick check for the two swords that were usually attached to her sides.

"Please! They are almost here! In the mist, I need your help, brother!" Eric's voice came through the mist again as it swirled around them as though not wanting to close too tightly around them. Jarl and Sylfia could see around themselves in a small circle, but beyond that the mist had formed a moving wall too thick to see through at all.

Thankfully, Eric's words did not make Jarl break into another sprint, and instead he closed his eyes and Sylfia knew that he was doing everything he could to ignore the pleas of his once best friend.

"You are correct, Sylfia," Jarl said quietly under his breath. "The mist seeks to bring us into danger and to trap us. It may already be too late because of my foolishness, but you are right; Eric will be dining within the halls of Valhalla and not in this place, forsaken by the Gods."

"What do you think will happen?" Sylfia asked, looking around. She had already become disoriented and did not know from which direction they had run, and it quickly dawned on her that the mist had already taken them to exactly where it had planned.

Jarl and Sylfia stood motionless for a long while, waiting for anything to happen that would enlighten them of the intent of the place, but nothing happened, and neither did Eric's voice reach their ears again.

Jarl could take this torment no longer and took two steps towards the swirling wall before them but when he reached the mist, it retreated as though it was sentient and with each step that Jarl took, it allowed him free passage. Just as it was about to close behind him, cutting him off from Sylfia's vision, she quickly moved to join him in stride.

Of course, neither of them knew where they were going, but there was little difference between standing still and moving forward, wherever that would take them.

"Sigrid! Hilda!" Jarl called loudly into the mist. Sylfia wondered if sound would carry through the thick mist, but she joined in with the call nonetheless.

"Can you hear me?" Jarl called.

Then a scream cut through the mist. It was shrill and filled with pain and anguish, and both Sylfia and Jarl spun around to look at the direction it had come from.

"Sigrid! Hilda!" Jarl called again with a pang of desperation to his tone.

"Help me!" Sigrid begged, and as Jarl was about to set off running again Sylfia grabbed his arm.

"How do we know that this is not another trick?" Sylfia asked with wide eyes.

"Does it matter? If there is a chance that your mother is in danger and we did nothing to help..." Jarl started.

"They are coming!" Sigrid's voice came filled with terror.

"What is coming?" Sylfia called back into the mist, making sure that neither she nor her father would take a single step before she was certain this was not another trick.

"Please! Help me!" Sigrid's voice returned shriller than ever, and as Sylfia watched closely, she could see that with each frantic word, the mist vibrated slightly. If she had not been looking for it, she might not have seen it, but she tried her best to decide if the mist moved in such a way because it was generating the sound or if the sound was loud enough to affect it.

What was not lost on Sylfia, though, was that her mother's words mimicked those of Eric's when he had begged for their help.

"Tell us what the problem is and we will come to help!" Sylfia called into the mist.

A moment passed, and then the mist carried her mother's words again.

"They will be here, and it will all be over if you do not come now!"

Sylfia watched as her father searched the mist frantically, his face twisted in tormented anguish. As she watched, his eyes suddenly glazed over into a milky white, his pupils suddenly disappearing.

Jarl's head whipped back and forth as he searched frantically in the mist for the source of Sigrid's voice.

"She is here. She needs our help," he said, but as Sylfia tried her best to hold onto Jarl's arm, he wrenched it away from her and ran blindly towards the mist.

"Father, stop!" Sylfia called out, but her father was as a man possessed. "The mist tries to trick us. This is not real!"

But it was too late. Jarl was beyond reason, and Sylfia realised that the mist was affecting him in some magical way.

Sylfia raced after Jarl again before he was lost to her into the mist forever and struggled to keep up with him as he stumbled blindly into the darkness, his new cries and shouts becoming more and more frenzied as he moved.

Sylfia felt her heart fill with worry as she followed as closely as possible. She did not know why her father was so badly affected by whatever magic the mist contained, and she did not know why she seemed to be somehow immune to it.

The stench of death and decay filled her nostrils, and the ground underfoot became tacky and moist as though something in this place was changing.

"Father, we must stop. You must awaken from whatever this is!" she begged, but the mist simply called back in the guise of Sigrid again, but now seeming to be even more distressed.

It was as though Jarl could not hear his daughter. She did not think he could see her through his milky-white eyes, but the more she called out to him to stop this madness, the more frantic he became in his search.

Sylfia knew that even if she could do nothing to bring her father back to his senses, the very least she could do was to follow him until whatever was going to happen, or she found some way to snap him out of it.

As Sylfia followed Jarl through the mist, the ground underfoot became wetter, thicker and deeper, and the stench made her wretch. If she had thought that the smell of death and decay had been terrible before, now it was as though it was seeping in through every pore of her being. Eventually, the area where the mist was thinning started to become larger until Sylfia could see the deadened branches of long-forgotten trees standing sparsely around them. The ground was turning a brown-grey, too, as though the very life that it was clinging onto was no longer present.

As though he was spurred on by the clearing mist, Jarl increased his pace and his shouts grew more frantic as he became sure that this new dimension meant that he was nearing his destination. The responses from the voice of Sylfia's mother were still distant and scared, although they did not offer anything more than a general call for aid. Sylfia wondered if the calls would still have come if she too had been entrapped by this spell, or whether they would have been deemed unnecessary.

Then Sylfia felt the ground hold onto her leg as her foot sank into it. The wet mud seemed to be growing thicker and deeper as she moved, and before she realised that it was not simply mud beneath her feet, she already knew it was too late.

The black ooze beneath her had begun to feel like tar, and she watched as it attempted to root her to the spot. It was now also hot against her ankles where the black liquid touched them, and she knew that the one thing that she needed to do now was to escape from this place.

Sylfia looked up to see where her father had managed to reach, and realised that the mist had shrunk so much that she could now see the entire landscape before her. For miles and miles to the left and right, Sylfia could see the steaming blackened tar pit, inter-spliced with the odd branches of long-dead trees. A stone bridge crossed the pit off in the distance, but her vision was drawn to what she could now see was causing the stench of death and decay that would not leave her nostrils.

Hundreds, possibly thousands of bodies were littered throughout the tar pit, each of them nearer to Sylfia's side than the other, as though they had attempted to cross and had simply become stuck. Some of them were complete skeletons with grey and dull bones forming their structure, but some still had chunks of flesh hanging from them as though they were a dire warning to others.

Sylfia looked over to where her father stood, and although she could see that he was already stuck fast in the ground, he was still trying blindly to bury himself further into the pit. The tar was past his knees, and he was a good few metres in front of Sylfia, just out of reach.

"Father! The mist has led you here to kill you!" Sylfia called out, but he did not seem to care.

"Can you not see what is happening? You are stuck in this pit and if we remain here, we will never complete our task! You will die here, father, and if we wait much longer then I shall die too! I shall die, and Ragnarök will come to pass!"

With relief Sylfia saw that her words had hit home and Jarl's struggle to continue to his death had abated slightly. To Jarl it was as though he was trying to hear her words, but they were off in the distance, and he was unsure if they were real.

He could hear words cutting through the darkness. They were twisted somehow, and although he was sure that he recognised the voice from somewhere, he was convinced that this was some trick that Hel was playing on him. He needed to keep his focus, to get to his wife and save her from whatever it was that he knew lurked within the mist and darkness. He tried to form words of encouragement to call out to Sigrid, but when he opened his mouth, his jaw felt heavy, and all that he could manage was a terrible roar.

And then he heard the twisted voice again, cutting through the fog that occupied his mind. It was certainly familiar; it was his daughter's voice!

"Father, this needs to stop now!" He could hear Sylfia practically screaming at him, begging him to see reason and as her words permeated his skull, the milky white of his pupil-less eyes dissolved away to reveal his dark brown eyes one again.

"S... Sylfia?" Jarl called back, looking behind to search for his daughter. His surroundings were not as they had been the last time he could remember, and a mild panic washed over his entire body.

"Sylfia, I cannot move!" Jarl announced as he located his daughter, ankle-deep in the tar that held his own legs. It was above his knees and with every second that passed, he could feel his legs burning.

"Do not move, father!" Sylfia called out as she saw that her father had returned to his senses. She could see that he was slowly sinking into the tar, but she thought that struggling would do neither of them any good. The tar around her own ankles was almost too hot to bear, so she could only imagine that Jarl's legs felt far worse than hers.

Sylfia looked all around and noticed a few dead trees nearby. It would be a risk to try to reach them because they were a little deeper into the tar than where she was standing, but if she left her father without aid then he would surely find no escape.

With all the effort that Sylfia thought she could muster, she tugged at her right leg with both hands. The tar seemed to tighten as she pulled as if some terrible hand was wrapped around her ankle, but with a grunt and a loud slap, her foot was finally freed. She then spread as much weight as she could through her freed foot atop the tar and repeated the action with her left leg.

By the time her left foot was freed, her right had started to sink again with the effort, although it was considerably shallower, and much easier to release a second time. She prayed that she could reach the trees and find something that would help her father break free from the tar. An added bonus was that there did not seem to be any rotting corpses between the trees and where she was standing. As it was, Jarl was sinking a few millimetres every few moments, so she knew that she needed to hurry.

"Do not move, father. I am coming to help!" Sylfia called, and began moving quickly towards the trees, not allowing her legs to remain still for too long and sink.

With a fair amount of effort, Sylfia made it to the closest copse of trees. She was sweating and her legs and feet were steaming from the repeated contact with the tar but she reached up to the lowest hanging branch, which she thought was long enough at least to reach her father from a respectable distance but not so heavy that she would not be able to carry it.

Sylfia reached up and took a firm hold of it, yanking it hard and fast. Thankfully, as the tree had been dead and dry for only the Gods knew how long, the branch snapped cleanly off where it met the tree trunk, and Sylfia was left holding it high over her head. She had been right; it was not overly heavy, but the added weight did increase the speed at which she was sinking into the tar.

Then Sylfia felt something hard touch her toes, and she shuddered in horror. She could only assume that it was some kind of bone, but she did not want to wait to find out so she picked her feet up and did her best facsimile of a run back towards where her father was now thigh-deep in the tar. Around his body, steam was rising as though he was being boiled alive, and although his face did not betray any pain, his expression told of the horror he was experiencing.

"Stay there, father. I will be with you in a moment!" Sylfia called back.

Her voice echoed away into the tar plains and beyond, and she wondered for a moment if her raised voice would stir some horror lurking in the depths, but she instinctively knew that this place was surely a place of death where no creature would survive.

"I am sinking, daughter. Do not put yourself in danger if you do not need to!" Jarl called back. He knew that if this was to be his end, he would rather Sylfia not risk her life trying to save him.

"It is OK, father. I have freed myself, and I will not go deep enough into the tar to get as stuck as you. Perhaps the Gods of the underworld wish to cling to you but are not yet ready to accept me!" Sylfia joked. Her words did lighten the mood somewhat, and Jarl smiled and did not object.

Sylfia managed to bring herself close enough to her father to lay the branch out on the tar between them. It threatened to sink into the black ooze, but once the substance realised it was not made of flesh, it seemed not to grip it so tightly.

Jarl turned within the tar slowly so that he faced Sylfia full-on and grabbed hold of the branch. He was still sinking and the tar threatened to reach his waist, but what was more concerning was that his legs were burning from the heat. He knew that if he was not freed soon, he would suffer an injury more agonising than simply suffocating in the tar.

Jarl used all the strength he could muster to try to pull himself free of the tar with just his arms but the problem was that pulling himself sideways seemed like an insurmountable task in itself. If there had been a branch overhead to pull himself up with, it would have been achievable.

Despite all of Jarl's efforts, he did not move more than an inch or two.

"Sylfia, this is no good. I cannot break free from this tar!" Jarl called to Sylfia, who had been watching and had seen that her father had been unsuccessful.

"Wait a second," Sylfia said and took hold of the branch in both hands. "We count to three, and then we both pull," she announced, and Jarl nodded.

"One... two..." they both counted together, and on three, they both conjured up as much strength and determination as they each could.

At first Jarl did not move, but after a second, he felt the tight grip around his toes start to relinquish.

"Do not stop Sylfia, I am moving!" he roared, and with redoubled effort, Jarl was pulled free of the tar that had sought to consume him. He was still in the pit, but now, as long as he was quick, he would be able to join Sylfia in the shallower area and ultimately out of the viscous fluid.

Free from the tar, the pair sat panting on the side of the long black sea before them, and now that Jarl could concentrate properly, the stench of death and decay assaulted his nostrils.

"This is a terrible place," Jarl managed to grumble as he had got his breath back after the monumental effort of freeing himself.

Sylfia nodded as she looked out across the long tar pit. It was clear now that it was similar to a moat. It spanned the area between the barren, cold wasteland where they sat and reached the base of a high stone wall, not unlike a fort. The bridge she could see in the distance clearly crossed over the tar pit and entered the inner wall.

"Do you think that is how we pass over into the next circle of this domain?" Sylfia asked as she pointed to the bridge.

Jarl followed her hand, and he too concluded that it would take them into the second ring of Helheim, where they would find all those who died of sickness or old age.

"I do not see where else we could go... and I think that you are correct. If we are to lead the charge into the centre of this domain so that we may free Baldur from his chains, this must be the way we shall go."

Jarl walked over to a dead and dry tree and broke off a long branch. He snapped off all of the small protrusions along its length so that it was as straight as possible and looked at Sylfia, who was watching him with mild confusion.

"Do you think this looks like a weapon, daughter?" he smiled as he spoke, and Sylfia appraised the long branch.

"Maybe? I do not know if it is supposed to be a spear or a staff, though. Do you think we will need such a weapon inside the second ring?"

"I do not know, but I only hope that the Gods will see this spear for what it truly is!" and with those words, he launched it high into the air above the tar pits, and as it left his fingertips it ignited with a burst of orange-red flame. It flew through the air in a tight spiral, hit its parabola's peak, and fell downwards into the thick black tar.

For a long moment, nothing happened. Then, as though somebody had ignited an enormous bonfire, the tar where the spear had landed exploded into a burst of flames and smoke. The air above the blaze quickly turned black, and the flames began to spread faster than Sylfia had ever seen any fire spread before.

The blaze snaked away from the point of impact and ignited the tar as it moved. Eventually, one of the blazing tendrils reached one of the static rotting corpses, and Sylfia wondered exactly what would happen when it caught fire. To her surprise, it exploded into a bright flame and a puff of black smoke - whatever gasses were released from the creature were far more flammable than Sylfia had expected.

The explosion was quickly followed by three more at the extremities of the fire that was still spreading faster than Sylfia could watch, and after each, the fire spread quicker still. Within a few moments, the flames had reached far out of sight and lapped against the stone wall of the second circle of Helheim, the entire tar pits aflame without any sign of the fuel being exhausted.

"Now we must head to the second circle," Jarl instructed. "We can await the others on the bridge - they will see the beacon we have lit for miles and they will find us, of that, I have no doubt."

Sylfia opened her mouth to complain, but the smell of death and decay was increasing as it heated the insides of her nostrils, and she could feel the heat rising exponentially. It was becoming uncomfortable. Instead, she simply nodded, and the pair made their way to the start of the bridge.

"Is it not strange that we have not met another living soul in this place?" Sylfia asked as they stopped, standing clear of the flames that lapped at the bottom of the stone bridge. On the far side, they could see that the stone wall had a large round archway and was straddled by two open iron gates, but beyond that was simply darkness.

Jarl thought for a moment and tousled his beard. The gesture made Sylfia smile as again it had been a while since she had seen her father comfortable enough to let his guard down and the familiar gesture return.

"I think that perhaps this place is made for people to be killed within," he mused. "I think that most souls do not enter Helheim in the way that we have done. While we entered the first ring, perhaps others are placed exactly where they are supposed to be. I do know, though, what this place did to me and I do not want to experience again."

Sylfia could understand that. The whole experience had been unnerving, and she could only assume that something within her, perhaps her divine power or the path that she walked, had prevented her from succumbing to the will of the mist.

"I agree, father, though what of mother and Hilda? Will they not have suffered the same fate? Without one of them with a clear mind, they would be stuck in this tar to burn to death!"

Jarl peered out into the flames that still seemed to be both growing and spreading. His expression was blank, and when he spoke, it was as though he was trying to convince himself.

"I do not think your mother would be so easily led, and Hilda has a divine gift. They will be safe. The end of their journey is not here, and we will await them. Your mother has a way of surviving when she is not supposed to."

Sylfia was not happy with that answer; she did not want to simply 'wait and see', but she knew that she had no choice, so instead of complaining, she looked out into the dark wilderness as far as she could will her eyes and waited to see if she could detect any movement.

A sudden noise behind them on the far side of the bridge made them both spin around. It was the loud clanging of iron against stone, along with a grinding, scraping sound and Sylfia and Jarl both saw something that quickened their pulses. The large iron gates had begun to slowly close, and the flames that lapped at the stone bridge were now much higher than the edges of the bridge and were curling inwards - before long, there would be no safe crossing to be had here.

"What do we do, father?" Sylfia asked in a shout over the noises that were now reaching them, but before Jarl could answer, a voice came from behind them. It was not a familiar voice calling for help this time though; rather, it was a deep, gravelly voice that made both Sylfia and Jarl turn away from the closing gate for just a moment.

The mist was now rolling quickly across the desolate plains before them, and the voice came from within.

"I have killed your friends. Do you not wish to avenge them? Come and fight me. Show me what kind of warriors you are."

Jarl placed a hand on Sylfia's shoulder and her eyes met his. Hers were filled with tears, but her father's betrayed only strength and determination.

"We run, Sylfia. We cross this bridge, and we do not look back, not even for one second."

Before she could object, Jarl swung her forward, and they ran. They kept to the centre of the stone bridge, while the searing heat of the flames grew ever higher, threatening every step they took, but they kept moving with stalwart determination.

The gates ahead were still slowly closing, and Sylfia was sure that if they kept at this pace, there was a good chance that they would not make it – they would be trapped outside with both the mist and the flames that would surely not let them back across the bridge.

The gap between the gates was just three feet, and the pair were still a few steps away. The darkness still hid whatever lay beyond, but neither cared. Nothing could be worse than this place.

Two feet.

Sylfia reached out her hand towards the gap in the gates, begging them to remain open just enough for both of them to fit through.

One foot.

Sylfia felt her father's hand on her arm and then her back as he pushed her with all his might, and she slotted through the gap in the gates with little room to spare.

Sylfia hit the darkness and felt her corporeal form disappear. The last thought that ran through her head was that she hoped more than anything else in the world that her father had made it through. She did not know if she could continue without him.

28

Jarl and Sylfia stepped out of the darkness and onto the solid stone ground of the second ring of Helheim. They were both immediately struck by the unfamiliar sights and sounds that greeted them. The sickly, elderly dead that they had expected to find here, along with a sense of death and decay, were nowhere to be seen, replaced instead by what seemed like a bright, bustling, thriving city.

"What... what is this place?" Sylfia asked with wide eyes, trying not to let her mind believe that what she was seeing was actually real. The sun shone in the sky above and by all accounts if she had not just entered this place through one of the gates of Helheim, she would have assumed that she was right back home.

Jarl looked all around too, his mouth slightly open. He fingered his thick beard before he mustered up a response for Sylfia.

"I do not know, but I cannot trust what I am seeing. This place plays tricks on the mind and I think that this is another, sent simply to entrap us once more.

Sylfia could agree with that statement, but there was something far more important playing on her mind.

"Father... why did you say that you knew mother was alive? You risked everything to follow her to the north and you did not even know that she would be there... what has changed now?" Sylfia asked with wide, teary eyes. She had never questioned her father's motives before, but turning to run from the mist and crossing the bridge was something that she could not comprehend.

Jarl met Sylfia's eyes and she could see that they were filled with both truth and compassion.

"There is something between your mother and I Sylfia, something that I do not know if anybody else can feel. Since the day we met, we have not parted in mind or soul. When we are apart in body, I know that she is safe and well, though the feeling is not one that I can explain. Your mother and I share a bond that is deeper than any other I know. When she is in danger or in pain I can feel it deep within my heart, and this is why I know that she is alive now, how I knew that she was alive in the north. When we met, we both made a promise to the Gods themselves. We would always be together, even through physical absence. I can feel her as a part of my very heart and soul and that is also how I knew that the mist lied when it told us that she had been killed. I knew the mist lied, and that could only mean that we would be safe to continue, doing the opposite of whatever that being wanted."

"But how can this be true?" Sylfia asked with a confused expression on her face.

"Of all the things that you have asked me to believe in of late, of the things you have seen with your own eyes, of the Gods we have met... this you find difficult to believe, daughter?" Jarl asked with a knowing expression.

Jarl was of course correct, between the four of their little family, nothing should ever be unbelievable or incomprehensible ever again, they had simply gone through too much already.

"OK," Sylfia said, forcing a cleansing exhale. "So what is this place, and what are we doing here?"

Jarl looked around with a look of mild confusion on his face as he began to lead the way towards the bustling city before them, and as Sylfia clutched at his arm in awe. He had never seen such a place in all his years – so many buildings all made of stone, so close together, so many people walking about as though they had nothing to do.

"Where are we, Father?" Sylfia asked, her voice barely above a whisper. "This does not look like what I had been expecting of the second ring of Helheim at all."

Jarl shook his head, unable to find words to express the confusion and disbelief that he too was feeling. He had simply assumed that the second ring of Helheim would be another place of decay and despair, a place where they had been told that the sick and elderly were sent once their days had come to an end and they had no use in battle. But this was anything but miserable.

The streets before them had stone-lined pavements and were straddled with vendors selling all manner of goods, from fresh produce to finely crafted weapons. The houses and buildings were well-maintained, with gardens and fountains decorating their fronts. And everywhere that Jarl and Sylfia looked, they saw happy, healthy people going about their daily lives.

Jarl and Sylfia walked straight forward without making any contact with another soul and to their surprise and relief, nobody attempted to talk to them, and in fact, barely even looked at them. They made their way further into the city, now receiving errant friendly smiles and warm welcomes. No one seemed to be surprised nor alarmed by their presence, but these people certainly knew that Jarl and Sylfia were new to the place.

"Father, I really do not like this place. It is so different to what I had been expecting. I do not know what their goal is but surely nothing good can come from this," Sylfia whispered.

A deep and booming voice reached them from somewhere ahead and Sylfia's gaze snapped upwards to see from where it had come.

"Come and have a drink! You will not find another place like this in all the nine realms!" It was a large man wearing what appeared to be a genuine smile on his face. He had no hair on his head and his dark beard had been braided into two long twists.

He seemed to be gesturing to what looked like an inn. The building was of stone construction like the rest, but hanging above the wooden door was a sign showing a tankard of some kind of drink painted upon it in multiple colours.

"Do not be shy! We have all been new members of the second ring at some point or another! Come, drink and talk and you will see that this place is nothing like what you have been expecting!"

Jarl looked around at the other people all going about their usual business. It felt as though this conversation was just between the large bald man and he and Sylfia as no one else seemed to even glance in their direction. The people though, did not seem elderly or sick in the slightest, with almost all of them being middle-aged and fighting fit.

"I do not think that we have any other choice but to see what is happening here," Jarl said. "I do not feel as though I am being controlled and as long as we remain cautious and suspicious, I think we should follow this man and learn what we can. Then if Sigrid and Hilda arrive and are offered the same, we may see them sooner than we expected."

That logic did make sense to Sylfia but she was still worried. Her father had seemed to take the 'wait and see' stance where she would have definitely preferred to have gone back to look for her friend and mother.

Regardless of Sylfia's worries, they followed the man into the inn. As soon as they entered through the door they were greeted with a pleasant warmth of an open fire, the smell of a delicious meal cooking slowly and the low hum of happy people going about their usual conversations. There was nothing negative or untoward about the place, but Sylfia could not help but remain suspicious.

"Here, take this and join me at my table," the same man said as he handed both Sylfia and Jarl a tankard of an amber looking liquid. Neither intended to drink though, having learnt the lesson from Baldur's Circle of not taking anything unless they were sure what it was – or what it could do.

"My name is Magnus," he said without hesitation as they all sat at a round wooden table, placing their drinks down with dull thuds.

Magnus took a long swig from his tankard and the amber liquid dripped out of the sides of his mouth as he drank, and down his long braided beard.

"Jarl. And Sylfia," Jarl replied shortly, offering no smile or kindness along with his words.

"Welcome to the second ring," Magnus said. "Second ring, second life. I think that you will like it here. What did you die of in your first life?"

Sylfia looked at Jarl questioningly, but her father did not take his eyes off Magnus.

"We are here by choice," Jarl said honestly. "Why are you here?"

Magnus' face lit up in a beaming smile. "I died a long time ago from a sickness that I never recovered from, and look at me now!"

"How can this be?" Sylfia asked in shock. "You do not look sick, elderly or frail but we already know that this ring is the dying destination of those who perish outside of combat."

"Ah, this is the way of the second ring," Magnus said with open palms. It is said that many centuries ago, a group of sickly men and women were sent to this place to meet their fate. They did not accept their end and bargained with Hel for mercy. They were granted a true second life where they built this city that you see all around you, and since that day this is where the old and sick arrive once their mortal lives have come to an end. When we arrive we are freed from what ended us, and we are allowed to live and appear as we choose. The second ring is filled with hope and happiness and that is the deal with Hel that we have struck."

"Could this be true father?" Sylfia asked with wide eyes. "Is this truly a place that could grant true happiness and everlasting life?"

"If there is one thing that I have learnt of Hel, daughter, it is that there is never an offering that is so simply one sided. Magnus is not telling us the extent of this bargain, are you Magnus?" Jarl asked, still not dropping his gaze from the large man.

Magnus' smile flashed from existence for a single second before returning, though now it did not quite meet his eyes.

"Your father is right, Sylfia," Magnus said. "The deal that the second ring has with Hel is not as one sided as it may seem, though what we have here in our everlasting life far exceeds the cost that we have paid, and continue to pay."

Sylfia watched Jarl as Magnus spoke and was amazed to see his stern furrowed brow loosen at Magnus' admission of a deal. Clearly he had been expecting to be lied to again but the man was being unexpectedly straight and up front about this deal with Hel.

"So what is the deal?" Sylfia asked when Magnus did not conclude his own sentence.

"It is that the people who reside within the second ring of Helheim may never touch each other," Magnus said flatly.

Sylfia and Jarl looked at each other for a moment, both trying to understand the implications of such a restriction, but before they could explore the fullness of this law, Magnus continued.

"We may never comfort, hug, shake hands, or make love to each other whilst we reside within the second ring. We can never kiss a loved one or fight with an enemy. It is the way it was bargained and the way it must be forever."

"Why is it that these rules are never taught before we enter such places, Sylfia?" Jarl asked loudly. "I could have tapped your back and then... what would happen if these rules are broken?" Jarl asked with a sideways glance to Magnus.

"If this one rule is broken, you will be taken from this place and never be seen nor heard from again... though if you had touched your daughter before learning of this rule, it would not be enforced."

"So why do you not simply tell nobody of the rule if it is not enforced in ignorance?" Sylfia asked.

"It is not the way it is done," Magnus answered. "We enjoy our eternal life here and we would not want to jeopardise that. Also, if one person knows the rule and is touched by one who does not, the one with the knowledge is still punished."

"That does not seem like such a bad trade for eternal life," Sylfia said.

"To you perhaps, daughter," Jarl replied. "Though to some, that cost would be far too high. If I could never hold my wife's hand again, hug her or even sleep beside her in bed without the fear that one wrong move could end my very life... I do not think that I could make that choice. After all, an unending life without love when bet against a short life with the one person who you truly love with all of your heart..." Jarl trailed off as though he was thinking about that very scenario and he shuddered.

"Indeed," Magnus replied. "Where many think that unending life is a gift above any other, some such as yourself see the truth in the bargain. Life here is long, but those who have known love may see out their existence in perpetual pain, never forgetting those who they have known before."

The three were silent for a moment as they let those words sink in, then Sylfia spoke.

"And those who break this rule, you do not know what happens to them?" she asked.

Magnus shook his head. "I do not, though some think that their souls are taken away and milked for their very life essence and it is this process that fuels our eternal life. If you ask me, I do not know what happens and I do not know the source of our everlasting life. These are questions that can raise problems, so I do not ask them." Then he took another long drink, emptying his tankard and slamming the metal vessel down on the wooden table with a loud thud.

"So this place... is just like the mortal realm?" Jarl asked slowly.

"More or less," Magnus replied. "You do not need to eat or drink here, though it is almost always pleasurable to do so. The vendors that you see throughout this ring will give you anything that you ask for and there is no need to trade – they are simply there as a mechanism for you to take what you need or want."

"What does this even mean?" Jarl asked. "That I can ask for whatever I want and I will be given it without cost?"

"Exactly," Magnus replied. "This place is a paradise... and you will soon learn that the things that you once wanted in the mortal realm are not the same here, for what good would gold and riches be when you can obtain anything that you would like without them?" He opened his arms wide as he spoke and smiled. If Jarl was being honest, the man did seem genuinely happy.

"So I can go out to a weaponsmith and ask for every weapon that I have ever trained with, and that would be OK?" Sylfia asked.

"Of course you can!" Magnus said with laughter in his voice, "but you would be unable to use weapons here, unless you would like to be taken away to the unknown. Mostly people ask for things to make their lives more comfortable, and food and drink! Forgetting your life in the mortal realm is not easy, but here you will have a new life without struggles and hardships. The way I see things is that all of us here have arrived because we grew too old or too sick and we were not offered the chance to die in combat so that we could reach the glorious halls of Valhalla. We struggled through hardships and our mortal lives were not easy... so this place is our recompense for that. Where once we had difficult lives, now we can live for all eternity in peace and luxury."

Sylfia looked at her father and they shared the mental agreement not to tell this man that they had not arrived through either old age or sickness, they were both aware that he was the type to shun anything out of the ordinary and they did not need that kind of enemy appearing before they had a plan of what to do next.

"So that is it, the welcome speech," Magnus said with a smile. "Remember not to touch anyone else, and try to have fun. I guarantee that you will have forgotten your mortal lives in no time." Then he stood up from the table, turned his back on Sylfia and Jarl, and walked away.

No one else in the inn seemed to care that Jarl and Sylfia remained. They were all talking amongst themselves merrily, though now the father and daughter could see that it was with an obvious yet small safety gap between each of them. It was strange - if the no touching rule had not been mentioned, they may not have noticed that anything was amiss.

"I think that Magnus was telling us the truth... this place is truly an eternal paradise for these people..." Sylfia said quietly to her father as he eyed the tankard on the table before him. "And if it is true that we can get anything we want from this place, then we can generate an entire stockpile of weaponry, ready for when we take the third ring."

Jarl did not respond and picked up the tankard. He raised it gingerly to his lips, sniffed audibly and then took a deep swig of the amber liquid. He swallowed loudly and then peered into the tankard as though trying to determine what was inside. Then his eyes widened in shock.

"This is the most unbelievable thing that I have ever drunk in my entire life, Sylfia! Come, you must try this!" Jarl announced loudly.

"No father, I do not wish to sit and drink; we must make our plans and continue along our path!" Sylfia replied though almost in a whisper. She could not believe that her father could become so easily distracted when there was still so much to be done.

"Sylfia, daughter," Jarl said placatingly. "Every once in a while it is important to step away from the hardships of life and battle and appreciate the world around you. Sit, take a drink and let your mind wander for a moment, daughter. I think that we have earned it."

Sylfia could not believe her ears and stared at her father with her mouth hanging open and Jarl then pushed his tankard into her hands and commanded her to drink. She took a moment to try to understand what was happening, but eventually could see no harm in it. Her expression did not change as she let the amber liquid fill her mouth.

Then it hit her.

It was cool and sweet and without a doubt, drinking it was the most pleasant experience she had ever felt in her entire life. Immediately her scowl melted away and she too smiled as she peered into the tankard to examine its contents.

"Do you feel any different?" Jarl asked.

Sylfia examined herself as best she could. "I do not think so. My desire is still to continue onwards, away from this place so that the end of my path can be reached."

Jarl nodded. "This drink has not clouded my vision as the mist did. I believe that we are indeed safe here, so perhaps we should wait until your mother and Hilda arrive and, in the meantime, make our plans whilst enjoying all that we can."

"I think... I think that it is a good idea to sit and await their arrival. But know that if they are not here within a day or two we must continue and plan to meet them in the third ring. We must not forget what we are here to do, no matter the choices we have."

"You are correct daughter. But perhaps there is some truth to what Magnus has said... perhaps that the reward for a life of struggle and hardship that ended without battle and the glory of Valhalla, is this very place. Perhaps we should not be so hasty as to ignore the life that we could lead in this place as a family, together and forever."

"You said yourself that you could not live without touching mother, without a hug or a kiss... this is not the place for us to sit and decay in father and you know that is the case... you will see before long, as with every temptation, as with Baldur's Circle, these things are never as they seem."

"I know Sylfia, but a man may dream of simpler things. It is just all so tiring. It has all been so tiring."

29

Neither Sigrid nor Hilda saw what had happened within the mists before them. One moment, Jarl and Sylfia were both there in front of them, and the next they had disappeared without a trace. They had both waited for a long while, not wanting to move in case the pair could retrace their steps and make their way back to them, but after a short while the realisation hit that they would not be returning.

"What do you think has happened? Hilda asked Sigrid in a worried tone. She felt a little awkward being left alone with Sigrid, as they had never really had the chance to talk without the other two around.

"I do not know; do you think we should follow after them?" Sigrid replied.

"Sylfia! Jarl!" Sigrid called at the top of her voice, but her words echoed away from them before disappearing entirely beyond the swirling mists.

"They must have heard that, no?" Hilda said. "But if I know both Jarl and Sylfia, they will do whatever they need to do to survive out there. Maybe we should follow in their path and see if we can reach them before anything happens."

Sigrid nodded once. "We can track their steps as the ground is soft and they have left tracks behind them," she said pointing to the ground. Hilda could see that she was correct, the soft, moist ground had held the indentations of their footprints almost exactly as they had been made – a tracker's dream.

Both Hilda and Sigrid walked slowly beside one another as they followed the path that Sylfia and Jarl had made before them. Neither of the women seemed too concerned that the pair ahead of them were in any kind of trouble, but neither wanted to wait too long so that trouble could reach them before they did.

"You came from the north, Hilda?" Sigrid asked.

"I do... I mean I did before I was trapped within Baldur's Circle. It was a long time ago and I miss my family, but I know that they are long passed."

"You know that they have passed?"

"I do. From everything I have seen since leaving the settlement, and the reasons why I left in the first place... there would be no way that they would survive another fruitless winter," Hilda said.

"What do you mean?" Sigrid asked, now turning to look at Hilda and where she had expected to see some sorrow on the woman's face, she was met with a blank expression.

"When I left, it was to search for a new place to settle, or for new hunting grounds as for many seasons the crops and the animals all around us had been dying out. Each year the winters had grown colder. I was the only one of my party to survive and without my report of new and better horizons, my clan was doomed. Because I did not return to my people, they are all dead. My husband... my friends... they will never return."

"That is awful, Hilda. But you must know that it is not your fault... you had become trapped and even if you had found a way to escape that place, what would you have done? Would you have brought your entire settlement to Baldur's Circle so that they too could be enslaved there, or perhaps even killed by their army? There was nothing that you could have done, Hilda, and blaming yourself serves no purpose."

"I do not blame myself. Not fully at least," Hilda replied, her expression now becoming harsher. "I blame the Gods that did this to my people. The Gods that welcome the coming of Ragnarök without lifting a finger to help those in need and the Gods who gave me this divine gift to create food whenever I choose, but held me back from the people who needed it the most. That is the sad fact of my story; I now have the gift that would have saved my family. I will never let anything like this happen again though. Your husband, your daughter and you... you are now my brothers and sisters and I will never let any of you go hungry. That is the gift I now have to share, and the gift that will not be wasted."

Sigrid did not quite know how to respond. Hilda had been so caught up in her recitation it was almost as though it was some mantra that she had been telling herself over and over.

"It... it is normal for someone who has gone through what you have, to want to help others Hilda, but it was not your fault, and it is not your calling to protect us all. You do realise that we are as a family and we are all there for each other. If one of us falls down then it is upon the other three to lift them back up again."

"I know," Hilda replied. "It is just that sometimes... sometimes I cannot help but feel as though I could have done better. Sylfia, you and Jarl have all given me a second chance at life. You have welcomed me into your family without a second thought and I feel as though I will never be able to do enough to repay you. Most women in your place would be cautious of my arrival with your husband, but you have shown no signs of jealousy, worry or even any animosity towards me at all, in fact it has been the opposite!"

Sigrid smiled. "Jarl and I share a bond that cannot be broken, and this bond is the reason that I know that I can trust you. Jarl and I have been one since the day we met; he knows my soul like no other and he mine. If Jarl tells me that you are as family to us, then that is the truth in as much as it would be the same if it were the other way around."

Hilda stared down at the ground as they continued to follow the footprints in the ever dampening muddy surface. The imprints were sometimes erratic but generally they all seemed to go in the same direction.

A voice suddenly reached them through the mist that surrounded them and Hilda peered out in front of her.

"Go back!" Jarl shouted. "It is not safe, go back and await our return!"

"Jarl? What happened? Where are you?" Sigrid called back into the mist. She was about to start running in the direction from which Jarl's voice was coming when Hilda placed a hand on her arm and gestured down to the ground.

"What are you..." Sigrid started and then realised what Hilda was indicating: Jarl's voice was coming from their right, where his footsteps clearly led straight on.

Sigrid thought for a moment, then called out into the mist. "Is that you, husband?"

"Yes! Go back! It is not safe!" came the reply from the mist.

"You do not want us to come and help you? What is the problem?" she called back, not taking another step forward.

"Just go back!" Jarl replied. "It is not safe!"

With those words, Sigrid made her decision - whatever this voice was, it was not her husband. With that in mind, she knew that the voice or whatever was attached to it was almost certainly a threat to her entire family, so she turned away from the imprints of her husband's feet in the ground and moved towards the voice's direction.

Sigrid had barely taken three steps before the voice called out to them again.

"I said stop!" Jarl boomed as commandingly as he had ever shouted.

"If you were my husband perhaps I would listen to your command... though that is debatable actually," Sigrid called into the mist. It made Hilda snort as she held her laughter. "I know that you are a danger, so why not show yourself and we can solve whatever this situation is?"

Sigrid reached down to her waist where her weapon had been sheathed, but it was not there. She looked down to see if there was any trace of it, or if it had shifted around her body slightly but it was clearly missing.

"Do you have a weapon, Hilda?" Sigrid asked almost in a whisper. She heard Hilda pat her sides and back and Hilda replied with her own whisper.

"No... I do not know what has happened, but I have nothing!"

The mist before them swirled violently as though it had been lifted by a freak updraft and disappeared to reveal a desolate wasteland beyond and a man walking towards them although neither could discern his features.

The man's outline was just like Jarl's; he was the same size, he had the same broad shoulders and he even mimicked the man's gait somewhat but as he came closer Sigrid could see that this was not her husband. It was a creature crafted entirely of mist and shadow.

The figure stopped a metre away from Sigrid and Hilda and the mist that constituted its human-like form swirled to give the impression that it was smiling.

"You want to fight against us as you pretend to be my husband? Do not think that will give you any advantage," Sigrid said.

"And I have watched Jarl fight, if I were you I would have chosen to become a fighter with much more skill!" Hilda added. This time she made Sigrid chuckle and it was evident to both that neither wanted to show any weakness to this apparition.

The mist-Jarl lopped its head to one side as though trying to figure out what the pair were saying, but did nothing to move against them. Eventually, when neither Sigrid nor Hilda did nothing to make the first move, from the mist a pair of identical shimmering silver swords dropped to the ground. They landed with a wet thud and a small amount of moist mud leapt into the air. Hilda and Sigrid looked at each other, each trying to decide if they were supposed to pick up the weapons or not.

"Sylfia said that the Gods are not allowed to attack mortals unless they are defending themselves," Hilda said.

"Do you think that this creature is a God?" Sigrid asked.

Hilda looked the mist-Jarl up and down appraisingly before shaking her head slowly. Before she could reply though, the creature floated back and away from the weapons so that the women could retrieve them without the threat of being attacked prematurely. A low, guttural sound rumbled from it and the voice was Jarl's, though it was strained as though it had never formed these words before.

"Fight. Win. Go," it said. "Lose. Stay."

The message was clear; if Sigrid and Hilda could beat the mist creature in combat then they would be free to leave this place, otherwise they would be condemned to stay, possibly forever.

Sigrid was the first to move. She lunged at the sword on the ground, picking the weapon up easily and in one single movement, swung it in a straight, upwards arch that betrayed her years of practise. The blade cut through the mist creature from where its right hip should have been, all the way up and through its left shoulder. There was no resistance and the cut was clean. Sigrid felt no remorse for cutting the facsimile of her husband in two as she knew that it had no bearing on the real man himself.

Sigrid watched as the mist-Jarl swirled and dissipated into nothingness, then turned to face Hilda, who was yet to make a move.

"That was far easier than I would have expected..." Sigrid said as she moved to sheathe her new sword.

"Jarl is too slow, he would never defeat you in battle and I think he knows that!" Hilda replied. "You should..." she started to say with a smile on her face, but it immediately vanished as she watched the mist reform into the shape of Jarl, though now clearly without the dire wound that Sigrid had inflicted.

"Move!" Hilda shouted as she dived for the second sword still on the ground. She too managed to collect it with ease but as she swung it at the creature's midsection, it bore down on her sword with a single hand axe made of mist and blocked her strike. A moment later, a second hand axe swung directly at her head and she had to flatten herself against the ground to avoid it.

Hilda was coated with wet, putrid mud and she wiped her eyes clear as she rolled to the side, narrowly avoiding another heavy strike from the mist.

"Why is it solid when it attacks, but our strikes pass right through?" Hilda shouted to Sigrid, though her partner had no good answer. Instead, as the mist-Jarl swung again at Hilda who was still rolling on the ground, Sigrid swung her sword at the thing's left arm, cutting it in two. The arm and weapon both dissipated and faded into nothingness before they hit the ground and within another moment they had reformed to the main mass.

Hilda used the time to leap back up to her feet and the two women stood shoulder to shoulder, weapons in their right hands in ready stances. The mist was already reformed into a perfect though grey facsimile of Jarl and now it held its two mist axes in its hands.

"It takes a moment to reform once you hit it, maybe if we cut it up enough it will not be able to become whole again?" Hilda suggested.

"There is nothing else to try," Sigrid said, "we attack together and do not stop!"

Both women nodded once and as Sigrid juked to the left, Hilda stepped right to present their opponent with two angles of attack for it to defend itself. Both Hilda and Sigrid struck out at the trunk of the creature and on both sides the mist axes blocked the strikes with ferocious strength. Only the fact that there were two attacks to block meant that their opponent could not retaliate with a counterattack again.

On either side of the mist-Jarl, the women attempted a repeated barrage of attacks, but their opponent simply parried without difficulty. It was both fast and strong and as the battle progressed it showed no sign of fatigue or weakness.

"We must work together!" Hilda called across the beast. "It is too fast and too strong for us to best on our own, but I would be willing to wager it has never fought a pair properly before!"

Hilda dodged an uppercut from one of the grey axes and leant into the movement, placing one hand on the ground and used her momentum to kick out at the misty form. Her leg met no resistance from the creature, but its head split in two as her appendage travelled through it and by the time its head had reassembled itself a moment later, Hilda and Sigrid stood shoulder to shoulder again.

"We need to attack together," Hilda said. "Do not let it reform!"

The mist-Jarl then began to swing its hand axes in downward overhead strikes one at a time over and over. With each strike, one of the two women parried with their own swords and as the weapons collided, the axes took solid form and forced the blocker to the ground, ready for the next to take over.

They took it in turns to block and duck so that neither were becoming overwhelmed by the strength of the mist creature. Sigrid had trained with Jarl many times and although their opponent somewhat matched his technique, its strength had definitely increased over the original.

Then finally Sigrid saw an opening. Just like Jarl, their opponent was leaving its leading leg exposed as it swung. Most combatants would not have noticed the oversight, being fully occupied with the strength and ferocity of the strikes from the hand axes, but as Sigrid had a partner in her defence, she had the time to exploit such a weakness. Instead of blocking and moving, this time Sigrid jumped back out of the way of the downward axe swing and cut the mist creature's leg in two.

It stumbled backwards and Hilda immediately pressed her advantage. She jumped over the top of the crouching Sigrid to deliver a surprise overhead blow and again the mist-Jarl had not seen it coming. Hilda's attack cut the creature in two and before it even had the chance to reform, Sigrid followed up with a strike of her own.

With the creature now unable to take the time to reform, the two warriors sliced through its form repeatedly, stepping forward over and over until they faced off against a swirling mass of mist.

Then instead of reforming into Jarl and holding corporeal weapons, the mist seemed to relinquish its human-shape and instead became a swirling dark mass of ether.

Suddenly, black tendrils, as though they were the arms of a dire octopus, shot out from the mass, grasping the wrists and ankles of the two women tightly and lifting them both up into the air.

There was nothing that they could do to prevent themselves being completely restrained and rendered helpless; it was far too late for that.

"Hilda! What do we do now?" Sigrid called out in a panic.

"There is nothing we can do, unless you are hiding some more weapons over there?" Hilda replied. The joke was in poor taste, but there was nothing that either of them could do. They had lost and they knew that this was to be their end.

A flicker of light in the distance momentarily caught Sigrid's attention. It was strange, as though it was a divine spark, and as she watched it grew into a bright orange glow.

"Do you see that?" Sigrid gasped.

Hilda peered out into the distance and saw the glow but it was now far more clear what it was: it was a growing blaze that had begun to spew deep black smoke high into the air above it.

The creature could not help but let its attention divert from the women that it had bested and to this new threat to its domain. The tendrils that held the pair lost their solidity without warning and both Hilda and Sigrid fell to the wet mud with a loud slap.

"Run Hilda!" Sigrid shouted. She did not need to specify where to as it was clear - if this creature was not expecting the fire at the least, or was scared of it at the most, then that was where they needed to go.

Their feet slapped the wet ground as their legs pumped, taking them hopefully away from the mist that they knew they could not beat. Neither of them took the time nor the risk to look back over their shoulders to see if they were escaping from it or not.

They could see more clearly now. The fire that was spreading faster was actually a black lake, filled with tar that seemed to span an expanse between the desolate wilds that they ran through and a high stone wall. The stench of both death and burning tar filled Sigrid's nostrils and as she ran, the inside of her nose burned in complaint.

"We are here, now what?" Sigrid panted but as she looked to where she thought Hilda was, she saw nothing but empty space.

Her blood ran cold and as she looked back, she saw that the creature had caught up with Hilda, who was again captured in its terrible tendrils.

"Hilda!" Sigrid called. With only one opponent to occupy, the tendrils had covered Hilda's throat and mouth to prevent her for calling for help.

Sigrid had but a moment to act. She had reached close enough to the burning tar pit that she could feel her skin burning, but she had a new plan now. Swiping her sword through the tar, the blade was coated in the thick black goo and along with the rest of the burning river, it had ignited to burn a bright orange red.

Sigrid did not waste any time and raced back to her friend. She did not know if it was too late or not but she knew she had to complete her task one way or another. As soon as she was within range of the dark creature, she sliced through it with her burning blade.

To Sigrid's amazement, the mist ignited, the incorporeal ether clinging to the tar as though it could not escape and as it stuck, the flames burnt and spread. Hilda was dropped to the ground once more with another wet slap and the two women watched as their opponent burned away to nothing but smoke and ash.

30

"Mother!" Sylfia called in delight as she watched Sigrid and Hilda walk through the gates that she and Jarl had done less than an hour previously. They had left the inn after finishing their drinks and had decided to await the arrival of the second half of their family at these exact gates because Jarl had been adamant that if they simply waited, they would all be back together in no time.

Hilda looked as though she had been dragged through the mud, where Sigrid had somehow retained some of her classical elegance. As the group approached each other though, Jarl was the first to speak.

"Do not come any closer," he commanded when they were just a few metres apart.

"It is us husband, you do not need to worry…" Sigrid started.

"No, there is a rule here," Jarl explained. "No two people can touch. It is the price they pay to live in such a beautiful and bountiful place."

Sigrid looked about herself for the first time. The moment she had come through the gateway into the second ring of Helheim, her gaze had been entirely focussed on Jarl and Sylfia. Now she could see that the place was indeed beautiful. Somehow in this second ring of Helheim, the sun was shining high in the sky and there were people moving in and out of stone buildings, crossing the streets, talking to vendors at their stalls, and generally they all looked happy and content.

"What is happening here?" Sigrid asked, her mouth hanging slightly open.

"And what happens if we touch each other?" Hilda added.

"They did not exactly say," Sylfia said. "Just that those people disappear and that they may be used to fuel the eternal lives of the people here. These people here are the ones who died who did not make it to Valhalla - they have been given eternal life and the freedom to do as they wish.

"This is everyone who did not make it to Valhalla?" Hilda asked slowly whilst peering about herself. "Everyone? How big is this place? How many are there?"

"We are not sure," Jarl said. "This place seems so big… but these people seem happy Hilda. If it were not for Valhalla, when I do eventually pass I think that I would be happy here, if it were not for that one rule. To live in a place so close to my wife and to not be able to touch her… it seems as though it could be a fate worse than torture."

"Hilda nodded slowly. "I can see how you may think that, but think of those…" her breath caught as she struggled to continue and Jarl recognised the look in her face as tears filled her eyes. It was the look of loss, mourning and regret.

"Think of those who have not had the chance to see the ones who they love for days, weeks, months... years..." her voice grew smaller and tears began to wet her cheeks.

Both Sylfia and Sigrid moved to comfort her, though they stopped when Jarl held up a single hand.

"You see how this is a curse?" Jarl Asked, "A man or woman can be left with tears in their eyes and not a single person can lend them either an arm or a shoulder."

Hilda brought her hands to her face and her shoulders rose and fell a few times as her sadness engulfed her. Then, wiping her eyes and cheeks, she managed to ask: "do you think they are here?"

"If they are here then they will be happy," Sylfia answered. She knew that Hilda's search party for new land and settlements had not died in battle so they could reside within the second ring of Helheim, but the rest of her settlement and her family was another matter.

"If they are not here they will have made it to the great halls of Valhalla, to dine with the Gods in eternal happiness," Sylfia reassured her.

The group stood beside Hilda as best they could to show their support and kindness for her sorrow, but deep down they each now knew that this place was truly cursed and those that lived there were simply living half-lives.

"We must leave this place and continue along our path," Jarl said in a low tone. "There is no good to come from staying here a moment longer than we must."

Sylfia nodded in agreement. "We have a duty, a task to complete and it is not here. We must find a way into the third ring of Helheim and then beyond again and again. The curse that Ragnarök will bring to all of the mortal realms must be stopped."

"So where do we go?" Sigrid asked. "Do we continue on through the streets until we find a doorway that leads us to the next ring?"

"I do not believe that it will be that simple," Hilda said. "If it was possible to cross back and forth across the rings, why would those dishonoured men and women of the third ring not simply cross into this place and take it for their own? I do not think that they would live in such luxury as this."

Hilda's words made a lot of sense to Sylfia, who was trying to remember if Hel had given them any clues or explanations when they had spoken, but eventually she realised that there was nothing. She had no more information to draw upon than the rest of her family.

"If it is information that we need, perhaps we should simply ask for it," Jarl said as he set off walking towards the nearest vendor: a short man with wild red hair and a bushy beard who seemed to be standing at an empty wooden stall with empty crates and baskets all around.

"Good day to you!" the man announced with a giant smile. "Is there anything that you are looking for in particular, or was it just to wish me a fine day today?"

Jarl peered into the crates and baskets with a bemused expression on his face.

"Why do you have nothing to trade?" he asked.

"Why that is not strictly true. But I guess it would seem like that if you are new to the second ring. I have anything and everything that you could ever want or need, but to say that my goods are for trade is definitely wrong for I take no payment and expect none either."

"What does that mean?" Hilda asked. "You will give us anything for free? But where does it come from?"

"Now that is a good question," the vendor said still beaming. "Why not ask for something and see what happens.

"Give me an apple," Jarl said without any pause or pleasantries.

The vendor reached down into a wooden crate - still smiling – and when he retracted his arm, he was holding the shiniest, juiciest looking red apple that Jarl had ever seen. He placed it on his wooden counter and gestured for Jarl to take it.

Without hesitating, Jarl took a large bite of the appetising fruit and the vendor and the three woman watched as golden apple juice spilled from his mouth and coated his beard.

Not wanting to betray his delight, Jarl held back his moans of pleasure at just how good this fruit was, swallowed, and dropped the rest of the apple to his side.

"Ah that is nothing," Hilda said with a grin as she cupped her own hands together and in a moment parted them to reveal an exact copy of the very same apple, placing it on the wooden counter.

The vendor's eyes grew wide. "You should not be able to do that," he exclaimed in a whispered shout. "The vendors here are sanctioned to provide any items that the people desire, but to pull something from the empty air… it is unheard of!"

"Do not worry, this is a gift that my friend Hilda had before we came to this place. But now tell me… why do you fulfil this role if it is of no benefit to you?"

"We… we all take it in turns here as vendors so that it is always fair. I am here for a few days then another will take my place. It is as fair as it can be," then looking at Hilda with wide eyes he asked: "can you bring anything into being?"

"Just food," Jarl answered before Hilda could reply. "Can you make me a pair of hand axes?"

The vendor reached under the counter and placed a pair of shining silver headed hand axes on top with a thud but the entire time he did not let his gaze fall from Hilda.

Jarl picked up the axes and appraised them. They were without a doubt the most beautiful weapons that he had ever seen, perfectly balanced for his hands, with runes carved into the wooden handles that were sized to fit his hands exactly. More runes and swirling patterns were expertly cast into the flat silver sides of the axe heads that themselves were ground to an almost unbelievably perfect razor's edge.

"These axes... they are the most beautiful that I have ever seen," Jarl mumbled, finding it difficult to keep the shock and wonder from his voice. "They are as though they have been crafted by the very Gods themselves, forged for my hands alone..."

"That is because these weapons are forged by the Gods themselves!" the vendor replied with a wide smile, with a tone as though this was the most normal thing in the world. "Where else would they come from? We are no magical beings with the ability to create items as though from nothing. The things that we ask for, no matter how menial they may seem, are created to fill our need. An apple is not simply an apple, rather it is a cure for hunger with a single bite." Then the vendor turned his attention back to Hilda as though he had not uttered a single word to Jarl. "Does your gift have a limit?" he asked Hilda.

"It is whatever will fit between my palms," Hilda said. "And a pair of short sword for me please."

The two swords that appeared on the counter from beneath were beautiful beyond Hilda's wildest dreams. If she had been asked to imagine a pair of swords so perfect, so beautiful, yet still so functional, this pair would have eclipsed even those. She quickly attached them to her sides and placed the sword that the mist-Jarl had given her and Sigrid on the counter in place of the new pair.

"You know that you cannot fight here... weapons are not strictly necessary..." the vendor said slowly.

"We like the way they feel," Jarl said. "Now two more swords and two more axes and I think that we will be ready to go."

Just like before, the weapons were retrieved from somewhere out of sight and again they were beyond perfect. It was as though the Gods themselves had forged them specifically for each of the group, there was not a single thing any of them would have changed.

"What if we were to use them here?" Sigrid asked. "What if we were to kill someone?"

"If you touch someone here..." the vendor started.

"No, not touch," Sigrid repeated, "Kill. I mean if I were to throw this sword at that woman over there," she gestured behind herself, "and cut her head clean off, what would happen?"

The vendor glanced at the woman who Sigrid had gestured to with his mouth slightly open. "I do... I am not sure... exactly... but why would you do such a thing in a place where there is no reason to fight, or kill?"

"For fun," Jarl said. "What if I cut your head off right now? Would you grow a new one? Wake up in your bed in the morning as though it had never happened?" As he spoke, he raised one of his new axes and pointed it at the vendor as though he was carrying out the very act in his mind at that very moment.

"I... uh... I do not know..." the man replied with a stutter. "But you surely would not wish to risk..."

"It would be most unwise," a voice came from behind the group and as one they turned to come face to face with Magnus.

"Sigrid, Hilda, this is Magnus," Jarl said with a smile. "I had a feeling that if we were to keep asking uncomfortable questions he would show himself.

Magnus smiled at the group and nodded to Sigrid and Hilda. "I can assume that Jarl has told you about the one rule we have here?"

Both women nodded wordlessly.

"And why may I ask, are you tormenting this vendor?" Magnus asked.

"Because it is fun, is it not?" Jarl said with a smile of his own. "This place you think is a paradise is not all it seems, not at all," Jarl explained. "Can you tell me how we may leave and find ourselves within the third ring of Helheim?"

Magnus did not stop smiling as he spoke, but this time again his smile did not reach his eyes.

"You already know the answer to this question, do you not?" he asked. "You know that those who reside within the third ring are the dishonoured, and the only way to become one of them is through the gutter."

Jarl gave a sarcastic smile to the large man. "Yes of course, and do you know how we can reach the gutter? After all, it would not do to have this paradise you have created tarnished with people who become dishonoured after death."

Sylfia looked at Jarl and suddenly comprehended what he had been doing up to this point: he was trying to push the vendor to see what would happen if one were to step out of line within the second ring. There must be some internal system to deal with those individuals who became unruly or difficult, but without technically breaking the one most important rule.

"So this is not the way to progress onward to the next ring of Helheim?" Jarl asked, a little disheartened with his own words.

Magnus clicked his tongue and looked thoughtful. "What do you mean, progress to the next ring?" he asked. "The nine rings of Helheim are not there to be traversed. They are there to keep the inhabitants separated depending upon their status in the mortal realms... I do not see why you would want to leave this place and move on to the third ring."

"Because we do not want to stay in this place," Sigrid said sweetly and added a smile for good measure. "This place is not for us, and we have a task to complete that involves us moving on and away from here. Surely there is a way to get to the next ring? We promise that we would not cause any trouble."

"I... I do not know," Magnus replied and his words at least seemed truthful. "When people leave this place it is usually for breaking the single rule that we hold and not because they wish to move to another place, and when they do leave, they do not report back to us. I have told you already, we have theories about what comes next but there is no way to prove them one way or another."

"But people *do* leave this place?" Sylfia pressed.

"Yes, they do," Magnus said, "but after they have broken the single rule that we impose."

"OK," Jarl said. "Then what happens if I wish to fight in this place, if battle is what makes me happy ?"

Then a new voice spoke from behind the group. It was smarmy, slick even, and the tone betrayed an air of superiority over his fellow man.

"Come now Magnus, you can tell them. If they want to fight then who are we to stop them?" the man said.

Hilda, Sylfia, Jarl and Sigrid turned as one and there behind them stood a tall, thin man with straight white hair and a crooked smile. He wore a shirt with buttons and a thick gold chain around his neck.

"Forgive the intrusion, but there is some place that the *other* things that you may wish for can happen. After all, not everybody has the same wishes and desires, right?" the man said cryptically.

"No, that place is not for them. They are new here and they do not know what they are asking for," Magnus almost whispered to the man.

"But they *are* asking, are they not?" the man replied.

"We are," Jarl interrupted before Magnus could respond again. "What is this place of which you speak? Is there a way for us to leave this second ring and find ourselves progressing onwards through Helheim?"

"There is indeed a way," the man responded. "My name is Frode." He held out a hand for Jarl to take, though Jarl made no move to make any contact with the offered appendage.

"See Magnus, this man knows what he is doing here, he knows the rules," Frode said with a smile.

"He does not know!" Magnus said, failing to keep his voice low and controlled. "He is a fool for asking such questions and you are not going to make things any easier for him!"

"Do you wish to know how to leave this place?" Frode said, ignoring Magnus' outburst.

"Yes, we do," Jarl said in a low and even tone. "We must leave this place and move onward, none of us wish to stay here."

"Then you must come with me," Frode announced. "Follow along and do not drag your heels, all of you. There is a place that you must see."

"Do not do this Frode," Magnus growled, though he made no move to stop the man. Jarl could not tell if Magnus had no power to dissuade him because of some hierarchical structure within the second ring, or if it was simply that because these people could not touch each other and therefore fight, anyone could pretty much do as they pleased.

"Father I do not know if this is right," Sylfia whispered to Jarl. "Should we trust this man and go with him?"

"I do not see another path, though I think that you are correct to be cautious. We must keep our minds focussed and sharp, and then we will fight for whatever we have to, if we have to," Jarl replied.

Frode led the group away from the busy entranceway to the second ring of Helheim whilst Sylfia and her family followed in silence. There was nothing that they could do or say other than to follow, and discussing what may be to come would serve no one any good.

"The thing about the second ring is," Frode cooed back from the front of the group as though this was his happiest day, "is that if you enjoy living your life as you are supposed to - quiet and friendly - then it is definitely a beautiful place to be. And by all accounts, if you lived your life in sickness and died without marvelling in what is *normal*, then perhaps it is something that you would crave. But some of us were destined for better things and were never given the chance to die properly, to join our families in the halls of Valhalla. You will see soon that we have a way to remedy all of this and we will all gain a second chance at eternal happiness in battle and in victory."

"It sounds like you are saying that we have a chance to reach Valhalla from within Helheim?" Hilda asked. "But Magnus said that…"

"Magnus likes what he has become accustomed to," Frode practically scoffed. "He does not wish for change or for anything neither different nor better. I can tell that you do not share this view. I can tell that you are each warriors, destined to dine with the Gods in Valhalla!"

"We have met the Gods and I am not sure if I would wish to dine with them," Jarl sneered, though kept his voice low enough for Frode not to hear him.

Frode turned away from the bright streets that were still lined with tall stone buildings and into a narrow alleyway, wide enough for just two to walk side by side. The sun struggled to penetrate the high walls and it made the alleyway dark. It made Sylfia feel as though the walls were closing in all around her.

"Is this place safe?" Sigrid asked loudly and her voice echoed away into the darkness over and over.

"Of course not! But that is the beauty of it, is it not?" Frode shouted back, his voice echoing equally as distantly as Sigrid's had. "If you are looking to make a change to your surroundings, if you have grown tired of day to day monotony, then this place will help you as you look to move on."

"Move on…" Sylfia repeated and as she spoke, she realised that there was a question that needed answering that she hadn't yet thought to ask. "Can we… can we die in this place?"

"That is a bit of an odd question," Frode said. "By coming here, you know that everyone and everything has already passed. To die is moot. But I do understand what you are asking of course. In this place, those who are unfortunate enough to find themselves at the wrong end of a mishap, or who manage to die in battle do not find themselves with the freedom to leave this place and find themselves within Valhalla. The dead of Helheim become the Draugr, damned to fester in the eighth ring for all eternity."

"And how would you know this?" Hilda asked. "If their torment is eternal how would you know?"

"Because it is written in the rules of the third and fourth rings of Helheim, where the cut-throats and the damned fight for their very survival. It is actually something that I confess to being rather familiar with myself, having the ability to cross through these three rings, from second to forth."

"You can cross the rings? You must show us the way!" Sylfia exclaimed as a ray of hope glimmered for her future.

"You will see soon enough, all you have to do is keep following me," Frode replied as he began to walk down a flight of carved stone steps into the silent darkness below.

With no alternative path to take, the group followed Frode. Jarl drew his axes and was about to use his divine gift to light them, but a steady hand from Sigrid stopped him. He was about to object when realised that she was telling him not to let these people know what he could do before it was advantageous to do so. Instead they descended the staircase in silence and darkness, the only sound their echoing steps as their feet clacked against the stone beneath them.

The path beyond the staircase was thankfully flat although it did wind left and right which caused Jarl to keep one hand on the cold hard wall to ensure he didn't walk into anything.

"You should be hearing them in just a moment," Frode said chirpily.

Jarl was about to ask what he should be hearing, when he heard the distant murmur of a cheering crowd, the banging of weaponry and the tell-tale sounds of battle.

"Where are you taking us," Jarl whispered, as he drew his weapons and his knuckles turned white around their handles.

"This tunnel connects the second and third rings of Helheim. A part of my duty, as I have already told you, is to travel between the second and third rings, as well as the fourth," he added as a slight afterthought. "You, and anyone else within the second and third rings, are allowed into this tunnel but no further. Furthermore, the tunnel itself is considered something of a grey area where the rules are concerned - go ahead, you can touch each other now that we are far enough in."

Not one of them made any move to touch another, which made Frode exhale loudly.

"Never mind, you will soon see. As I have said, there is one single place that you can go to as a resident of the second ring and that is right here." Frode's voice started to move away from the group as he walked and they continued to follow, the sounds of battle growing louder as they moved towards it.

"Life is just not enough when people are not able to touch. I know that your first instinct may be that you require the touch of your loved ones, your family... but the fact is, it is more often than not that people find themselves craving the touch of battle above anything else. *That* is what the pit is all about."

"The pit?" Hilda asked in a small voice, but Frode did not need to explain any further because as the group made one last turn, they arrived at what they immediately knew was 'The Pit'."

31

"This place is barbaric!" Hilda practically cried as she realised what the place was. Bright burning torches lit a wide, round area where hundreds of men and women cheered and jeered down towards two men fighting each other with bare fists ten feet below them. It lived up to its name; the arena where the two warriors fought was indeed a pit.

The stench of blood, sweat and decay was thick in the air as the group reached the edge of the area that had clearly been made for spectators. The two men were trading blows as though each of them could not have cared less about being struck. Neither of them blocked a strike, but as each took their punches in turn, the cracking of knuckles against jaw and nose filled the air along with the roars of the crowd. Deep red blood splattered and stained the walls of the pit that seemed to be constructed of some bright solid sand, though they were already covered in the stains of previous battles.

"No, not barbaric!" Frode replied with a smile on his lips, "This is exactly what these people want. The crowds are watching and getting their fill of violence and bloodshed, and the warriors will battle until their own desire for inflicting harm on others is satiated, and at the end of the day, the men leave to recover from their wounds."

"One of them doesn't die?" Hilda asked in a small voice as though it was a silly question.

"Have you not already been told that all in this place are already dead?" Frode asked, then quickly added: "It matters not. In most of the battles within The Pit, the warriors do not battle to the death. After all, there would be no point. There is no prize for the common man in winning or losing in the pit, only the promise that if you are killed, you leave this place."

"Then why do people fight?" Sylfia asked "It makes no sense."

"Because people are basic creatures," Frode said, now intently watching the warriors still trading blows as though they were taking turns. "People need to fight and to struggle. To give mortal beings everything they need, but not everything they desire, is to some a fate worse than death. Look around you now, are these people not happy? Are the warriors not smiling as their teeth are broken and their bodies bruised?"

Sylfia scanned the crowd and looked for anyone who seemed as though they were not enjoying themselves, but she came up wanting.

"These people... they are all pleased to be here. Every single one of them," she muttered under her breath. "But why?" Then she raised her voice to ask aloud: "What do they fight for? What is the prize?"

Frode let out a laugh. "There is no prize for these men! The prize has already been won the moment they arrived here at The Pit! It is the freedom to do as they please, to live by no rules except for those they set for themselves!"

"And what if they wish to kill, or to be killed?" Jarl asked.

Frode's face fell into a thoughtful frown for the first time since the group had set eyes on him. "It is a strange thing for a man to wish for death, is it not?"

"But still, to want to come here and to fight, the risk is there, is it not?" Jarl asked. "And there is no doubt that some will come here because they wish for death."

"It is true, warrior," Frode said. "Some come here to fight to the death, but these battles are agreed upon before they begin. The fight that you see before you now is between two men who wish not to die, but who wish to live, and the battle will be concluded as such. Their wounds will heal within a few days, and when they are ready, they will return to fight another day."

"And who is there to ensure that these matches are fought fairly and with honour?" Jarl asked.

"The vendors throughout the second ring would not favour those who break the rules here in The Pit. And the residents of the third and fourth rings would not dare to betray their masters, or else their existence would be forever filled with unending pain and torture. The rules here are always obeyed, and that is the way that it shall always be."

"What happens when somebody dies in The Pit?" Sylfia asked.

"What happens when anybody dies?" Frode asked in response. "Their existence within the realm comes to an end, and they move on as they are supposed. From here, though, I am sad to report that a warrior who has fought and died does not join the ranks of the mighty fallen warriors in Valhalla. No, the fallen from this place join the ranks of the Draugr within the eighth ring of Helheim, or so I am led to believe. I have not actually been there, of course, so you will have to forgive my ignorance."

"Then why would anyone fight in a battle to the death?" Sigrid asked with a bemused look on her face. "If the battle is the reward itself and the penalty for death is so steep, why would anybody wish to play with that risk?"

Frode smiled a devilish smile as he spoke softly and smoothly. "What is life, if there is no risk of death?" he asked. "But of course, there is a second reason. The third ring of Helheim houses all of the miscreants, the murderers, the rapists, and the worst of all the mortal realm, but who do you think is there to guide their hands? The kings of the foul, the masters of these low lives. These are the inhabitants of the fourth ring, and their lives are filled with luxury beyond compare. And they have no rules. These masters though, will live in fear of being usurped at any moment and so treat their bodyguards and loyal servants with the luxuries that they enjoy themselves. The winners of the most brutal battles, those who prove themselves able to fend off their opponents and win, these are the ones who are recruited to work their way into the houses of these kings, and these are the ones who will one day inherit their thrones, one way or another. This is the prize for the victorious warriors, and I can tell you now I have seen nothing better."

"You have seen these kings?" Sigrid asked.

"Of course I have seen them!" Frode laughed. "Who do you think sends me to recruit the warriors from this place?! I must admit however, that the quality of the victors of late has been a little, shall we say, lacking?"

"And this is what you wish to do with us?" Sigrid asked incredulously. "You wish for us to fight to the death in this place so that we may become the servants of some king?"

"No!" Frode cried. "If you are truly the warriors that I believe you to be and with the desire to fight burning in your eyes, I believe that you have the ability to destroy all who you meet in The Pit, and move on to become kings and queens in your own right! It has been foretold that there will be a cataclysmic change in the rings of man and that it will be brought forward by a mighty group of warriors. I believe that you four are those warriors, and that you will all play a part in the changes that are supposed to come to the rings of mortal men. Do you not believe in such prophecies?" His eyes scanned the group as he spoke and stopped for a second on Sylfia, who searched for deeper meaning in his words.

"Father I... I believe that this could be our only chance. And I have spent my entire life with the belief that a path has been laid out before me... if there is indeed such a prophecy, then I must believe that it speaks of us."

Jarl brought a hand up to his beard and wrapped it around his fingers until they had disappeared inside its depths. He thought for a long while before he spoke and when he did, he addressed the group as a whole.

"This place, this second ring. It is as a paradise, and each of us can live a long, possibly eternal life if we stay here. Our choice is now to turn back and stay in comfort, or to embrace the unknown. Each of you is free to make your own decision, but my decision is to stand by my daughter and continue onward as we have planned for so many days."

Sigrid stepped forward. "And I stand with my husband and daughter."

Hilda followed suit and took a step forward of her own. "I stand with my family."

"Ah, then it is settled then, is it not?" Frode announced with a wide grin and as he did so, Sylfia was sure that she heard the flutter of a bird's wing somewhere overhead, away from the burning torches, hidden within the darkness.

"So what do we do now? Who do we fight?" Jarl asked.

"I am afraid that the test of The Pit is an event between two warriors only, so there is no 'we' here. You are tested as individuals and will be weighed as such," Frode said with a smile.

Although all of the group would have preferred to fight alongside one another, they each were skilled fighters in their own right and would never shy away from such a challenge. They had fought supernatural beings, giant wolves, Hel herself and by all accounts, The Pit was there for mortal beings to fight within. There should be no test in this place any greater than those they had already bested.

"If this is the way that this needs to happen, then so be it," Jarl said slowly, keeping an eye on the rest of his group to ensure that they were all in agreement, and not a single one gave him any impression to think that they were unhappy with him.

"We will fight, one at a time, until we have bested each of our opponents within this place, then you will take us onward to the fourth ring so that we may talk to these kings of men. Perhaps then we will find a way to continue our path further and find what we are looking for," Jarl said, and this time the rest of his family nodded in agreement.

"This is excellent news," Frode said with a sparkling glint in his eye. "If you would be so kind as to remain here for a short moment, I will go and find your opponents for the upcoming matches."

"We are to fight today? Now?" Hilda asked in surprise. "There are people awaiting fights to the death here now?"

"There are always those awaiting such battles," Frode said. "Most of the issue is finding suitable opponents. But I think that I should be able to produce an opponent for each of you."

"This all sounds a little convenient, does it not?" Hilda asked, mostly talking to Jarl. "There are people here that will fight against us, but not against each other?"

"If I may," Frode interrupted. "There are always people such as this. For example, there are four of you here now willing to fight to the death, though I presume that none of you would like to fight each other?"

Jarl nodded. "This is true. Perhaps this is simply the way that it has to be. Do not worry though; I know that we are ready to fight this battle." Then he looked at Sylfia. "You still have a way to go before you will be able to best your father, but these mere mortals will have nothing when compared to your skill and strength." He patted the top of Sylfia's head sarcastically, and she batted it away with an open palm.

"It is not myself I worry for, father. Perhaps in your advancing age and widening stomach, you will not be able to fight as you once could," Sylfia joked, though Jarl made a decided effort to suck in his gut with a smile.

"I shall be right back," Frode said and swiftly disappeared into the roaring crowds as they watched the two men still trading punches below and within The Pit.

"Who do you think that we will be fighting against?" Sylfia asked the group as they watched the fight with mild disinterest.

"I would say that these will be regular people who had gained the itch for something more. It will not be an issue, so if they ask for death, we will have no choice but to give them what they ask for," Jarl said.

"Are you sure this is the right thing to do?" Sigrid asked. "To end the lives of these people and to damn them to eternity, it seems as though the cost that they risk is so high."

"There does not seem to be any alternative," Sylfia said. "We must fight to reach further into Helheim, and these people willingly gamble with their lives. If things were the other way around, we would not risk everything without forethought. These people know what they do, and it is not for us to pass judgement."

"I have found an opponent for each of you!" Frode's voice cut through the crowds. "Four fights to behold until the defeated warrior is no more!"

"How can this be?" Hilda asked in shock, "You have been gone but a minute, and you have found four willing to gamble with their lives already?"

"As I have said, there are plenty of souls here willing to gamble with their lives. It is simply a matter of being in the correct place at the correct time."

The murmurs had already started coming from the crowds around the edge of the pit as the group spoke, with some even removing their attention from the fight still underway to see who these people were that wanted to fight to the death.

"Well, are you ready to move onwards and upwards?" Frode asked.

32

Sylfia had been told that she would be the first of the group to fight, so she stood to one side of The Pit, having climbed down the sheer wall moments before. She had been offered a change of weapons, but had chosen to bring with her the two brand new, razor-sharp shimmering swords that she had procured from the vendor less than an hour ago.

She found it strange that she had been told to enter the pit first and to await her opponent, though she was confident that whatever this challenge would bring, she would be up to the task.

Eventually, a thin man climbed carefully down into the pit, holding a round wooden shield and a single hand axe to the ready, as though Sylfia was going to pounce the moment his feet hit the ground. He wore no helmet or armour; rather he was topless, wearing simple leather trousers and a belt to hold them up. His face did not betray the fearsome gaze of a warrior, more the nervous disposition of somebody who did not wish to be there.

"Are you sure that this is my opponent?" Sylfia asked up at the crowd, who were now watching with an uneasy silence. She had meant to ask her family specifically, but Frode answered loudly and before anyone else.

"Come now, do not insult your opponent. He may look as though a strong breeze would knock him down, but I am sure that you will both give these fine people a worthy show, no?"

Sylfia looked back towards her opponent, who still held his shield and axe up to the ready, and still as though she was about to pounce on him. His behaviour was strange to her, mainly because her weapons were currently sheathed by her sides and she could not have been farther from a combat stance unless she was sitting down.

"Kill her!" a female member of the crowd screeched, and it seemed as though this was the signal for the fight to begin. The rest of the crowd immediately began to cheer and whistle, as though something important had happened, but Sylfia could still not see what it was.

Her opponent took a step towards her and raised his axe a little higher.

Sylfia squinted one eye at the man, who she was now sure she could see was shaking, but she still did not take a hold of her two swords.

The man took another shuffled step towards her, Sylfia moved her foot a minuscule amount towards him, and he almost fell over. She smiled at her opponent and spoke softly. "Are you sure that you want to do this?" she asked.

The man did not respond though her attempt to calm him appeared to have stirred something within, and he released a loud, shrill scream and ran straight at Sylfia without any semblance of technique or forethought. Sylfia simply stepped out of the way and he ran right past her. She was also quite sure that he had closed his eyes at the last moment.

He turned and lowered his shield so that he could swing his axe wildly at the unarmed woman, but again she read his intentions and stepped out of the way again and again as he swung with all his might at where he thought she might have been.

Sylfia still did not draw her swords.

"I do not know what you are doing here. You are clearly not a fighter," she said softly and low enough so that the crowds around them could not hear. "I do not wish to kill you, but you may leave me with no choice if you continue."

"Then kill me and end this. I am here to die so let it be," the man grunted as he repeatedly swung his axe harmlessly. "One of us here is to die, and I welcome death. If you do not fight me soon, the crowd may see fit to join in."

Sylfia did not understand what he meant, but she did not see an alternative to actually engaging in combat. The crowd had indeed already started booing at the lack of violence in the fight and again, she knew that this task was necessary for her to continue along her path.

"Fight or I shall come down there and kill you both!" a loud voice came from the spectators. Sylfia looked up into the crowd to see if she could determine who had shouted but she could not tell, but as she let her attention wander from the fight, her opponent attempted to seize the opportunity to attack, and he stepped to within a foot of the unarmed woman.

Sylfia, sensing sudden danger, planted a foot on the man's leading knee, breaking his stride expertly and sending him howling to his knees. Then, in an action so fast that if the blade had not shone in the firelight it may have been missed, Sylfia both drew and slid her sword into the man's neck from above in one fluid movement, then releasing it smoothly to allow him to flop lifelessly to the ground. Sylfia had won her battle though she took no pleasure in this simple victory.

"Was that not wonderful?" Frode announced to the crowd who had eventually stopped cheering for Sylfia once she had climbed out of The Pit. She had wondered what would happen to her opponent's body, but as she had let him lie, within moments he had evaporated into a black mist and dissipated into the air above. She could only conclude that it was just the way things were within Helheim.

"Father, that was no battle to be proud of," Sylfia said as she re-joined her family. "That man was no skilled warrior and I do not believe that it was his choice to be there with me."

Jarl nodded in response. "We must carry out the actions as we are supposed. And be thankful that your fight bore you no wounds, daughter."

"But father," Sylfia started, but before she could protest any further, Frode tapped Sigrid on the shoulder and gestured for her to descend into The Pit for her challenge.

The man who jumped down a second after Sigrid had climbed down into The Pit did not look nervous as Sylfia's opponent had. Sigrid's opponent was a topless man made of bulging muscles, cuts across his body from what must have been many fights, and some even recent as dry blood stained his body. His midsection was covered by a narrow cloth, and in his hands, he held two large battle axes that looked as though they would have been too heavy for Sigrid herself to wield without using both of her hands on each.

The man held his axes high in the air, threw his head back into the air and roared. The sound was so loud and so filled with emotion that the crowds silenced before eventually roaring back with cheers and whistles of their own.

Sigrid held her sword before her in one hand parallel to the ground. She had contemplated bringing a shield with her, but she had always liked keeping one hand free when fighting. It was an unknown to most opponents and allowed her to grab or grapple when she needed to.

The battle began almost instantaneously as Sigrid's large opponent held one battle axe before him and swung the other in a powerful arch towards her. She watched as his muscles bulged and rippled as though they were dancing to the tune of his ferocious attack. The axe caught Sigrid's sword, and she rolled her body and shoulder to allow the strike to sweep by her without requiring her to use any strength to block or parry.

But before Sigrid could right herself and regain her footing, the second axe came at her in a low sweep, threatening to separate her feet from her legs. She only just managed to leap the axe and land in a forward roll, out of the way of any follow-up attacks.

The crowd was deafening. Their shrill calls for blood could be heard above everything else in The Pit, and although Hilda, Sylfia and Jarl all shouted both words of encouragement and warning, they would never be heard above the cacophony.

The brute swung his axe again at chest height and Sigrid jerked her body back and out of its path, only to have to back away again as he spun and unleashed a deadly backhand strike.

Her back was now against the wall and Sigrid knew that she needed to move, to escape from this position as quickly as possible, but her opponent was so relentless and did not seem to be tiring even for a second. Another swing at head height this time caused Sigrid to drop to the ground as fast as she could, and the huge battle axe bit deeply into the soft stone wall above her, showering her with sand and dust.

In the explosion of particles and the surprise that the brute had made contact with the wall, Sigrid managed to raise her blade and strike out at the man's chest, spilling first blood within the fight, which sprayed out to stain the loose ground. As he howled in pain, the noise from the crowd practically doubled.

Sigrid returned to a ready stance, moving away from the wall, and she saw that the brute had dropped one of his heavy battle axes, leaving just one to wield in both hands. Again he charged, though this time with his single weapon held high above his head. Sigrid had seen this charge many times as it was an attack that Jarl preferred to use when he was in trouble, and quickly she levelled her blade in another horizontal slash across his chest, more blood spurting from his body which this time reached her own arms, turning them slick and red.

The man did not seem deterred and once again, as Sigrid sat back into a ready stance, he attacked single-handedly with his one remaining axe. His wounds did not seem to give him any trouble but Sigrid knew that if she could hit them again, the man would surely fall.

Sigrid rolled her shoulder with another overhead strike as she had done the first and ducked under the backhand that followed. The man's strikes were powerful and deadly, but also slow and telegraphed. As she ducked the last strike, she brought her sword up in an upswing, the blade reflecting the light of the burning torches around The Pit and the tip of the weapon cut a deep, dark line into her opponent's stomach and chest.

He staggered backwards, his arms out to either side and his eyes almost closed, and Sigrid knew that she had to take this opportunity. She raised her sword again and stepped in to deliver the final killing blow.

But the man managed to lower his axe and block the strike and as he did so, he used the contact point between sword and axe to pivot his fist around and into Sigrid's jaw. Her world exploded into pain and a moment of darkness, and when she regained her senses, her opponent's other fist powered into her face. Blood and spit flew from her mouth as her head was turned with the force of the punch, and at that moment, she had no idea what to do.

But things were about to get far worse. The larger man used the moment of Sigrid's pain and hesitation to wrench her sword from her and he flung it to the ground, way out of reach. He then feigned a now unblockable swing with his axe to Sigrid's head, and as she made a half-hearted attempt to duck under the strike, he kicked out at her unbalanced leg, sending her to the ground and onto her back, winding her.

Sigrid's opponent could taste victory now and as she lay on the ground looking up at him, she could only watch as he raised his arms to the crowds, roaring once more in victory. She could see their faces calling for the end and more bloodshed. She could hear their taunts and their laughter, and then she saw Frode standing next to Hilda with a wide grin on his face.

Finally, the time arrived for the man to strike the killing blow, but again it was so slow and it took so long to arrive that Sigrid had regained her breath and rolled out of the way at the last moment so that the battle axe impacted the ground with a loud thud. She spun up onto her feet to stand toe to toe with the man again. His face betrayed his shock that Sigrid was still willing to fight, but he readied his stance and grasped his axe in both hands.

Sigrid knew that she had just one option left to take: she had to attack, and with that thought in mind she leapt at her opponent. He did not have the time to bring his heavy axe up to defend himself this time, and Sigrid kicked him hard directly on the wound she had caused earlier, snaked around to his right and attached herself tightly to his back. As the brute howled in pain and could not return his attention to the fight, Sigrid took a hold of the shaft of his axe in both of her hands and pulled it tight against his neck.

Her opponent grabbed hold of the weapon to try to wrench it free, but Sigrid shifted it into the crook of her elbows and cupped her hands on the back of the man's head so that the harder he tried to pull the weapon away, the more he choked himself. Sigrid knew that she had won this fight, and it was simply a matter of seconds before her opponent would fade and then pass.

Then suddenly a flash of light caught her eye, and she looked up and into the crowd to see what had interrupted her. Standing next to Hilda was Frode, now not smiling; no, now he was scowling, and she could see that within his right hand he held a short, shining dagger so tightly that his knuckles had turned white. At that moment, Sigrid knew that her whole family was not supposed to make it through this test.

Sigrid released her grip on one end of the axe and quickly swung it about herself as she kicked off her opponent's back, and launched the weapon into the crowd directly at Frode, who did not even see the danger coming. The crowd went deathly silent as the heavy weapon buried itself into Frode's face and he hit the ground before he even had the chance to gasp in surprise.

"Sigrid, look out!" Jarl called to break the silence surrounding The Pit, but it was too late. She had not seen it, but Frode's knife had fallen into The Pit, and her opponent had since recovered, picked up the weapon and before she could do anything to stop him, he slit Sigrid's throat in one clean strike. She grasped at the wound with both of her hands, wearing a silent expression of surprise before she eventually fell to the ground in a heap. Then, her body simply evaporated to dust and floated away into the air above her and into nothingness.

"Sigrid!" Jarl cried louder than any voice that could be heard within The Pit, and he leapt down to where his wife's body had lay just a few seconds ago.

"My wife! You cannot leave me again!" he cried. He felt a hand on his shoulder and was about to strike but he caught himself just in time, realising that it was his daughter, Sylfia, who had followed him down into The Pit.

"Father, I..." she started, tears filling her eyes.

"No, do not say anything more," Jarl said through broken words and gritted teeth. "I can still feel her. The bond that we have... she is not gone..."

"Then we must leave this place," Sylfia said. "We will find her wherever she is, but we cannot stay here!"

Jarl looked up at the crowds around The Pit, and he could now see what Sylfia meant. The people there now all held weapons and looked directly at the father and daughter standing together in the arena of battle. Perhaps the act of killing Frode had caused them all to take up arms, or maybe it was the fact that a spectator was killed when he was clearly not a part of the fight, either way, if they did not move quickly then they would be in big trouble.

Jarl looked up to where he knew Hilda was standing and called to her to join them, but before she could move to Jarl, an arm blocked her path.

"Husband?" Hilda practically screeched as she gazed into the face of the man who blocked her path. "How..." she started, but she could not contain her emotion any longer. She buried her face into the man's shoulder, and her gait betrayed her tears.

"Hilda, we must leave now!" Jarl called up to her, but when she resurfaced from her embrace, Jarl could see in her eyes that she would not be joining them.

"I will catch up with you - go!" she called, though her words lacked conviction. "Save yourselves while you still can!"

Jarl looked back at Sylfia, who was smiling up at Hilda. She knew what this meant to her friend, and she knew that if she could, she would come back to this place to ensure that she was with her family again before the end of her days.

"To the third ring?" Sylfia said with a forced smirk. Then she hunched over to allow Jarl to springboard from her back and into the crowd above.

Sylfia took a second to peer at the space on the ground where her mother's body had fallen, but she trusted her father's words. If he said that her mother was still alive out there somewhere, then that would be what she believed until it was proven otherwise.

Sylfia quickly clambered up the wall of The Pit to join her father who awaited her on the ledge. He held both of his hand axes and was swinging them in wild arcs to keep the spectators at bay, but it looked as if they were already closing in on him. Once Sylfia had joined him with her two swords drawn though, the people all seemed to be a little warier, having watched her fight and seen her skill already.

The arc of warriors who stood between Jarl and Sylfia seemed far warier of Sylfia than they did of her father, and the pair took advantage of that. Sylfia feinted forward, and the ten or so warriors rippled back and away from her as though she would be able to kill them with a single swing of her sword, and she and her father did not squander the opportunity.

Jarl lowered his shoulder and charged at the centre of the warriors with Sylfia following just behind. When they made contact with the line, although each person held weapons to the ready, there was not much they could do to prevent the pair from breaking through, which they did with relative ease before sprinting towards the tunnel that led away from The Pit, and surely towards the third ring of Helheim.

33

The tunnel in front of Sylfia and Jarl looked as though it was going to be long, dark and cold. It seemed there would be no more warriors from the third ring trying to stand in their way, so Jarl ignited one of his hand axes to light the way ahead.

The tunnel itself seemed to be lined with stone, as though it had been built to serve people going to and coming from The Pit and had been made to last. There were unlit torches attached to the walls, but when Jarl checked them to see if they had been lit recently, they were cold to the touch.

"Father? What do you think has happened to mother?" Sylfia asked quietly once they were sure that they were not being followed. The group that had tried to stop them from leaving The Pit seemed to want to avoid following them into this tunnel, and that suited both Jarl and Sylfia.

"I do not know," Jarl replied in a level tone. "But I can still feel her presence within my soul. I do not know how this connection works, but I know that she has not simply perished, never to be seen again." Jarl did not look at Sylfia as he spoke calmly, and she had no choice but to believe her father. Besides, his voice betrayed nothing other than complete trust in his words. If she had thought he had not fully believed his words, she may have simply laid down on the ground where she stood and sobbed.

"Then we will collect her on the way to the Naglfar ship," Sylfia announced confidently. "Then we will bring her back and out of this place once our task is complete."

"Did you say Naglfar ship?" a voice cut through the darkness ahead as Frode strode confidently towards them with a smile.

Sylfia drew both of her swords, and Jarl retrieved his second axe, igniting it as he slipped it from its sheathe.

"Now now, there is no need for any of that," Frode said, still smiling.

"Then talk, quickly," Jarl growled. "And how is it that you are not dead after we watched your body taken away by the wind?"

"Ok Ok, but lower your weapons, please," Frode said. "I admit that it was my intention to create a situation where some of your little group would make it away from that place and some would not. I wanted to see what would happen if you did not have each other to depend upon. But your wife would not simply accept a loss, would she?"

Neither Jarl nor Sylfia lowered their weapons from the ready. "So you took it upon yourself to kill Hilda, but Sigrid stopped you, did she?" Jarl said. "What do you think gives you the right to attempt what you did?"

"Are you not surprised that I am back?" Frode asked. "That you watched my body dissipate as your wife's body did, but here I am moments later, talking to you once more?"

"No," Jarl said. "I do not care to know how you have done what you have done. I do not care that you think that you are able to interfere with battles to the death, and I do not care that you are here now, blocking our path. I suggest that you either move now and never let me see you again, or die where you stand."

Frode lopped his head to one side. "I do like that. Maybe we should see if you are able to kill what you do not know the full truth about."

Jarl shrugged his shoulders and walked towards Frode, raising both of his axes high above his head, but as he began his swing, Frode raised a long, silver sword of his own and blocked the attack with seemingly little difficulty or effort.

"Listen, what I told you was not untrue," Frode said conversationally as Jarl strained against his parry. "I can take you onward, closer to where you need to go. I know this place well, and if you can simply see fit to ignore what has happened thus far, I will take you there."

"Why?" Sylfia asked through gritted teeth. "Why would you take us and why should we trust you?"

"Because it is what I would like to do," Frode said. "Besides, if I wished your death, I could kill you both right here, right now."

Sylfia looked into Frode's eyes as he spoke, and within them she could see nothing but total and complete truth. She did not know who this person was, but it seemed very much as though he was far more powerful than she could have ever imagined.

"But I must tell you," Frode said with his smile widening. "What lies in the rings beyond is nothing compared to what you have already faced. The Pit is a terrible place, and you are lucky to have survived your battles there. Everything else will seem easy in comparison, I am sure."

Frode pushed Jarl's axes away with little effort and sheathed his own weapon. Jarl looked as though he was going to attack again, although he thought better of it when he saw that Sylfia did not look like she was going to join the fight.

"None of this makes sense," Sylfia said almost to herself. "I do not understand why you wished to separate us before and why you will help us now. Who are you? I mean, who are you really?"

With those words, the visage of Frode evaporated into the ether and after a second, a figure reformed before Sylfia and Jarl. Her skin was a pale blue, and the woman stood shorter than both Jarl and Sylfia. Hel still looked exactly as she had done before – as though she had been frozen and thawed out again.

Sylfia's eyes bulged. "Hel!?" She exclaimed and took a step back. "What...?" she tried to form new questions, but nothing came to mind. Jarl lifted his axes up before himself again as though Hel's presence in itself was a threat.

"About The Pit," Hel said softly. "I wanted to see what would happen if your family was torn apart. To see if you would continue along your path or simply surrender. I wanted to know... what it would be like to lose a daughter, a mother... a friend. After all, for me... you cannot kill what is already dead."

"You have said this before," Sylfia said. "That you cannot die. Tell me though, why do you harbour such interest in family connections?"

"Do you know who my father is?" Hel rasped. "He gave me this domain to preside over but never has he spent any time with me here as your family does with each other. I do not understand why mortals can love each other as your family does, while my own father takes no interest in me or my domain."

"But your father gave you everything, did he not?" Sylfia asked.

"No! my father gave me a task and left me to it. I know the journey that you are on, the things that you seek here in my domain, but your family is with you now and will be with you until they are taken from you against their will. Even Hilda, who is no real family of yours yearns to reconnect with you even when I have given her the opportunity to stay with her blood. I... I do not understand why I am so forsaken."

Jarl dropped his weapons to his sides and stepped forward to stand by Sylfia. Then he sighed.

"Blood does not make family. And a man who gives none of himself, his time, his teachings, his love and care to his daughter is no father. A father, a family... and even friends are those who love you regardless of when, where or how they entered your life. Listen to my words, Hel," Jarl placed an arm around Sylfia. "Sylfia is my daughter not by blood but through love. This is what you do not understand. It is not family that you lack. It is love."

Sylfia smiled at Jarl and nodded. "If your father does not wish to spend his time with you, then he is no father."

Hel looked down at the ground, and any semblance of the smile that Frode had shown was long gone. It was almost as though her eyes had filled with tears.

Then Hel abruptly evaporated into dust again, reforming into the visage of Frode, smile present once more.

"I do not wish to hinder your path, for it is not my way. You are free to do as you will in this domain as long as you abide by any rules you encounter. I manipulated your journey to this point in a small way, but I will not do so again. My repayment to you will be to deliver what I promised to you, to take you to the fourth ring so that you may speak with the kings of men," Frode said.

Sylfia blinked twice at Frode before she spoke. "Does anyone else know who you truly are?" she asked.

Frode smiled. "Of course not. Nobody would speak freely with a God, but with an indentured servant, lips tend to be looser.

"And you will help us, with no ties or repayment owed?" Jarl asked.

Frode nodded.

"Then tell me," Jarl growled. "Where is my wife? Where is Sigrid?"

"Ah yes, of course," Frode said. "I am afraid that when one dies in this domain, they are taken to join the ranks of the Draugr within the eighth ring."

"Because one cannot kill what is already dead?" Jarl asked with a growl.

Frode nodded.

"Will you return her to me?" he asked.

"When you reach what it is that you seek, you will be given the chance to have her returned. Until that time, she will have to defend herself, but I feel that she is more than capable, no?" Frode answered.

"Why will you not just bring her back if you have the power!?" Jarl practically shouted.

"Because I do not wish to do so," Frode replied. "It is within your power to have everything that you want. You can have your family back if you choose to fight for that. You can complete this task to find the Naglfar ship within my domain if you choose to do so, but some paths will be difficult to the point of almost impossibility. The salient point is, though, that I will neither help nor hinder you on your path."

"But you already hindered!" Sylfia exclaimed. "You would have killed Hilda, and you were the reason that my mother was taken to wherever these Draugr are!"

"You are correct, those actions were my own. But I did not expect to be caught in carrying them out. And the facts are that I did not kill your Hilda, nor did I kill your mother."

"And how does that make any of this any better?" Sylfia asked, her voice falling to a more sociable volume.

"If I had not been discovered to have done these things, would it have made your path any different? Would we not be exactly where we are right now, the only difference being that you would not be asking me these questions?"

"Yes! But that is not the point! I do not understand why you would choose to interfere then for your own curiosity, and now you are choosing not to help, but for no reason?!" Sylfia said.

"There is a reason," Frode said with another smile. "When we were in The Pit, actions can be missed, overlooked or otherwise ignored. In this place now, as we head into the innermost rings of my domain, I can and will be judged on my actions. As you will see from ring to ring, the rules of my domain differ, so where I may have free reign to do what I like in some places, in others that fact is not true. In theory, I could help you now, but whatever action that I would take could be countered by another, and it would leave you exactly where you were in the beginning."

"So this is a God thing?" Sylfia asked. "Like how Odin's raven prevented Loki from killing me before?"

Frode let a thoughtful look wash across his face as he pondered the question for a moment. Sylfia could not tell what he was thinking, but if she had to guess, he was finding it fascinating that Sylfia had encountered Loki so intimately already and had some knowledge of how the Gods worked when within the mortal realms.

"Yes, something like that," Frode said distantly. "Let us forget these... inner workings of my domain for now and focus on what you are trying to do next. I believe that you are looking to reach the Naglfar ship, if memory serves? It is placed within the eighth and ring of Helheim as I have already disclosed, but I wonder if you know what you will find there, and if you are equipped to deal with them."

"It is a ship of the dead," Sylfia said confidently. "And when it launches it will signal the beginning of Ragnarök. It will be launched by a great tremor. We have to stop the ship so that Ragnarök will not come to pass."

Frode clicked his tongue. "But the Naglfar ship's launch..." he started, then chose to hold back whatever information that he was about to give. "It does not matter. Ragnarök and its passing is not something that can be prevented, and if you wish to give your lives - though I suppose that you already have - in some feeble attempt to stop it, then these lives are yours to give."

"This is the difference between man and God, is it not?" Jarl asked with a scowl. "Everything you do, not interfering, only defending yourselves, playing these silly games. You do these things to keep yourselves safe and happy. You do not care for one another and you do not care what happens to the realms of men, just as long as you are still here at the end of it. Do you not know that once Ragnarök has passed, everything will be removed from existence?"

"That is not entirely true," Frode said. "Ragnarök will pass, and I shall remain. After all, those who fall in the afterward will need some place to go, will they not? I will remain eternal as shepherd to my flock and that is the way it shall be for all eternity, Ragnarök or not."

"So you do not care?" Sylfia said. "If hundreds of thousands of people die in the mortal realm? If the Gods and demons are killed to bring about the end of days?"

"It is how it is meant to be," Frode said with a shrug. "I do not interfere, rather I carry out my charge and oversee my domain as I am supposed."

"And what will you do, when one day the wolves are at your door?" Jarl asked.

"I am not worried, because the wolves are my children and my siblings. But my time is eternal and that is a promise."

"Then if you have no cares, send us to the Naglfar ship now so that we may carry out our task and be done with all of this!" Sylfia pleaded.

"No," Frode said, "and I have given you my reasons."

"Your reasons count for nothing!" Jarl said angrily and Sylfia placed a comforting hand on his shoulder.

"I am sorry that you feel this way, Jarl, though I know you have the conviction and strength to follow through with the tasks you give yourself. You will see soon enough, I am sure. Now come, I do not wish to spend any more time here than I have to," Frode said.

Then he turned and began to walk away and into the darkness, with Jarl and Sylfia following quickly behind. Jarl made to light his axes again, but Frode spoke before he had the chance.

"I would prefer if you did not illuminate our path at this moment."

Jarl was about to ask why, but then as though from nowhere a light up ahead faded into view. He was not sure, but he had the distinct feeling that the three of them had just travelled a great distance in a very short space of time.

"Where..." Sylfia started to ask, though she shut her mouth as she realised that the light they had seen was now much, much closer and was coming from torches burning either side of a large door, which was attached to a huge wooden longhouse.

"As I promised, I have brought you to one of the kings of men within the fourth ring of Helheim. Unlike some of the others, this man, his name is..." Frode thought for a moment,

"Erling. Erling is not in a position to be able to turn warriors away who come to him with the desire to fight."

"We do not have the desire to fight for some king!" Sylfia objected.

"Oh, that is not true," Frode said. "At least when you hear what this fight is about. You see, Erling and his domain within the fourth ring is at war with the Jötnar."

"The Jötnar are a story told to scare young children. They do not exist in this place any more than the..." Jarl stopped himself as he realised that he was about to say something very foolish.

Frode smiled again. "The Jötnar are indeed very real, and they remain within the fifth and sixth rings of my domain. I know that you mortals enjoy closing your eyes to the larger actions of the universe, but oftentimes you still manage to surprise me."

"So, the Jötnar?" Sylfia said. "They wage war with man?"

Frode nodded. "Indeed they do. Helheim is not an infinite amount of space and as both men and the Jötnar die within their realms, their space here becomes crowded and filled. Waging war against each other is a good way for each to increase their territory, but also it serves as a manner of population control, shall we say."

Sylfia almost heard Hilda exclaim 'that is barbaric!' again in her mind, though she kept her own mouth firmly shut.

"The thing is," Frode said, "since the beginning of the war between man and Jötnar, throughout the tens of thousands who have given their lives so that their people may be afforded a little more space, not a single inch of land has been gained or lost by either side."

Sylfia could not help but retaliate now. "This is all a game to you, is it not? They think that what they are doing makes a difference, but it is just a way for you to keep their populations down so that you do not run out of space!"

"NO!" Frode raised his voice above Sylfia's, interrupting her. "It is not as simple as population control. Where do you think the lost souls go once they are taken from this place? Do you even know what Ragnarök will bring? It seems that you have missed one vital piece of the puzzle, mortal girl."

Then Jarl spoke low and slowly. "When Ragnarök arrives, the armies of the dead will rise back to earth to join in the battle for the end of days. The fallen here, these will form the army that is called forward."

"The Draugr?" Sylfia asked incredulously. "But there would be so, so many... "

"That is exactly the point, is it not? My armies will be the difference, to turn the tide of war, and that fact alone will force my father to see what use I am, and the good I can do if he just simply looks at me." Frode turned his head with the last words though not before Sylfia saw his eyes fill with tears.

"This is not the way," Sylfia started to say in a soft voice but in a moment, Frode had turned his head back to Sylfia and Jarl with a renewed smile on his face.

"Anyway, none of this matters to us right now, does it?" Frode said. "I have promised to find you a place with a king here in the fourth ring, and that is what I have done. I will leave you here and it is up to you both to speak to Erling and petition him for your conscription."

"And why do you think that we would join this futile army after what you have told us?" Sylfia said. "You have said that no ground can be won, so why would we fight? Why would we risk our lives in a battle that cannot be won?"

"Because," Frode said. "If you do not fight, if you do not believe that there is a small shred of hope, some small difference that you can make here, then you accept that you, Sylfia, and you Jarl, you will never see your mother and your wife, ever again."

Then Frode evaporated into shreds of dark mist that wafted for a moment, then simply disappeared.

Sylfia looked behind herself to see only a sheer, flat rock wall and then looked to her father. "What do we do now?" she asked.

"There is only one path before us this time daughter. And while we are in the company of men, we should see what we can do here." Jarl spoke as though he had already been defeated, but deep down inside he knew that if there was any slight chance that he could continue on through the rings of Helheim to eventually find Sigrid, then he would not rest until he took that chance.

After entering the longhouse only to find it empty, Jarl and Sylfia found that they could leave through the far end. There they were greeted with a huge, dark campsite filled with cloth tents and burning fires as far as the eye could see. In the distance, Jarl could see a wooden wall, and if he squinted, he was sure he could see some movement along the top.

"I have never seen a warrior turn up here with their own weapons before, and certainly not ones as good-looking as that," a young man said as he strode up towards the pair. "Usually, I would send you over to the armoury and something would be provided for you, but, well, I guess follow me."

Sylfia and Jarl both kept their mouths shut and followed the man. He seemed small, ill-equipped and a little nervous, which told them that he was no warrior. Perhaps he was a servant or simply the one who greeted newcomers to this place. Whatever or whoever he was, there was no way that he was this king, Erling.

"It is nearly light, so we shall be sending out our raiding party soon," the man said as he walked. "This place is a little quiet because of it, but if we hurry now, you should be able to make up the distance."

"Excuse me," Sylfia said in as sweet a voice as she could manage. "But where are we going? And who are you?"

"You are going out on the raid of course," the young man said, "and my name is Ari."

"But we know nothing of this place or of what we are supposed to be doing. We know nothing about the land or the rules here, and we know nothing of our enemies," Sylfia explained.

"Ah, do not worry. You will catch on quickly. It is a very simple place here. We are warring with the Jötnar, who seek to take our land as their warriors become too numerous. It is our task to thin their ranks every now and then to ensure that everyone has enough space here."

"You know about the population control?" Sylfia asked in surprise.

"Of course! It is why we are here – as I have said to keep the Jötnar to a low enough number to remain under control."

"That is not..." Sylfia began to say, though Jarl interrupted her.

"That is not a bad idea, Ari, but I must ask, how many of these Jötnar are there?"

"Oh, there are thousands. Thousands upon thousands. But they do not come all at once," he added quickly. "Most are not warriors – though the same can be said of man of course, but we built the wall you see. We keep them out at night and retaliate in the daylight when they are at their weakest."

Sylfia blinked a few times, trying to force her mind to keep up with the conversation.

"So the Jötnar raid at night and attempt to break the wall, and in the daylight, you raid their settlements so that they have fewer ranks with which to attack," Jarl summarised.

"Exactly!" Ari said, raising a single digit into the air. "It is not an easy existence here on the battlefield between the fourth and fifth, but it is a duty that we must provide so that the rest of mankind and the mortal realms can remain free."

Sylfia did not even want to touch that statement. Whatever these people had either been told - or believed – was none of her business as she had one task and one task alone: to leave this place and to move on towards the centre of Helheim.

"And the Jötnar? They are as we would expect to see them?" Sylfia asked.

Ari nodded animatedly. "If you have never seen one before, then your first viewing will be something that will never leave you. As big as three or four men each, they are grotesque creatures who prefer large clubbing weapons. They will either wear furs to cover themselves, making them look like ginormous beasts, or they will be without clothing at all. The things that you will see are enough to haunt your dreams forever." He shivered.

"You have fought them?" Jarl asked.

"Not me. I have seen them and I have defended the wall when they have come, but I would not stand toe to toe with a Jötnar, not for one moment."

"Then why are you here?" Sylfia asked.

"Every army needs its runners," Ari said nonchalantly. "Information is key; without it, the Jötnar could attack where and when they liked, and nobody would know about it. That is where people like me come in."

"How many are the army of man?" Jarl asked.

"We are over one hundred thousand at this point, but it goes up and down as you may imagine."

"One... hundred... thousand..." Sylfia repeated again in shock. "There are so many..."

"I know, impressive, is it not?" Ari said. "Now the wall is just up ahead. The gates will still be open, so just go on through and join the ranks at the back."

34

As soon as Jarl and Sylfia had passed through the large wooden gates and had joined the ranks of the unimaginably massive army that stood before them, each man and woman holding old and rusty-looking weapons, a loud bang signified that no more warriors would be exiting from the campsite. Looking behind and above, Sylfia could see a cursory complement of archers along the top of the high wall that stood at least fifteen feet tall. It seemed to her a little moot though, as if anyone was able to pass through this army, a few archers would be little good in preventing ingress to the campsite.

Far away in the distance and past the ranks upon ranks of soldiers, a man stood atop a wooden platform and addressed the amassed warriors with a loud voice. His words carried across the distance between them all as though it was magically amplified.

"Today, we take our revenge for what the despicable Jötnar have done to us each night. We thin their ranks as a warning to stop their attempt to expand their homestead. They wish to take our land and kill us all, but we shall never let that happen. We stand as the last line of defence between these grotesque and belligerent beings and our fellow man - our friends, our families and our kin. Without us, these Jötnar will not stop until they have destroyed the human race, but will we not let that happen, will we!"

The sound that the warriors returned shook Sylfia to her very soul. The clash of weapons and the calls of "NO!" reverberated across the open lands and beyond, and Sylfia could not help but feel a sense of complete camaraderie.

"We will take them from their beds in the daylight as they sleep!"

"Yes!" The call returned from the army.

"We will kill them before they kill us!"

"Yes!"

"We will not let them set one foot on human land again!"

"NO!" the call returned.

Sylfia saw that her father had been enthralled too, joining in with the call and return from the man that could only have been Erling. His face was contorted in hatred and determination, and he held both of his shining hand axes tightly above his head. His weapons stood out against the rest of the weapons that his army wielded, as his were beautiful by comparison.

"Father, are you sure that this is the right thing to do? This is a war that we have no part in," Sylfia asked.

"We have no alternative, daughter," Jarl said out of the corner of his mouth. "Besides, these creatures threaten our kin, our families and our friends. It is our moral duty to prevent them from being able to kill humans without retaliation."

Sylfia found it strange that Jarl had repeated the same words as Erling's but decided it was best not to delve too deeply into what was actually happening in this place.

"Our own family needs our help too, father. We must remember that this war is not something that we are a big part of. It simply stands between us and the next ring of Helheim, nothing more."

Jarl looked down at Sylfia with a glint in his eye. "Of course. But if we can kill a few of these despicable Jötnar along the way, then it is all for the better, is it not?"

Sylfia shrugged. It was a fair point: If they could thin the ranks of a race that was attempting to kill humans and take their land, then where was the harm?

Erling called out a few more instructions, and a moment later the army of fallen men surged forward and into the open plains before them. Sylfia could not see where they were going as for miles around, all that she could see were flat, barren lands, illuminated by the rising sun. In the distance though, rolling hills became mountains although there was no sign of any of the apparent Jötnar that threatened their existence.

The army swiftly crossed the barren plains and within a few minutes reached the beginnings of the hills. It was here that the first of the Jötnar came into view, and the first of the creatures that Sylfia and Jarl would ever lay eyes upon.

The creature was indeed grotesque. A thing the size of three men at least and just as wide, it scratched its dark grey head wearily as it stumbled towards the approaching army of men. It seemed as though it had not seen the men approaching, though to Sylfia the noise their feet made against the ground was a deafening thunder.

This Jötnar had a short tuft of hair atop its head, and when it finally realised that something odd was happening before it, it opened its eyes fully and a look of shock washed across its face.

Then the creature opened its mouth and roared. The sound was unlike anything that Sylfia had ever heard in her life, and it carried over and above the sound of the army all around her. She did not know exactly how far this sound would carry, but she immediately recognised it for what it was: this was an alarm call, and being this loud, she was sure that it would not go unnoticed.

As if in response to the call, the army of men immediately swarmed over the Jötnar as though they were a colony of ants. It managed to swing the long branch it was holding in its hands just once before it was entirely enveloped by the human warriors, the giant creature falling to the ground with a thud, deep red blood spurting into the air even before it had stumbled and fallen. The warriors of man had hit it with arrows, spears and thrown axes in what had seemed like a tremendous amount of overkill, but it had definitely been effective.

Then the ground began to shake.

From the hills in the distance, dust began to rise, and Sylfia peered onwards to see if she could determine what was happening. She did not have to think very hard though, for approaching them now came its kin in response to the alarm call, those who would look to serve their revenge on mankind.

"Raise your weapons and be ready!" Erling's voice again cut through the sound of approaching thunder and the victorious calls of the warriors who were still celebrating felling the first Jötnar of the day.

"Do not loose your arrows until you can see the whites of their eyes!" Erling shouted, and those of the army who held longbows replied with the sound of thousands of bows being pulled taught. The army then fell silent, and the sound of the approaching Jötnar filled the air.

"Hold!" Erling commanded, and the warriors obediently made no moves or sounds.

The Jötnar were now within a few hundred metres, and Sylfia peered across the battlefield at them. They were huge creatures, much like the first one that had already been killed, but these did not look tired and confused. These looked angry and ready for battle.

"The Jötnar will be tired!" Erling shouted. "They do not like to fight in the light of day, so we will take our advantage and fight until each and every one of them has fallen, or they retreat like the cowards that they are!"

Sylfia couldn't help but feel as though each time Erling gave a shout or a command, a warmth was building inside of her. It was as though it gave her the courage to fight until her last breath, and focussing her mind on the warmth, it made her smile.

"Are you ready for this, father?" Sylfia asked.

"It would seem as though my entire life has been building to this very battle, Sylfia. Just stay close to me, and we will see how many of these beasts we can destroy."

Then everything happened in a flurry of activity. The charging Jötnar were hit by the initial volley of arrows, and although they were densely packed as they charged and there were so, so many arrows launched towards them, only a small portion fell and were left behind on the ground as their huge number continued onwards. Then the first Jötnar impacted the front line of men. The warriors did their best to absorb the tremendous charge, but the Jötnar were so big and so strong that the initial impact sent hundreds of men flying into the air with horrified screams ringing out. The Jötnar weapons, too, were so large and heavy that the blunt ones that resembled tree trunks could carve an arch of the humans around the Jötnar that wielded them and send their opponents flying, mostly unconscious. The ones that carried bladed weapons, though, these weapons could cut ten men in half in a single attack.

"Encircle them!" Erling ordered. "Do not stand before them and let them hit you!"

The Jötnar were edging their way closer to Sylfia and Jarl, although it would take them a while to breach the entire line of men.

It seemed to Sylfia that there were at least ten times the number of humans as Jötnar in the battle, though she did not know if one Jötnar warrior was equal to ten men. As far as she could see from the battle so far, despite the size of this army, the Jötnar looked to have the upper hand.

"I thought that this was to be a raid, where the Jötnar would not be fighting back so hard," Sylfia said to Jarl, though another man replied before her father had the chance.

"The Jötnar usually sleep during the day. It was unfortunate that the first one was awake and managed to wake the rest. Usually we would kill a few hundred in their sleep before the rest have even picked up their weapons."

"Usually?" Sylfia asked. "This happens often?"

"Yes," the man replied. "I have seen a few days of battle like this. Truthfully I cannot remember past the last few, but I know how these battles go. We fight, some of us will die, and the rest will live to fight another day."

"How long have you been here?" Sylfia asked with a look of shock on her face.

The man grimaced as he tried to remember. Sylfia waited for him to reply for a short while and was about to ask again when he managed to reply.

"I... do not know. My memory is not as good as it once was. All I know is that we must fight to stop these beasts from spilling over into our lands."

The crash of metal on metal interrupted their conversation as a Jötnar warrior trundled into view just a few metres away.

It seemed as if the battle had finally reached Sylfia and Jarl's position.

"Are you ready, Sylfia?" Jarl asked again, and Sylfia nodded silently, holding her two short swords out in a ready stance. She could see that Jarl was already prepared for what was to come but still, with their short reach and the size of these creatures, she was unsure of how they could actually be prepared for anything.

Then, as though it was from a tree that had been uprooted and dropped upon them, a giant club cascaded down from above so large that it cast a shadow over them both.

Jarl was the first to see the attack and he pushed Sylfia hard at the shoulder, causing her to fall to the ground and she used the momentum to roll out of the way of the club. Similarly, Jarl used his own momentum to dive from the path of the attack and narrowly missed the club aimed at the back of his legs.

As Sylfia met the ground, she was thankful that it was hard. Tufts of grass littered the surface but it was mostly dry dirt, so she was able to regain her footing after the roll, and she saw her father running in a wide arc around their enemy.

At least a dozen warriors littered the ground around the Jötnar that had nearly killed Sylfia and her father, and it looked as though none of them would ever stand again.

In front of the creature grouped a few more warriors equipped with a range of weapons, although none seemed as useful as the range afforded by the longbows, and this Jötnar had already been punctured by at least twenty arrows, yet it still stood.

The Jötnar roared as it hefted its mighty club into the air again, but both Jarl and Sylfia had managed to reach past its opposite sides and were far away from the attack that followed, an attack that caved in the bodies of another five human warriors.

As soon as the ground rumbled when the mighty club impacted it, both Jarl and Sylfia darted towards the Jötnar. The weapon was too large and heavy to be drawn again before they would make at least one attack, but they would make it count. Sylfia drove her perfect, razor-sharp blades into the Jötnar's legs in the hope that their weakness mirrored that of man, and Jarl swung both of his axes from behind his head into the thing's lower back. It howled in pain, a sound that shook Sylfia's very bones, before it gave up on lifting its club for a third time and fell backwards onto the ground with a loud thud.

The moment the Jötnar hit the ground, it was swarmed by warriors who took the opportunity to bury their weapons into its flesh without the worry of retaliation. It died within seconds.

Clearly this Jötnar was a fine warrior because it had made its way deep into the human lines, but it was quickly followed up by three more, two holding clubs like the first and a third holding a large, rusty cleaver the size of an oar. Men and women were flying high into the air and in all directions as the three Jötnar ruined the ranks of men, but not a single person turned to flee in fear; they met their end with ferocity and pride.

"Sylfia!" Jarl cried above the sound of battle and death.

"I am here, father!" Sylfia replied. She knew that his call was irrelevant as they could clearly see each other; it was more a check to see if she was prepared for what was to come or not. It was a mild surprise to her, though, and the warmth that she had felt grow within her when Erling had spoken was still evident. It comforted her, gave her the desire and the courage to fight on, and the distant hope that in some way, all of this was going to work out for the best.

Another swing of a huge club sent warriors flying off in all directions, and it cleared the path between Sylfia, Jarl and the approaching Jötnar.

The foremost of the three giants seemed to lock eyes with Sylfia, and upon seeing her standing to the ready, it began to lumber towards her with interest. Sylfia gripped her bloodied swords tightly and prepared to dive out of the way again, but before it made it to within range, it suddenly stopped.

Having seen the creature heading for his daughter, Jarl let out a shout that was nowhere near as loud or as fearsome as the creatures had managed, but he had one advantage that they did not. Jarl had held his axes high above his head and ignited them in a bright orange-red blaze, ready to defend Sylfia.

"Father, no!" Sylfia shouted, but it was too late. All three of the Jötnar had their attention ripped away from Sylfia as they saw this new addition to the battlefield. Jarl was now a beacon that attracted not just one Jötnar, but the attention of all three. They lurched towards him as though they were moths to a flame and when the first one reached within range, Jarl swung his axes around himself ferociously.

Jarl's reach, though, was nothing compared to his attackers. The first giant Jötnar initially seemed cautious not to be hit by the white-hot axes, but it soon realised that the short range of the human that held them meant that it really was in no danger. Eventually, the leading Jötnar shrugged and wound his huge club behind himself, and swung it in a semi-circle the height of a human midriff.

Jarl did not have the opportunity to dodge the strike, but deep down he had known what he had been doing all along. These Jötnar were not to be toyed with, and if they had reached Sylfia she would not have made it out of this place alive. He was happy that the last thought he would ever have was that he would give his life so that Sylfia may continue along her own path.

As the club connected with Jarl, it carried him along with its momentum for a second or so before Sylfia watched her father's limp body fly through the air and off into the distance, towards the Jötnar's own lands. He flew for at least a few hundred metres before he disappeared, and Sylfia knew that save for some divine miracle, her father was gone.

Rage built up inside her, and it fought for dominance over her grief and the desire to do something to avenge her father. She closed her eyes and willed her mind to whirr into action, and then something distant came to her. Her father had used the ability that the Gods had given him, so why could she not use her own? It was not as straightforward as Jarl's ability, but she knew what she had and if there was ever a time that it was to be useful, then now was it.

Sylfia opened her eyes and looked at the army of men that surrounded her, now scattered by pockets of giant Jötnar all around. The three that had come to deal with her and her father still lumbered close by, though now they were dealing with uncoordinated and scared-looking warriors with no trouble at all. Sylfia knew that a disorganised mass of warriors did not make a proper army, so she did the one thing that she thought could make a difference. She opened her mouth and shouted.

"I need your help, all of you, NOW!" she ordered. Her voice sounded alien to her as the words left her mouth, but she could sense that they had been imbued with the gift that she had inside of her. She could feel the power that she had intended for them to carry, and within an instant, the scattered men and women nearby who had looked both unsure and nervous within their battles formed perfectly straight and silent ranks before her.

The three Jötnar close by were confused at first, thinking that their opponents had simply withdrawn from the battle, but when the warriors of man began to walk towards them as one with their weapons held to the ready, the Jötnar themselves felt the first stirrings of worry. Sylfia watched as the first warriors came into range and began to land blows on their enemies, thick red blood spraying into the air, and the howls of the Jötnar filled the battlefield once more.

Sylfia took the opportunity to sneak away while the battle before her escalated. She knew that she was only human. She would make a little difference to the outcome of this war, if any, and she knew that if there was any chance that her father had survived his own ordeal, he was going to be gravely wounded and in desperate need of her help.

Sylfia did her best to skirt the edge of the battle, keeping her distance so that she did not get dragged into any of the fighting as she moved further and further away from the human line. To her delight, as she moved and the Jötnar became more numerous, ranks of men and woman filled the gap between her and the giant creatures as though they were forming a defensive barrier that would allow her to move freely in the general direction that her father had flown after he had been struck.

Sylfia continued along her path towards where she thought her father could be, and the warriors that blocked the space between her and the Jötnar continued to do so until there were no Jötnar left to protect her from, each of them now engrossed in their individual battles against the ranks of warriors who looked far more ready for battle than they had done moments ago.

As soon as Sylfia realised that before her, to the left and to the right, there was nothing but empty space, she broke into a run. She still held her two swords in her hands just in case she found herself in a position where she needed to fight, but she was relatively sure she would be safe if she just kept moving.

The land had evolved into the rolling hills that she had already seen in the distance, and now not too far away, she could see the mountains that looked so large even at her previous range. Now they looked monstrous, unpassable, except for where one mountain met the next and a high, secluded path ran between them.

Sylfia resisted the urge to call out to her father; she knew that although she had travelled in the right direction, it would still be difficult to find him without a proper line of sight across the landscape. Instead of calling, she ran to the top of the first hill and looked into the trough below.

The land below was not simply more of the same dry earth, though. Within the lull between hills, there seemed to be a dense mixture of vegetation growing. Everything from mosses, flowers, and giant leaves that resembled lettuces covered the ground, and it was so thick that Sylfia could not see the land beneath.

It was as though the land had a clear divide between the battlefield and a thriving ecosystem beyond, as if there was a line where the death would stop, and a peaceful place was there just beyond.

Sylfia peered down into the vegetation to see if Jarl was anywhere to be seen, or even if there was any evidence that he had landed in this place after he had been launched by the Jötnar, but there was nothing. What was even stranger now, was that as she looked across the landscape from this new elevation, she could see that these pockets of growth, or whatever they were, spanned off away from her in both directions and for some distance ahead. But then she concentrated on what she was actually looking at, and it was not as straightforward as her first assumption: some of the pockets of vegetation were not thriving and vibrant; there were swathes of blackened decay at seemingly random intervals where huge sections of the plants had been cut down, destroyed of burnt. She had no idea why anything would grow in such an unusual and irregular pattern, but knew that now was not the time to stop and ponder.

Sylfia descended the hill and walked into the vegetation that she found so large that it was above her head height when she reached it.

Walking up and down the hills through the dense vegetation, Sylfia was beginning to lose any hope that she would ever find her father. If he had been killed and landed somewhere within one of these patches, there was a good chance that she would never be able to find him. What was worse was the fact that if he was injured or unconscious, he would not know that she was there to find him and would most likely not call out to her and she could not call out to him in case it brought the attention of any Jötnar warriors that happened to be nearby. It made Sylfia grit her teeth as she walked in silence - she could be within feet of her dying father and she would never even know it.

Eventually, Sylfia realised that she had to do something different if she truly wanted to find her father for better or for worse, so she trudged to the top of the next hill, readying her lungs to let out a call that would either bring her father's location to light or alert anything else that lurked out of sight.

Sylfia opened her mouth to call out, but in the moment before she could even produce a single squeak, a black raven fluttered down from out of sight, flew within an inch of her right ear and continued on forward towards the tall mountains that had been growing closer and closer as she had searched. She knew there was no way she could be sure that this was the same raven that had been aiding her on her path thus far, but it was simply too much of a coincidence to ignore.

She watched as it glided onwards towards the mountains and then suddenly disappeared into the background. She could not tell if the bird had actually disappeared or if it had simply landed and was now too far away and too camouflaged against the backdrop of the rough rock for her to see, but the message she took from it gave her no alternative: she needed to push on and reach these mountains.

Looking around herself somewhat frantically now, Sylfia wanted to make sure that she wasn't going to simply follow the lead of the bird and away from her father. Of course, the raven could have been looking to help her find Jarl, but equally, it could have been telling her that it was time to leave this place and continue along her path. There was simply no way to know.

Inhaling sharply, Sylfia decided that as usual, the raven would not have appeared if it was not indeed necessary. Making her mind up, she started walking directly towards the mountains where she had last seen it, though she made an effort to keep an eye out for her father, or at least any evidence that he had landed there within the dense vegetation.

Eventually, Sylfia exited the final section of plant life and vegetables and found that she was within a short clearance before the foot of the closest mountain. To her surprise, though, at this distance she could now see that the cut into the jagged wall that spanned away high and into the distance was an opening, not much larger than that of a human. The jet-black raven sat perched above the entrance, and Sylfia sensed it was telling her to go inside.

35

The moment Sylfia entered the cave she could hear voices. It was not exactly voices though, more like pained grunting and the sound of somebody biting down on a piece of leather to stop themselves from screaming. It suddenly dawned on her what that meant – whoever was here had most likely been gagged to prevent them from calling for help.

Sylfia knew there was a chance that this person would not be her father, but something inside her was fanning the ever-growing flame of hope. Even if it was not Jarl, though, she would not have turned her back and left this place; whoever was inside was in trouble, and they needed her help whether she knew them or not.

Sylfia broke into a sprint, ignoring her new surroundings. The tunnel that had either been carved from the cave mouth or had occurred naturally, was far too small for the Jötnar to have entered, so her thought was that whoever was inside was under threat from something else.

The path was long, straight and dark, although the light that filtered in through the entrance at least illuminated the walls around her enough so that she did not bump into anything.

The muffled howls grew louder as Sylfia moved. It sounded as though the person was being tortured, and this spurred her on to move faster and faster until she reached the end of the path and her first turn. She could now see two shadows dancing on the wall in front of her, illuminated by a flickering orange glow.

"Father!" Sylfia could not help but call out in the hope that Jarl had survived and had made it to this place. The orange flickering before her nudged the link between the flame and her father, but as she called out, she quickly brought her hands to her mouth.

The sound before her stopped for a moment and then continued. It was as though whoever it was ahead was not sure whether they had actually heard a noise or not.

Sylfia dropped her hands from her mouth, took a tight hold of both of her swords and stepped out from around the corner.

Two large beings were hunched over something slumped on the ground. They were grunting as they continued to do whatever it was that they were doing, and they seemed way too interested in that to want to turn to look at Sylfia. The pair were Jötnar for sure. They looked exactly as the others did, dark grey skin with tufts of hair, with large furs covering their bodies, and they were massive - not as large as the others but larger than the average human and certainly broader.

Sylfia made sure that her footsteps were as quiet as she could make them as she tiptoed around to the side to see if she could discover what they were doing without them noticing. Eventually, she could see a person lying before them. It was her father.

Jarl was biting down on a piece of cloth, and as the Jötnar continued to do whatever it was they were doing, he let out another muffled scream. Sylfia inhaled sharply at the sound, overcome with both surprise that she had found her father so easily and shared pain for his ordeal.

Jarl's eyes opened and met Sylfia's. Normally, his trained ears would not let such a betrayal of her stealth go unpunished, but it was clear that he was unable to move. Sylfia's face morphed into a grimace and she leapt forward to help her father.

Jarl spat the cloth from his mouth and managed to cry, "Sylfia, no!" as she moved and if he had been but a moment later, Sylfia's sword would have skewered the closest Jötnar. Sylfia skidded to a halt with a look of confusion on her face, and both of the Jötnar turned to see what had happened. They did not seem to be in any rush, and the look on their faces betrayed the fact that even once they had seen Sylfia, they still did not fully know what was happening.

"Father I...?" Sylfia said but could not form a coherent question. The two faces of the Jötnar that looked at her were undeniably the faces of children. She could now see, too, that the flame that illuminated the small clearing was coming from a burning hand axe, held in Jarl's outstretched hand.

"Sylfia, come here," Jarl ordered and gestured with his free hand. "You do not have to worry. Sheathe your swords and come." His tone was sincere and calming, and Sylfia could see no underlying reason to object. The two Jötnar children stared at her in silence as she moved, and when she reached her father she took a moment to appraise his condition.

Jarl had been propped up against a rock, with his head cushioned by a thick bundle of furs and the rest of his body laid out before him. His head and torso looked undamaged, but his right leg had been placed between two straight, thick branches that stopped at the ankle and were lashed tightly together by something bright and green that Sylfia recognised as a part of the vegetation that she had already travelled through.

Her face betrayed the emotions that she felt in a rush - relief that she had found him, anger and sadness at the fact that he had been hurt, and confusion at the presence of these two Jötnar children.

"You see that they are no threat to us," Jarl said in almost a whisper. "They have not said much, but they carried me from where I fell and brought me here. They have bandaged my wounds and the only pain that they have caused, I believe, has been for my own good. Do not judge them for what they are, daughter."

Sylfia looked at the pair of Jötnar children that were clearly a male and a female. They simply watched her in cautious silence and made no moves to speak or even to approach either Sylfia or Jarl, and Sylfia wondered exactly what it was that they had planned for them both.

"Hello?" Sylfia said in a careful tone. She realised that she had to make an effort to look past their appearance and to treat them more like children than the monsters that they appeared to be.

"Hello," the male Jötnar said back and the female kicked him lightly in the shin, the contact making an audible thud.

"Thank you for helping my father," Sylfia said, gesturing to Jarl, who remained on the ground. "Where did you learn to do that?"

The male Jötnar was about to speak again, but a glare from the female stopped him before he could begin.

"Is there anything that I can do to thank you, anything that you need?" Sylfia asked, but again was met with cautious silence.

"They have not said a word since they brought me here," Jarl explained. "I landed awkwardly after the blow I took in the battle. These two saw me land, picked me up and carried me into this cave. They have strapped my leg which I think is broken." He smiled at the Jötnar, who watched him in silence. "Thank you," he said, repeating Sylfia's words.

"Do they understand us?" Sylfia asked when she realised that there may be a language barrier between them.

"Yes, they speak as we do," Jarl said. "I have heard them speaking to each other and they seem to know what they are saying,"

"We understand," the male Jötnar said with a cautious grin. "We are very smart. We know to carry hurt warriors from battlefield and to heal them!"

"We are not supposed to heal the human warriors, Hern," the female said in a far more eloquent sentence than the male had constructed. Her voice was still slightly off and certainly not usual for a human but she had clearly had more practice than her counterpart.

"It not matter," the male who was apparently called Hern replied. "Heal them all up is what I say!"

"And where did you hear that?" the female asked. "This is why you are always getting into trouble."

Hern lowered his head as though he had been soundly told off and Sylfia spoke quickly to reassure him.

"No, no. You are not in trouble. You did the right thing in helping my father. Honestly, I do not know what I would do without him," she said.

"Me either," Hern said. "My father is out at battle today. I hope he comes back this time."

"What do you mean?" Jarl asked. "He has not come back before?"

The female Jötnar kicked Hern again, but it did not stop him from speaking.

"Many time he not come back. He die many time," Hern said.

"You must be mistaken," Sylfia said with a confused look on her face. She glanced back to Jarl and shrugged her shoulders. "Do you think it means something different to them?"

"No, he not come back. He die," Hern repeated and made a slicing motion with a finger across his throat. The female kicked him again. "Will you stop doing that Hrit!?" he exclaimed.

"You tell them too much!" Hrit said, though now that she had spoken again, she seemed unable to stop herself.

"My brother is telling the truth. Our father has been in many battles and died many times. Some days he comes back alive, some days he comes back hurt, and some days he does not come back at all. It is the way that it is."

Sylfia stared at the two Jötnar again with her mouth slightly open. She turned the words over and over in her mind, but no matter how hard she tried, she could not figure out what Hrit had meant to say.

"You not know what this place is?" Hern asked, smiling as though he was the cock of the walk.

"This is the expanse between the fourth and fifth ring of Helheim, is it not?" Jarl asked, now very worried that he was not in the place that he had expected.

Hern nodded emphatically. "Yes, that where we are," he said. "But what you know about here?" he asked.

"We were told," Sylfia started to say, then stopped to think if she should be telling them the information she had about this place, but finally deciding that it could really do no harm. "We were told that this was a place designed to keep the populations of the humans and the Jötnar down so that they do not overspill from their lands. We were told that the war waged here is a way of controlling both populations so that they do not become too numerous."

Hrit snorted loudly. "Did you not see how many warriors were out there on that battlefield?" she asked.

"Well, yes," Sylfia said.

"And how many do you think have fallen, hundreds? Thousands?"

"I think that... yes perhaps," Sylfia replied thoughtfully.

"Then how many humans and Jötnar do you think die each day outside of battle so that they may come to this place and not be sent somewhere else?" Hrit asked.

"Wait... these battles happen every day?" Sylfia asked incredulously. "There is a battle the size of what we have just been a part of every single day?"

"Yes," Hrit said. "Each day, a battle is brought here beside our farms. Sometimes the food is destroyed, but we have enough to keep our people fed. Each night, the Jötnar raiders attempt to break down the walls of the human settlement, and sometimes they are successful."

"I do not understand," Sylfia admitted. "There are huge battles every single day with more deaths than I could ever imagine happening... and there are enough souls arriving each day to replenish those ranks on both sides? It is not something that I can believe!"

"That is because it is not how it happens," Hrit said. "The warriors fall in the battles, and each day a handful of new souls await their place in the ranks. The new souls take the places of the fallen so that the total numbers on either side remain the same, and then the rest awaken in their beds the next day to fight again."

"This... I do not understand," Sylfia said again. "So new warriors replace the fallen, and then the rest are resurrected the next day?"

"Yes," Hern said and stamped his foot once with glee.

"Do they remember dying? And how are the warriors that do not awaken chosen? And where do they go? And what is all of this for?" Sylfia asked without taking a breath.

"Most do not remember that they have been here before, but some have faint memories," Hrit explained. "How they are chosen is a mystery, but the ones that do not awaken are sent on to join the ranks of the Draugr." Hrit took a deep breath. "And all of this, it is believed, is simply to keep us all busy while the time passes both here and in the other realms until Ragnarök comes to pass."

"This... this cannot be simply a waste of time!" Sylfia exclaimed as the information penetrated her mind. "These people fight and die over and over and you say that they do not even remember any of it?"

"It is, it is!" Hern said as he bounded up and down, the ground shaking slightly with each leap.

"Does Erling know?" Sylfia asked, remembering the human commander who had seemed to have some divine ability to instil hope and morale into his troops. "Or is he simply another who has been forsaken to repeat his own actions over and over for the rest of time?"

"Ha!" Hern exclaimed. "You mean Bergelmir!"

"What?" Jarl asked.

Hrit sighed. "Will you be quiet, brother? Once again, my brother has told you more information than you should know. Erling's real name is indeed Bergelmir. He is a Jötnar like us."

"A Jötnar?" Jarl asked slowly.

"Bergelmir is a very powerful being," Hrit said. "He is a great warrior, but his greatest ability is to keep his warriors focussed on their task. Once he led the Jötnar in battle against the armies of man, but when he realised what this place was, he decided to join the humans. Sometimes he comes back though and fights with the Jötnar. He kind of enjoys all of the fighting and the killing, especially knowing that there are no consequences."

Jarl stroked his beard. In a strange, twisted way, he could see the allure of fighting in battles that had no true outcome.

It was almost as though this place was a facsimile of Valhalla, where the glory of battle was forever lasting.

"But he looks like a human," Sylfia asked.

"Sometimes he looks human," Hern said, smiling. "Sometimes he look Jötnar. Depend on the day."

Jarl closed his eyes and rubbed his forehead with the back of his fist.

"Then why did you save me," he asked. "If none of this matters, why did you bother?"

"First," Hrit held up a chubby grey finger. "If you die, there is a chance that you do not come back, so it does matter. Second, we help anyone who needs it. We are not a fearsome warrior people as you may believe. We are farmers and builders. We are just here because it is where we were placed. And last, if you do not die, then you will remember. The more who remember, the more who will know what this place truly is."

"Why does that matter?" Sylfia asked.

"Because like you have done," Hrit explained, "the battle in this place is fought daily because that is what they all think is supposed to happen. Nobody has a choice. But if more and more know that there is no need to fight, eventually the spell that is keeping this place alive could fail."

"But would that not change if Erling... I mean Bergelmir were to fall? Wouldn't his game be reduced to nothing?" Sylfia asked.

"Bergelmir will never be sent away from this place. He has been killed before in battle, but he has always awoken to fight again another day. I do not know if this is a rule of the battle or not, but it has never been broken."

Jarl and Sylfia remained silent once Hrit had finished speaking. What she had told them seemed so far-fetched and yet still somehow believable. This place provided a battle to be fought over and over again and the warriors mostly did not know that it was even happening. This was a prison, a hold to keep the souls within, and when they were eventually freed, they were sent to eternal servitude as a Draugr.

"I... I do not know if we are able to help," Jarl said, anticipating his daughter's next wish. "We cannot stay in this place any longer, and we cannot afford the time to get stuck here. I am sorry, Hrit, Hern. I am thankful that you have helped me, but we have a path on which to walk, and it is larger than this battle."

Sylfia opened her mouth to speak but snapped it shut again. She wanted to object, to help both the humans and the Jötnar that could not leave this place, but Jarl was right. This was an occasion where their path was more significant than the needs of these few – even if it meant leaving so many people in a state of perpetual war. At least, she thought, they would not all die.

"But you remember! You help!" Hern said, his smile fading as he realised what Jarl had said. "That how this supposed to work!"

Sylfia turned her attention to the smaller male Jötnar, and she could see in his face both disappointment and upset. She adapted her tone of voice to that when speaking to a child.

"I am sorry Hern. Our goal is to stop Ragnarök from happening. If we stay, everyone in all of the realms will be killed but if we go and manage to carry out our task, it will save so many. I know a few may die here on the battlefield, but the longer we wait then more will not wake up to fight another day."

"But..." Hern said, but his sister interrupted him with an outstretched arm around his shoulder.

"Do not worry, brother. If these people can stop Ragnarök, then all of this will come to an end, and we will not have to worry about father ever again! Imagine that there will be no more fighting, just playtime and all the food we can eat!"

Hern could not help but smile at Hrit's words. It was clear that the promise of brighter horizons was enough to bring him on board.

"But will you tell us how you will stop Ragnarök from coming?" Hrit asked.

A flash of uncertainty washed across Sylfia's face before she replied, and she only hoped that the Jötnar had not seen it. The truth was, she knew that she needed to reach the Naglfar ship and somehow prevent it from being launched, but she did not know what that would actually achieve, or how to even complete that task. It was as though she was being led by her complete faith in the fact that the Gods had set her along this path, so the end would inevitably somehow become clear.

"I cannot say," Sylfia replied truthfully. It was the only way she could be sure this pair would not think she had lied to them. "I must continue as I have been charged by the Gods, and when I reach the Naglfar ship, I hope that they will guide me on what I will have to do. Beyond that, I cannot answer your question."

Hern looked saddened at the fact that he was not going to play a part in knowing the future, although Hrit's face twisted as she travelled through a number of different emotions.

"I know that you must not tell us your plans... but are you truly saying that you have none?" Hrit asked. "That we must simply wait and see what is to happen? Even for the Jötnar, this seems like a plan destined to fail. We may look as though we are feral creatures of little intelligence, but we are more intelligent than you may give us credit for."

Sylfia exhaled. "It is true. The plan is to keep going and hope that guidance from the Gods shines its light on our path. So far I have been steered well and it has brought me this far, to this very cave, actually. Without the help of the Gods, I would have lost my father more than once, so I have faith that my path will be properly illuminated when the time is right."

"Your path has brought you to the depths of Helheim!" Hrit exclaimed, then visibly reeled her emotions back in. "But OK... if you do not wish to tell us your true plan, just promise us now that if we help you, you will do everything that you can to close this place down so that no more Jötnar... or humans," she added thoughtfully, "will be trapped to fight in a never-ending battle filled with pain and death."

Sylfia nodded. "I promise that I will do all I can. If it is the will of the Gods that this place is to be no more, then I know that it shall be."

Jarl called up from the ground and it made Sylfia jump. "What do you mean, help us?" he asked. Sylfia almost kicked herself for missing the statement that Hrit had made.

Hrit kicked at the ground, releasing a puff of dirt as she contemplated her next statement. Eventually, she spoke. "Well... I guess it would be OK to tell you because you promised to do what you can to help us..." she trailed off as though still unsure if she should tell this pair of humans what she had been hiding.

"We will do what we can," Sylfia affirmed again. "But please, any help that you can give will be greatly appreciated." Sylfia felt a dull warmth in her chest as she pleaded with Hrit to help them. The sensation was strange, similar to the one she had felt when Erling – or Bergelmir – had given his speech before the battle. She did her best to ignore it and forced her eyes to meet Hrit's own so that she could see Sylfia's sincerity.

"OK," Hrit said again as she peered at Sylfia. It seemed as though she had concluded that this human could be trusted, and that she would be able to help. "This place... the fifth ring... it is my home. I know that it may seem strange, but we do not live atop the ground like you may expect," She glanced down to the floor. "My people live underground where it is dark and cool, we do not enjoy the light of day."

"Right, that makes sense," Sylfia said.

"The connection between the fifth and sixth ring – where the mightiest of the Jötnar live - that is also underground. In fact it is the only way to pass into the sixth ring."

"So we would need to pass through your domain and then through an underground settlement where everyone within is a mighty Jötnar warrior?" Sylfia asked, her eyes widening with the realisation that things were about to get a lot more complicated for her and her father.

"Not... not exactly," Hrit replied slowly. "This is not easy for me to say... it makes me feel like I am betraying my people... but I suppose it does not matter..." she was almost talking to herself at this point. "It is possible to travel through our underground settlement, as you say, but there is another way. It is not an easy path, and eventually, you will have to deal with the beasts... I... I do not know if it is even possible..."

"Another way? Is it quicker? Does it bypass your people and take us directly into the seventh ring, then?" Sylfia asked quickly and excitedly. If there was a way that she and her father could shorten the length of their ordeal, she really wanted to know about it.

Hrit nodded. "The path will lead you to the seventh ring without facing another Jötnar. I can make you this promise, but you must listen to me. If you were to travel through our underground settlements, you would arrive at the eighth ring, having bypassed the seventh. If you take this path above ground, then you will bypass all of the Jötnar and find yourselves within the seventh ring, and that is the hunting grounds of Garmr and his pack. It is a terrible place that the Jötnar do not even attempt to step a single foot on..."

Sylfia turned to look at her father. She had not missed the fact that Hern had crouched down low and had begun go shiver at the mention of the great wolf's name, but this was not a choice that she could make alone.

"So our choice is to go underground and risk facing the full might of the Jötnar people and arrive at the eighth ring, or we go over the mountains and arrive at the seventh ring and bypass the Jötnar?" her words formed a question that she directed to Jarl and Sylfia turned the words over in her mind as she spoke them.

"Then how will you help us?" Jarl asked the Jötnar female as she awaited Sylfia's decision.

"If you choose to try to take the path underground, we can come with you and attempt to let everyone know what it is that you have planned. I think that at least some of the people will want to help, but if you choose the other way, we will show you where to go. But you must take the path alone. No Jötnar has ever faced off against the great wolf and his pack and lived." She stopped and looked thoughtful for a moment. "The seventh ring, Garmr's hunting grounds... you should not go there. It is simply a place that will bring about your death. At least if we were to try to argue your task to our people, you might stand a chance."

"What would happen if your people would not agree with you and decide not to help us?" Jarl asked.

Hrit grimaced. "It is not something that would be pleasant for you..." she trailed off. "Maybe then one benefit of going to the seventh ring would be that your deaths would most likely be quick and painless?"

Jarl turned back to Sylfia, who was still looking to him for guidance, but in truth, both of the options before them sounded terrible. It would be death either way for sure, but he had trusted his daughter for all this time, and he was not about to change that now.

"Sylfia. You have always said that you were supposed to take the most difficult of paths as they presented themselves. Of the two paths we are presented with now," Jarl stroked his braided beard thoughtfully, "I believe that facing Garmr would be the most difficult. The beast is mighty, and I am unable to run with my leg like this. If we are to place our lives in the hands of the Gods once more, then let us do it in the way that we are supposed. There is also another thing: the Jötnar who have faced Garmr and were killed - they visited the seventh ring with the aim of fighting the beast and his pack in battle?" his question was directed towards Hrit, who nodded in response.

"There was a time when the strongest and mightiest of the Jötnar people strode into the seventh ring to face the beasts so that their torment of any who crossed their paths could end. Not more than a handful of wolves fell in the battle, and only a single Jötnar warrior returned. It was our father. I am glad that he had the sense to run from that place and never return."

"Then this is how we are different," Jarl announced. "We do not look to take the land from these beasts, nor do we wish to meet them on the battlefield; we look to cross the ring to reach the far side. We will not make such a noise as the Jötnar warriors will have done in their approach, and we are much smaller and quieter than your people."

Sylfia closed her eyes. She hated the wolves, hated the battles that they had already had, and she just simply wished that they could go and meet the Jötnar people underground and ask them for help all the way to the end. She knew that her father was correct, though; Sylfia was supposed to be tested over and over until the time that she knew how she could stop Ragnarök. It was the way that she had been told by Elder Wise, and by always following the most difficult of paths, she had always been steered right. Jarl had made a good point, though. The Jötnar that had been killed by Garmr and his pack had presented the wolves with a large and loud target. All Sylfia and Jarl had to do was to remain as quiet as possible and attempt to sneak across the seventh ring.

"My father is right," Sylfia announced, turning back to the Jötnar pair. "If you think it is impossible to best Garmr, then that is the path we must take. I will ask, though, that you spread the word to your people that not all humans are bloodthirsty monsters. If we are to be victorious in our task, then the world will need to heal, I am sure of it. I am so tired of war, death and battle, and I am sure that many others are as well."

Hrit nodded. "We will do as you ask. But I am not sure that your plan will work; these creatures are hunters, and they will know the moment that you arrive within their territory. They will hunt you until you are found, and then they will kill you without question."

Jarl raised himself gingerly to his feet with a grunt and wobbled slightly as he tried to get used to the binding on his leg.

"Do not worry about us," he said. "We have fought the wolves before, and seeing how slowly I will be able to move, I doubt that they will waste their time on us."

36

"We will tell our people what you are planning to do," Hrit said quietly as she, Hern, Jarl and Sylfia looked out at the desolate, dry entrance to the domain where Garmr and his kin roamed free.

The sky above the expanse that seemed to have no end was a brownish grey and the ground before them was dry and cracked, like a desert. The strangest thing, though, was that after a few feet of arid ground, there appeared to be a vibrant green forest that rolled away as far as the eye could see. The colour of the leaves stood out against the dire backdrop of the sky above, almost as though there was a huge blaze off in the distance that was giving everything a dark brown hue with its smoke. The only sound was of rumbling thunder somewhere off in the distance. Strangely, behind them the sky over the battlefield between man and Jötnar was clear and bright still, but with a portion of white mist that had rolled down the mountains to cover the pass where the group now stood. It seemed as though each ring of Helheim had its own weather and light and dark cycle, and there was little crossover between them.

"How many do you think there are here?" Jarl asked the two Jötnar.

"It is not known," Hrit replied. "Garmr is head of the pack though there could be as little as ten or as many as fifty."

Hern let out a small whimper and Hrit looked to comfort him. "Do not worry brother, we will not take another step further; this is where we will turn back and await father."

Hern's face lit up at the mention of their father. "You think he play with me today?" he said with a hopeful expression on his face.

"I hope so Hern," Hrit said. "But if he does not then I will play with you." Her words seemed to placate Hern, who turned to look back along the mountain pass excitedly as though he could not wait to get back to his family.

"We will do what we can to tell our people about you," Hrit said looking back to Jarl and Sylfia. "But I doubt that you will be heard from again."

"And we will do what we can to end the war that your people are stuck within," Sylfia assured the Jötnar. "Thank you for your help. And thank you for saving my father." She gave them both a genuine smile and watched as the pair turned away from them silently and started the journey back towards their underground settlement.

"How do you think we should proceed?" Sylfia asked Jarl, trying her best not to look worried at the task that lay before them. Although they could see no wolves or indeed any other threat from the seventh ring of Helheim, she knew that this test was sure to be much more difficult than any they had faced thus far.

"I do not know, but I do not see any of the beasts nearby. We will have to attempt to remain quiet and unseen as we move. I do not know if this place will experience night and day but we must assume that what we see now is the best chance we have to remain unseen. We must cross this place," Jarl said, his voice heavy with determination, "but with my leg the way it is... I do not know if I will be able to make it all the way without your help."

"You have helped me every day of my life father, it is about time that I repaid a little of your kindness, is it not?" Sylfia said and she placed an arm around her father's torso and gave him a squeeze. Jarl winced slightly through some unseen injury but did not object to Sylfia's embrace.

Sylfia held on to her father as the pair took their first steps out into the seventh ring of Helheim and the moment their feet touched the dry, cracked ground beneath them, they were both assaulted by a dense warmth and the smell of wet dog in the air.

"Do you..." Sylfia started to ask, but Jarl gave her a look that she knew told her to be quiet. She shut her mouth and looked all around to see if she could see any danger approaching, but the world was silent and offered nothing past the sensations that she was already feeling.

After a moment, Jarl spoke. "We must conceal ourselves within the forest," he said. "We must not be seen entering or our plan to remain hidden will be over before it has even begun."

Sylfia nodded silently. Again, Jarl was right; the last thing either of them wanted was to be seen this early on, making their crossing of the seventh ring one long escape from a hunt, when they could have remained undetected.

The pair shuffled towards the treeline, with Sylfia helping her father walk and when they had entered the dense cover that the forest provided, they released the breaths that each of them had been unconsciously holding. They did not know if they had already been seen, but nothing around them suggested that they were in any immediate danger.

"We must move from this place," Jarl said quietly once they had regained their breath and the adrenaline that coursed through their bodies had started to abate. "If we have been seen this is the first place they will look. It is better to be safe and to move rather than stay in one place and risk discovery."

Jarl did not wait for Sylfia to reply, but simply started to hobble away into the treeline to their left. Sylfia caught up with him in a moment and wrapped her arm around him again to offer her support.

"Should we not be looking to cross this place as quickly as possible?" she asked in a hushed tone as she realised that they had made a sharp left turn, keeping the site where they had entered the forest on their left as they moved. They were evidently not making a beeline to the far side of the forest as she had expected, rather this seemed to be the long way round.

"If the wolves have seen us enter, they will attempt to head us off. We must travel along a different path just in case," Jarl explained.

Sylfia nodded in response. Her father had always been a great hunter so why would it have been any different to assume that he would be skilled in evading a hunt.

Then a noise that they had both been dreading reached them - the howls of a giant wolf. After a moment, another voice joined in, then another and any hope of discerning from which direction the howls had come were now entirely gone. It sounded as though there were hundreds of wolves out there in the forest, spread out before them as far as they could hear.

"Where..." Sylfia began, though a raised hand from Jarl silenced her until the crescendo of howls had finally stopped.

"None of them sounded near to us," Jarl announced as he dropped his hand. "And they are spread out across this land, throughout the forest. I do not know if we will be able to make it all the way across undetected... perhaps that is what they had planned all along."

"What should we do?" Sylfia asked with wide eyes. It had not occurred to her that there could have been so many wolves and she truly had believed that there was a possibility that they would have been able to cross this place undetected.

"We must move swiftly, but remain as quiet as possible," Jarl said. "All is not lost yet, but we must keep our minds with us."

The pair resumed walking for another few minutes before they turned inward, their path sending them deeper into the forest and away from the outskirts. Even if they had been seen entering the seventh ring, there would be no chance that anyone or anything within would know where they currently were, or indeed their eventual path from one side to the other.

The humid air about them was already making both Jarl and Sylfia sweat, and at times the vegetation from the forest was so dense that Sylfia needed to push or hold it out of the way so that Jarl could continue despite his limited mobility. Eventually, they had travelled for so long that they did not know how far they had come, or if indeed they were still travelling in the correct direction.

The light overhead seemed unchanged, the brown hued sky above struggling to breach the dense canopy overhead which meant that this was probably going to remain as the state of the light within the forest.

Another series of howls began and Jarl stopped to listen to calculate how close any of the beasts were to their position. The howls had started from far off into the distance and as more and more voices joined in the chorus again they seemed to be coming from literally everywhere. That was until one of the howls began from what sounded like within touching distance from Jarl and Sylfia.

The wolf that had joined the howl could only have been a few metres away from where Sylfia and Jarl crouched awaiting the end of the deafening noise. Sylfia was in two minds as to whether they should try to escape from it – either creeping or running – or if they should try to hide but looking at her father she knew he was in no fit state to try to outrun a giant wolf.

Jarl could read Sylfia's thoughts on her face and he too realised that he would not be able to escape quickly so he removed the choice from Sylfia and lowered himself to the ground slowly and quietly. Sylfia followed suit. They then gathered as much of the undergrowth and ground-level vegetation that surrounded them as they could, and pulled it over their prone backs as best they could without making any noise.

It seemed as though they had made the right decision in stopping and attempting to hide because the second that both Jarl and Sylfia stopped moving, two deep red eyes appeared above and in front of them, peering into the place where they had been standing.

The eyes, almost too huge to comprehend, belonged to an enormous grey wolf. Its fur was matted and damp where the atmosphere was heavy with moisture and its mouth hung open, drool spilling out over the edges. Sylfia struggled to keep from gasping as she realised that the wolf's terrible maw was certainly large enough to fit her entire head in.

The wolf lowered its mouth towards the ground, just a few feet away from where they were trying their best to remain silent, and it sniffed the air as though it knew that they were hiding nearby in the dense undergrowth. Sylfia held her breath as it edged closer and closer, still sniffing the air loudly. It must have known, there was no other explanation, but because the wolf was so huge and its muzzle so long, it was having trouble seeing what it thought it could smell.

Sylfia shifted her gaze taking care not to move any part of her being. She held her breath as she realised that Jarl was looking right back at her and he too was holding his own breath. As their eyes met she could read his very thoughts: above anything else, neither of them could make a single sound or it would mean their certain end.

The wolf must have heard something far in the distance because its ears pricked upright and it regained its stature, standing upright and proud. It waited a long second, then turned and darted away into the thick forest as though it had been called by its master.

Sylfia and Jarl waited for a moment until they could no longer hear the cracking of fallen branches as the beast disappeared without any attempt at stealth. Their last-minute plan had worked, and they both knew that if a similar thing were to happen again, they would not hesitate to drop and hide themselves. Sylfia could not help but think that the size of any of the Jötnar that had been to this place would have given them a much harder time concealing themselves.

"How did it get so close before we noticed?" Sylfia asked quietly as they began to walk again. It was the one thing that she could not figure out: the wolf was so large and when it ran from them it had made so much noise, but they had not known that it had been mere feet away from them in the first place. If it had not howled, they may have simply walked straight into the back of it.

"I do not know," Jarl replied. "But we must take more care. A creature that size... I will be of little use and if others come..." He did not have to finish his sentence as the meaning was clear: fighting one of these wolves was not something that they could do.

"Do you know which way we should go?" Sylfia asked, trying to figure out if they had continued to travel in the same direction or if they were now hopelessly lost.

"We carry on this way," Jarl gestured to the front of the pair. "Have a look at the way the plants are growing."

Sylfia frowned as she tried to remember her training, and then it hit her. The smaller plants, the tiny flowers and even the undergrowth itself seemed to be pointing all in one direction. Moss had grown on just one side of many of the thicker trees that she could see and she exclaimed in glee: "Yes! I remember! The plants... they always grow the same!"

Jarl smiled and placed a flat hand atop Sylfia's head. "Yes, that is it. But we must hope that it is also true of this place as it is in the mortal realm... so far it seems as though we have been lucky as I have been keeping a note of the growth. I hope that it continues."

"Then when we reach the other side of this ring we will find the Naglfar ship and all of this will be over before we know it," Sylfia said with a smile. It was a huge oversimplification, but her words made Jarl smile too. It was nice to think that although they still had so far to go, they had come so, so far already.

Jarl and Sylfia walked slowly in a straight line, following the growth of the plants for a long time. The light above them remained unchanged and the care that they needed to take now, combined with the density of the forest and Jarl's injury, meant that they had travelled a fraction of the distance that they would have otherwise, but they were making progress and that was all that mattered.

Then Jarl abruptly stopped and placed a hand over Sylfia's mouth before she could exclaim. He gestured to a thin screen of greenery and small bushes and although it took a second, Sylfia could now see the huge form of a deep brown wolf beyond. The creature was just standing there on all fours looking off to the side. It was clear that it did not know they were there, but they could not risk getting any closer or making any noise to alert it.

Sylfia took a step backwards, watching the ground carefully as she placed her feet to ensure there were no large branches that would snap or loudly crack. Fortunately this time they were just far enough away to turn back and circle around it rather than lie down and hide - they were very aware that if the previous wolf had not heard something off in the distance, with a little more effort it could have found them.

Sylfia and Jarl both watched the ground as they stepped, turning away from where the wolf stood but as their attention returned to the forest before them and not their feet, they found themselves face to face with the huge, snarling grey wolf that had been searching for them earlier.

Sylfia bit back a scream as the dripping maw of the enormous beast appeared only inches from her face and it bared its teeth, ready to strike. She knew that if she were to make a sound it would bring the attention of the second wolf, so instead she slowly let go of her father and almost undetectably slowly she began to lower her arms to her sides, where her two shimmering silver swords hung from her waist.

It would do no good to attempt to hide from the wolf now, it knew that Sylfia and Jarl were there and, if anything, she could only be grateful that it hadn't simply killed her already.

The wolf's teeth were each at least three inches long and as sharp as blades. It snarled so hard that it revealed its deep red gums and Sylfia inhaled its hot putrid breath. Then it moved almost imperceptibly, but Sylfia saw her chance and she threw herself back onto the ground, evading the wolf's strike that would have taken her life in one devastating bite.

In an instant Jarl leapt into action. He did not know and did not care if the wolf had simply ignored him because it saw him as less of a threat, but he was about to prove the creature wrong. As the wolf's head followed Sylfia as she fell back to the ground, he swung both of his axes with all of his might, igniting them with his divine gift and they cut through the air and both plunged deep into the wolf's neck.

The sharpened edges of the hand axes cut deeply into the wolf's flesh as though they met no resistance at all. The ease of the impact surprised Jarl and he momentarily appraised the weapons curiously, noticing that the runes etched into their handles and axe heads had a slight white glow to them. These weapons were certainly the mightiest that he had ever held before.

The wolf howled in pain and reared up and away from Sylfia. The sound gave Jarl goose bumps as he held tightly onto his axes to prevent himself from losing them. A long, thick line of blood followed the loud squelching sound as his axes released from their cut, but Jarl did not stop to wait and see what damage they had caused; he swung again and again and the howls of the wolf slowly died down to silence as it fell to the ground, finally dead, its body quickly fading away to the wind.

The battle had not gone unnoticed though and Sylfia's worst fear was realised as the second wolf had turned and was charging straight at them. Jarl did not spare a moment to stop and think and he launched both of his blazing axes simultaneously at it. This wolf was just as large as the first so it was difficult for Jarl to miss, but his aim could not have been truer. Each of the axes bypassed the wolf's snarling maw and struck the wolf in its two bright yellow eyes, blinding it before it could take another step.

It yelped and fell to the ground, not yet dead but seriously injured. It raised its head to the sky and let out a howl that made the very ground around Sylfia and Jarl shake.

"This is not good, Sylfia," Jarl said as his shoulders rose and fell. "There will be others with us soon."

Sylfia knew that what her father was saying was true, but her attention was focused on something far more threatening right now. The wolf panted and yelped as it attempted the shake off its injury in vain, but at its feet lay Jarl's axes, now extinguished although the dry ground beneath them was smoking as if about to burst into flames.

Sylfia took two slow, careful steps toward the wolf. She knew that it could not see her but would still be able to hear her. She wondered too if it would smell her approaching, but there was nothing that she could do to prevent that. All she knew was that if the forest was allowed to alight, they would be in far more trouble than only having to deal with the wolves – especially as Jarl could certainly not move with any kind of speed.

"What are you doing?" Jarl asked, but Sylfia held out a palm to quieten him. He obeyed her command and watched as she walked closer and closer to the still struggling wolf. He wanted to help, or to simply to dive at her and stop her from moving into harm's reach but he knew that in his state there was nothing that he could do. He could now also see what Sylfia was doing, as well as the white smoke rising in carefree wisps from the ground.

Sylfia took another step, then another and within a moment she had reached the feet of the beast. She remained as quiet as she could, choosing her steps carefully and to her relief, when she was finally within reach of the hand axes that had fallen to the ground, the wolf had still not noticed her proximity, being either too wounded or simply too preoccupied in whining and writhing to pay her any attention.

Sylfia picked up the axes and smiled to herself, this had gone far easier than she could have hoped.

But she had thought too soon, as within an instant the smoke near her feet turned to flames that rose to the height of her waist in a second and began to widen and spread. The wolf that had fallen began to burn and it yelped as it felt the heat against its body, its own fur alight and it ran. It clearly had no destination in mind, but it ran as fast as its legs would carry it and as it moved the flames licked the branches, trees, bushes and undergrowth to cause a trail of bright burning orange and red in its wake. The forest had begun to burn, and it was now too late for Sylfia to do anything about it.

Then things turned from bad to worse as Sylfia glanced back to her father and saw that behind him stood another giant, angry wolf. To its left and right there were two more and as she peered all around, she realised that she and her father were encircled by even more angry, snarling giant wolves. To make things worse, Sylfia and Jarl were separated by the flames that had been spread by the fleeing wolf.

Sylfia did the only thing that she could think of: she drew her own two short swords and tossed the pair of hand axes to Jarl, and as soon as they reached her father's hands they exploded into bright flame.

The world around the pair burned. It was becoming hotter and darker by the second, and Sylfia felt the sweat dripping from her head as she watched the wolves close in on her father as one. Those nearest her did not move, it was as though they wanted her to watch as her father fell.

The first attack came and as a wolf lunged at Jarl, and he swung his axes upwards in a mighty attack. The wolf turned to avoid the attack and leapt over the top of Jarl to stand between him and Sylfia, no one having won the first test.

A second wolf then lowered its head and charged, and it was all that Jarl could do to lower his axes and plant his feet. He knew that in his injured state there was no way that he would be able to remain stabilised against such a charge - even at full strength he most likely would have been pushed back, down or trampled.

The wolf impacted with Jarl and his axes bit into the beast, releasing a spray of blood that coated both of them in a deep red sheen. The creature yelled in pain but it did not matter; the charge had served its purpose – Jarl was on the ground and within the reach of the first attacker. The creature did not waste a second and opened its huge jaws wide enough to bite Jarl's head clean off.

"NO!" Sylfia screamed at the top of her lungs, with a shout so forceful that the flames that surrounded her flickered and danced as though they had been blown by some divine gust.

Jarl's headless body fell to the ground. The flames all around him engulfed his body and just as in the dream that Sylfia had seen that was incepted by Loki himself, she watched as her father's body burned, turning almost immediately to ash and then being carried off by the wind.

It all seemed so unreal, as if this was again the dream that Loki had given to her that now felt so long ago. There was no way that this was how her father was to meet his end, no way that the last time they would see each other would be surrounded by death and fire.

Sylfia fought the urge to fall down to her knees. She wanted to shout, to cry but a low rumbling growl brought her back to the reality which she was in. The wolves that had encircled the pair were still there, having awaited Jarl's end. It seemed as though they were enjoying the pain and torment that Sylfia felt more than the actual death of her father itself.

Sylfia looked at all of the glowing eyes surrounding her. They each spoke to her of pain and death and deep down inside, she knew that this was going to be her end too, just as it was her father's. She could not fight all of these creatures alone, the task was simply too difficult.

"Odin save me," Sylfia mumbled under her breath. She did not reach for her weapons nor make any sudden or aggressive movements; she knew that her only hope was that these wolves were bound by the same laws that had stopped the Gods from killing her already. If she was not a threat then perhaps they could not harm her.

This hope was shattered a moment later when one of the wolves, encouraged by its desire to kill, leapt forward, away from the rest and bore down on her.

She closed her eyes tightly and accepted her fate, the last thing she saw being the drool dripping from the long, sharp teeth of the giant wolf, and its tongue begging to taste her blood.

Then, as though the world had turned to silence around her, Sylfia heard and felt nothing. The pain that she expected to feel from the attacking wolf did not arrive. Instead she felt the warmth in her chest rising, rising above the heat of the flames that still threatened to destroy the forest around her and then she heard a thud.

Opening her eyes, Sylfia could now see that the wolf that had attacked lay on the ground before her, its head cleanly separated from its body. In addition, all around her the sounds of battle became clear as she watched a group of very large and very fearsome looking Jötnar warriors trading blows with the ferocious wolves.

The Jötnar looked as though they were the strongest of their people and each of them held a terrible bladed weapon, almost all of them coated in the thick red blood of the wolves which they were battling. At three or four times the size of a single human each, Sylfia wondered how exactly these warriors had managed to sneak up on her and the wolves, but the point was moot. They had saved her from certain death and she did not particularly care how that had arrived there.

"You are Sylfia?" a particularly large Jötnar asked as he stood next to Sylfia like he was her protector. His voice was so deep and loud that her very bones shook within her skin as he spoke.

Sylfia looked up at the almost-human giant but could only see the bottom half of his face. As he spoke, he watched his people battling the wolves instead of looking down at her.

Sylfia nodded. "I am," she said. She did not have the heart to say any more, still trying to comprehend what had just happened and still stunned into silence by the passing of her father.

"My daughter said that you would be here," the Jötnar said. "She said that you will try to stop Bergelmir... I told her that you would not be able to keep your promise if you came to this place alone."

Sylfia did not respond this time. She could hear the words that this Jötnar was speaking, but could simply not cope with any more information. She simply stared forward, watching as the wolves and the Jötnar fought to the death.

The wolves did not seem to have too much trouble in repelling the Jötnar's attacks, leaping and bounding, snapping and swiping back each time one of the Jötnar swung their mighty weapons at them. There were already more than a few Jötnar on the ground dead, with heads and limbs detached from their bodies, and Sylfia could see that only a handful of the wolves had fallen. She distantly worried that there would come a time when there would be no Jötnar left to fight.

As Sylfia did not respond, the Jötnar spoke again. "I do not know what your plans are, but I believe that we must take this chance. If you can put an end to the war that my people are stuck within... then please... I give you my life as my kin do. We will help you find your escape from these plains."

Again Sylfia heard the words but had trouble comprehending them. Why were these belligerent giants, these foes of man here to help her? Why did they care and why would they give their lives to protect her?

"Why?" Sylfia managed to croak out eventually, fully aware that her cheeks were wet with tears and more were overflowing from her bloodshot eyes.

"Does it matter!?" the Jötnar replied incredulously. "Look around you human, can you not see that if you are to stay here for much longer then you will die anyway, if not at the teeth of a great wolf then burned alive? My kin will do what they can but we must go now!"

Something that the Jötnar said made its way through to Sylfia now. The world seemed to move in slow motion and the blaze around her came into focus. Her nostrils were filled with smoke and she found herself struggling to breathe properly. She was dying, she knew it now. She was dying and if this Jötnar wanted to help her get far away from this place then who was she to resist? But her father though. She looked at the ground where the image of his headless, lifeless body remained scorched into her mind's eye.

The huge Jötnar evidently could not spare another moment to try to get Sylfia to snap out of whatever she was experiencing. Instead, he grabbed her by the arm and swept her off of her feet, dragging her behind him as he started to run.

"What are you doing?" Sylfia managed to call up to the huge Jötnar, though he did not respond.

As Sylfia was dragged along without her feet touching the ground, she realised the scale of what was happening all around her. There were so many Jötnar that she could not comprehend how they were having such trouble with the wolves. There were also more and more Jötnar streaming into the field of battle to engage the wolves as they too arrived from the forest. It was clear to Sylfia now that there were far more wolves than the hundred that she had thought of as the worst-case scenario; more likely there were thousands of the creatures.

The Jötnar looked as if they were in trouble though, and even where there were three or four of the warriors facing off against a single wolf, the wolves still seemed to hold the upper hand. Sylfia clung onto a hope that the tide of battle would ebb and flow and eventually the Jötnar would emerge victorious. Whatever the result would be though, it would be at a dire cost.

The Jötnar that pulled Sylfia along did not seem to be slowed by the forest as Sylfia and Jarl had been. Where they had found moving through dense vegetation a slow and tedious process, this Jötnar seemed to simply keep running at things and they either broke or moved out of his way. He was just so large and so strong that what would have held Sylfia and Jarl back did not even pose a mild inconvenience to this giant.

Sylfia watched as best she could to try to determine which way they were travelling and eventually to her relief, she realised that she was being carried along the same path that she and Jarl had walked. She could tell by the greenery that grew on the side of the tree trunks still facing in the same direction. The smell of smoke and ash was becoming weaker and she wondered how many lives had already been lost to the fire that she had played a part in starting, and whether she and Jarl would have even been able to outrun the blaze.

"OK... I think we can slow down now," Sylfia managed to call out after a long time had passed. She had thought over and over that the Jötnar was about to stop, but he had simply kept on going without slowing for even a moment. He seemed to have an infinite amount of stamina.

The Jötnar ran on for another few minutes but eventually he slowed and stopped in a small clearing, dropping to one knee and breathing heavily. It seemed as though he did need to rest eventually after all.

Neither Sylfia nor the Jötnar said anything for a long moment as the giant caught his breath. Sylfia now had the chance to look at him, and noticed that he had a long curved blade attached to his waist. Furs covered his shoulders and they were so large that she could have only guessed that they had come from the great wolves here.

"Your furs..." Sylfia said. "Did you get them from the wolves?"

The Jötnar looked a little confused at first, then looked at his shoulders and chuckled to himself.

"No, the furs that we wear do not come from the wolves in this place. You must have seen that the bodies of the fallen do not remain long enough for them to have their skin removed?" the Jötnar said.

Sylfia nodded silently.

"Why did you come for me?" she eventually asked.

"As I have said, we have come because we believe that there is a chance that you can save our people from the torment of everlasting war."

"But so many have fallen," Sylfia said quietly.

"My people have had too many years of war and death, we would all risk our lives to find an end; that is why we came."

"All of you came?" Sylfia asked in shock and disbelief.

"No, not all. But most. My kin do not wish to fight any longer, so we have come here in the hope that you will be successful in your quest, as you have told my children. My people have sacrificed the protection of their home in this hope... you are our one last hope I fear."

"My father trusted me," Sylfia said in a very small voice, "as did my mother, and our friends. Each of them has died and now it is just me. I do not know if I have the strength to continue along my path alone..."

This time the Jötnar turned to look down at Sylfia. His eyes were a deep dull grey and they seemed to penetrate Sylfia's very mind.

"As fathers and mothers, we must have the strength to believe in our children, for they are the ones who will carry the torch along into the next age. We have lived our lives but with each passing moment our time becomes shorter. The trust that your father has placed within you, to follow you on your path and aid you until his dying breath, has been his duty and his honour. It is not because you have been unworthy or because your choices have been poor, it is simply the fate of man and Jötnar alike." The Jötnar paused for a moment, then resumed speaking. "Do you know why we all came to help you? It is because my son Hern and my daughter Hrit came before our people with a message and a plea. They told us all that these two humans were unlike the others, that they had a divine task to prevent Ragnarök, and that they had promised to do what they could to end our war. Our people listened to their plea because each and every Jötnar has a voice that must be heard. I and many of the others felt the warmth and the sincerity of their message and it is because of that that I am with you here and now. It was my choice to make, it was the choice of each and every Jötnar that entered into the plains of Garmr, to face almost certain death to give you the chance to continue your journey. I tell you this not because you should feel the death that your task has created, but so that you may feel the hope and strength that moves you forward. The people who aid you in your task do so because it is their choice, and you should not feel the weight or the burden of their passing."

Sylfia opened and closed her mouth a few times before she could arrange her thoughts properly. On the one hand she still could not believe that the Jötnar had so freely chosen to help her, and on the other, no matter the kind words this Jötnar spoke, she could not help feel the weight of guilt bearing down on her.

"But now I have brought you to the path between the seventh and eight ring of Helheim," the Jötnar said as he pulled back some of the vegetation in front of them to reveal the treeline where the forest ended and the dry cracked ground restarted. "I will join you as far as it is destined and when I fall, you must remember that this was my choice and I accept my own fate, as many others before me have done."

The Jötnar then walked out of the forest and away from the treeline and Sylfia scrambled to follow him although she had to run to match his walking pace.

Sylfia could see where she needed to go as soon as the forest had been removed from her line of sight and the world was clear again. Just a hundred metres or so in front of her she could see the edge of the arid ground drop down slightly and a waterfall cascaded downwards as though from some magical beginning.

But then when she looked closer she realised that this was no ordinary waterfall, the water that should have been flowing over the edge and downwards was actually flowing in reverse, travelling up the mountainside, and was lapping at the dry cracked ground at the top. As her gaze travelled upwards her heart skipped a beat as it fell on the giant form of Garmr standing guard at the top of the waterfall.

Before she could shout a word of warning, it was clear that her Jötnar protector had seen the wolf as he broke into a sprint directly towards the colossal beast. The pair were comparable in size, but Sylfia knew what this creature was capable of. As she too increased her speed, she spared a glance behind her to see if any help was arriving from the treeline, but the destruction that she had left behind shocked her.

The forest as a whole burned a bright orange as far as the eye could see with thick black smoke billowing high up and blotting out the brownish sky. Even the place where she and the Jötnar had just emerged from was already ablaze and Sylfia instinctively knew that anything that had been alive within the forest was now surely gone.

Sylfia blinked hard and pushed the thoughts from her head as she turned her attention back to the Jötnar and the giant wolf who were about to engage in combat, but there was nothing that she could do to reach them in time. She willed her legs to work harder and faster as she ran, though she knew that it was futile. She watched as the Jötnar pulled his blade from his side and Garmr reared up high onto its hind legs, snarling a deep, terrible snarl that made her shiver.

The Jötnar led with his blade held between both of his hands and Garmr's first attack was caught by the weapon, its maw closing down tightly upon it. It appeared to Sylfia as though the pair were of similar strength at first, but as she drew closer she could see the amount of effort that the Jötnar was putting into simply holding onto the blade, while the wolf looked as though it was simply toying with him.

"Go quickly!" The Jötnar shouted as Sylfia reached within his eyesight. She was not sure what she was supposed to do, but she wanted to help. "I will hold off the beast, you must continue!" His voice was strained and urgent and Sylfia did as she had been told: she ran towards the waterfall.

Garmr's eye slowly followed Sylfia as she passed the battle and it seemed as though the beast was waiting for her to join the fight, but when she did not, he whipped his head around to throw the Jötnar back and Garmr launched himself at Sylfia.

Sylfia knew that she could not reach the waterfall before Garmr would reach her and when he did, it would be her end. Then suddenly the wolf yelped - the Jötnar had lunged at Garmr before it had escaped, he had managed to impale the beast with his huge blade and was now hanging on as tightly as he could.

The Jötnar's feet scraped along the ground as he wrestled against Garmr's great strength, but Sylfia knew that the wolf would easily with the battle.

"Now!" The Jötnar practically screamed and Sylfia turned her attention back to the waterfall and redoubled her effort to sprint.

As she reached the waterfall, she spared a moment to look back at the wolf and the Jötnar who had saved her life again, just in time to see the wolf perform the killing bite on her saviour, his blood spraying up into the air. She looked away and without another thought, dived into the water before her that still seemed to be flowing the wrong way.

37

Jarl stood facing the archway that had clearly been intentionally carved from the ice that surrounded him. He was alone in wherever this new place was, and his body had returned to how it was before he had been killed. In fact, it was as it had been before he had been injured. Even his two perfect shimmering axes hung down by his legs from his waist, and it made him feel strong.

He was in a small cavern constructed of ice. There was no fire and no torches, rather the ice itself seemed to generate its own dull blue glow. It was not overly bright, but certainly bright enough for Jarl to comfortably see everything around him.

The archway led onward, away from where he stood and into a wide tunnel that snaked off around a bend that prevented him from divining anything further from where he stood. The air was cold but not offensively so, and he could not help but think that there was an undertone of something putrid or rotten within the air.

Jarl took one step forward, not seeing any alternative course of action, but as he did so, something made him stop, a prickling sensation on the back of his neck as though he was being watched and there was something standing behind him. He gingerly took another step forward, acting as casually as possible while reaching down towards his axes. As his fingers reached the cold, carved wood of their handles, he spun on his heels and drew them to the ready.

He could never have been prepared for what he was faced with in that very moment.

At first glance, there appeared to be a man who must have been following behind him somehow, but as Jarl's eyes focused, he could now see exactly what this being was.

Bright blue neon eyes, a metal, horned helmet atop his head and a long white wispy beard and moustache did nothing to hide the reality of the man's skin beneath. It was torn and black through necrosis, although the man still smiled a terrible smile nonetheless. He wore tattered rags and furs and did not say or do anything until Jarl made his first move.

Jarl knew that this could only have been a Draugr, residing in this eighth ring of Helheim, but he did not know if he could fight it, or even if he should. His nostrils were filled with the rotting stench of decaying flesh, but none of this seemed to goad him into raising his weapons to the ready. The creature simply looked so far removed from anything that he had ever experienced before that for the longest time, Jarl did not know what to do.

"Hello, weary traveller," the Draugr said in a half rasped, half-proper tone. "Welcome to the eighth ring of Helheim. I am sorry to be the one to tell you, but this is to be your resting place from now until the end of time." The Draugr held out an open hand but Jarl did not want to touch it as he could see the skin hanging from it. "Come with me now and join the ranks of my Draugr. I will keep you safe forevermore."

"Am... am I a Draugr?" Jarl asked.

The Draugr laughed slowly and wearily as if this was not the first time the question had been asked.

"No, you are not yet a Draugr. You have come to this place to join the ranks of my Draugr, but the choice has not yet been made."

"You are saying that I can choose not to become a Draugr? That I can remain a mortal man?" Jarl asked, not quite believing what this being had to say.

"As unlikely as it may seem to you, the choice, as I have said, is yours. I do not desire unwilling souls to dwell within my army of the dead, so I give all who come to me this choice: you can become a Draugr and live forever, or you can choose to try to live within this realm as you are now. It is as simple as that," the being said. He was still smiling, and although it sounded as though he was giving Jarl a choice, somehow Jarl knew that all was not as it seemed on the surface.

"And what does it mean to try to live in this place without becoming a Draugr?" he asked. "Are there others who are alive now that have made this choice?"

The man's smile grew even wider at the question. "I will tell you no lies," he said. "There are others that have made the choice not to become Draugr, and some are still here and are not of the Draugr. There are also others that made the choice to remain as they were, and they are now Draugr themselves. There are also those here who made the choice to become

Draugr, and as promised, they continue on in their chosen role."

Jarl instinctively grabbed a hold of his beard and lightly twisted it. He was trying to figure out what this thing was leaving out, or why he was being given this choice when every part of his being was screaming at him that this was a trap. He could not help acknowledging, though, that within his heart he could feel that Sigrid was still alive and that she was somewhere in this place.

When Jarl did not answer for a long moment, the thing spoke again.

"Maybe if I tell you about myself and my Draugr, it will help you to understand your choice a little better?" he asked, though Jarl did not respond. The Draugr took that as confirmation that he may continue.

"My name is Glam." He paused for a moment to see if Jarl's expression betrayed any comprehension of what that statement meant, but nothing came so he continued. "I was once a normal, mortal man such as yourself. A brave warrior I was, strong, fearless. Overconfident, it could be said. I was untouchable in every battle that I ever participated in. No enemy blade touched my skin for years and years, and with each fight my confidence continued to grow. Eventually, my time as a warrior was drawing to an end though, and I looked for work across the mortal realm that would provide a suitable challenge for me. Eventually, I heard a story of a farmer who could not find a shepherd because the people within his settlement believed that his farm was haunted by spirits. I, of course, told him that I did not fear man or ghost."

Jarl kept his mouth shut and listened, although he was still unsure of why this conversation was happening.

"Nothing supernatural came to the farm for the year that I spent there, and eventually, it came to Christmas Eve. Being headstrong and unafraid, I ignored the traditions of my people and ate when I was supposed to fast. I announced my intent to the settlement that I would feast and not fast, and I did so as they all watched with hunger in their eyes. They sensed my betrayal of the Gods, though neither man nor woman attempted to stop me. I remember the words I spoke to the people of the settlement that night. "You have many restrictions, when I see no good come of it. I do not know that men fare better now than when they did not heed such things. It seems to me that the customs of men were better when they were called heathens, and now I want my meat and no foolishness." Glam looked as though the words pained him, or that he was embarrassed that he had been the one to speak them, though there was still at least a semblance of a smile on his face.

"Then you went out into the fields the next day, and a storm came," Jarl said, recounting the story that he had been told as a child. "The storm was sent by the Gods as punishment for the breaking of traditions, and the next day and the next, people searched the lands for any sign of you after you did not return. On the third day, a body was found. No man or beast had managed to fell the mighty Glam, but his body was found nonetheless, as blue as Hel and as bloated as an ox."

Glam's smile grew as Jarl recounted the version of the story that he had been brought up with. "Do you know what happened next?" Glam asked.

Jarl tousled his beard again before he replied. "They tried to move the body, to take it back to the settlement, but it was not possible. The flesh was thin and would tear if they tried, so they lay Glam to rest where he had fallen," he recounted.

"But this was the beginning of my next life, did you know?" Glam asked, and Jarl shook his head. "I remained with the farm as a spectre, a spirit that could turn men insane at the very sight of me. Many of the residents of the settlement fled because they could not deal with my haunting of their home, and eventually I drew heroes from all across the land who would try to rid me of my home. But none succeeded."

"But that is not true," Jarl said. "I have been told this story as a child, and there was one who succeeded in stopping you in your terrorising. Grettir..."

"Grettir was cursed and remained so until the end of his days," Glam spat, though he quickly regained his composure. "But that is not important. The reason that I am recounting this story for you is simple: you have heard my story before and you know what I became. But you have never heard what happened between my death and my resurrection as a ghoul, able to torment those weakened people."

Jarl shook his head slowly.

"I was given a choice. One simple choice, and it was that I could either return to the lands of mortal men, although being stuck out in the raging storm, I would have to make my own way back to the settlement or face the possibility of dying in the attempt, or I could become a champion of the Gods. An unlikely mortal, raised higher than the rest, who could stand toe to toe with any mortal man or woman in the land."

"So this is the choice that you are giving me now?" Jarl asked, "the same choice that you were presented with and took, to become more than simply mortal?"

Glam said nothing for a moment as he peered into Jarl's eyes.

"No," he said eventually. "I told the Gods that I would not take their deal. I told them that I was Glam! I did not need some divine intervention to become higher than a base man because I was already better and stronger than every single man or woman that I had ever encountered. I chose to fight and remain as I had always been."

"You turned them down?" Jarl asked, confused by Glam's admission. "Then what happened?"

"Yes, of course I turned them down!" Glam said in a half hiss and half roar, as though he was proud of himself but also regretted his decision. "And now, given the very same choice, I am telling you my story so that you do not make the same mistake that I made in my past."

"Then how did you die?" Jarl asked. He could now tell that Glam simply loved himself, and if he could get him to keep talking, to keep telling his story, there might be something to be learnt from it.

"I died because I made the wrong choice," Glam said. "I turned down the Gods' most precious of gifts and was taken from the mortal realm because of it. Do not make the same mistake I did."

"How though?" Jarl asked. "How did you die? Please, I ask this of you so that I may understand fully how one as powerful as yourself can be taken by nothing but a winter's storm."

"It was no storm!" Glam practically roared, and his voice echoed away through the iced tunnels. "Because within was the first of the Draugr. Those cursed by the Gods to wander undying for all of time. The creatures were nothing like the Draugr that I oversee now though. They were slow and bumbling, but in the storm, I could not see them all. I killed each and every Draugr until there were none left... but I was wounded. The cut festered and boiled until it overtook my very soul, and within the hour I had changed into the thing that I was destined to become."

"Then forgive me," Jarl said. "Why is there a choice if the result is the same regardless of the choices we make?"

"Because I was mighty as a man!" Glam replied. "I made the wrong decision, but I was able to turn that into something so much more. The choice is yours because if you choose to accept your fate and join the ranks of my Draugr, you will be stronger and more powerful than you could ever have thought possible as a mortal man. However, if you choose incorrectly to remain as you are and to fight as I did once, when the Draugr turn you to my cause through injury, you will not be afforded the same luxury."

"I... do not understand," Jarl said slowly. "If you chose incorrectly, then how did you become what you are now? How did you become this legend that is told to children through the ages?"

"That is... not important," Glam said, clearly not wanting to talk about himself and his life anymore. "We have exhausted our time here though mortal, so now it is time to make your choice. Become a Draugr now by my own hand, or fight and become a lesser cursed when my children eventually catch up with you."

"How do you expect me to make such a decision if I do not know what it means to be either Draugr or cursed?" Jarl asked. "The decision is..."

"The decision is yours to make right now, mortal, though do not think that if you are not swift with your next words, I will not remove the luxury from you," Glam interrupted quickly. "Now, make your choice."

Jarl ran his fingers through his beard once more. He knew what he wanted to say to this king of the Draugr, but he did not know what would happen when he finally uttered his answer.

"What will you do with me?" he asked.

"If you choose to join my legion of undead warriors, you will be given your place amongst the ranks. Your duty will be sworn to me, and if you prove yourself worthy you will be given the chance to raise yourself through the ranks and become a chieftain amongst the Draugr."

"And if I choose to remain as I am, to fight for my mortality?" Jarl asked.

"Then I shall leave you where you stand, and it will be up to you to fight for your... mortality... as you say," Glam replied with a smile that revealed his black, decaying gums.

Jarl looked to find any deception from the Draugr, to see if there was anything within his dead eyes that said he was not being entirely truthful, but he could see nothing. Eventually, he had no choice but to give his answer.

"I will stay as I am, and I will fight," Jarl said. "I kneel to no man or God, not any longer."

Glam smiled again. It was strange, as though Jarl had issued a challenge to him and that he was happy about it.

"I look forward to speaking with you again soon," Glam said, and as Jarl watched, the Draugr morphed into an orb of white light, the size of which would fit easily within Jarl's hand. Then the orb flew away from Jarl and disappeared into the tunnel before him.

Before Jarl could gather his thoughts and opinions on what had just happened, he heard a low moaning, groaning sound coming from the tunnels ahead and he knew that there could be no good coming from it.

As he watched, a creature the size and shape of a man rounded the nearest corner to Jarl, and he watched as it stumbled towards him, followed by another and another. Three of the things that he already knew to be Draugr walked towards him as best they could with their necrotic flesh falling from their bodies. They were covered in tattered leather bindings, their eyes white and milky, and their teeth bared. One of the Draugr was missing half the skin that had once covered its head and face, and Jarl could see through its empty eye socket and most of its jaw bone.

Jarl pulled his shimmering axes free from his sides and held them to the ready, setting them alight as he swung them upwards. He did not know how this fight was about to go, but he would use every advantage he had to win.

The first Draugr lunged at Jarl as soon as it had reached within a few feet of where he stood ready. If he had not been holding his hand axes at head height, he may not have been able to raise them between himself and the creature in time to fend off the attack, but as it was, he managed to hold off the attack simply because it did not seem to comprehend that Jarl would be able to place his weapons between him and it.

Despite the flesh falling away from the Draugr, and even though it had stumbled as though it could not hold its body weight up adequately, the Draugr's strength caught Jarl off guard. He had not been expecting to have to struggle so much with this undead foe but had expected to shrug off its attack with relative ease. The Draugr though, he now remembered, were said to have supernatural strength to call upon.

Jarl was still holding the Draugr back by crossing his hand axes across its face, and it snapped at the shafts of the weapons in a frenzied, bloodthirsty state. The axes, though, were at least causing it a fair amount of damage as he let them remain alight so that they scorched and burned the Draugr's skin. Sweat beaded onto Jarl's forehead both from the effort that he exuded and the heat from his axes, though in a straight battle of strength, he knew that eventually he would tire and lose. He could also see that imminently the two other Draugr would enter the fight and that would surely mean that he would be overpowered.

Gritting his teeth and pushing all of his rage into his axes, the orange flames that engulfed them turned to a brilliant white. Jarl had to squint his eyes to keep the bright light from burning into his retinas, and as soon as he felt his foe take a small amount of its pressure off of his axes, he pulled them away from it, cocked them both back to his ears and drove them straight into the Draugr's face. He heard the sickening sound of skin tearing, bones breaking and the weight of his enemy falling to the ground after a final and killing blow.

Jarl knew that he did not have the time to stop now. He pulled his axes back again, and this time he readied them both to his right side and swept them into the next Draugr. One of the axes took the creature's jaw off entirely, and the second bit into its ribcage, getting stuck in the process. Jarl took a moment to try to dislodge his axe, but gave up on the effort as he realised that the third Draugr was much closer than he had anticipated. This Draugr, held a rusted, curved blade in its decaying hand and swung it swiftly and directly at Jarl's face.

Seeing the attack coming at him, at the very last second Jarl let his legs bend fully underneath him. The blade cut through the air and he felt the wind pass over his head where he had managed to avoid the attack, and then he waited until the strike had passed over completely before launching into an uppercut with his one remaining axe. With all of the power afforded by his knees bent in his crouching position, the razor-sharp blade of the axe bit into the Draugr's chin and sliced its head in half as it travelled all the way up and out the top of the creature's skull.

All that was left in the iced hallway now was the sound of the second Draugr, who had been almost fatally injured, but was on the ground attempting to bite out at Jarl's feet. Jarl's axe was still embedded into its side, so he slammed his other axe through its head, hitting the ground on the other side with a loud metallic thud, and then wrenched the lost axe free.

Jarl's shoulders rose and fell as he breathed heavily. The smell of the rotting corpses filled his nostrils, and unlike in the other rings of Helheim, these fallen foes did not evaporate into nothingness but remained slumped in position, festering just as they had done when they had been animated.

"Is that all you have to send?!" Jarl shouted, and his voice echoed away into the system of tunnels that evidently laid before him. He grimaced at the thought that perhaps he had been a little too hasty and that his shout could have called more Draugr to his position, but he also believed that he would have to eventually fight them all anyway.

Jarl took a moment to extinguish his axes and wipe the blood from them onto his clothes. He noticed that it was a deep red with some parts almost black and he wondered if this fluid was cursed, although again he could do nothing about that right now.

Deep in his heart, Jarl could again feel the presence of Sigrid. Something inside him was telling him that she was in this place, and if she was then he was going to find her. If she had been given the same choice as Jarl had, he knew that she would have responded in the same way, and that meant that she could be in grave danger. The quicker he moved and the sooner he found her, the safer they would both be.

With the thought of his wife in danger firmly etched into the front of his mind, Jarl took a deep breath and started to run. He relit his axes and carried them as he ran so that he could see where the tunnel led him and ensured that he did not run into anything that he would rather not.

The tunnel that had been wide and tall enough for Jarl and the first three Draugr now widened to accommodate at least a large group, but Jarl did not stop moving. That was of course, until he ran into a group of Draugr who seemed to be ambling about without any real purpose.

Jarl did not stop. He had the advantage afforded by surprise and knew that it was not best to waste such a thing. The closest Draugr had its back to Jarl, so he took the opportunity in both hands literally. Both of Jarl's hand axes were buried into the back of the Draugr, making it fold to the ground, and straight away the sound of breaking bones and the smell of burning rotten flesh alerted the rest of their attention to Jarl.

Eight pairs of bright, milky white eyes turned as one to meet Jarl's murderous, determined gaze. All thoughts of his own safety had left the fearsome warrior now, and all that was left that stood to face these supernatural beings was a base, primal creature.

Jarl took no time to set himself or to assess his situation in any great detail; he was now relying on his years of training and his body's desire to both kill and survive so that he could be reunited with Sigrid. The first three Draugr fell easily, having attacked one at a time which gave Jarl the time to drop them all to the ground in man-sized piles of flesh, blood and bone. The remaining five, though, stood together and seemed to await Jarl's own action before they made any of their own.

"Come then! Come and take what you want from me!" Jarl cried through gritted teeth.

The Draugr gave no sign that they had heard Jarl's shout, and neither did they move an inch closer to him.

Jarl panted, his shoulders rising and falling, his knuckles white around the handles of his axes, and he tried to will his body to just pick a route to attack. His face, weapons and hands were slick with blood and the smell of death was almost overpowering. He was about to simply pick his next target at random, when another leapt over the top of the still Draugr in a blur as the rest watched on.

This Draugr was not like the others. Its flesh was as rotten and decaying as the rest, but this one seemed to be wearing a kind of mixture of wooden and leather body armour. Its weapon, too, was definitely of a higher quality, not shimmering like Jarl's own but certainly less rusty and far sharper than those the rest of the Draugr carried.

Jarl just about managed to raise his axes above his head and cross them defensively, but the force of the incoming blow made his knees buckle and he fell backwards. He tried to will the flame in his axes to burn as brightly as it had ever done before, but it seemed that they were giving him everything they had left.

The new Draugr stepped forward to bear down over Jarl, not in an aggressive stance, but rather more one of victory. Jarl could now see that the skin on this one's face was indeed torn and damaged, although it was in far better shape than any he had seen as of yet.

"You see now how I am different to these others, no?" The Draugr hissed. "It is because I became what I am through choice. You see, there are two ways to become a Draugr."

Jarl had no intention of lying on his back and listening as it spoke, so he kicked out at its shin, hoping to sweep it to the ground. But it was as though he had tried to kick a solid stone wall.

"I am no festering mound of decay," the Draugr said. "If you become a Draugr by choice, the powers that you receive are almost unimaginable. If you are turned by the masses, then you become no better than they."

Jarl scrambled back and away from the Draugr and back to his feet. He knew he needed to keep away from this creature until he knew how to fight it properly, but he had no idea what to do. The thing seemed just too strong and too powerful.

Silently bringing his axes back up to the ready, Jarl regained his fighting stance, though it seemed as though the Draugr had no intention of stopping him.

The Draugr then, in the blink of an eye, appeared within an inch of Jarl's face, and its fist impacted his chest. Jarl flew back again and hit the ground with a loud thud. He was winded and his mind struggled to grasp what he was supposed to do to beat this foe.

Again Jarl raised himself back to his feet. This time though, he was much slower, and the action was accompanied by pain through his chest and back. He did not raise his axes back to the ready this time, leaving them in his hands still but hanging down by his sides.

"What... what does it mean to yield to you?" he asked slowly, defeated.

The Draugr dropped his axe to the side nonchalantly, stepped forward slowly as though it was making a show of it for the rest, who still watched on with their empty milky eyes, and came to a halt before Jarl.

"You will kneel before me and I will take your soul for my own," the Draugr rasped.

Jarl felt the weight of the being's words bearing down upon him. He could feel the desire - no - the need to drop to his knees and accept his fate. He had no other options now, so he fell down to one knee and placed his axes on the ground on either side of him, extinguishing them into darkness. Thankfully the dim light around them was still bright enough for Jarl to be able to see.

The Draugr stood and watched Jarl. It was clear that it was enjoying simply watching him yield and would do nothing to speed up this process. It wanted to savour the moment, and that would be fine with Jarl because as every second passed, he was willing every ounce of strength within his body to flow into his muscles. He was still not ready to die.

Jarl's thoughts turned again to Sigrid, who he knew still wandered this place. He knew that she was still safe in his heart, but these beings were so, so powerful that he knew she would not last long alone. He needed to reach her, to help her, and to continue on as Sylfia had done over and over, no matter the obstacles before them.

The Draugr then placed a hand on Jarl's chin to force him to look up at the terrible rotting face that it had assumed would be the last thing that Jarl would ever see in his mortal form.

"Do you not see? No mortal man can best the Draugr," it said almost in a whisper.

Tasting the putrification on the air, Jarl channelled every last shred of energy he had into his arms, forearms and hands, and tightened his grip around his axes until his knuckles burned from the action. He was practically shaking although he did nothing to betray his intent to this enemy.

The Draugr then reached back over its own shoulder as though it was about to unsheathe an unseen weapon. The large battle axe still held loosely to the side, and Jarl took his opportunity to strike.

Jarl pushed down through his heels down into the ground and raised his axes up, igniting them the second they were within the upward motion that hurtled towards their intended target. The speed of the action, the surprise of the light and the heat caught the Draugr off guard, as before it could make any move to defend itself, the axe in Jarl's right hand had cut clean through its face, and when the swing had reached its crescendo, he brought his left axe down onto the creature's neck.

The sound that the impact made was sickening, though at the same time it forced Jarl's defeated grimace into a smile. He knew that this time, no matter if his actions had been underhanded and perhaps not strictly honourable, he had managed to defeat his foe, or at least he could do so now with relative ease.

At the ferocity of the attack, the Draugr fell to one knee. Jarl could simply not believe that this being, now bloodied and broken, could still remain upright before him but he knew he must not give his enemy even the slightest chance of retaliation. He pulled an axe back and chopped it down into the Draugr's neck over and over until its head finally fell to the ground, detached from its body.

Only a moment later, when the Draugr's body had made a dull thud on the ground, the remaining five spectators all lurched forwards as one.

38

The sensation that Sylfia felt as soon as she dived into the waterfall that flowed upwards was nothing like she had ever felt before. As soon as she hit the water, it felt as though it was pushing her upwards, back into the seventh ring and back into Garmr's domain, and it was cold to the touch, which she actually found to be a little refreshing. She was determined though, that she would not allow the Jötnar to have fallen in vain; she would not allow herself to be turned back to face her fate when Hrit and Hern would now be without their father. With all that in mind, Sylfia held her breath, forced herself beneath the flowing water and swam.

She swam as fast as she could against the rising current, knowing that this was the way that she needed to go to reach that next place on her path. As she struggled, it occurred to her that with each new step on her path, everything always seemed to become so much more difficult. There were new and stronger challenges, death and loss... and she did not know how much more of it she could take. Her body ached and her mind fared no better. She knew that it would only be a matter of time before something fractured entirely.

A minute had passed and Sylfia could see no end to the waterfall. She did not know if it would end soon, but she knew she would not be able to hold her breath for much longer.

The water around her seemed to sense the beginnings of her panic and it began to flow faster and louder, the sound of water rotating, churning, blocking out all other sounds in the world. It was deafening and the movement now also took away Sylfia's ability to see which way that she was supposed to be going.

Sylfia struggled, kicking her legs and flapping her arms, trying to divine which way was up. She knew that with the new effort that she was exerting and the panic coursing through her body she had but moments before she would be unable to hold her breath any longer.

Then abruptly, the water turned to a serene calm. The difference was night and day and Sylfia burst free from the water and inhaled loudly, filling her lungs with no regard for anyone or anything that may have been there to greet her. The water flowed away from her as though it did not want to stick to her body and she stood upright to find that she was now standing in still, calm water that reached only up to her waist.

The atmosphere around her was cold, much colder than the water had been and it made her want to plunge herself back in rather than have to wait until she was dry to warm up. It reminded her of her father, and how he would have been able to provide her with a warming blaze if he was here.

Lowering herself back into the water so that it reached up to her neck, Sylfia took a moment to appraise her new surroundings. She could tell that she was inside a cavern that appeared to have an innate glow rather than a single source of light. Behind her she could see where she had emerged from, though rather than being a waterfall that went up a cliff face, the water that she had come from flowed down and away from her, as though during her journey she had been turned upside down. Within the water there were rock formations at the edges that could provide cover if it was required, though there seemed to be nothing living lurking within the depths.

The walls were of stone and rock and in many places there was a dark green moss covering portions of them, as though this was an underground cave. The water that she was standing in was a part of a river that spanned away from her and through another rock archway, off into the distance.

Sylfia realised that she had two options before her: she could emerge from the water and pick a tunnel in this cave system to walk down, or remain in the water and swim away, under the stone archway and into whatever this place was proper.

The choice was about to be taken away from her though, as she heard a noise coming from the tunnel system before her on the dry land. In fact it was more than simply a noise and as it approached, she recognised it for what it was: the sound of something metallic being dragged along the ground.

Sylfia dropped herself down deeper into the water to hide herself from whatever was approaching and moved to lurk behind one of the rock formations at the edge of her lake. She listened as the thing drew nearer and hoped beyond hope that whatever it was had not seen her, or would not approach the water only to discover her hiding place. She held her breath so as to not make any sound and slowly lowered her arms under the water, searching for the swords that were attached to her waist.

The scraping sound drew closer, then stopped for a moment and Sylfia could feel her heart beating in her chest. Abruptly the noise began again and it was clear to her that whatever this was, it was now moving away. When she was sure that the sound was far enough away that it would be safe to have a look to see what she was potentially dealing with, she saw the back of a Draugr walking away. She knew that it was a Draugr because it was the size of a man, although half of its body was covered in tattered old rags and the other half seemed to be a skeleton with no skin attached at all. It was dragging a rusty old spear along the ground in its skeletal hand and Sylfia could not decide if it was unable to hold the weapon up - not having any muscles – or if it simply could not be bothered to carry it properly.

Sylfia was almost certain that she was safe to allow herself a breath now that the Draugr was far away from her so she let out the breath that she had been holding and relaxed. As soon as she did, though, she realised her mistake. The Draugr stopped walking and turned its head ever so slightly in her direction.

Knowing she had only a moment to act, she slipped silently under the water. From beneath the surface it was difficult to see what was happening above and she only hoped that it was the same for the Draugr if it was to investigate the water more closely. She desperately hoped that when slipping under the water, she hadn't disturbed the surface notably.

Watching the world above her as best she could as she again held her breath, Sylfia remained as still as she had ever done before. She could not see any movement or any indication that the Draugr was looking for her or even that it suspected that there was another individual nearby, but she knew that it was not something that she wished to risk.

Sylfia waited under the water for as long as she could before her lungs burnt and she had no other choice but to surface and take in a new breath. She grit her teeth, hoping and praying that the Draugr had simply left and slowly rose until her head was free from the water.

The terrible bright blue eyes and half-skeletal face that greeted her told her that her prayers had not been answered. The Draugr must have seen her and had waited for her mere inches from where she surfaced.

Grabbing her throat with a hand that had turned necrotic but not yet skeletal, the Draugr lifted her out of the water as though it had no trouble with her weight at all. Sylfia kicked out with her legs but could not reach the Draugr to attack.

Her arms still free, Sylfia reached her right hand down to one of her shining short swords and released it from her waist. She could feel the life being squeezed from her throat as the Draugr's grip tightened more and more with each second that passed.

Then as her vision turned blurry, Sylfia summoned every ounce of strength that still remained within her body and swung her blade at the Draugr's arm. It was easily and immediately severed at the elbow.

Sylfia felt the Draugr's grip loosen as the connection to its muscles was lost and she fell into the water with a loud splash, the hand finally releasing her. She heard the Draugr's loud, ear-piercing high-pitched scream before her head went under the water again.

She knew now that she only had the one choice left to her: she would have to swim away from the Draugr and the shore because she knew that its scream could not go unnoticed. The creature had been so strong too - if there were more of them, she would stand no chance in a fight.

Keeping her head underwater and holding onto her sword, Sylfia began to swim directly away from where the Draugr had stood and further away into the lake. The water was still not deep though it was getting deeper as she swam, and she kept close to the bottom so that she would have been difficult to track from the surface if indeed the Draugr were to attempt it.

Sylfia had swam for at least a minute when she felt the need to rise to the surface for air again but in the moment that she decided that it was time to rise, she felt something wrap around her left ankle. She tried to gently kick it off, then with more force but it would not budge. She tried to swim up to the surface but whatever was holding onto her was keeping her close to the bottom and now the depth of the water had increased so that she could not reach the top.

She looked back, panic beginning to set in, and she could now see what it was. A decaying hand had risen from this riverbed, the body that it was attached to evidently hidden by years of sediment and muck, but still it had somehow sensed her and now it was stopping her from taking her one lifesaving breath.

Instinctively, Sylfia swung her sword down to try to separate this arm from the being that owned it as she had done with the last Draugr that had grabbed her. The problem was though that swinging a sword underwater well enough to cut through bone, no matter how sharp the blade was, was a feat that Sylfia was unable to manage.

She could feel the life leaving her again, though this time from gradual drowning rather than strangulation by an incredibly strong foe, and she panicked now. This was worse because she had already tried to swing her sword and had failed and in her frantic state she could not think how to escape. Eventually she shut her eyes and stopped struggling, and she entered a quiet and serene state. She did not know if this was because she had willed it to happen, or if she was approaching her end and this was her own personal acceptance of her fate.

Sylfia shifted her free leg so that the bottom of her foot rested on the skeletal hand that held her down and away from the surface, found where the fingers ended and wrenched the hand from her ankle as though it was the easiest thing in the world.

Immediately she swam up the few feet to the surface and this time made the effort to be as quiet as she could when taking in her well awaited breath. The sensation was more satisfying than anything she had felt previously as she felt the cool air filling her lungs.

After gathering her thoughts, Sylfia took a moment to appreciate her new surroundings. She was within what looked like a wide-open lake that narrowed before her into a river that was gently flowing away. It was the only direction that she had available to her and because the mossy walls all around her were straight and high, she could not have left the water even if she had wanted to. Regardless of what lurked beneath the surface, Sylfia knew that she was going to have to remain in the water.

Taking the straight path across the lake and into the river-like exit, Sylfia continued to swim on the surface. It was where she would have usually remained but knowing that there could be an unknown number of sunken Draugr beneath her, ready to drag her down to a watery grave it made her feel anxious.

The water thankfully remained cool and manageable and as she reached the river, nothing else at the bottom had attempted to drag her down. The further she swam, the more confident she felt and the fact that the water was moving with a current meant that she was neither making any noise in an otherwise silent and calm body of water, nor did she have to put all of her effort into swimming, being slowly pulled along by the current.

In the beginning, the river was straddled by two high, black walls that spanned off high above her before curving to meet each other. Sylfia was in one great tunnel and had no option but to simply keep swimming. She had no idea where this water would take her, but she had the feeling that as the waterfall had begun – or ended – within the seventh ring of Helheim, there was a good chance that it would lead all the way to the centre of the eighth. If not, she was sure that she would eventually get her bearings and figure out which way she was supposed to go. After all, she reasoned, she had already been told that the Naglfar ship resided within the eighth ring, and if the boat was indeed built to remain on water, then following any water that she could find seemed to be a good idea.

As she swam quietly along the river, Sylfia let her mind wander back to a story that she had been told as a child by her father. She had not yet thought about it because it had no relevance to her situation, but now submerged in water and away from the mortal realm, it did seem as though there was some meaning to it.

The story as she remembered it, was that there were three major springs beneath the roots of Yggdrasil, from which all water in all the lands came. The first of these springs was called Uroarbrunnr. This great well spanned far and wide, providing water to distant lands. The second spring, Mimisbrunnr, lay beneath the root of Yggdrasil that provided water to the realm of the Jötnar. This spring was said to have been blessed by Odin himself, the water it provided containing much wisdom and thought.

The last of the three great springs was called Hvergelmir. This spring provided water to all of man within the mortal realm and was where all rivers, lakes and seas on earth found their beginnings. The one piece of information that Sylfia had forgotten until this very moment though, was the fact that this spring was said to lie deep within Helheim, at the base of one of the great roots of Yggdrasil.

Sylfia had also heard that the great watercourse that ran from Helheim into the mortal realm contained a great many snakes, although she had seen no evidence of this is this was where she swam. She hoped that at least this part of the story she remembered had been embellished, or perhaps she had simply remembered it incorrectly. She knew though that the water that she was currently in, whether or not it was the great spring, was not without its dangers.

As Sylfia swam and still keeping at the surface of the water, she became aware of echoes coming from above her, as though there were people moving about, or more likely she thought, the Draugr. She could not even begin to wonder what the creatures actually did on a day-to-day basis, but it did not matter; whatever they were doing up there she wanted no part of it.

The stone walls around her remained flat and sharp, although now she could see that there were ledges high above her which she assumed was where the things were walking. Ahead in the distance, she could also see a series of wooden and rope bridges spanning from one side to the other.

Again Sylfia was thankful that the river flowed with a current and that there were outcroppings of rock and stone placed around the banks; if the waters had been still and open there would have been no way that she could have remained hidden and her movements within the water would have been identified immediately.

Sylfia swam to the edge of the river though she knew it was a risk; as with any river the waters would run shallower, so the risk of capture by anything hiding beneath the surface would be increased. She knew though that if there were Draugr above her, she would be wise to utilise as much of the cover as she could. Besides, if another hand were to reach out and grab her, in shallower waters she would have much less of a risk of being pulled under the surface to her watery grave.

Moving gingerly along the edge of the river with one hand placed flat against the wall of the cavern, Sylfia was relieved that no rotten or skeletal hands emerged to attempt to grab her, though she remained vigilant and moved slowly. As she rounded a corner in the cavern, she could see more of the path that lay before her.

In the distance, she could now see a ship the size of which made her mouth hang agape; her vision was now in front of her and she had to convince herself that what lay ahead was actually real.

Even though it was so far away, the ship was so large that it almost seemed as though she could reach out and touch it. Even from this distance, she knew that it was the one she had seen before, with distant signs of activity as its crew moved back and forth upon it. She knew too that this Naglfar ship had been constructed of bones and finger or toenails, and that discarded body parts covered it as though they were in unlimited supply. Once again Sylfia had to stop herself from retching at the sight.

The back end of the ship looked as though it had been engulfed in a block of ice and snow as though the ages that it had remained in place had begun to swallow it up. The front of the ship though, was very much in the water.

To the side of the immense galleon, where the ice threatened to overtake it, Sylfia could see that the land was white with snow and atop it stood an entire army of the Draugr, ready and unmoving.

She was still too far away to make out any real details, but the army was clearly Draugr. Their weapons hung down by their sides and even at this distance their clothes looked as though they were falling from their bodies.

Sylfia had no idea what she was supposed to do next. She knew that her goal was to destroy the ship, but without her father's burning axes any small hope of setting it alight had now gone and between her and the ship now stood an army that she had no hope of defeating.

Then, as though her plight had been answered by the Gods, Sylfia watched in amazement as the Draugr readied their weapons, and from the white caverns beyond, a second army arrived to engage them.

This army though, with their impressive size and huge, terrible weapons, was unmistakably that of the Jötnar.

39

Jarl stared at the five Draugr as they moved towards him and truly he did not know what he was supposed to do. The Draugr that he had already fought had been so strong on its own, and the prospect of facing five together was frightening. He had never been one to feel afraid of a battle though.

The Draugr all held old and rusted looking swords that paled in comparison with Jarl's own shining silver axes. The blades did not look sharp and if anything, that could mean a more painful death for Jarl, if that was to be the result of this battle.

The flames of Jarl's axes lit up the tunnels around him as he held them to the ready, telling of the twists and turns that would await him if he could best these opponents.

The first of the Draugr reached him quickly and it was all that he could do not to be bowled over by the sheer strength of the attack. Instead he was pushed backwards and he leaned into the motion, regaining his balance a foot or so behind where he had begun. The Draugr then unleashed a fierce upwards swipe with his sword which Jarl only just managed to dodge, but while doing so he felt a burning, searing pain as his enemy lashed out with a clawed hand. The blackened fingernails of the Draugr cut into Jarl's shoulder leaving three bloody red lines on his skin. The smell of blood and the sense of a new weakness sent the rest of the enemies into a frenzy, clambering to attack.

If anything, the increased number of Draugr trying to reach him actually worked in his favour because as he stepped back again to keep out of the range of the Draugr that seemed hell-bent on taking his life, whether it be by sword or claw, his enemies were having to clamber over each other to try to reach him. One of the Draugr was actually pulling another back to get closer to its prey and Jarl saw an opportunity that he could not afford to miss.

"You want my blood?" he shouted loudly. "Then come and take it!"

The Draugr that had already landed a blow on Jarl lunged again. It attacked with its sword and as the reach the weapon afforded bridged the gap between them and the swing came towards him, Jarl dodged the blade and allowed it to clang loudly into the wall beside him. With the Draugr now off-balance he struck out with a front kick into its the chest and it fell backwards into the mass of its huddled comrades. Jarl was surprised that his kick had been so effective, although he had felt the strength of the Draugr and knew that if it had not been off-balance, he probably would not have been able to even move it.

The group of Draugr now seemed to be in even further disarray as they struggled with the problem of another one of their own getting in their way, and also having to deal with its momentum as it fell back into them. Jarl took his advantage and stepped forward.

The Draugr that had fallen into the group was still struggling when Jarl reached them and it seemed to him as though some of the other Draugr were holding its arms back as if they were offering it to him. He could not know if it was simply a matter of circumstance, or if they were truly so bloodthirsty that they would allow him to kill one of their kin, but he would not stop to ask the question. Jarl raised one of his burning axes and buried it into the skull of the Draugr who had injured him, retrieving it quickly before any of the others could grab him.

The Draugr crumpled to the ground and the others let it fall. It seemed to Jarl as if they had indeed been offering it up to him and he realised that these creatures, although incredibly strong, were somewhat lacking in intelligence.

The remaining four Draugr were still fighting for their rightful place before the others, and when one eventually managed to break through past its kin, Jarl quickly cut it back by swiping one of his axes just inches from its face. The Draugr managed to dodge the swipe, although the action caused it to fall back among its ranks.

Another of the Draugr stepped forwards and lunged for Jarl with its sword just as the first had. This time though, the Draugr dropped its sword and Jarl almost fell for the diversion, watching it as it clattered loudly to the ground. By the time his gaze had returned to his enemy, the Draugr had begun to move towards him with its blackened lips withdrawn and its teeth bared, snapping wildly at the air between them.

Luckily for Jarl, he had not been too consumed by the sight of the sword falling to the ground and he regained his senses just in time to step out of the way. The Draugr tripped and fell to the ground. Jarl had no option now but to shift to the offensive and before any of his enemies could compose themselves into a proper defensive stance, he threw himself into range.

The first Draugr fell a moment later after taking a flaming axe to the skull and a second took a ferocious backswing that also took its life immediately without response. That left Jarl standing before one lone Draugr, while the other was slowly raising itself back to its feet behind him. It was the worst place for him to be – between two enemies that individually were almost too much for him – it was an added complication that he now stood between them.

Making a decision on instinct rather than thought, Jarl did something that he knew could be very stupid if the move did not work out, but he did it before his mind could stop him nonetheless. He threw one of his axes at the Draugr who had almost risen to his feet. It would leave him with just one axe to face the other Draugr, but he knew that he could not afford to let them both enter range with him at the same time.

The axe hit the Draugr before it even knew what was happening and the crunching sound of the creature's skull being split in two by Jarl's expertly thrown, razor-sharp axe reverberated into the tunnels in both directions. Jarl now had just one opponent left to deal with.

The Draugr faced Jarl, its eyes blazing a burning bright blue, and on its face Jarl could see the thought process behind them. It was ferocious, ravenous and desperate to attack, but it had just watched this mortal kill four of its brothers and was therefore not an enemy to rush into battle with. The Draugr's head listed from side to side as it watched Jarl, wondering if he was going to make the first move.

Jarl's hand tightened around the handle of his one single hand axe, his huge arms tensing as he prepared for the fight of his life against an enemy that he knew was stronger than him.

The Draugr then let out a deep, guttural growl and without warning it charged forward, swinging its rusty sword about itself with deadly precision directly toward Jarl's face. Jarl ducked to avoid the first swipe and weaved side to side avoiding a second, then a third from the open hand of the creature. He narrowly avoided each of the blows but he could feel that with each strike the Draugr's blade was getting closer and closer to him.

Suddenly, instead of a fourth swing, the Draugr lunged forward with its sword outstretched, aiming for a killing blow. Jarl quickly managed to sidestep the attack and drove his burning axe into the Draugr's side. The axe bit into his enemy deeply, and Jarl heard the sound of flesh sizzling as the heat added to the strength of the blow. The Draugr howled in pain and stumbled backwards.

With the opportunity presented, Jarl charged forward, striking again and again with his one axe. The Draugr howled in rage, swinging its sword around wildly as it tried to fend off the relentless attacks, and on a few occasions the rusted sword met the shining axe in their arching paths, metal clashing against metal and ringing out through the tunnel system.

Jarl knew that he could not keep up this relentless attack for long and he could already feel that he was beginning to tire. His movements were slowing and his attacks had begun to lose their ferocity. The Draugr had noticed this as well.

With the tide of battle turning, the Draugr's sword began to rain down on Jarl as blow after blow pushed him swiftly back, the strength of the attacks simply too much for him to bear. Jarl grunted in pain as he deflected each blow with his one available axe, his hand, arm and shoulder aching under the immense force that he was having to contend with. He wished dimly for a shield, but he knew that wishful thinking would not save him now.

The only thing he could do was to launch an attack while he still had a little strength left in his body.

He stepped back repeatedly to allow himself a little breathing room from the wild swipes of the Draugr and its sword, as blocking was simply sapping all of his energy, and to his delight he realised that the battle had moved closer to the axe he had thrown. His second weapon would be a useful addition to this fight.

Sensing a possible route to victory, Jarl mustered one last burst of energy, dropped to one knee to duck under the attack that the Draugr launched and buried his axe as hard as he could into the Draugr's leg, just below the knee.

The soft, decaying flesh of the Draugr's leg did nothing to withstand the blow and neither did the dry, brittle bone beneath. The terrible creature's leg broke cleanly in two in the centre of the fireball that was Jarl's deadly axe.

The Draugr howled as its leg was removed from the rest of its body although Jarl could not tell if the sound was borne of pain or anger. He did not wait to find out and reaching down to the ground with his free hand, he swung his reclaimed axe in a deadly attack that impacted his enemy on the base of its chin, splitting its jaw in two in the blink of an eye.

Jarl pressed on as the Draugr remained off balance and he swung his second axe down from behind his head to split the rest of his enemy's head apart, the creature falling to the ground in a lifeless heap.

Panting heavily, Jarl stood over his fallen opponent, his hand axe still held tightly and he allowed the adrenaline of the battle to seep out of him and the realities of the world around to return to his attention. The tunnels before him spanned off in multiple directions and Jarl again felt the cold radiating from the ice all around him.

The world again had turned to silence and Jarl took a moment to try to divine which way he was supposed to go, but also to regain his energy and strength. He could feel that Sigrid was not so far away that she was beyond his grasp, so he did the only thing he could think to do: he placed his left hand against the cold wall and started walking. His plan was that if he simply held the left wall and took every left turn that he was presented with, then he would not unknowingly circle back on himself without discovering if there was another way out of this place, and especially before he found Sigrid.

Jarl walked as slowly and quietly as he could for a long time. He did not know if there were any dangers ahead, but he knew that he had already been lucky to have survived tense battles with the Draugr here. He was not sure if he would be lucky for a third time.

Holding his burning axes before him, Jarl looked for any indication that there was anyone else nearby, or if there was some clue that would lead him to Sigrid. The problem was that this place did not seem to change no matter how far he walked or in what direction; there were simply cold ice walls and a deep foreboding ahead. The smell of rotten matter that constantly assaulted his nostrils also constantly occupied his mind and kept him from thinking clearly on the problems he faced.

Eventually Jarl could hear a sound travelling along the tunnels before him. It was quiet at first but as he kept moving it became louder. It came in waves and as it became clearer the closer Jarl came to it, he knew what it was - steel upon steel, as though warriors were locked in battle.

The sound filled Jarl with dread because he knew that it could only mean one thing: there were more Draugr ahead, and more than he could possibly care to imagine.

Jarl moved as slowly as he could along the cold wall, flattening himself against it to remain as small and as unnoticeable as possible. He did not want another fight, especially as he knew how strong and ferocious these beasts could be. He was also worried that Sigrid could be out there alone and if her experience had been similar to his, with each passing moment her life she could be in increasing danger. These sounds of battle did nothing to settle his nerves.

Keeping his back to the wall as he rounded the last corner to where the sounds were coming from, Jarl remembered to extinguish his axes so as to not betray his presence with their bright light. The walls still radiated a dull glow that illuminated the tunnel slightly, and it was enough to see a few feet ahead but not much more than that. As he rounded the final corner though, he was astounded to see a huddle of Draugr with their backs to him, all attempting to break through a small gap in the ice that spanned upwards, which looked just wide enough for one person to fit through. Beyond the Draugr too, Jarl could hear the telltale grunts of a woman engaged in battle. Jarl had finally found Sigrid.

The clanging of blade upon blade and blade upon ice did not stop for one moment as Jarl watched, and he could now see that what was happening before him was similar to what he had already experienced. The Draugr were fighting each other to be the first to breach the gap in the wall and reach their prey beyond, but Sylfia had been using this to her advantage, and was systematically destroying them one by one. Jarl took a quiet step closer to the rear of the Draugr and could now see that they were clambering over a mound of broken bones and the body parts of their fallen kin. There must have been tens or even hundreds of the Draugr that had already been killed, and there was no sign that they had reached Sigrid through the gap.

Jarl felt a smile creep across his face. It was just like Sigrid to find a way to defend herself against such insurmountable odds, to use her intelligence to her advantage in battle where he had relied on pure technique and strength. It made him remember why exactly he had fallen in love with his wife in the first place; they were simply the perfect team.

Taking another cautious step forward, Jarl's blood ran cold as he felt a large hand press down on his shoulder and a second one cover his face entirely. Struggling to breathe but also not wishing to make a sound that would garner the attention of the Draugr before him, Jarl thrashed his arms about himself silently, but there was nothing he could do to reach whatever had a hold of him. He could feel the life fading from him as his lungs burnt with their lack of oxygen and eventually there was nothing he could do other than to accept the fact that this was to be his end. Whatever had found him and had managed to sneak up on him had won, and there was nothing that he could do about it.

But then the hand over his face fell away and Jarl was turned by the shoulder to stand face to face with a huge, muscular Jötnar. The warrior was three times Jarl's size and it was no wonder that its hand covered his entire face. It was clear though that this Jötnar was certainly no Draugr, and it wished Jarl no harm.

The Jötnar raised a hand up to its own mouth and extended a single finger, telling Jarl to remain silent. Jarl dutifully obliged and allowed his gaze to fall to the huge, curved blade hanging down by its side.

Jarl had no idea how the giant creature had managed to sneak up on him so effectively, but he could not focus on that right now. The Jötnar was gesturing to the Draugr and silently unsheathing his huge weapon, evidently ready for a fight, and with two fingers it indicated that they should each approach the Draugr from behind, Jarl from the left and the Jötnar from the right.

Nodding once, Jarl moved into position slowly and quietly and watched as the Jötnar followed suit. Again he wondered how the giant was able to move so quietly, but as the sound of the frantic Draugr attempting to reach Sigrid was so loud, perhaps it had concealed their approach.

The Jötnar and Jarl had reached so close to the rear of the Draugr that Jarl could smell the stench of the closest rotten foe at the back of the group. The Draugr's attention and gaze was so focussed on the gap in the wall ahead that not a single one even turned around when Jarl removed the closest Draugr's head from its shoulders. Then the Jötnar struck and five heads fell to the ground at once, making a slightly louder thud.

Jarl held his breath as there was no way that the sound could have gone unnoticed, but to his delight, not a single head turned back to see what was happening behind them. This was then the perfect opportunity for Jarl and the Jötnar to destroy all of the Draugr that still remained and after a few minutes there was nothing left before the gap but a pile of broken bones, rotten flesh and decapitated heads. A moment of quiet passed before Sigrid walked through the gap in the ice, both of her shoulders brushing the walls as she moved.

"I would have killed them all given a little more time," Sigrid protested, wiping blood and a black stain from her sword. Then she looked Jarl in the eye and smiled.

Jarl took his wife in his arms as tightly as he had ever done and held her for as long as he could before letting her go and holding her at an arm's length to look at her.

"Are you hurt, wife? I knew that you were here!" Jarl exclaimed.

"No I am not hurt, I managed to find this place quite quickly and have been hiding here for a while. The tunnel does not lead anywhere but it funnels those creatures in one by one and it makes them very easy to kill."

"Were you offered the chance to become of the Draugr?" Jarl asked, recalling what had happened to him; he had always known that if Sigrid had been given the choice, she would have made the same decision that he had.

"I was given a choice, but I ran from the Draugr at first. It was only when I found this place that I began to fight back." She looked down at her arm that was smeared with dirt and blood. "I do not know what this means, but I see you have it too."

On Sigrid's forearm sat a dark, round mark with tendrils of black spanning off towards her wrist and elbow. Jarl looked down at his own arm and held the identical mark he had next to Sigrid's.

"It can be nothing good," the Jötnar rumbled and his words reminded Jarl that he was still present. Sigrid jumped but when she saw that the Jötnar was holding out his own arm with another identical dark mark upon it, she recognised that he was not of the enemy.

"This Jötnar I have just met. We killed all the Draugr trying to reach you but that is all," Jarl said.

"Then I must thank you," Sigrid replied, facing the Jötnar, though her words seemed to mean nothing to him and he turned away and began to walk back along the tunnel leading up to where the Draugr had been.

Jarl and Sigrid shared a quick look before walking behind it. It was difficult for them to keep up with the giant though, as each step it took was worth at least three of their own.

"Where did you come from?" Jarl called up as they walked.

"Are there more of you?" Sigrid added.

"Do you know of a way out of this place?" Jarl called.

The Jötnar stopped in his tracks and looked down at both Jarl and Sigrid. "You must be quiet," he said. "There are Draugr everywhere and we do not want to alert them. Yes, there are more and we came from the plains of Garmr, all together. We will talk when we reach the others."

Sigrid smiled to herself. The fact that there were more of these giants was going to make survival a lot more possible, as long as they did not simply kill the humans when they arrived. Her instinct though was that this one had helped to save her and that meant something.

"You come from the forest?" Jarl said, not able to hold his question back as the group started walking again.

"Yes. Later," the Jötnar replied shortly. Jarl had so many questions to ask, but he could wait a little longer. Instead he simply enjoyed the fact that he had Sigrid back by his side, and that the Draugr had not managed to kill either of them. Not yet at least anyway.

Eventually, after passing a few more Jötnar along the way and joining up with a small group, they reached a wide-open clearing in the tunnels where hundreds of Jötnar seemed to be awaiting them. Some were sitting on the ground, some were talking in hushed voices and some were even hugging, but not a single one of them gave the two mortals a second glance.

Then a Jötnar, who was even bigger than most of the others approached and Jarl had to make a concerted effort not to reach for his axes. He glanced quickly about the cavern at all of the Jötnar to see if there were any that he recognised, but unfortunately there were just so many that it was an impossible task.

"Are you the ones who came to stop Ragnarök?" the Jötnar asked in a deep, booming voice. It was all that Sigrid could do to nod her head in response.

"Then we must talk," the Jötnar said. "My name is Mego and I have arrived in this place along with my warriors from the forests that house Garmr and his pack. My people decided to help your daughter on her quest, but I am sorry to say that the forest was burned to ash and tinder before we could escort her to safety. I do not know what has become of her."

"The forest was burned?" Jarl asked. He had not yet been able to bring Sigrid up to date on what had happened since she had fallen in the fighting pits, so he hoped that she catch up by listening to his conversation with the Jötnar.

Mego nodded solemnly. "I too know the pain of losing a loved one."

"But that makes no sense," Jarl said. "How did the forest burn? And were the wolves all killed?"

"Some of the wolves fell, but the fires would have surely taken everything away from that place. From the fragments of information that we can put together, we do not believe that anything could have survived. This is why there are so many Jötnar here now, and this is the reason that we have been able to keep the Draugr at bay for now."

The large Jötnar went on to explain that the Jötnar had all arrived at the Draugr's domain in a short space of time and had managed to group up and use their strength to overpower the bloodthirsty creatures. It stood to reason that this place was not designed to accommodate the arrival of so many skilled warriors at once, but the circumstance had served everyone well.

Scouts had been sent along the tunnels so the Jötnar had a very good idea of the layout of the iced labyrinth. Their homes being underground must have played a part in their ability to map a place this large so quickly. The main point of interest, Mego told Jarl and Sigrid, was a huge old ship at one end of the tunnel system that seemed to house an army of Draugr on board.

"The army sits idle as though it awaits its true purpose. Our scouts were not found," the Jötnar explained. "I do not know how many Draugr are within the cavern, but I believe that it may be too many for us to face and survive out in the open. It is the belief of the Jötnar that this is a place of significance."

"Yes!" Jarl exclaimed. "This is the Naglfar ship, the ship that will be launched at the beginning of Ragnarök! We *must* destroy it as quickly as we can!"

Mego held up a massive hand to stop Jarl. "As I have said, there are many Draugr there and I think that it may be too many for us to face alone."

"It does not matter how many enemy stand before us." Jarl said. "We must continue in our struggle to keep Ragnarök from passing, do you not see? We have all come so far and with this very task in mind!"

Jarl's voice rose as he spoke and Sigrid placed a single hand on his shoulder to calm him and he abruptly shut his mouth.

"I fear that time may be running out for us all," Sigrid said, turning her arm over to show the Jötnar the mark that seemed to have grown since the last time she had looked. Mego looked down at Sigrid and slowly turned his own giant arm over to reveal an identical mark.

"Each of the Jötnar in this place has this mark upon their skin and it grows with every passing minute. Do you know what it means?" Mego asked.

"In truth, we cannot be sure," Sigrid replied carefully. "But I believe that as it grows it is the curse of this place taking over our physical bodies and when it has done so it will begin its work on our minds. I believe that the moment we came to this place, our lives were already over. All our lives," she stared pointedly at Mego.

The Jötnar looked down at the mark and closed his eyes tightly. It seemed as though he was trying to decide if Sigrid was being truthful, and if so, what they could do about any of this.

"It appears we have but one path left before us to take," Mego grumbled. "There are a few Jötnar to return from their patrols. When they return we will begin the last war that the Jötnar will fight, and we will do so alongside two human warriors."

It took a little while, but eventually the army of Jötnar was mustered and the cavern that had been filled with meandering souls with little purpose was now a place where ranks upon ranks of fierce, ready warriors stood ready to face their final battle. Sigrid and Jarl joined the first line at the front of the cavern, and as one the mass of warriors lurched forwards.

Through winding tunnels with ice covered walls, the army marched and did not encounter a single Draugr on their journey. Eventually, they came to a halt and Jarl could see that before them, blocking the exit to the place where the Naglfar ship lay beyond, stood Glam. The king of the Draugr held a huge mace in one hand that was covered with two-inch deadly looking spikes and in the other he held a long straight sword to the ready.

"You are all my children," Glam said loudly with a wide grin on his face, "and you will do as I say!"

Jarl remained still, not wanting to step forward to challenge the fabled warrior, but he did not need to do so because three huge Jötnar warriors stepped up to remove this Draugr from their path.

The three Jötnar warriors looked so powerful that Jarl wondered if Glam was going to be able to withstand even one blow from any of them, but the Draugr looked as though he had not even a single care; he held his mace before him to the ready and the first Jötnar struck.

The Jötnar attacked with a battle axe that was larger than Jarl himself and as the first attack swung towards the mighty Glam, the Draugr simply shifted slightly to place his mace between him and the deadly looking axe.

Jarl waited for the loud clang of weapon biting into weapon but to his shock, as soon as the axe met the iron shaft of the mace, the steel exploded into thousands of tiny pieces and the Jötnar was left holding nothing but a short stump where his axe used to be.

Glam smiled.

He swung his mace about in one hand and it hit the Jötnar with sickening force that filled the tunnel with its impact. A moment later the Jötnar smashed into the ice wall, imbedded in it so far that just his hands and feet protruded. The huge giant was well and truly dispatched.

Glam then stepped forward and began to systematically destroy the ranks of Jötnar before him as he swung his terrible mace over and over. Not a single one of the giants could stand against the attacks, being launched into the walls or ceiling, or otherwise crushed to pulp into the ground.

With Glam's attention focused solely on the Jötnar, who certainly posed the greater threat, Jarl and Sigrid had no choice but to stand and watch as their army had no chance of progressing whilst Glam stood before them.

But Jarl could no longer stand by and watch as Glam began to laugh, a sound that made his blood boil. He ignited his axes and leapt forward to stand before the Draugr. Glam, still laughing, turned his attention to the man wielding shining burning axes.

"You have already lost, so yield before your king," Glam growled, though he still smiled as though he was enjoying all the death and destruction.

Jarl did not respond. Instead he swung his axe at his enemy but as it impacted against the heavy black mace, it did not break apart as the Jötnar's weapons had; the two weapons clanged and remained together as Jarl put all of his effort into besting Glam in a test of strength.

The act, though, was futile. Glam tensed his muscles and whipped the mace about, sending Jarl flying back into the huddle of Jötnar, and thankfully their density and strength meant that he was caught without injury.

While Jarl had flown through the air though, he had initially heard Glam laughing at his victory but before being caught by the ever-helpful Jötnar, the tunnel ahead fell deathly silent.

Jarl quickly regained his footing and ran back to the front of the army, igniting his axes as he moved, ready to fight again, but he skidded to a stop, being faced with a very unexpected sight.

Glam was looking down at his chest in shock and silence, where the tip of a straight silver sword protruded, coated in his own deep, red blood. He opened his mouth to try to speak, but no sound would come.

Over Glam's shoulder, Sigrid appeared and said loudly for all to hear: "It has been said that we cannot kill what is already dead, let us put that to the test shall we?" and she drew her blade back to allow Glam to fall in a lifeless heap to the ground at her feet. She waited for a moment before announcing to the rest of the army before her: "sometimes it is not the strongest or the bravest who win the fight. Sometimes speed and a delicate touch is all that is required to fell the mightiest of opponents.

40

Sylfia knew that whatever was happening, it was to her advantage. The Jötnar that she could see engaging with the Draugr did not look as though they were decaying or had become a part of this place – they looked as though they were intent on fighting the dreadful Draugr with every last breath they had.

Their attack was not quiet either. The deafening sounds of battle reached Sylfia with the clang of steel on steel ringing out from their weapons and echoing off in all directions, atop the waters and through every tunnel it met. Sylfia knew that she either needed to join in this fight or use its distraction to gain access to the Naglfar ship, but she still had no idea how she was going to destroy such a colossal construction. Her only hope was that there would be something on board that she could use to achieve that feat.

Dipping her head under the water and beginning her approach to the Naglfar ship, Sylfia swam slowly and quietly in case there were any lookouts watching, but if there were, none made their presence known. Moments later, Sylfia made it to the ship and peered up from the waters at it.

Now within full view, the monstrosity that was the Naglfar ship presented itself in its full horrific glory. A long, wide ship with years of decay sat firmly stuck half within the ice and half breaching the water as though it was already half-launched. Sylfia could now make out the individual fingernails and teeth that constituted the hull, and the multitude of sails above that could only have been made from rotting rags and decaying skin. On the deck of the ship, she could now see Draugr of all shapes and sizes streaming back and forth to retrieve weapons or armour, then running quickly to join the back of the battle that had begun below, between Jötnar and Draugr.

Where the boarding ramps were too narrow to cater for all of the Draugr at once, some were even leaping from the ship onto the ice, breaking every bone in their festering bodies only to rise again, shift their broken bodies back into position, and join the fight.

Sylfia knew that she could not simply stand by and let these Jötnar fight in a battle against these Draugr whilst she snuck in behind them to attempt to destroy the ship. She did not know if they had come to help her or not, but she already knew that she would do anything within her power to keep as many of them alive as she could.

Sylfia quickly swam to the shore at the back of the ship and waded out of the water onto the white ground. It took a moment for her to find her feet on solid ground again, but within a moment she was holding her twin short swords in her hands and sprinting towards the battle at the point where the Draugr had met the Jötnar. Sylfia ignored the few that were trying to recover from their fall from the ship to the ground, as she needed to reach the battle as quickly as she could.

Her wet clothing was a slight annoyance as she moved, but it would not cause her too much difficulty in the battle to come.

Within a moment, Sylfia was within reach of the Draugr's front line, and regardless of the fact that she was at least one-third the size of the giant Jötnar warriors, she leapt high up into the air and inserted her blades into the closest enemy. The Draugr crumpled to the ground at the end of Sylfia's ferocious attack, and before any of the others could turn to look at her, she had decapitated a second with a clean sweep of her sword.

The Draugr barely made a sound as they fell; it was simply as though their souls had been removed from their reanimated corpses and as Sylfia moved on to the next enemy combatant, she was relieved to note that the fallen Draugr were not rising back to their feet as the ones who had fallen from the ship had.

The Jötnar fought as they had done against the humans, with great sweeping strikes that threw swathes of the creatures back, sometimes even as far as the water. Some were being crushed to ash where they stood, and others were being cut in half by the Jötnar who carried terrible bladed weapons. If the battle had been fought against opposing armies of similar sizes, the size of the Jötnar and their power would have certainly been enough to sway the outcome in their favour.

The problem was though, that there were just so many Draugr. No matter how many were decimated by the Jötnar, they simply kept coming. They moved before the Jötnar like an ocean with an ebb and flow, and eventually when one or two made it to within touching distance of the mighty Jötnar, the Draugr managed to overpower the giants and bring them down to the ground, plunging their own rusted weapons, hands, feet or teeth into the defenceless Jötnar.

The stench of death and decay had already filled Sylfia's nostrils, but it was not until this moment that she realised the actual scale of the death that was happening all around her. It was as though the world went instantly silent as she looked out across the battlefield, and everything seemed to move in slow motion. The Jötnar were dying. The Draugr were falling too, but it was not going to be enough and Sylfia knew in that moment that this battle would end in the death of every single Jötnar here.

And then Sylfia saw something across the battlefield within the front lines. It was like a shining beacon of hope sent by the Gods to remind her of who she was and what she was supposed to be doing: there was a human warrior holding two burning axes high above his head. Her father had finally returned to her.

The sight of Jarl instantly washed away all the hopelessness and pain she had suffered over the last few hours. She had missed him dearly and had wept more than she had taken the time to realise. But that was done now. Jarl was back and her heart filled with a warmth that she did not know had been missing.

There were hundreds of both Draugr and Jötnar engaged in fierce battles between her and Jarl, but she knew that she needed to reach him; it would be his ability to conjure flame from nothing that she had planned on being the downfall of the Naglfar ship, and seeing the ship up close, she already knew that without him, destroying it was going to be almost impossible. It would be impossible too, though, if the Jötnar failed in their battle with the Draugr.

Just as Sylfia was trying to figure out a way to get to Jarl that did not involve skirting the entire battlefield and coming up to him from behind, a Draugr that was essentially a skeleton launched itself at her. Had she been paying attention, she may have been able to stop it as it approached, but in her distracted state there was nothing that she could do to stop her new opponent before it sank its rotten teeth into her shoulder.

The Draugr's teeth cut through her cloth top as though it was not even there, and Sylfia let out an ear-piercing scream as she struggled to get it off of her. Her scream had the opposite effect. It seemed as though the attention of all the Draugr around her turned to her at once. All of their heads turned to her, their milky-white dead eyes boring into her soul as she struggled to free herself from the jaws of her enemy.

Sylfia knew that she had made a mistake. She had shown weakness to an enemy that would forgive no weakness, and it was all that she could do to place a boot into the rib cage of the Draugr who still bit into her shoulder to try to wrench herself free. Then she felt her flesh tear and a small chunk of it pull away from her shoulder within the disgusting maw of the Draugr. She was free, it she was injured.

Sylfia raised her swords up before a handful of the now interested Draugr reached her. Her only saving grace was the fact that as they had all come at her at once so, none of them could effectively swing their weapons, electing instead to attempt to bite her as the first had done. Perhaps it was because they all saw how effective the first Draugr's attack had been.

Tightly packed as her enemy was, and defending herself with her swords as best she could, Sylfia was relieved to note that not a single one of the terrible angry faces were able to reach her, and what had looked like an immediate and painful death had quickly turned into a situation where the number of Draugr attacking her had become their downfall.

Regardless of the fact that Sylfia was still relatively unhurt, she could do nothing in retaliation and things were about to get far worse when she realised that she was being pushed back by the sheer weight of the Draugr trying to reach her.

Then abruptly, their unholy strength came into play and Sylfia tripped and fell to her back, winding her as she hit the ground.

The Draugr were on her within a second, still trying to reach her with their terrible teeth. There were so many on top of her that the light from the cavern was blotted out, and it was all she could do to grit her teeth and close her eyes; she knew that she did not have the strength to hold off these enemies for much longer.

Then Sylfia felt the warmth inside her chest again. No, not a warmth. This time it was an explosion of white-hot heat and she had no idea if the Draugr had reached her and this pain was borne of their attacks, or if the feeling was coming from within. The pain grew and grew until she could bear it no longer, and she could feel the scream rising in her throat and coming out of her mouth. She screamed louder than she had ever screamed before, and as the pain reached its crescendo, her eyes snapped open.

Sylfia's eyes had turned a deep orange, and as she looked past the Draugr still attempting to sink their teeth into her face, she watched as the front line of the Jötnar that she could see from her position, held their weapons out before them and as one they exploded into a thick line of fire.

The Jötnar's weapons had burst into flames, just like her father's did when he activated his divine power, and the sheer heat and surprise of the action made the sea of Draugr fall back as one as it they had been blown over by a huge explosion. The Jötnar pressed forward in response, now with their weapons ablaze.

Sylfia immediately felt the heat from the weapons around her remove the last of the Draugr that had managed to cling on through the explosion and in a moment she was free. The Jötnar who had taken the life from the Draugr had been careful not to hurt her during their attack, something that she was very thankful for.

As the Jötnar pressed forward and bore down on the Draugr, who had still had not managed to return to their feet, Sylfia stood up and brushed herself down, checking for any more injuries. Her shoulder burnt with a white-hot pain where she had already been bitten, but she knew that it could have been far, far worse.

Then before she could snap her attention back to her father, Jarl clattered into her, wrapping his arms tightly around her and almost knocking her over.

"Sylfia! I knew that you would make it to this place! We have almost made it through, have we not? And do you see the Jötnar?" Jarl barely knew where to start. He had missed Sylfia dearly, but not for a moment did he think that she would have fallen on the plains of Garmr.

"Yes, father..." Sylfia began to say, but she stopped in mid-sentence and her eyes filled with tears of joy as Sigrid approached casually from behind Jarl. She held her own single sword held down by her side, dripping with a combination of red and black blood.

Sigrid stopped to stand next to Jarl, placing her free hand around his waist. "You cannot kill what is already dead, Sylfia, did you not know?" she asked with a smile on her face, and Sylfia could not help but burst into a combination of tears and laughter. Sylfia's very soul had warmed at the sight of her two parents standing before her. It was as though the sun had illuminated her world again, and everything that had wronged her had been erased.

"We are so close..." Sylfia managed to say, "but we must destroy the ship..."

Jarl placed his hands on Sylfia's shoulders and turned her so that she was facing the Naglfar ship. It took her a second to figure out what he was trying to show her, but then she realised. The Draugr were retreating from the Jötnar. They still had the advantage of strength and numbers, but the addition of their white-hot flaming weapons all ablaze at once, combined with the Draugr's momentary misstep, had given the Jötnar the ability to seize their advantage.

"But where... and how..." Sylfia tried to ask as she watched the Jötnar cut through swathes of unorganised and routing Draugr.

Jarl smiled at Sylfia, clearly delighted that they had managed to regroup as a family. "When I arrived here I was alone, but then the Jötnar began to arrive from the plains of Garmr. When they were killed in battle, they could not reach Valhalla so they were sent here, and all at once!"

"So why did they not simply become more Draugr?" Sylfia asked.

Jarl let out a small chuckle. "Because, Sylfia, this place had been designed with the premise that when people arrive here, they do so alone or in smaller numbers. The Draugr would then be able to convince them to join their ranks as though it was their own choice. But then if the fallen decided not to join, the Draugr would simply outnumber them and kill them, which would add them to their ranks anyway."

Sylfia did not know how her father knew any of this, but he seemed to be very sure of what he was saying and it did make sense. How many people, after all, would die all at once and arrive in the Draugr's domain willing to fight together against their common foe? This was most likely the first time that an army had managed to make it through to the eighth ring of Helheim, and by all accounts it was because of her.

"The Jötnar have helped us so much Sylfia," Jarl said. "And then I found your mother. I knew that she was still with us, and when I found her she had managed to defend herself against so many. I would not have believed it if I had not seen it for myself."

Sigrid punched Jarl in the shoulder and it looked to Sylfia as though it had some power behind it. Jarl smiled at Sigrid apologetically.

"It takes more than a few undead spirits to keep me from putting my family back together," Sylfia said with a smile of her own.

A loud cracking sound interrupted the family reunion and all three of them turned to see what it was.

The Jötnar had made it all the way to the Naglfar ship although they had not yet managed to set foot on the narrow wooden planks that led up onto the deck. The Draugr, now concentrated, seemed to be able to use each other as shields and their sheer density combined with their strength was making it almost impossible for the Jötnar to push them back. It was clear though that the Jötnar were definitely chipping away at the Draugr as they continued their attack, even if they were being funnelled into a narrower and narrower force.

What made the most noise though, had not come from the battle between the Jötnar and the Draugr. The Jötnar were still brandishing their blazing weapons and Sylfia could feel the sheer heat coming from the group even at their distance of a hundred metres or so. The heat had caused the sound. The ice that had engulfed the Naglfar ship at the back end that held it in place, had begun to melt and the great galleon was slowly pulling itself free, although the movement was subtle.

Sylfia had no idea what she was supposed to do. She knew that the launching of the ship would signify the beginning of Ragnarök, but she did not know if the fact that the launch was being spurred on by the Jötnar was a good thing or not, as the launch of the Naglfar ship was supposed to be because of the waves caused by the uncoiling of Jörmungandr and not some mortal act. She fretted that the ship would be launched too early or in the wrong way.

In her heart though, Sylfia knew that no matter how the Naglfar ship was launched, the fact that it would come to pass would be the only fact of relevance.

"Father, we need to destroy the ship," Sylfia said slowly.

"That is why we are here, it is not?" Jarl asked. "The Jötnar have given us the opportunity that we needed and we must take it now."

Jarl held his hand out and Sylfia wrapped her fingers around her father's wrist. Then Sigrid added her hand and between the three of them, they formed their clasped hands into a triangle, an unbreakable bond that only a family can maintain.

"Then how do we do it?" Sylfia asked.

Jarl looked out at the ship, at the Jötnar engaged in combat with the Draugr at the rear of the ship, and the ice holding it steadfast slowly melting. He ran his fingers through his braided beard as he thought and eventually he came to a conclusion.

"We wade out into the water while the Draugr are occupied," he said. "Then we quietly climb up the front of the ship and slip into the boughs, as deep as we can, and we start the fire that will engulf it. I do not care what the Naglfar ship is constructed of, but a fire started deep within will sink even the mightiest of vessels."

Sylfia could offer no alternatives to the plan, but there was one thing that worried her.

"But what of the Draugr that may be still within the ship? The ship is so big that there could be thousands inside, and we cannot hope to fight against that many."

"Look to the deck," Jarl said as he pointed Sylfia towards the open space atop the great ship. She could not see what he was trying to show her, so he spoke again. "Do you see any Draugr atop the ship awaiting the arrival of a new enemy from elsewhere? Or do you see every single Draugr that was within this place streaming forward to the ramps where they meet the Jötnar?"

Now Sylfia could see, and her father was correct: It was clear that all of the Draugr that may have been inside the ship had turned their attention towards the battle that was already raging. The plan, therefore, made sense. If they could sneak onto the ship, at least they had a chance to burn it to the ground, especially now that they had Jarl with them and his ability to generate fire with nothing but his hand axes.

"And you, mother?" Sylfia asked Sigrid. "Do you think that this is the best plan for us?"

Sigrid hugged Jarl, pulling her body close against his. "What matters, Sylfia, is not what I think, nor whatever the future will hold for our plans or of Ragnarök. The only thing that I care about is that we stay together as a family. I feel as though we have already lost each other too many times, and if we are to continue along this path, I only care that we do it together. I will follow you, Sylfia, in whatever you decide."

"But do you think that it will work?" Sylfia asked again. She knew what her mother was saying to her, but she wanted to be sure that she was doing the right thing before she made any decisions.

Sigrid nodded. "I think it is the best that we can do with what we can see before us," she said. It was the truth, Sigrid did believe that the plan Jarl had concocted was the best chance that they would have to sink the Naglfar ship.

41

Sylfia, Jarl and Sigrid moved away from the battle and stepped into the water that Sylfia had arrived from. To their surprise and relief, not a single one of the Draugr, still engrossed in their battle with the Jötnar, seemed interested in what they were doing, and within a moment all three of them had waded into the water so far that none of their enemies could have even followed them if they had wanted to.

The water was cool and deep enough that Sylfia did not have to place her feet on the ground, which was a good thing because all she could think about was the hand that had grabbed her earlier when she had strayed too close to the bottom.

"Do not go down too deep," Sylfia said quietly, though loud enough for her parents to hear. "There are things at the bottom that are better left to rest."

Neither Jarl nor Sylfia answered her, though she did see them both glance down and paddle a little more frantically than they had been.

To all of their delight, nothing happened in the space between the front of the ship and the shore where they had launched from, and all three came to a halt below a long piece of rope that was hanging down from the ship, touching the water almost as though it was made to be climbed up.

The rope itself looked old, as did most of the ship and it looked both green and slippery – as if it had been there for centuries. Sylfia had reservations about how strong it was going to be, although it was in the best place to climb if they wanted to remain out of sight of the Draugr.

On either side of the ship, great horns protruded as though they were the tusks of some colossal beast and below them hung netting and sheets. Sylfia had initially thought to scale these parts as climbing would have proven much simpler, but Jarl had said that climbing the sides of the ship would be far riskier. After all, if the Draugr saw them and paid them any attention, their plan would fail before it had even begun.

Jarl took hold of the rope before either of the women, and as he did so, Sylfia noticed that the bare flesh of his forearm had a deep black mark on it, with tendrils of black beginning to snake away from the mass and up his arm. It was small, and the tendrils were thin, but whatever it was, she knew it would certainly not be good.

Sylfia grabbed hold of Jarl's arm as he pulled himself from the water, and he looked down at his daughter. She gestured to his arm, but he simply looked away and started again pulling himself up the rope with his arms, and when he was out of the water, he wrapped his legs around the base of it to aid in his ascent.

Sylfia looked at her mother after Jarl had clearly avoided her questioning glance. To her horror, Sigrid raised a single arm from the water and showed Sylfia that she, too, had a mark on her wrist that was apparently spreading as though it was a plague that could not be stopped.

"Mother... what is this?" Sylfia asked slowly. She moved to touch the mark but Sigrid pulled her arm away as though it was contagious.

"Sylfia I..." Sigrid began, but stopped when she could not find the words. She inhaled and tried again. "You know how we arrived here, daughter." Sylfia waited but eventually nodded when it became clear that Sigrid awaited a response. "It is impossible to kill that which is already dead," Sigrid said. "Your father and I, we both arrived in this place because our lives came to an end. To die in this place is a sentence that has no end. It does not matter if you agree to become Draugr or not, the mortal bodies that we inhabit are already beginning to rot and eventually our end will come. We are Draugr now, and that is what awaits us both in our future."

"No, it cannot be true!" Sylfia choked out, doing her best to stop the tears from welling in her eyes. "There must be something that can be done... we did not arrive in Helheim because we died in the mortal realm so surely..."

"But it is what happened after we arrived, Sylfia," Sigrid interrupted. "There is nothing that can be done, and in the fullness of time your father and I will rot as the rest have done. This is how it shall be, but for now we must fulfil your destiny. We will help you on your path, and when all is done, we will leave you, and there is nothing more to be said on the matter."

Sylfia felt her tears begin to fall and wet her cheeks. It was a terrible thing to be given her parents back, only to be told they would not last as she had expected. Her heart pounded and her chest hurt, and she knew there was nothing she could do about it.

She gritted her teeth as she heard her mother's words but she could not accept them; there was no way that the Gods could send her on this journey only to take everything away from her that she had ever cared about. She had already lost so much.

"I will stop this, mother," Sylfia said through her gritted teeth. "I swear this to you on my life, to the Gods and any other being that sees fit to listen. I will give my own life before I let you and father perish and decay within the ranks of the Draugr."

Sigrid gave a half-hearted smile, which Sylfia knew immediately was a smile of pity and disbelief rather than one of thanks. Sylfia did not care though; she had given her oath that she would not let this happen and breaking an oath was not a practice that she was about to start. She did not know yet how exactly she would stop the necrosis that threatened her parents' mortal bodies, but she would find a way. She did not have a choice.

Trying to ignore the state of her parents, Sylfia turned her attention back to the task at hand. After all, none of it would matter if they could not prevent the Naglfar ship from launching, and then they would need to figure out how to reach Baldur and undo all of the things that Loki had done to bring about Ragnarök.

Sylfia placed her hands on the rope up to the ship as soon as Jarl had made it to the top. It had taken him a long while, not because he had ascended slowly but rather because the ship was larger than anything she had ever seen before in all her life. As she began her own ascent, her mind wandered to everything that had happened to her so far, and the thought of Loki occupied a large part of her mind. He had sought to stop her in her path, but she was yet to see him again. She wondered if he had just assumed that Hel would deal with her and her family, or perhaps he could simply not enter into this domain as freely as she had supposed. After all, everything that she had encountered in this place so far, other than she, Jarl and Sigrid, had truly been dead in one way or another.

Sylfia struggled as she climbed, as the pain from the wound on her shoulder burned, but she struggled on and eventually, after a fair amount of effort and pain, she breached the top of the ship where Jarl was waiting. When she climbed over the edge with her father's help, she again saw the mark on his arm, and the twang of guilt and sorrow returned, although she said nothing.

The deck of the Naglfar ship was twice the size of any settlement that Sylfia had ever seen. It spanned so far away from her that the sounds of battle from over the edge sounded muffled and distant, and between her and her father and the far end of the ship, not a single soul stood, human, Draugr, nor Jötnar. It was an eerie and unexpected sight, as though the ship should have been crewed by tens of thousands, but Sylfia would not complain; as far as she was concerned if she never saw another Draugr for as long as she lived that would be too soon.

A few moments later, while Sylfia took stock of the ship before her, Sigrid pulled herself over the edge of the ship and climbed onto the deck to join her husband and daughter. She gave Jarl a look that he read immediately as she had told Sylfia about the mark and what it meant. Jarl did not say a word.

As one, Jarl, Sylfia and Sigrid drew their weapons, Jarl his pair of hand axes, Sylfia her pair of short swords and Sigrid her own single sword, and they moved forwards in search of the stairs or ladder that would lead them downwards into the belly of the ship. It was clear that there were no Draugr on the deck before them, but they knew that now was not the time to take any chances, and holding their weapons to the ready could potentially save them precious seconds if they were taken by surprise.

Thankfully, the ship had been built much like the vessels in the mortal realm, and the wooden stairs down to the lower decks sat not far from where they had arrived. For a vessel that looked so decrepit from the outside, the deck and what they had already seen of the stairs looked like had been kept in good repair, and certainly not as though everything had been rotting away as Sylfia had expected.

They descended the stairs as slowly and as quietly as they could, and once they had gone down fourteen flights, they found themselves at the very bottom of the ship without having seen a single Draugr.

In fact, they had seen nothing except wide open spaces as they had moved - no provisions, boxes, barrels or anything else that ships usually contained below deck. It did make sense though, once Sylfia took a moment to think about it; this ship was designed for just one simple purpose: to bring the terrible army of the Draugr to the mortal realm so that they could play their part in Ragnarök, and they didn't need the normal creature comforts that the living preferred.

"We are at the bottom of the ship now, Sylfia," Sigrid said quietly. "If we start the fires here, they will cause the most damage as they grow and expand upwards. But we must be ready to run if the flames grow too quickly."

Sylfia nodded to her mother. "I am ready, but mother, father, we must speak about the marks on your arms properly. Do not expect that I will just allow you to become one of those creatures. I mean, how long do you think you have before it spreads? And will your mind follow? Let us find a way to stop all of this."

"There is no stopping this," Jarl said quickly, stepping forward. "The deed has already been done. It was done before we even stepped a single foot within this place, and I can tell that it is already growing. I truly do not know how long we have left, but when the time comes and our minds begin to fail, you must do what is right, Sylfia."

"I will not!" Sylfia replied sternly, picking up on what her father was implying. "I will find a way to undo this, and then... and then you will apologise for making these foolish demands of me!"

Sigrid took hold of Sylfia's arm, and Jarl placed a hand on her shoulder.

"Sylfia," Sigrid said softly. "We will look for a different path, and we have not given up all hope as of yet, but what your father is asking, or should I say telling you, is that sometimes the most difficult thing to do is the right thing. If we do not find a way to undo this and it becomes clear that we will become one of those creatures, you *must* show us the mercy that you know in your heart is right."

Sylfia barely listened to her mother's words because all she could think about was finding out which Gods may have the power to undo this so that she may petition them for their mercy. She had already dealt with Hodur, Hel, Loki and Odin to a lesser extent, so was this beyond the realms of possibility? Of the things they had witnessed that should not have been possible, one small act of mercy to undo a curse on her parents should not be too much to ask, should it?

"Anyway, this has no bearing on what we are to do here now, does it?" Jarl asked with a wide grin. "Let us set our fires and watch the eternal souls of Helheim burn before our very eyes."

It sounded as though Jarl was taking all of this very lightly, but Sylfia knew no matter how jovial his tone was, he was taking this task very seriously.

"But one last thing Sylfia," Jarl said, and Sylfia nodded for her to continue. "If we sink this ship, burn it to tinder and everything on or within, tell me again how this will prevent Ragnarök?"

Sylfia thought for a long moment before she replied. She had never truly thought it through in fine detail as she had always just thought that it would become obvious.

"The ship will launch when Ragnarök begins, and it will bring along with it the army of the damned. If we sink the ship now, then if Ragnarök does come to pass, this part of the prophecy will not happen. It will ruin the order of Ragnarök, and that is not something that the end of days will be able to abide by. But this act alone does not prevent Ragnarök. The only way that we can achieve that is to free the God Baldur from Hel. This we will still have to do even after the Naglfar ship has fallen."

Jarl tousled his beard as he thought. "And Baldur still resides within the central circle of Helheim?" he asked.

Sylfia nodded. "I do not know how we will get there yet, but I have faith that our path will become clear as it always has."

Jarl nodded. "Then let us waste no more time, daughter. Let us sink this ship and move along into the centre of Helheim itself so that we may put a stop to all of this."

Then Jarl drew both of his axes and ignited them with a thought. They burnt a bright orange as he held them to his sides, and in a moment he pushed them against the inner curved wooden wall of the bottom of the belly of the Naglfar ship.

The ship seemed to inhale the flames as the aged and dried wood felt light and warmth for the first time in centuries. Jarl then moved along the ship away from Sylfia and Sigrid, igniting small fires all the way along the wall before crossing over to the other side and doing the same thing all the way back. By the time he had reached the two women again, the heat from the growing flames was already uncomfortable, and the fires were spreading quickly.

"Come, we must leave this place," Jarl said commandingly as he returned to his family, and as one they began to ascend the wooden staircases back up to the surface of the Naglfar ship.

The ascent was much quicker than the descent into the ship had been, mainly because they spared no time to check each floor they landed on for Draugr; they reasoned that the ship had been empty before, so it made sense that it still would be. Eventually, they reached the surface and breathed a sigh of relief: They had made it.

"I cannot believe that we have made it back up!" Sylfia exclaimed once they were back on the deck of the great ship. "Perhaps this was not the most difficult of tasks after all!"

Jarl grinned down at Sylfia as she rejoiced, although Sigrid had a far more serious look on her face.

"Sylfia, I do not think we have made it out just yet," Sigrid said.

Sylfia turned to see where her mother was looking. Nothing seemed obvious at first, until she saw what her mother had been talking about: The ice that held the Naglfar ship in place had all but melted, and the battle between the Draugr and the Jötnar with their flaming weapons was still in dire throws. Sylfia watched as a vast block of ice that curved around and hung high above the ship suddenly cracked.

The sound as it cracked was so deafening that it echoed away and into the caverns all around over and over and then, as though it was a spear sent down to earth from the very Gods themselves, the ice broke and fell.

The block of ice that broke away must have been the size of ten longhouses and it fell onto the back of the Naglfar ship just behind the battle between the Jötnar and the Draugr. Sylfia watched as the ice cut through the ship and some of the Draugr on the boarding ramps, breaking them away and sending them down to the ground below.

The battle for the eighth ring of Helheim, Sylfia realised, had come to a disastrous end as the Draugr and the Jötnar were either crushed by falling ice, or fell from the great heights they fought on while the ramps and parts of the ship fell away. The ice spared neither race, and both fell without bias.

Then a second deafening cracking sound came from the back of the ship, and this time it was accompanied by a great jolt within the vessel. The ice that had held it in place was gone. The ship had launched.

Sylfia almost fell as the ship lurched forwards, and the sound of the water beneath it was so loud that she did not hear her father shouting for her to take hold of something. Sigrid, Jarl and Sylfia took hold of each other and huddled together as though they were able to protect each other from whatever was to come next.

"What do we do?!" Sylfia shouted as the noise of the launch dissipated.

"We must leave the ship!" Jarl called back, "Quickly, to the front and back down the rope!"

They staggered towards the front of the ship where they had climbed up, with a fair amount of difficulty as their bodies attempted to acclimatise to the ship now moving atop the water.

"You are too late!" A voice boomed above all of the other sounds that were still loud enough that they needed to be shouted over. Sylfia knew that she recognised it, and as the hairs on the back of her neck stood on end, she turned to look behind her. There in the very centre of the ship stood the God Loki.

This time, the trickster God wore no mask. He did not pretend to be a great wolf, nor did he pretend to be the visage of old age; he was simply Loki. His hair was golden-red, and he had no facial hair to tousle as Jarl enjoyed. He wore a long, flowing tunic made of rich, velvety fabric in a deep golden hue. He wore a belt around his waist studded with what looked like precious gems, embellished with intricate golden knotwork designs. Over the tunic, Loki wore a full-length cape of deep-blue fox fur, trimmed with gold and fastened at the throat with a brooch in the shape of a snarling wolf's head. The look that Loki had chosen for himself was clearly one of power. He was telling the world that he had arrived and was better than everyone else.

In addition to his lustrous attire, Loki was also adorned with a variety of jewellery. He wore shining gold arm rings and a thick necklace and his long, flowing golden-red hair was crowned with a circle of beaten gold.

Loki's piercing blue eyes surveyed the scene before him with a mixture of amusement and menace.

"I have arrived!" he announced loudly. "Kneel before your God!" Then he raised his arms to his sides as though he was waiting for adoration to be showered down upon him.

At this point, Jarl, Sigrid and Sylfia had turned to face the trickster God. He was quite far away from them, but his words reached them as though he was standing right next to them.

With an arrogant smirk on his face, Loki began to speak again, now that he had garnered the attention of the three mortals and the only other beings on board the great Naglfar ship.

"Greetings, mortals. I am Loki, the God of mischief and fire, and I stand before you as the harbinger of Ragnarök, the end of all things. You may ask yourselves, why have I brought you here? Why have I chosen you to bear witness to the end of the world? You may believe yourselves not worthy to stand in the presence of a God such as I. But it is simply because I wish to show you now the power and majesty of the Gods, to demonstrate that even the mightiest of you are but mere mortals before us. You may think that you can make changes to the nine realms, but the scope of the Gods is simply beyond your comprehension." Loki looked all about the ship with a mild look of confusion on his face. "What you have achieved here is nothing. You think that by felling but a handful of the army of the dead, it will change anything?"

Sylfia felt the urge to reply, but as she opened her mouth to interrupt him, the God quickly continued before she could utter even a sound. "I want you to watch, mortals, watch as the world around you becomes what it has always meant to be. See the armies of the dead marching on, led by my daughter Hel and the demon wolf Fenrir. See the skies darken with the flight of the eagle, Jörmungandr, the World's Serpent. See the oceans of your mortal realm swirl and crash in a torrent of never-ending turmoil. This is how the world was always meant to be and how things will come to pass. You have failed, my mortal friends." Then he continued quickly again: "And know this, mortals: all of this is because of me. I, Loki, have brought about the end of the world, and I stand here on the brink of victory, revelling in the chaos and destruction I have wrought. So bow down, mortals, and pay homage to the might and power of the Gods, for we are the masters of the universe, and you are but mere pawns in our game."

Sylfia felt the Naglfar ship lurch again as it listed violently to one side, and running over to the edge, she looked down to the still waters below to see what was happening.

The waters, though, were not still. They had begun to thrash and crash loudly against the bough of the ship, and as she watched they flowed into a wide spiral, the white edges of the crashing waves carving through each other as they fought to spin in the same direction. The ship now sat in the centre of a great whirlpool and Sylfia had no idea what any of this meant, or what was truly happening.

"You came here to prevent Ragnarök!" Loki shouted above the now deafening waves below. "But you have been a part of my plans for longer than you could possibly imagine! It is the flames that you have brought along with you that launched my ship and brought about the end of days!"

Jarl, having heard enough from the trickster God, coiled his arm behind his head and launched a single hand axe directly at Loki as he spoke, hoping that Loki was so absorbed in his own words that he would not see the weapon approaching.

The God did not stop speaking as he casually caught the axe by its blade and peered down at it, turning it over and over. Then he laughed.

"To think that you would attempt to harm me is not an insult," Loki shouted over the sound of the seas below, though his words were calm. "I do not take it as an insult because you have no comprehension of what you have attempted. It is as though the ant has bitten the wolf. There is no blame there, just simply futility."

"Sylfia stepped forward and both Jarl and Sigrid moved to hold her back, but she simply shrugged them off, and they had no choice but to follow her. She came to a halt a few feet from Loki, and he looked at her with a look of overconfidence on his face.

"I know of the rules of the Gods!" Sylfia called. "I know that you cannot interfere with us mortals unless you see us as a threat to you, and I know that you have tried to stop me on my path at every opportunity! You are nothing but a trickster, a liar, and you will stand in my way no longer!"

"NO!" Loki cried back. "You are a fool that has been directed exactly as I had planned before you were even born! Every step on your path has been crafted by my hand, and just look at where you have arrived. You are correct that I could not bring about Ragnarök alone, but you have now done that for me, have you not?"

Sylfia felt her heart sink at those words. Could this be the truth? Could Loki really have manufactured her entire life so that she would be the one to launch the Naglfar ship and begin the end of days?

"And about me not being able to stop you? Do you seriously think that you will be able to fight against me when you have no weapons?" Loki held out his hands, still holding onto Jarl's axe, and all of their weapons detached themselves from their belts and flew through the air towards the trickster God.

With the weapons floating in the air before him, Loki smiled. "There is nothing that you can do, and nowhere you can run to," and then he gestured to the ground and each of the weapons, Jarls' axes and Sylfia and Sigrid's swords, hurtled towards the deck of the ship.

Sylfia gasped as her swords stuck deep into the wooden floor in front of Loki and watched as her father's heavy axes cut through the deck, exposing black smoke and the tips of deep red flames as the fires that they had set deep below finally reached the surface of the ship.

Loki, who clearly had not expected this fire, or indeed for the axes to have breached the thick wooden deck, took a large step backwards. Then the Naglfar ship began to rise as the swirling waters swelled upwards from beneath them, and the ceiling of the caverns started coming closer and closer towards them.

Suddenly, the ceiling of Helheim burst open above them, and the waters inside the caverns spilt forth into the mortal realm, with Sylfia, Sigrid and Jarl the only beings to bear witness to the beginning of Ragnarök as all the realms began to collide.

The ship was clearly in a bad state, and the flames lapped hungrily at the dry and decaying wood from which the deck was constructed. The cut that the axes had caused had allowed the flames to climb up onto the surface, and within a moment, a large crack had started to open up to allow the deep red glow of the fires beneath to illuminate the God of mischief.

The sky was bright and warm above, and Sylfia enjoyed the feeling of the mortal realm on her face, and when she took a deep breath, she realised how much she had missed clean air.

Sylfia did not have much time to revel in her new surroundings though, because the ship was not the only thing to rise from the depths of Helheim up into the mortal realm. Far behind the ship, a huge mountain also rose, but it did not stop when it reached the surface of the water. This mountain, Sylfia knew, was the centre of Helheim, the cage in which Baldur resided.

42

"Helheim has risen!" Loki shouted above the sound of the water still swirling around the ship. It seemed as though he had chosen to ignore the fire still raging below the ship's deck, and Sylfia wondered how long it would be until the entire vessel would be engulfed in flame.

"Do you not see that your army of the dead is all gone?" Jarl shouted back. "Your ship is empty and your Draugr remain in the caverns below and are now surely all dead!"

"It does not matter the fate of the Draugr in all of this. What matters is that Ragnarök has arrived!" Loki called back, still smiling. "Midgard will fall under my rule, and any who oppose me will not be able to withstand my divine might!"

Another voice suddenly boomed from beyond the ship, and it was one that none of them had ever heard before. The sound was so loud that the very ship shook as whoever this was spoke. Everyone on the Naglfar ship, including Loki, turned to look overboard and in the distance, they could see a man running towards them on top of the swirling waters. He had obviously come from the mountain that was the centre of Helheim and it was clear that this man was the shining God Baldur himself.

Baldur wore simply a cape of bright gold, his hair was long and as yellow as the sun, and his beard was thicker perhaps than even Jarl's. Baldur seemed to exude a shining light, like a beacon of the sun itself, and he ran across the top of the water as though it was as solid as the land. On his back was strapped a long wooden spear.

"Can you not see that you are too late, brother?" Loki shouted over the edge of the ship towards Baldur. "The time has come for me to take my rightful place within this world, and you may either kneel or die where you stand."

Baldur remained silent as he approached as though he had not heard Loki speak at all. He came to within reach of the Naglfar ship and Sylfia wondered if they were going to have to watch and wait as the shining God climbed up the huge height onto the deck, but Baldur leapt from the water and came crashing down to within a few feet of Loki, who for the first time seemed little fazed by what was happening before him.

"There is still time to stop this," Baldur said in a gruff tone. "It has not yet gone too far."

Loki could not help but throw his head back and laugh. "This is not some spur-of-the-moment decision that I have made brother! Years of planning, coercing and scheming have brought us to this very moment, more so than you could ever hope to understand, is that not right, Sylfia?"

Sylfia was shocked that Loki had stopped his gloating to address her directly, and as she looked at the two Gods who were both awaiting her answer, she saw Loki's eyes flash a bright golden hue. She knew she had seen a pair of eyes do this before, but she was could not remember exactly when.

"I... I do not know how any of this has come to pass," Sylfia replied truthfully, "but it seems that this was Loki's plan all along. I set out on my path to free you from Helheim, the shining God that was wrongly imprisoned by Hel..."

Loki scoffed at Sylfia's words, but she continued nonetheless. "My journey has been filled with difficulties, death and struggles and it seems now that it could all have been at the will of the trickster God. If I have done wrong, I apologise, and I give my life and my oath to you, Baldur." Sylfia dropped to one knee and crossed her arms across her chest.

Jarl and Sigrid stood behind their daughter but did not kneel as she had done. They did not know what the Gods had planned, but they were certainly not about to kneel before one who could easily punish their daughter for attempting to follow their instructions.

"Do not kneel, child," Baldur said with a stern expression. "You have struggled to do what you thought was right for all of Midgard, and that warrants no apology. Baldur turned to face Loki again. "Let us settle this matter in the way that the Gods have settled matters in ages past. Pick your champion to face my own in battle and let the victor do as they must." As he spoke, he unstrapped the spear from his back and threw it onto the ship's deck where it stuck and stood upright as though it had been placed as a marker.

Loki looked at the spear and smiled so widely that Sylfia thought it was impossible for any mortal being to look so happy. She had a terrible feeling that this was what Loki had hoped for the entire time.

"I agree to your terms, brother," Loki announced clearly. "So choose your champion."

Baldur turned to Sylfia again. She had risen to her feet and was awaiting the words of the God that she knew would come to her.

"Within you, child, I can sense a great determination but also a great power. You would make a fine champion if you only would accept, so I ask you to willingly give your mortal soul. Know that this is no small thing that I ask..."

Then Loki interrupted Baldur's speech. "There is one small problem if you wish any of these mortals to become your champion. The mother and the father here are of the Draugr, having already passed. They are not yours to turn to your cause." Then before anyone could object, he turned his attention to Sylfia, "And this one... this one is my champion already, is that not correct, Sylfia?" And as Loki spoke, his eyes once again shone a bright gold as though he was punctuating his question.

Then Sylfia remembered where she had seen these eyes before. They were the eyes that she had seen flash on Elder Wise, and she remembered the last words she had ever spoken to the Elder before she had passed into the next realm. "I swear it," Sylfia whispered to herself.

"You see! You have no champions here and none to choose from!" Loki cried in happiness. "You have lost already, brother!"

"That is not true!" Jarl boomed making Sylfia jump. "Baldur has his champion. In fact, Baldur has an army to his name, does he not? Baldur's Children have sworn to fight for the freedom of the shining God, and if you bring them here, you will see the power that this God wields within Midgard."

"And what is more," Sigrid added, "Our daughter will not fight on your behalf, trickster God. The army of Baldur's Children will face no opponent and will stand victorious as champions of Baldur. Your fight is over before it has even begun."

It seemed to them all as though Loki's plans had been foiled but surprisingly, Baldur placed a hand on his forehead as though something had gone very, very wrong.

Loki then spoke clearly and loudly. "If the champions of the Gods refuse to battle in the name of their sworn deities, then let the Gods themselves decide their fate!"

The Naglfar ship creaked as though answering Loki's dire call to action, and Sylfia wondered exactly how long it had left before it was entirely engulfed in the flames that her family had set deep below deck. Right now, though, it did not matter; the two Gods that stood before them were about to battle, and there was nothing that she could do to help.

"You always were a fool, Baldur," Loki sneered, "thinking that your beauty and light could protect you from the world's dangers."

"You speak as though you know me," Baldur replied, his voice calm and measured, "but you know nothing of me or the power I possess."

Loki laughed a harsh and mirthless sound. "Power? You have no power here, in this place, surrounded by the forces that I control."

The two Gods abruptly lunged at each other, their movements swift and graceful as they began to fight with the ferocity of beasts. They traded blows with closed fists, their bodies slamming into each other with the force of the waves around the ship. The sound of each punch landing on flesh cracked like thunder above and the entire battle was deafening.

The speed of the battle seemed incomprehensible, too, with Loki dancing swiftly around Baldur in the blink of an eye and Baldur raising his forearms to block blows that no mortal man could have seen coming.

Baldur smashed his fist into Loki's jaw as he approached, then landed a lightning-fast jab and the trickster God stumbled and fell backwards, holding his face in his hands.

"You are weak, brother," Baldur said as he stood over Loki. "All of your planning, your scheming and yet here we are again. You have been found wanting, so accept your loss and return to where you came from before this goes any further than it has to."

Loki nodded slowly behind his hands and Baldur stood up straight. What Baldur could not see, though, was that there was now a second Loki standing behind Baldur, silently wielding a short dagger with a menacingly sharp blade.

"Look out!" Sylfia's scream reached Baldur a fraction before Loki began his attack. Baldur was quick but Loki was quicker still, and as he lunged, Baldur could only move slightly so that the blade would not plunge fatally into his heart. The dagger sank deep into his flesh and the God reeled, falling backwards through the clone of Loki that evaporated immediately into dark mist before Baldur hit the wooden deck with a crunch.

"You see, brother, it is not just the mistletoe that can harm you now. You are nothing, as weak as you have always been, so now you must accept your fate and your end," Loki goaded loudly.

Baldur gave no response and simply hung his head in shame. He knew he had lost the fight and there was nothing more that he could do. Loki had won.

Loki then wrapped a single hand around Baldur's throat, picked him up off the ground and held him high up in the air, pulling his knife back ready to deliver the killing blow.

Sylfia wanted to help, to do something, anything to aid the shining God, but before she could move Jarl had run past her, picked up the spear that Baldur had thrown into the deck which still stood upright and launched it at Loki whilst the God's back was turned.

The world seemed to move slowly as the spear rotated as it approached its target. There was no chance that it could miss.

But at the last second, Loki dropped Baldur to the ground, spun on his heels and cut the spear in two with his forearm.

The action was swift, but it had given the shining God enough time to make his escape, and when Loki turned to look back to where he had dropped Baldur, his foe was gone.

"This is the end for you, Baldur," Loki shouted. "You thought yourself invincible, but you were wrong. Your beauty and light mean nothing in the face of my cunning and power! You have lost, and if you do not show yourself, you are a coward too!"

Sylfia watched as a shining bright light fell from the mast of the ship above. It shone with the brightness of the sun, and as Loki whirled around, trying to locate the arrival of his enemy, Baldur fell upon the trickster God, crashing him through the burning deck of the ship towards the furnace below.

As they fell, with Baldur gasping for air, his eyes met Loki's with a look of defiance. "You may have taken my life, Loki," he rasped in obvious pain, "but the war is far from over. The light will always shine, even in the darkest of places." Then Baldur spiralled forward into the depths that had swallowed Loki before him.

The Naglfar ship could take no more punishment, and the great galleon crackled and creaked before the flames abruptly burst upwards from the ever-growing burning hole in the deck.

The ship lurched again, and this time the loud cracking sound that accompanied it was unmistakable. The Naglfar ship was failing, and as though it could not proceed without the two Gods who had fallen atop its deck, it broke cleanly in two.

The front half began to raise high into the air as it began its descent into the tumultuous waters below. Sylfia, Jarl and Sigrid raced up the ship hoping to find something to grab hold of or to leave the ship, away from the flames and the whirlpool below. They ran as fast and as hard as they could, and Sylfia was the first to grab hold of one of the old, decaying ropes that hung down, now flapping against the deck as though it was some divine lifeline. Sylfia managed to grab the rope in one hand as her feet began to slip on the deck but her purchase lessened with the ever-increasing gradient of the sinking Naglfar ship.

"Take my hand!" Sylfia called back to her mother, who was within touching distance of her, but as she turned, she realised that Jarl was a few steps too far away, and he was already slowing as he did his best not to slip and fall to his death.

Sylfia held the rope in her left hand, and in her right she took Sigrid's, clasping her fingers around her mother's wrist and her mother returning the action. The grip was strong, but the wound that Sylfia still carried within her shoulder was already burning, begging her to stop this madness.

Looking past her mother she could see that her father was so close to Sigrid. He needed to take but a few more small steps and she would be able to take his hand.

"Come, father! Quickly! You can make it!" Sylfia called out in the hope that her words would bring her father new strength.

But Jarl's steps were growing shorter for fear of slipping, and the front of the ship was still rising up higher into the air, making each step more difficult.

"Here husband!" Sigrid shouted and reached her hand out as far as she could manage. Sylfia too gave everything that she had to increase the length of their human chain, but with each new movement, her body and shoulder cried out in pain. She gritted her teeth and did her best to shut out all thoughts of hurt or failure.

Abruptly, Jarl's foot slipped and Sylfia's heart stopped. He had begun to fall and if it had not been for Sigrid's outstretched arm, he would have certainly fallen to his death. Instead though, Sigrid and Jarl linked their wrists as Sylfia and her mother had and held on. By now though, the ship was almost vertical and with the heat from the flames below them evident and reaching their bodies, Sylfia did not know how long she could hold on for.

Sylfia looked down at her parents' faces as she gripped the rope in one hand as tightly as she could. She would easily have been able to climb the rope and reach the front of the ship where she would find a place to rest, but not with both of her parents holding her arm. Neither could she pull their weight up alone, although it may have been possible if she were not badly injured or if she at least had both hands free.

Her parents' faces looked back up at her as they hung there helplessly, and she could see nothing but love and adoration in their eyes. They knew that they had done everything for their daughter, and she saw at that moment the level of pride that they both had for her with every part of their being.

Sylfia did not know it, but tears streamed down her face. She knew that she was stuck in a situation where she was without any choices, and no hope.

"I promise... I will save you! I promise!" Sylfia shouted, the last words breaking, being spoken through floods of tears. In reply, her parents simply smiled.

Sigrid was the first to respond to Sylfia's promise. She knew that it was not a promise that she could keep, and she could see that with every passing moment that her daughter's struggle was drawing closer and closer to an end.

"We are your parents, Sylfia. Our job is to protect you and help you grow into the person you have become. We have watched you grow and we could be no prouder. You have done great things with your life, much more than any person we have ever known... but it is time that now..."

"NO!" Sylfia cried, struggling to speak through the pain.

"Yes Sylfia," Sigrid replied softly. "We knew how this journey was going to end from the moment we left our home. It is by the mercy of the Gods that your father and I have been given this one last opportunity to save your life and we gladly give our lives so that you may take but a single breath more. You are our daughter Sylfia, and it does not matter if we are living or of the afterlife."

"No... please do not leave me," Sylfia whispered, her voice filled with every ounce of pain that she was experiencing, both physical and emotional. "I can hold on."

"And then what, Sylfia?" Jarl called up from below Sigrid. "Look at our arms, daughter! You know what we have already become. There is no place for us in the mortal realms any longer. The infection is already spreading. Show us this one mercy but take us with you in your heart and in your mind."

Sylfia shut her eyes as tightly as she could. She shut out the pain in her shoulder, the sounds of the oceans below, the crackling of the fire burning and the splintering of the great ship as it continued to buckle and break. She thought back to the moment that she had first seen her father and her mother. It all seemed so long ago, and she was just so tired. Not just of body but of her mind, and she had one desire above everything: for all of this to stop and that they could all simply be back at home, within the Rakki settlement with the rest of their clan, eating and drinking happily, with the only task before them being to guard the God's Chasm.

But she knew that such thoughts were futile. The past remained in the past.

"My daughter, my darling... you have been the light in our lives. The one thing that we could be truly thankful to the Gods for," Jarl's voice shook as he spoke, and Sylfia watched the tears wetting his own cheeks. "You know what you must do next. You are strong, much stronger than your mother or I have ever been, and you will survive this; you have an entire lifetime ahead of you and a future that I know will make us prouder than we already are. I wish that I could be there to witness all of the amazing things that you are going to do and achieve in your life, but for now, we must say goodbye and hope that we will meet again in another life."

Sylfia kept her eyes closed and shook her head back and forth, not wanting to hear another word of goodbye.

"Daughter..." Sigrid said softly, and the tone of her caring, loving voice made Sylfia look down at her mother, their eyes meeting again. "We will always love you with all of our hearts and souls."

Then the ship lurched, the rope whipped and Sigrid's grip slipped away from Sylfia's. Sylfia had no choice but to watch as both of her parents fell away from her, down into the depths of the ship, into the fires that they had set themselves, and away from any world that Sylfia had ever known or wanted to be a part of.

Sylfia screamed until her voice turned hoarse. Her tears fell freely to where her parents had fallen, and she made no effort to pull herself up the rope and away to her own safety although deep inside she knew that this was not what her parents had wanted for her. She could simply not bring herself to accept what had just happened.

The waters below the Naglfar ship then belched loudly, and the ship began to sink slowly into the depths.

The movement abruptly brought Sylfia back to herself, and she began to climb deftly up the rope to the top of the Naglfar ship.

The ship was now sinking with no sign of slowing down, and Sylfia knew that she had just one option available to her: she was going to have to wait until the waters came closer and then leap as far as she could away from the ship. If she leapt too early, the fall from that height would kill her, but if she waited too long, there was a risk that she would be pulled down with the ship itself.

Sylfia waited for as long as she could until she was sure that diving into the waters from such a height would not take her life. She willed all of her might into her legs, bent her knees and dove from the ship. A moment later, she impacted the water. It was cold, but she knew that she needed to keep moving to get out of the way of the ship as it sank, so she swam as far and as fast as she could, her only thoughts focused on what was happening to her right now and everything else pushed to the back of her mind for another time. If she stopped to think about her parents any longer, she would be killed, and she could not bear for their sacrifices to be for nothing.

Ragnarök

43

Sylfia had been swimming for a reasonable distance before she turned behind her to look at where the Naglfar ship had been and, by all accounts, she had been expecting to see a burning ship, a thrashing ocean and dark clouds above as though it was the end of days. Instead, what she saw, was nothing. The ship had apparently disappeared under the waters, the sky above was clear, and the ocean waters were calm. The only sign that there had even been a ship there was the debris floating on the surface of the water.

Sylfia quickly turned and swam back to where the ship had been, feeling that the danger had now passed, and when she arrived she began searching desperately through the debris for her parents. She knew that the chances of finding them were slim, and that they could still be alive were even slimmer, but she knew that she would not be able to forgive herself if she did not even take the time to look.

After a long while of searching, Sylfia climbed onto a wide section of the great mast that was still floating in the sea of debris and accepted the truth for what it was: she was truly alone. Her parents had gone, and she needed to accept that fact, no matter how much it hurt.

In the distance, the central spire of Helheim still stood proud against the sea of nothingness all around her, and she wondered if any other Gods had escaped from that place along with the shining God Baldur. There was no way she could find out, though, and a large part of her felt that she had had enough dealings with the Gods and such things to last a lifetime.

Her thought process was quickly interrupted by the sound of thunder. It was strange as no clouds were overhead, but the sound was unmistakably thunder, rumbling high above.

The rumbling increased in volume, and along with it came the sound of metal smashing together as though some great chains were being tested somewhere miles away. Sylfia winced as a great flash lit up the skies around her and she looked up into the sky and straight into two deep red eyes, peering down on the earth, seemingly as large as the sun or the moon.

Great chains the size of the sky itself fell down in front of the terrible eyes, and then without notice, the eyes started to move.

The terrible red eyes were not all that bore down from the sky, though, and as they moved closer, Sylfia could see the foreboding muzzle and dripping, snarling maw of the great wolf, Fenrir.

Sylfia's heart stopped. She had known that Ragnarök would bring along with it the great wolf, but she had no idea that it would be so huge. It was larger than any mountain she had ever seen, and she only hoped beyond hope that the creature's size would mean that it would not see her floating on her tiny piece of wood on the calm waters down on earth.

Fenrir lifted his head upwards, now in full view, and howled into the sky. The howl was so loud that it threatened to deafen Sylfia, and she had to cover her ears simply to try to keep a small amount of the howl out. The water around her rippled with the sound, and when Fenrir had finished, his great mouth remained open, expelling a thick, black mist into the sky that covered the sun and the blue skies above. The world turned grey and cold, with no sun to warm the surface, and the wolf's deep red eyes were all that shone from above.

The howl did more than threaten to deafen Sylfia, though. From the sea at the base of the central spire of Helheim, the waters began to stir. They thrashed back and forth until a great whirlpool began to form, and slowly the head of a great beast emerged. Jörmungandr, the world's serpent, had arrived to take its rightful place beside its brother Fenrir and father, Loki.

The serpent had bright orange eyes, dark green skin, and each of its razor-sharp fangs looked to be the size of a mountain. Again, the size of this beast gave Sylfia a tiny amount of hope that it simply could not see a person so small in comparison and so would not look to kill her immediately.

Jörmungandr raised its head high into the air and opened its mouth as Fenrir had done, although this time, instead of a black mist that blocked out the sun, the world's serpent exhaled a cloud of bright green mist that Sylfia instinctively knew would be very deadly to any who inhaled it.

Between the great wolf and the world's serpent, Sylfia knew that there was nothing that she could do. She had brought the realm of Helheim to this very place, but she was still simply a mortal being. All she could do was sit, watch, and hope that her end would be quick and not too painful.

The two great beasts of Ragnarök did not look as though they were about to kill her, though. In fact, they looked as though they were waiting for something to happen or for someone to arrive, and it suddenly dawned on Sylfia what had happened: in every single story that she had ever been told of Ragnarök, the two sons of Loki would reunite with their father and with Hel, their sister. Then the Naglfar ship would bring forth the armies of the damned. What was happening now though was that Loki, who was essentially the leader in this battle, had not arrived, and the Naglfar ship had already been destroyed. The two great beasts had been left without direction.

Really it did not matter; Fenrir and Jörmungandr had been bred for destruction, and even without direction, that was indeed what they would achieve – simply by their size if nothing else. If their father was not present, what difference would that really make in the fullness of time?

Things were about to change once more though, because the end of days did not just bring Fenrir and Jörmungandr to Midgard so that they could reign supreme freely. Ragnarök was not, in fact, the end; it was the beginning of a great battle between good and evil, and that fact became apparent with the arrival of the Gods.

As though riding on divine clouds that cut through the mists high above the earth, three great figures descended from the sky above the terrible beasts of Ragnarök. As huge as Fenrir and Jörmungandr themselves, Sylfia watched in awe as the Gods hurtled towards the earth. She could see Odin, the Allfather, holding his great spear Gungnir with his two great ravens swirling about his head. She could see Thor, the mightiest of all the Gods, holding his great hammer Mjolnir high in the air, ready for the battle to come.

It took Sylfia a while to figure out the third God. He was almost as big as Thor, although he held a sword and a great round shield. When Sylfia saw that he wore boots that snaked up his legs and looked like they were made of stone, she knew. Unmistakably, this was Vidar, the God of revenge and silence, wearing his divine boots that allowed him to move silently throughout each of the realms as he traversed them.

The Gods stepped from the clouds and faced the great beasts of Ragnarök. Sylfia could not see what they were all actually standing upon - except for the World Serpent who was half submerged underwater – though she thought it would not be beyond the realms of possibility that they did not require a physical surface to stand upon; they were Gods after all and all of a size that she could not ever have even imagined before.

The Gods spared no time in engaging with Fenrir and Jörmungandr. Odin and Vidar stood before the great wolf, Fenrir, whilst Thor paired off against the giant serpent Jörmungandr.

Odin waved Vidar to stand back so that he may face the wolf alone. It was a mistake, Sylfia thought, not to rely on the aid that his son would be able to bring to this battle, but she understood the desire for a father to protect his child.

The Allfather stood with his spear Gungnir in hand, ready to defend Midgard and all of the other realms that these beasts threatened to consume. He was ready to face his own demise if it meant that he could save his son and his family from Ragnarök, the end of the world.

Fenrir, the son of Loki, had no father to defend him and he stood on his own two feet with his massive jaws wide open, his sharp teeth glistening in the dim light. His eyes burned a deep hate-filled red, and he let out a second deafening roar that echoed through the sky, and the very surface of the earth shook beneath his feet.

Odin took a step forward, held his hands wide apart and with a firm voice, he spoke. His voice was so loud and clear that Sylfia could hear every word as though the God was standing right next to her. "Fenrir, it is not too late. I offer you a chance to spare yourself and this world from the inevitable destruction that Ragnarök brings. Surrender now and I will spare your life!"

Sylfia hoped more than anything that Fenrir would simply sit down and obey the Allfather, for all of this to end so that the world could return to the way it was.

But to her dismay, the wolf simply laughed. His deep and menacing laughter sent shivers down her spine. Then he spoke. It was as though he had been able to for his entire life, and Sylfia's mouth hung agape.

"Surrender? To you, Odin? You and your pitiful Gods are no match for me. I will devour you, just as I will devour all of Midgard. Ragnarök has already begun and there is no stopping it, with or without my father present."

With those words, the battle began. Odin charged forward with Gungnir raised high, ready to strike. But Fenrir was quick, and he easily dodged the opening strike, his massive jaws clamping quickly down around Odin's head.

The Allfather was quick to react and he brought his spear up, thrusting it deep into the inside of Fenrir's mouth. The wolf let out a roar of pain, but he was not deterred. He simply tore the spear from Odin's hands and cast it aside, his jaws closing in on Odin once more. The Allfather had attempted to hold onto his faithful spear, but the wolf had been far too strong, so strong that Sylfia wondered what could stop such a beast if not Odin himself.

The Allfather, undaunted, pulled out his sword Hofund, and held it high. It shimmered as though it held the sun within its blade and Sylfia recalled the stories she had heard of the weapon in her past. Odin's sword was said to be so sharp that it could cut through anything with ease. It represented the power and the wisdom of the Gods, and with this blade she knew that Fenrir would fall.

Odin swung Hofund at the wolf's neck but Fenrir was again too quick and he dodged the strike, biting down on Odin's arm and tossing him aside like a ragdoll. The God flew across the sky and landed with a crash that reverberated through Sylfia's very bones.

The Allfather eventually stood up clutching his arm, which was now badly injured and covered in his blood. But he was not defeated yet. He summoned the power of the Gods, and a brilliant light shone upon him, rejuvenating him once more and afforded him renewed divine strength.

With a fierce battle cry, Odin charged at Fenrir once more, his sword held high and ready to strike out at the beast's neck. The wolf was ready for him again, though, and he lunged forward, his jaws wide open. The two clashed in a final showdown, the sound of their impact ringing throughout the sky as though it was the loudest of thunderclaps.

Fenrir bore down on Odin, and the Allfather did what he could to keep his sword wedged into the great maw of the beast so that it could not swallow him, but as Sylfia watched she could see that the wolf was winning this battle of strength, and inch by inch the sword was being forced down, closer and closer to Odin. His muscles strained and sweat beaded on his forehead. Odin grimaced darkly as he knew that his own end was approaching. He was simply too weak to hold on for much longer, and then suddenly, with one great growl of defiance, the great wolf Fenrir snapped his mouth shut, swallowing the Allfather and taking him from this world forever.

"No!" screamed Sylfia and covered her mouth before her exclamation could bring the attention of the beasts towards her. She need not have worried, though, as even if the beasts were not already enthralled in battle, they were unlikely to have heard her from where they stood. She could simply not believe that the great wolf had killed Odin. She was so sure that if anyone could have brought an end to Ragnarök, it would have been the Allfather.

As Sylfia would have done if it were her father facing the wolf and he had just been killed in battle, Odin's son Vidar stepped forward and presented himself as a new opponent for Fenrir. He held his sword and shield to the ready and shouted his fierce war cry.

"Fenrir! I am the God of vengeance, and I will make you pay for taking my father from this world!"

The wolf sneered but did not reply.

Vidar crashed his sword against his shield, releasing a great shockwave across the world and the sheer force of it almost threw Sylfia from her debris and into the water.

The great wolf bared its fangs, its eyes shining with a wild, feral light. It let out a deep growl, its massive body coiling as it prepared to spring, but Vidar was not intimidated. He stood tall, his eyes fixed on the wolf and his sword held steady in his hand.

"I will not let you destroy this world!" Vidar roared, his voice carrying loud and true, just as his fathers before him had. "I will not let you bring about the end of all that we hold dear. I will stand against you, and I will defeat you no matter how great the cost."

And with that, Vidar charged forward, his stone boots pounding against the ground as he leapt towards the great wolf. He did not attack as the wolf had supposed though, and his feet found some divine purchase at the last moment. He leapt as though using the very air itself to dart from the path of Fenrir's snapping maw and landed on the wolf's back. Fenrir thrashed and snapped, his massive jaws finding only air as he tried to shake Vidar from his back, but Vidar held on, his grip firm and unyielding.

Vidar raised his sword high, the blade shining as though imbued with the power of each of the Gods, but Fenrir took his opportunity to lurch forwards and throw the God onto the ground before him.

Vidar's landing on the ground did not cause tremors as Odin's had. In fact, it was though Vidar had not hit the ground at all. The wolf then pressed his own advantage once more and moved to bite down on the fallen God.

Fenrir's bottom jaw scraped along the ground as he tried to scoop up Vidar before he could right himself, but as he reached Vidar, the God lifted his foot and stamped his stone boot down onto the front most teeth of the wolf's bottom jaw. Fenrir jolted to a halt, well and truly pinned down by the magical boot.

The wolf's mouth was still open, and it looked to Sylfia as though he was straining to lift Vidar into his mouth but was unable to, no matter how hard he tried. The wolf struggled, growled and huffed, covering Vidar with foul spittle, but he could simply not bring his jaw up off the ground to end the God's life.

Fenrir had two other options: he could swipe at the God with his fearsome paws, or he could bring the top of his head down to bite off Vidar's leg between his razor-sharp teeth. Not usually one to favour the use of his paws, Fenrir allowed the top of his head to fall down to shut his mouth around the annoying God, but lacking the strength of his jaw to reinforce his bite, Fenrir pushed up with his back legs to give the motion as much strength as he could possibly muster.

This was the moment that Vidar had been waiting for and with a mighty cry, as the wolf's head came crashing towards him from above, he raised his sword high into the air and braced himself to stand within Fenrir's mouth. It was too late for the wolf to change his plans.

Fenrir howled for a moment as he felt the tip of the sword cut through the roof of his mouth and then fell abruptly silent. The great wolf of Ragnarök had been slain, and the Gods had marked their first victory.

But the victory itself was bittersweet, because as Fenrir's mouth closed shut over the top of the sword, not only did the weapon protrude from the great wolf's muzzle, but the huge, razor-sharp teeth within penetrated straight through the standing form of Vidar, killing the God during his final attack. Both Fenrir and the God of vengeance and silence had been killed, and that left only the battle between the mighty Thor and the World Serpent, Jörmungandr, to decide the fate of Midgard.

Sylfia was shocked that in felling the great wolf Fenrir, two of the Gods had been killed. She was still not sure what actually happened when a God died; the only experience she had was of Baldur, who had resided in Helheim until freed, only to die at the hands of Loki – another God who she had witnessed perish. She had seen so much death and destruction in her life, and with each passing day it seemed that death came on a larger scale.

She wondered vaguely if all of these Gods would go to Valhalla to spend the rest of eternity as they had died in glorious battle, or if they would be confined to some eternal damnation for failing to achieve victory in their one sacred task. Sylfia knew that she would never learn the answer to these questions, but it put her own mortality into perspective.

While Odin and Vidar had fought and died with the great wolf Fenrir, Thor had been keeping the World Serpent at bay. The huge creature would dive under the water, disappear for a long moment, then reappear with its jaws open wide to attempt to swallow the God of thunder whole. Thor, though, could see these attacks coming and would dart out of the way at the last moment, hurtling through the sky and leaping with such strength that he was almost flying.

Thor turned and swung Mjolnir with all his might, but Jörmungandr was too quick and agile for the great hammer to make contact. The serpent slithered away, his massive body rippling with power as he dove back beneath the ocean, causing a tidal wave to cascade away from the battle.

A moment later, the serpent breached the waters below Thor and lunged forward, his jaws opening wide to reveal his own razor-sharp teeth. Thor quickly sidestepped the attack and used his hammer to deflect the serpent's jaws, keeping them from injecting him with their terrible poison. Jörmungandr hissed in anger and swung his tail out of the water, but again Thor was quick to react, jumping over the massive appendage and landing ready to swing Mjolnir once more.

With a loud, booming roar, Thor brought Mjolnir down onto Jörmungandr's back as the serpent tried to slither away once more, the force of the blow sending the terrible creature sprawling down to the surface of the water though not beneath. The World Serpent was clearly in pain but Jörmungandr was not defeated yet and he quickly regained his posture, his eyes glowing with a fierce intensity, most of his body once again submerged.

The serpent lunged forward again, though slightly slower this time as his injuries took their toll. His jaws were open wide as he aimed to crush Thor between his massive teeth, but Thor was ready and he swung Mjolnir again with all his might, sending a shockwave through the air that sent Jörmungandr flying backwards as it impacted the serpent with a deafening crack.

Thor did not allow the serpent a moment to gather itself and pressed his advantage, raining blow after blow down upon it, each one echoing like thunder across the battlefield. Jörmungandr fought back with frenzied ferocity, his jaws snapping and his tail whipping through the air, but his attacks were frantic, uncoordinated and inaccurate. Thor was just so quick and too powerful and he soon had Jörmungandr on the defensive.

With a final roar, Thor held the mighty hammer above his head, drawing of the thunder that he commanded, and Mjolnir began to glow brightly as it absorbed the power of the sky above. Thor then brought Mjolnir down upon Jörmungandr's head with a flash of lightning and a thunderclap that almost deafened Sylfia. The World Serpent flew back away from Thor and came to rest atop the oceans that began to grow calm and still without the great serpent's writhing presence.

Thor looked down at the great serpent with disgust etched onto his face, and then he noticed the tiniest red speck of blood on his muscular shoulder. He grimaced slightly at the sight of Jörmungandr's body before turning to walk away.

Sylfia watched as the one remaining God, the champion of Ragnarök, began to walk slowly away from Jörmungandr. He took nine steps away from the battle that had seen him victorious, and then fell to his knees before falling flat onto the ground before him. Jörmungandr had managed to strike one fatal blow in the great battle, and it was enough to bring down the mightiest of the Gods.

Sylfia sat on her floating mast, part of the wreckage from the destroyed Naglfar ship for a long time. She had no idea what she was supposed to do or where she was supposed to go, but after a while, she saw the bodies of the Gods and the great beasts of Ragnarök slowly fading away into nothing. The dark mist that Fenrir had sprayed into the sky and the foul green smoke that the World Serpent had exuded slowly dissipated, and the sun, high up in the sky above, returned in all its glory to bathe Sylfia in its warming glow.

The world had returned to a quiet normality. The ocean was still and the lands were at peace, and after a long while of nothing happening, and despite the worry that this was all too good to be true, Sylfia realised that she was hungry. And tired.

Epilogue: Sylfia

As she sat and pondered in silence, Sylfia looked out across the calm waters at the huge mountain, the centre of Helheim that had erupted into the mortal realm. She was wondering if she could reach it by paddling on her floating mast, or if she could swim there in the hope that the land it provided would also bring some food that she could eat.

While she sat there thinking, she saw movement in the sky above the huge mountain. She watched as it listed back and forth and swirled around the mountain for a while, and then something in her stomach dropped as it began to fly directly towards her. It took her a moment to realise what this thing was, but as it drew closer, it became clear that this thing was a jet-black raven. One of Odin's ravens.

The sight of the bird took Sylfia back to the fact that she had just witnessed the death of its master, and that brought back the faces of her own parents as they had slipped from her grasp. She feared that it would be a sight that she would never be able to erase from her mind's eye.

The raven seemed to take its time as it flew towards Sylfia as though it was enjoying the cool breeze, the warm sun and the calmness that seemed to engulf the world as a whole. Eventually it reached her and landed delicately on her shoulder. As she turned to look at the black raven, it turned its head to allow her to again see into the place where its missing eye had once been.

Sylfia was absorbed by the flashing images and lights within the raven's eye, and as the world around her faded to darkness, she was presented with a new reality. One in which she could watch the events of the past as they had occurred.

The scene that unfolded was one that she had already witnessed in the past: the visage of the giant God Hodur, hunched over with his great axe embedded deep into the ground as he sobbed for his brother, who he had unwittingly killed. Sylfia wondered why it was that the raven was showing her this information, but kept quiet as the scene panned and rotated so that Sylfia could see the huge tears falling from the giant God onto the ground, saturating the dry earth beneath. The God slowly disappeared, fading away along with his great axe, and the great God's Chasm was all that was left behind as a reminder of what had come before.

The scene then changed to what must have been centuries later and, as though in fast forward, the settlement began to spring up and grow atop the lands where the God had once sobbed. The buildings grew and the people who arrived and remained within Baldur's Circle safely thrived with their newfound abilities, until eventually the scene slowed to a move regular pace. Sylfia watched as her mother, her real mother, gave birth to her and held her against her chest, sobbing as she rocked the baby back and forth.

"I do not want this life for my little baby girl," Sylfia's mother whispered to the woman who had helped her bring Sylfia into the world. "This place is no good for a child, but I do not know what I can do about it. I hope, and I pray that the Gods see it in their mercy to protect my daughter."

Sylfia then watched as a few short months later, her mother lifted her from her crib and prepared to leave Baldur's Circle. As she reached the boundary that she knew had killed so many who had tried to leave in the past, she paused just before crossing the invisible barrier and uttered another short prayer. Sylfia felt her own breath catch as she watched her mother then stride onward and begin to climb down into the God's Chasm.

Having been told this story by her father, Sylfia already knew what was to happen next. Of course, his recitation had only ever begun from the moment that he had accepted the baby girl from her desperate mother, but Sylfia could have guessed what was going to happen next. She watched her mother strap her to her chest with a length of fabric, and Sylfia gritted her teeth as her mother descended the sheer wall of the God's Chasm. Sylfia knew so well how difficult this climb was, having completed it twice in her life already.

Once she had reached the bottom, Sylfia's mother crossed the Chasm slowly. The world around her was dark, misty and cold, and it seemed to be getting worse as she moved. Sylfia silently willed her mother onwards as though she was watching her journey in real-time. She clenched her fists as the woman began her climb on the western wall of the Chasm, and her heart leapt each time her mother's hand or foot slipped on the difficult surface.

Eventually, her mother reached just feet from the top of the Chasm, so close to salvation, and Sylfia watched herself meet her father for the very first time in her life, her mother pushing the baby Sylfia up towards the open arms of Jarl. She had never seen it before, and in the stories she had been told of her passing over to the western side of the Chasm, it was never mentioned that Jarl had tears in his eyes when he first saw Sylfia as a helpless baby, and as he reached down to take her from her mother, Jarl did not hesitate for even one second.

As soon as Sylfia's mother was free from the burden that she had carried, she faded away into the wind as though her task had been completed and she could finally be at peace. Sylfia couldn't help a great feeling of sorrow wash over her entire being. Her mother had given everything so that she could have a chance for a better life.

Sylfia watched the vision fade away and to be replaced by a new one, although this time she did not recognise the setting. Her point of view was within a great stone hall with torches burning all along the walls to either side of her, and two people were talking in hushed tones. She tried to move but realised that she was simply stuck in position, so she did her best to listen to their conversation. A moment later, they each turned their heads, and it was clear that the pair were Loki and Baldur's mother, Frigg.

"Can you not see what you have done to this family, Loki? What you continue to do with your schemes and your tricks? You must change your ways or you will quickly find that you will not belong of this world," Frigg said, almost in a whisper.

"I will not weep for the shining God," Loki spat back loudly, not caring who would overhear them. "That fool thought he was unbeatable, but what finally killed him was a simple piece of mistletoe. Baldur was clearly not strong enough to be placed amongst the Gods and I feel that he is far better suited with my daughter, away in Helheim."

"You call Hel your daughter, but you know nothing of family!" Frigg spat. "You are supposed to be of our own blood, but you refuse my one simple request! If you truly had love for your family, then you would not place your daughter so out of reach that you never have to lay your eyes upon her. Tell me Loki, are you so despised by her appearance, or do you simply not wish to accept the fact that you are no father to Hel. You gave her life, but that is all."

"You know nothing of my relationships with my children!" Loki interrupted with a shout. "And when Ragnarök comes to pass, you will see what my family and I can achieve!"

Loki turned and made to storm from the hall, heading directly towards Sylfia, but the trickster God abruptly stopped when Odin entered and stood before him, blocking his path.

"You know not what you say, Loki," Odin rumbled as he towered over his adopted son. "You speak of Ragnarök as though you will play a part in its passing. You know that I cannot allow this to happen."

Loki glanced up at Odin and did his best to mask the look of disgust that flashed on his face before looking forward once more and storming out of the hall.

"What do you think that he will do?" Frigg asked Odin quietly as he came to stand beside her.

"I do not know, but I will send my ravens to follow him if he travels into Midgard. He knows that we will all be watching him as he creates his plans, so I suspect that he may try to leverage the mortals to enact his plans. We must take great care not to interfere in such a way that he will recognise our presence. He must believe that he has won, up until the very moment that he has lost."

"What do you know, husband?" Frigg asked inquisitively. It was clear that she was well-versed in reading Odin. "What have you seen?"

Odin turned his head away from his wife and looked directly at Sylfia. It seemed as though he could see here standing there, watching this whole scene play out. She knew that it was absurd, but his gaze was unmistakably boring into her as though he was speaking directly to her.

"There will be a child born that will be given a divine gift. Loki seeks to turn this individual to his cause without her knowledge, to use her as she grows by instilling the thought that she alone may be able to prevent the passing of Ragnarök. But in doing so, she alone will be the cause for the beginning of the end of days."

"Then let us help this child!" Frigg shouted. "Let us simply tell her that she is being fooled, and Loki's plans will fail."

"It is not as simple as that, wife," Odin replied. "If we do indeed interfere, then Loki will have cause to petition others to his schemes. It is not our way to interfere with the dealings of mortals so openly." His gaze met Sylfia's and held it for a long moment again. "This child does not know what she is destined to do, and it will not be her fault."

Then Odin turned away from Sylfia and back to Frigg. "We must allow Loki to believe that his plan has been effective, right up until the very moment that he is most vulnerable. He is an intelligent being, but he is arrogant and will not believe that his demise will be manufactured by his own hand. We must see to it that the powers this girl receives are such that they will help her along her path, but also include others so that she has a force to stand behind her that Loki would never have seen coming. He believes mortals weak and stupid, but we can see to it that if they work together with a common purpose, they can shatter the plans of even the mighty Loki. After all wife, is it not the highest truth, that family conquers all?"

Frigg was silent for a long moment, pondering her husband's words. "And what will happen to this child? We are not as used to toying with the lives of mortals as Loki. Is she destined to fall after giving her life unknowingly to both us and Loki?"

Odin's head fell sadly at the question. It seemed as though he had always known the answer to this question, but had been dreading having to speak the words aloud.

"I cannot see her future, wife. For within the short lifetime of this girl, I am destined to fall in battle against the great wolf, Fenrir. It is the way that it has been told, and the way that it shall be," he added quickly before his wife could object. "In glorious battle I shall fall, and then I will grace the halls of Valhalla with my presence."

To Sylfia's surprise, Frigg, rather than object, took hold of Odin's head and held it against her chest as though to comfort him.

"You have always had a soft spot for these mortals, have you not husband?" she spoke softly. "There is nothing more beautiful than a life given so freely for others so that others may live, and in the end be happy and at peace."

Then as though in the blink of an eye, Sylfia's entire life flashed before her once more. The glowing golden eyes of Elder Wise, who she was now sure had been the trickster God in disguise, her crossing of the God's Chasm, her short life lived within Baldur's Circle, and her imagined meeting with Loki as she slept. She relived the deaths of all of the people who had helped her along her path towards Helheim, her parents, Sigrid and Jarl as they fell to the tumultuous depths of the thrashing seas below the Naglfar ship. She saw it all but in some strange way, it gave her peace; she had not asked for any of this, but the path that she had walked, the most difficult of paths to prevent Ragnarök, was finally over and she knew that she had been successful. She had won.

Sylfia opened her eyes as though she had awoken from a deep sleep and was confronted with the black raven staring back at her. It looked calm and still, peering about itself as though it was looking for food or at least something to entertain it. Then abruptly, it leapt from her shoulder and flew off high into the sky.

Sylfia followed the raven with her gaze as it ascended into the warm, cloudless sky above until she could no longer see it; she knew it had completed its own task and she wondered idly where it would go next, whether it would remain within the mortal realm or would follow its master into Valhalla and remain there for the rest of its days.

"They are very intelligent birds, are they not?" a voice came from Sylfia's side. It startled her so much that she instinctively reached for her swords and rushed to stand up. She had forgotten that her swords were long gone though, and as she turned to the owner of the voice, she found herself face-to-face with the keeper of Helheim: Hel.

Hel still looked young to Sylfia, and her straight, jet-black hair was still as perfect as it had ever been. In the light of the day, her skin shimmered with its blue tint as if it had been woven from some divine gem.

"Please, can we talk?" Hel asked softly, and Sylfia could detect no malice within the question so sat back down. In reality, she had no choice but to sit and listen to the overseer of the underworld anyway, as her only other option was to dive from the broken mast and attempt to swim to the mountain in the distance.

Eventually, Sylfia replied.

"Your father tried to take everything from Midgard. He is the reason that I have no family. He is the reason that I am alone," Sylfia's words pained her, but she continued. "Tell me, are you here to claim my soul, to bring me back to your domain and keep me trapped within forever?"

"My father was not a great man," Hel replied, ignoring Sylfia's question. "He did many bad things to so many people, mortals and Gods, and I fear that all of the nine realms will be better off without his presence. Your parents gave their lives willingly so that you may live and without any idea how long that life would be, but I feel they would have given their lives so that you would remain for another single second if that was the choice they had been presented with."

Sylfia nodded silently.

"I do not feel that my father would have made the same decision, given the same choices if our roles were reversed," Hel said. "He has never been a father as Jarl was to you, and that is something that I deeply regret."

"My father was a great man," Sylfia agreed, unable to hold her silence. "I will miss him, and my mother, along with everyone else who has fallen because of the actions of your father."

Hel clicked her tongue as she sat, apparently deep in thought. She closed and opened her hands a few times, and it was in that moment that Sylfia could see that the overseer of Helheim was not a being to be avoided and feared; Hel was, above anything else, a daughter. She should not have been judged by the actions of her father, nor by the duty that she had been tasked with.

"Hel..." Sylfia began. She suddenly felt such apathy for her counterpart but did not know exactly how one was supposed to comfort a being such as Hel. In the end, she simply decided to treat her as a person. "I am sorry that you have lost your father. And I am sorry that he was not more present in your life. I have been lucky to have what I have loved in my life, and I truly hope that you will find what you are looking for as time passes."

Sylfia looked at Hel as she spoke to gauge if any of her words held any weight with the supernatural being, and to her surprise, Hel did look as though she was hurt. As if she was just another young girl crying out for the love of her parents.

"Do you know why I am here?" Hel said abruptly, changing the subject.

Sylfia shook her head. "Unless you are truly here to collect me and to bring me back to Helheim, but honestly, I have never died."

Hel smiled. It was genuine and warm and again Sylfia saw the humanity within her. "I am not here to bring you back into Helheim, Sylfia. I am here to ask a favour of you. I must admit, though, it is not lightly asked and I do not know how you will react."

Before Sylfia could respond either negatively or positively, Hel blurted out: "I would like you to take my place as overseer of Helheim." Then she took a deep breath as though expecting Sylfia to scream back at her in outrage.

Sylfia, though, did nothing of the sort. She simply leant her head to one side and asked: "Why?"

Hel looked back out to the open waters and lowered her shoulders. "Do you know how long it has been since I have enjoyed the warmth of the sun on my skin? How long it has been since I have had the chance to simply stop and enjoy what life has to offer? I was created to be the overseer of death, and it is a wonder that it has not consumed me completely as yet."

"But that does not..." Sylfia started to say but was interrupted by Hel again.

"I would like to spend some time to figure out what it means to be alive. What it means to love and to be loved by a family. Surely you can understand that desire of all people?"

"Well, yes," Sylfia said and again Hel interrupted her.

"What I can offer you is something that no mortal has been offered before, and that no mortal will ever be given the chance of again. Tell me Sylfia, what is it that you want most, more than anything else in the world?"

Sylfia did not even have to think about her answer. "I want my family back," she said assuredly. "Is it within your power to give me that?"

Hel listed her head from side to side and eventually shook it. "I cannot give you that. But I can do something that is close to it, if you would keep an open mind?"

Sylfia narrowed her eyes. She did not know what could be 'close to' having her parents back, but she would listen to Hel if there was any chance that she could see her parents again.

"Your parents are of the Draugr. It may not have seemed as though the infection had crossed over into their minds when you last saw them, but the transformation is unyielding and eventually they will join the ranks of the damned within Helheim."

"They are alive?" Sylfia asked, her eyes wide.

"You cannot kill what is already dead," Hel replied, "but the change that they will go through will render them unrecognisable in both body and mind. If you were to take the mantle of overseer, though, you could watch over them."

"Watch over them as they decay and become feral beasts?" Sylfia flared up.

"No... there is something more that I can do," Hel said slowly. Sylfia felt as though she had been avoiding giving her explanation of what exactly it was that she was offering, and wondered if it was somehow against the rules of the nine realms.

"If you were to take my mantle, the last action that I would carry out would be to give your parents new lives within Helheim. I could remove their memories of their past lives and allow them to live forever under your charge. They would not remember you though, nor your life or your accomplishments. They would be as they were in life, though confined to their place in Hel. As overseer, you would remember though. You would have to spend each day for the rest of eternity with the knowledge of your past and your family... you alone would know the truth as you watch them live their unending lives."

Sylfia remained silent for a long time as she turned Hel's words over in her mind, analysing them for truth, or underlying meaning, but as thoroughly as she could think on them, she could detect no real sense of deception.

"So I would become ruler of Helheim, and you would make it so that my parents would live forever within my domain... albeit with no knowledge of who I really am? What if I told them?"

"They would not believe you if you tried, but yes, this is my offer to you."

"And what of Midgard? And of the Gods? And you? What will the ruler of Helheim do once she is free of her chains?" Sylfia asked.

"Midgard will rise again as it has been foretold. The God Baldur has been freed from the central ring of Hel and he will regenerate the world with the help of what you call 'Baldur's Children'. They will as one usher in a new age of shining glory and bring an inherited divine power to the next generation of the mortals that follow."

Something suddenly struck Sylfia at the mention of Baldur's Children. "Is this to do with my divine gift?" she asked. "Is this why you are making me this offer?"

Hel let out a short laugh. "No, Sylfia. Your divine gift, as you call it, does not affect me, and it will not stay with you if you choose to take me up on my offer either. And of the Gods you ask? Some still remain, but the few who perished in battle have already arrived at Valhalla to spend eternity in glorious battle."

"Even your father?" Sylfia asked in a very small voice. "Will he grace Valhalla with his presence?"

Hel quickly shook her head. "Actually, that is why I wish to give up my place. My father now resides in the central ring of Helheim. It was to be his punishment for his misdeeds. I wish to spend my time there with him so that I may know what it means to be a family, what it means to be loved. I am sorry Sylfia, I am envious of what you have had in your life and I see the irony in the fact that I wish to gain what you have lost. Know though, that I will keep my promise and your parents will be safe in Helheim, even if you are not able to be a part of their lives as I have not been able to be a part of my father's."

"I do not understand," Sylfia said. "Can you not simply free your father from the central ring and get to know him better as you are now?"

Hel gave an awkward smile. "My father has had centuries to get to know me better, and not once has he come to visit me in my domain. The central ring of Helheim is locked to all those outside of it so if I go there, he has no choice but to know me. This is my chance at a family, Sylfia, this is my chance to gain a father."

Sylfia contemplated the fact that this whole plan seemed to hinge on the fact that Hel sought to imprison her father and then join him so that he would have no choice but to spend time with her. It was a terrible plan and certainly not one that Sylfia would have entertained, but in fact the very thought of Hel's plan clarified her mind: Sylfia would give up everything that she had ever known so that her parents could be happy, and that was exactly what Hel was offering.

Sylfia opened her mouth to accept Hel's offer, and after fighting her inability to make a single sound, she managed to croak out: "I will accept your offer. I will give my life in exchange for theirs and oversee the nine rings of Helheim as you have done for so long, but I wish for you to do one more thing for my parents, and one thing for all of the residents of the second ring."

Epilogue: Helheim

Initially, Sylfia had thought that she might be able to speak to her parents and her friend Hilda in order to reignite the bond that they had shared in life, but somewhere deep down she knew that no good would come of it. The favour she had asked of Hel was that the people within the second ring would be allowed to touch, as they would in the mortal realm, so that they may start their own families, and the one favour that she had asked for her parents was that they may conceive a child of their own as they had always wished. When the baby was born, she was surprised to learn that it had been named Sylfia. Perhaps it was simply the way it was always meant to be.

Sylfia came close to the central ring of Helheim to ask Hel what it was that she was supposed to do in her role, but decided it was best to keep her promise to Hel to let her and her father have their own time to create their family bond, so she left them be.

She placed her flat palm against the wall between the eighth and ninth rings before she turned away and wandered back into the domain of the Draugr. She had quickly realised that she could relocate in her domain at a thought, as Hel must have been able to, but she felt that for now it would be best to walk through the lands that she was now responsible for. After all, that would be the best way to learn everything she needed to know about her eternal home.

Sylfia walked the halls of the Draugr, past the great well where the Naglfar ship had been and what was now simply a wide-open cavern. She passed the Draugr as they meandered slowly through their rightful place in Helheim, and they seemed slow and unmotivated without any leaders to guide them. In one way, Sylfia was pleased with that; she longed that there would be no uprising from the eighth ring any time soon, but she also remembered who these souls were: they were once people, corrupted by the magic of this place, and one day she knew that she would do what she could to change what this place was.

The plains of Garmr spanned away from Sylfia as she entered the seventh ring of Helheim. From the moment that she stepped foot into the once lush forest, the devastation that she had caused as she had passed through was clear, and she could not help but feel responsible. Burnt husks of former trees and once vibrant plant life now stood testament to the total destruction that had been ignited by her father's once useful gift.

Sylfia felt tears come to her eyes, and the overwhelming feelings of guilt and dismay overcame her. She allowed her body to react in the way that it wanted to, falling down to sit on the hard, arid ground, and she shut her eyes tightly, wishing that she could undo all of the damage that she had caused.

Eventually she opened her eyes, and what now lay before her was the lush greenery that had once been. The forest had been reborn and had regrown as though nothing had ever happened in this place, and she could not help but laugh loudly at what had just happened. She had wished it, and therefore it was. And it was great.

A movement caught her eye and from the tree line, a great grey wolf came bounding towards her with its head and tail held high. She felt no danger in the presence of the great wolf, rather she knew instinctively that Garmr was coming to greet her as his master.

The wolf ran up to Sylfia and abruptly stopped just inches from where she sat on the ground. The wolf that had once looked so fierce, so deadly, now lowered its head to the ground so that Sylfia could stand up and stoke its long, soft fur. It then raised its head into the air and let out a deafening howl, and from all across the rejuvenated forest, the howls of his pack returned their answers.

Garmr then brushed his huge head against Sylfia's face before turning away from her and bounding back into the forest to join his pack.

Sylfia gave the place one last smile before she continued along her journey through her domain to the next place she needed to go to, the place where she had made a promise that needed to be kept.

The promise that Sylfia had made was to the Jötnar - Hrit, Hern and their father - and it was to put an end to the battle that had no conclusion, that seemed to recycle souls into the nothingness in a senseless, never-ending loop.

With this in mind, Sylfia disappeared from the plains of Garmr and reappeared in the centre of the battlefield that had seen so many souls stuck in their perpetual war. She looked over to the mountains that she knew housed the entirety of the fallen of the Jötnar race, and then to where the armies of man waited behind their high wooden walls until they were ready to foray out and wreak their renewed havoc onto their slumbering enemy.

Sylfia wondered exactly how she was going to stop all of this madness. It did not sound like a good idea to petition each side to leave each other alone; she needed to do something bigger.

The sky above in this place was grey and the land was dry and lacked the pleasantries, the beauty of life, so this was where Sylfia decided to begin making her changes.

She closed her eyes as she had done in Garmr's domain and visualised what she wanted to change. As she did so, the sky above abruptly split, and the grey-brown veil that coated the battlefield between the fourth and fifth rings of Helheim faded away, allowing bright sunshine to bathe the desolate ground in light and warmth.

Sylfia had not finished yet though and with her eyes still tightly shut, she remembered what the Jötnar had done with so little, how they had managed to grow fruits and vegetables even without the help of the life-giving sun. She decided to expand what they had started.

Beneath her feet sprouted thin independent strands of grass which quickly grew into thick clumps and then into a sea of green that rolled away as far as the dry ground stretched. It grew up past her ankles, and between the strands, small white and yellow flowers bloomed. Sylvia opened her eyes again and smiled as she now saw that the once dark, grey field of death was now a bright and vibrant place with the field of life and colour displayed beneath the warm glow of the yellow sun above.

Standing in the centre of the battlefield, Sylfia watched for signs of movement from both sides of her new paradise, and eventually she had to smile. The Jötnar, sensing the change in their atmosphere, slowly emerged from their caves and walked out past their small farms and onto the soft, lush grass.

The Jötnar did not appear to have seen Sylfia as they emerged from their underground homes, and once their feet touched the grass it was as though their curious demeanour simply melted away. The ones who had brought their weapons along with them, apparently expecting battle to accompany this new development, dropped them abruptly to the ground and ran forward with a chorus of laughter, playfully shoving each other as they went.

Sylfia turned her attention to the far side of the battlefield, where the huge wooden gates in front of the human camp-site had caught her attention as they creaked open. Slowly the gates revealed the ready armies of man, each of them holding their weapons to the ready although not a single person took a step forward.

Then out of the gates slowly walked Erling, or in reality, the Jötnar Bergelmir, who had played a large part in keeping the battle renewed and ongoing each day. He did not look as though he shared the Jötnar's willingness to throw down their weapons, and now held a great golden battle axe high above his head.

"This changes nothing!" he cried, his voice carrying across the battlefield and reaching Sylfia. He turned to face his army waiting behind him, but not a single soldier moved to follow him out onto the luscious green grass. Then slowly, the soldiers all began to drop their weapons to the ground with a sound that carried even further than Erling's shout, and they filtered out through the gates and walked onto the previous field of battle. Sylfia knew that she had done well and that this place was now free from the battles that had once plagued it.

She heard Erling shout out a few more words to try to bring his soldiers back to their task, but he was soundly ignored by the masses and eventually stood alone, his weapon dropped down by his side.

Sylfia decided that her work in the fourth ring was now complete and that she had kept her promise, so she turned her back on it and thought of the very first ring of Helheim. It was a terrible, foreboding place and she felt that it was time for change under her rule. If she was to be overseer of this realm, she would make a few more changes to how people were greeted when they arrived.

When Sylfia arrived in the mist that formed the first ring of Helheim, she wondered exactly what she could do to make it more inviting. She knew that only those who managed to wander into Helheim the way that she, Hilda and her parents had would see this part of her domain, and in reality, it was either there to keep people out or to scare those who needed to be scared, so she felt as though it really did not need to exist.

The mist creature in particular was something that Sylfia simply could not abide; there was just no place within her domain for a creature that used the emotions of its prey to lead them to their inevitable deaths. With this in mind, Sylfia started thinking about what exactly she could do here.

Sylfia knew that she could not simply remove the first ring of Helheim; it certainly had a purpose and she knew that she needed the place to keep those out who shouldn't enter. With that in mind, she decided to take a simpler approach.

Sylfia began by entirely removing the mist from the first ring of Helheim, because without the mist, there would be no mist creature. Rather than repeating what she had done with the battlefield between the fourth and fifth rings - transforming it with beauty - she decided to do the opposite in the first ring, so she emptied it of everything that resided within. She removed the tar pits that caught their unsuspecting victims, she removed the bridge across into the second ring, and she removed the bodies that had been left to rot as a warning to anyone venturing within.

As the first ring of Helheim was not supposed to be entered into from either the outside world or from the second ring itself, Sylfia took away the entrance that led in from the caverns of ice beyond. Lastly, she removed the ceiling of the cavern to allow the light from the outside world to flood in. The first ring of Helheim would forever remain desolate, but at least it would be bright.

The one place that tugged at Sylfia's chest had remained until last. A part of her felt as though she had been avoiding the second ring because she was afraid of what she would find there, but she knew that she needed to oversee all of her domain without prejudice.

Sylfia arrived within the second ring a moment later and slipped into the shadows between two of the stone buildings. It was as she had remembered it: people walking about in the bright sunlight without a care in the world. Merchants offered their wares, and everything seemed as normal as it had ever done. Then Sylfia overheard a voice that stopped her in her tracks and gave her goose bumps.

"The world outside this place has returned to normal. That is the word that is arriving from those new to this place," Jarl said as he stood shoulder to shoulder with Sigrid, looking up at the bright sky above as though he could see the mortal realm beyond. "Few people have been arriving, but they tell stories of Ragnarök coming and failing to pass. The shining God Baldur has returned to the land of the living, and he commands a great army, the likes of which has never been seen before. Magics have returned to the people, and the foul beasts of death and destruction have all been removed from Midgard."

Sigrid smiled at her husband's words. "The Gods would never allow Ragnarök to truly pass, would they husband? Good will always triumph over evil, and no matter how dark the darkest day is, the smallest flame of brightness will always shine through."

Laughter then reached Sylfia's ears and she watched as Jarl dropped to his knees as a small child ran up to him, her braided blonde hair flowing behind her as she ran. Jarl held his arms open wide and the girl leapt into his embrace. He held her tightly as he stood up with her in his arms.

"Sylfia, where have you been?" Sigrid called out in exasperation. "You are covered in mud!"

"Sorry, mother, I was just out playing with the other children," little Sylfia said. "I am sure it will come off easily," she said, unsuccessfully attempting to wipe a dirty mark from her face. "They said that the end of the world came and went and that people can do magic now! Could people do magic when you were out there in the mortal realm?"

Jarl shook his head. "There was no magic before," he said with a smile. "When we were there, people had to rely on hard work and their pride in battle to get by, not on some magic tricks!"

"I wish I could do magic," little Sylfia replied with a frown on her face.

"Do not worry, daughter, you can do anything that you put your mind to, only when you are older," Jarl said, and those words made Sylfia smile.

"Then I think that when I am older, I will learn magic. And I will use it to help people, and everyone will love me because of it!"

Jarl tousled his daughter's hair, and she leapt from his arms and ran off down the cobbled road towards a small group of children who were playing merrily.

"You should not tell her those things, Jarl," Sigrid said with a proud smile.

"Why should she not want more from life?" Jarl asked. "We may not remember the lives that we led before, but the Gods have seen it fit to bless us with a family here, and we would be foolish to believe that some things are simply impossible. I do wonder though, what we were like out there in the mortal realm... if we had left others behind who miss us even now..."

"Such things do not bear thinking about, husband," Sigrid said. "We are here, and we are together. One day that may not be so, but we live in the present, Jarl. Now come, it is time that we found ourselves with Hilda and her family; they have invited us to join them for lunch, and I do not want to miss out!"

"She is a very good cook," Jarl replied with a broad smile on his face and added: "I wonder if she was a cook in her old life."

Once Jarl, Sigrid and the little Sylfia had turned away towards Hilda and her family's home, the real Sylfia, overseer of Helheim, stepped out of the shadows and from between the two buildings.

Sigrid stopped abruptly, and Sylfia wondered if she should dive back into the shadows in case Sigrid would turn and see her standing there. She assumed that neither her mother nor her father would recognise her as was the deal that she had struck with Hel, but she could not bear having to look into the two pairs of eyes that she knew better than any others in the whole world, as they looked upon her as a total stranger.

Sylfia longed to tell her parents of their past, how they had been the most important people in the world to each other, and the same for Hilda too, but the one thing that she had come to realise as she had watched Jarl, Sigrid and little Sylfia, was that her family was happy, and there was nothing that she was ever going to do to put that happiness at risk.

Sigrid's gaze turned to Sylfia, and as their eyes met, Sylfia did not see someone who was regarding a stranger; she saw love, affection and possibly a flash of recognition. Sigrid then gave Sylfia a warm smile, which Sylfia returned, and then her mother spun on her heels and walked quickly away to catch up with Jarl and their daughter.

~ The End ~

A Thankyou

Again, your investment of your own time and money is always well appreciated and again, I ask that you **rate** and **review** everything that you read – and not just this book, so that lesser-known authors can grow their audience and gain the credibility that they deserve for their hard work.

Also, check out my website, it's usually kept up to date with current works, reviews and a few extra little bits. You'll find it at: www.davidlingard.com

Ingram Content Group UK Ltd.
Milton Keynes UK
UKHW021403250423
420747UK00015B/551